Beauty and The Best

JUDI FENNELL

MERJINN PRESS

PHILADELPHIA, PENNSYLVANIA

She cooks. He broods. The cat has a halo and an agenda.

Jolie Gardener needs this job. Personal chef to reclusive artist Todd Best isn't exactly her dream gig, but it pays the bills while she figures out her life — and her novel. Todd just wants to be left alone with his memories and his guilt. He's not painting anymore. He's not anything anymore.

Then Jolie shows up in his kitchen, talking too much, feeding him too well, and making him feel things he buried a long time ago.

He's the beast who lost everything. She's the beauty who won't stop showing up with lunch.

And Jonathan — that impossibly smug little kitten with the glowing halo — seems entirely too pleased with how this is all going.

Beauty and The Best is a warm, witty, grumpy/sunshine romance about two people who needed saving and were too stubborn to ask — and one very scheming angel in disguise.

Books By Judi Fennell

Royally Sunk
In Over Her Head
Wild Blue Under
Catch of a Lifetime
Love on the Rocks
~Making Waves ~ outtakes

Bottled Magic
I Dream of Genies
Genie Knows Best
My Fair Genie
~Your Wish Is His Command ~ outtake

Once Upon A Time Romance
Beauty and The Best
If The Shoe Fits
Through The Leaded Glass ~ prequel

BeefCake, Inc.
Beefcake & Cupcakes
Beefcake & Mistakes
Beefcake & Retakes
Beefcake & Snowflakes

Manley Maids
What a Woman Wants
What a Woman Needs
What a Woman Gets
What a Woman
What A Guy Wants

Once upon a time...

a long time ago,
there lived a beast of a man,
locked within a castle
with no one to love him.

This is not his story.

This is the story of another man,
locked within himself,
and the Beauty
who sets him free.

Chapter One

There's a naked man in my kitchen.

The thought registered just as the terse, "Who the hell are you?" had Jolie Gardener spinning around faster than a figure skater on speed.

He had the nerve to ask this? He of the broad shoulders, six-pack abs, and other, nice, um, parts...

Really. A naked man. In her kitchen.

Well, *technically*, she was in a naked man's kitchen. Even more technically, she was in a naked Todd Best's kitchen—and there wasn't one hint of self-consciousness or embarrassment on his part.

Of course with that body, there shouldn't be. The guy *should* flaunt his nudity for the world to see. Which, at present, consisted of one single, solitary person: Jolie Gardener, aspiring writer and personal chef extraordinaire.

"Well?" His hands slammed to his hips.

"You're naked," she squeaked, which, really, was the only way to state that kind of obvious.

"I'm what?" Mr. Six-Pack Abs glanced down.

Jolie tried not to—so unsuccessfully it was pitiful.

"Shit," he muttered. "I am. I, uh, fell asleep last night..."

As butter sizzled in the new super-slick omelet pan on the top-of-the-line range, Jolie's gaze alternated between some rock-hard abs and a scruffy eight a.m. shadow while her fingers danced along the granite countertop in search of a napkin, placemat, oven mitt... something.

Mercifully, they scooped up a thick dishtowel that, in her world, would constitute a very plush, very luxurious hand towel from The Ritz or The Four Seasons, but which, here, apparently, was used to soak up water from designer flatware. She dangled it in the direction of Mr. *Au Naturel.* "Here."

He placed an empty bottle of Jim Beam on the island countertop with a *clink*, then took the towel with a grunt. "So, who are you, what are you doing in my kitchen, and would you mind turning around?"

She turned. "I'm the new girl the agency sent over."

"Hell. There better be some aspirin left," he muttered beside her, his bare (of course) feet making no sound on the limestone floor.

She peeked over at him.

His eyebrow soared skyward.

Right.

She turned back to the sizzling butter. Which had started to burn. Sigh.

He rummaged around in one of the drawers as she carried the pan to the sink. Trying to impress the new boss on her first day with his favorite omelet ranchero and she burned the butter. Not good, but then, it wasn't exactly her fault because nowhere in those papers she'd signed with her employment agency, Domestic Gods & Goddesses, was mention made of an optional dress code. And she didn't care how much they were paying her, nudity did tend to throw one off. As for the alcohol-before-breakfast debacle, she wasn't even going to address that. His rudeness said it all.

And here, *she'd* been worried about making a good impression on *him*.

A click of plastic bottle cap followed by a shake of the bottle, the fridge opening, a gulp, then Naked Guy sighing punctuated the silence before she turned on the faucet. She cleaned out the pan, all the while the Naughty Girl side of her brain screaming, "Turn around!" with the other, Jolie side, going, "You *want* to keep this job?"

Self-preservation being the backbone of her existence since being dumped into the foster care system, she decided to listen to the Jolie side—no matter how much groaning Naughty Girl did.

Naughty Girl, however, couldn't resist a peek, and was rewarded with a swish of his longish golden hair, a flex of his well-defined arm, and an accompanying sizzle to her own nerve endings.

So not good. Jolie had known he was a hunk before she accepted this position. Had had quite the crush on him, too. How could she not? The guy had been plastered all over every magazine in the country for years, most especially here in his hometown.

Todd Best. *The* Best, as the media had dubbed him. And rightfully so. The man's landscape paintings were hanging in every high-end hotel, public library, and courtroom in the country. Even the White House, for Pete's sake. Not that she had an eye for art, but when a painting looked like the scene down the road and made her think she was standing there, feeling the leaves rustling by, smelling the fresh cut grass, hearing the birds singing in the trees and the ducks quacking on the pond, the whole set-up, that, to her, was talent.

And, of course, there'd been his fairytale marriage. But then, sadly, his wife had died suddenly and he'd moved out of their home, turned the reins of his company over to his brother, and put down his paint brushes.

Yes, Jolie had known *exactly* who she'd be working for. That'd been half the incentive.

"So, new girl, do you have a name? And what are you doing here today?"

Since he was talking, she assumed it was safe to turn around.

The old adage about making an "ASS out of U and ME" proved true.

Although he was the one with the A-S-S. And what a nice one it was. As was the muscled shoulder leaning against the stainless steel of the microwave above the stove, and the ninety-degree jut of his jaw line, the sculpted cheekbones, a perfectly proportioned brow, the fall of hair over his forehead…

She tore her gaze away from the visual smorgasbord and, traitors that they were, her eyes headed south.

Thank goodness he had the dish towel spread across his nether regions like a loincloth. But a hot guy in a loincloth was just as distracting as a naked hot guy. And she'd seen him in both. Or not in both. Whatever.

She ordered her eyes back on the pan. "Um yes, I do have a name, and as to what I'm doing here, I think that's obvious—burning the butter for your morning omelet." She raised the pan to illustrate and managed a quick push with her hip to get him to back away from the stove so she could start cooking again, praying all the while she wasn't hitting something vital.

Luckily, the guy had quick reflexes—or a good hunch—'cause he stepped out of the way before her hip came anywhere close to anything important, saving them the extreme embarrassment of *that*.

"How'd you get in?" Mr. Clothing-Optional asked.

Okay, what was the protocol here? How long did one actually have to converse with a buck-naked human being before someone said something about it? Or did a strategically placed dishtowel negate all observances of nudity?

"Look, um, *Mister*." What did one call their bare boss? Todd? Sir? *Big guy*? "How 'bout you go freshen up a bit and I'll make breakfast. We can have our chat when we're both, um, well, prepared for the day. 'Kay?"

"Fine. I'll get dressed. Then we'll talk."

"You do that."

As he sauntered—okay, maybe that was her overactive imagination, because could one *really* saunter with a Jim Beam-sized hangover?—from the fourteen-foot-ceiling kitchen with its state-of-the-art appliances that looked as if they'd come out of their packing boxes yesterday, so stainless steel shiny she could have used them as a mirror to fix her lipstick—if she'd worn lipstick—and she inhaled enough oxygen to jump-start primordial ooze.

Which posed a whole new set of problems for this job. How was she supposed to focus if she kept getting sidetracked by the physical?

But she would.

She could.

Heck, if she could outwit social workers and manage to keep her teenaged self out of the gutter, not to mention, actually *make* something of her life, she could certainly keep her own libido in check.

She had to. Her job, her livelihood, and all her dreams depended on it.

***

Each step up the goddamned grandiose stairway reverberated through Todd's skull, setting his teeth on edge and his stomach roiling. Why the hell hadn't the builder put carpet on these stairs?

Todd grabbed his head with one hand, keeping the other one hovering above his groin with the damned kitchen towel. It'd be funny if it weren't so ungodly pitiful.

He, a grown man, hiding his modesty behind a piece of eight-by-twelve cotton because he didn't have enough sense to pass out in his own bed.

He kicked open the bedroom door and grimaced. Bare, tan walls, minimal furniture, and the fucking king-sized bed mocked him.

He knew exactly why he'd chosen the couch.

And he wasn't about to dwell on it. He'd done enough dwelling last night. More than enough, apparently.

He barreled through to the bathroom, his refusal to dwell on the reason just one more part of the person he'd become in the past two years.

And the poor woman downstairs who'd had to witness the person he'd become last night... God, wasn't it just *perfect* she'd shown up this morning?

Todd grabbed the shower handle and turned the water full force to hot. He'd burn the alcohol out of his system if he had to. No one deserved that greeting her first day on the job. Even if it was his house.

Todd sucked in a breath as he stepped beneath the pelting liquid fire and realized he wasn't as tough as he pretended. He turned the spigot back to warm and leaned his forehead against the cool ivory tile, and listened to the phone ring in his bedroom. Let the machine get the fucking thing. He couldn't deal with the calls and the goddamned hounding.

Not today.

The water ran into his eyes and he wiped it away with the heels of his hands. Why *today*? Why'd she have to start *today*?

Why'd she have to start at all?

Why wouldn't they all just leave him alone?

***

"You see what you're up against, Jonathan?" The archangel, Raphael, waved his hand in front of the computer monitor in the executive office of Domestic Gods & Goddesses and the split-screen images of Todd and Jolie faded to a serene, heavenly blue screen saver. "Todd doesn't think he's ready to let go of his wife's memory and Jolie is still a work in progress. Getting these two together could be difficult."

Jonathan Griff took a seat on one of the burgundy chairs opposite the mahogany desk and sipped the lemonade Raphael had given him. Well, perhaps he gulped it. This was a big assignment. Todd was front-page news. Still. After two years out of the public eye, the man could have media coverage in an instant. He was high profile. He was hot.

What if Jonathan failed? Not only would Todd and Jolie, his Charges, suffer, but it'd be public. Then he'd never earn his wings.

Of course, personal aggrandizement was not what a Guardian should worry about. His Charges' happiness should be his sole focus.

He'd had some success in the past, but there always seemed to be *something* he never got quite right. Could he take that risk with such a prominent case?

"You can do this, Jonathan."

The archangel's words reverberated inside his mind—another talent Jonathan hadn't yet mastered. Why was Raphael offering him this assignment? The archangel had no malice in him so he couldn't want to see him fail. Perhaps he had an overabundance of Hope?

Jonathan, left eye twitching, touched the keypad and the close-up of Todd's face reappeared. The poor man was in so much pain and, while The Boss had a Plan for Todd, Jonathan couldn't bear to see someone hurting.

And then there was Jolie. No one should have to endure what she had as a child. She was trying so hard to be all right that she'd almost convinced herself she was.

But she wasn't. Not really. She played a good game, but she craved acceptance so much that she'd do anything to get it.

Well, almost anything.

Jonathan smiled, the twitch subsiding. He'd read her dossier. The girl had a fine moral character, as did Todd.

Character and a run of bad luck; that's what the two of them shared. Not to mention the wellspring of love in their souls. That's why the request for their happiness had been selected for fulfillment.

Now it was up to him to help them along.

Jonathan set the lemonade on an antique walnut-inlay table beside him and hopped off the chair to stand before the archangel. If Raphael thought he was capable of this job, then he owed it to his Charges to be the best Guardian possible.

"Yes, sir. I believe I can help them."

Chapter Two

As Jolie pulled the omelet ranchero together, complete with nice little lemon- and orange-rind garnishes courtesy of the Julienne peeler—a must-have in every kitchen—Mr. Best descended the hardwood stairs to the accompaniment of yet another phone call. That made five since he'd headed up. Amazing he had time for a shower.

She glanced through the arched doorway. More amazing was that he ended up looking like *that*. Even in a boring brown golf shirt and khaki shorts, you had to love summer and lots of skin. His was quite worth looking at.

Calm down. You need this job, remember?

Oh, yes, she remembered. She had enough memories from her unstable childhood with Mom flitting from man to man to know not to get involved with anyone to whom she owed her financial stability.

Heck, this job was for getting out from being under anyone's financial strings. She'd had enough of others dictating when, where, or how she could live or what she was going to do with her life, and she was determined to stand on her own two feet. She'd made that vow when she'd left the foster care system ten years ago, and though the road had been bumpy, it'd been her road. And once she had enough money to finish her education and open her own pastry shop, she would be finished being beholden to anyone. The only person responsible for her life, her happiness, and her bank account would be Hers Truly.

"Hey," her new employer said, his golden hair curling damply at his collar. "I'm sorry about the nudity. I obviously wasn't expecting anyone today."

She set a glass of orange juice at his place at the table. "I should hope not. That is, I should hope nudity isn't on the daily agenda. However, I am kind of confused as to why you weren't expecting me."

He ran a hand through that longish hair. A few strands fell forward onto his forehead. "I guess I got the dates mixed up. I thought I'd have the week to myself before the new girl started," he answered.

"To dance naked through the house?" She folded a napkin next to his plate. "Not that there's anything wrong with that, but honestly, it is kind of distracting."

Finally, a smile.

Whooooa.

"Promise." He raised his hand. "No more nudity. Back to wearing a robe and sleeping in pajamas."

She wasn't going to picture that—and with what she'd already seen, that was taking some major mental fortitude. But because of her mother's *wonderful* example of male-female relationships, she was sticking him in the look-but-don't-touch category. Heck, she shouldn't even look, but she *was* human.

"So—" He grabbed a chair as the phone rang for Phone Call Number Six.

"Do you want me to answer that?" She reached for the receiver.

"Let the machine get it." He scooted closer to the table. "So, do you really have a name, or am I just going to keep calling you 'new girl'?"

Jolie whipped a folded letter from the pocket of the apron her friend, Giuseppe, had made for her when she'd graduated culinary school that now accompanied her to every job. "Here's my letter of introduction from the agency, complete with references."

Mr. Best, no longer Naked Guy (pity), scanned the letter from the DeLeos. He'd probably be counting his lucky stars she'd deigned to work for him after reading that missive. Mrs. DeLeo had gone a bit overboard, but Jolie couldn't complain. She couldn't have asked for a better reference than one from someone who owned a food service company yet had still hired a personal chef for her at-home dining experience.

She also wasn't going to complain about Mrs. DeLeo's verbosity because it was the perfect opportunity to check out Mr. Dressed Guy—*vis-à-vis* the whole being-human-and-allowed-to-look thing. *Sans* the nudity awkwardness, thank goodness.

She'd already noticed the taut muscles and broad shoulders, and his freshly-shaven jaw reminded her of the male models in those cigarette ads with their cowboy hats and boots, open collared shirts, and sexy-as-all-get-out jeans. Yep, she could see ol' Todd here in the pages of a magazine. Those weren't shoulder pads under his shirt and he had a nice start on a summer tan.

She glanced out the French doors. Yep, a pool. Probably like every other home in the Mirror Lake development. A necessity, she guessed, like the housekeeper, nanny, and circular driveway. Their own veritable Stepford.

"The name fits," he said, tucking the letter in his back pocket.

Pretty nice place to be tucked.

"Uh… what?" She paused at the silverware drawer.

"Your name. Jolie."

"Okay?"

"It means 'pretty' in French," he explained with a smile.

Well if she didn't get all tingly at that. Which, again, was not a good thing.

She opened the drawer and found a sudden interest in selecting just the right fork and knife. "Oh. Thanks. But my name was supposed to be Julie."

He cocked his head and it was kinda cute.

She walked back to the table and set the utensils on the correct sides of his plate. "My mother knew absolutely no French." The language, anyhow. "She was just a bit too groggy, I guess, when she filled out my birth certificate and wrote J-O-L-I-E instead of J-U-L-I-E. It wasn't 'til grade school that a teacher called me 'Jolie' and I learned about the mix-up. So, I went with Jolie from then on."

Nothing said "I love you" like misspelling your own kid's name.

But she was over it.

Really.

"Well," said Todd, "it worked out, because, as I said, the name fits."

To which Jolie had no witty comeback without sounding like a teenager meeting her high school crush. Instead, she flourished the fluffiest three-egg white omelet ever under his nose, complete with perfectly done toast, a sprig of parsley and those little lemon and orange curlicues. Garnishes always made such a nice touch. Good for impressing the boss.

"Are you going to join me? Meals are included in your contract." He emptied a forkful of egg into his mouth and used the tines to point to the chair across from him.

Jolie sat. "I'll have to remember that." Especially since sitting there staring at him while he ate was more than a bit uncomfortable. Okay, maybe not quite as uncomfortable as the naked thing, but still…

Besides, she was a bit of a talker and silence kinda made her edgy. "So? Is that the best omelet you've ever had or what?"

His mouth had a little twisty move going like he'd just sucked on a lemon.

She checked his plate. Both garnishes accounted for.

Then he covered his mouth and coughed. Then coughed some more.

Oh no, he was choking.

She hopped up and started pounding him on the back. "Boy, oh, boy. First day on the job and I'm killing you. Not the best way to stay employed."

He waved his hands once his airway cleared, then coughed again. "Thanks." He cleared his throat. "Actually, it is the best I've ever had," he said around another cough. "So, awesome omelet aside, what else do you make, Jolie?"

His eyes got all crinkly around the edges when he smiled, sparkling like light colored emeralds.

She knew dozens of girls who'd kill for eyes like that. Herself included…well, maybe not. People had always told her that her violet eyes were unusual and she'd enjoyed the attention when she was younger. Nowadays, she'd love for *anyone* to be looking close enough to see she even *had* eyes.

But that was a thought for another lifetime. The one where she'd be able to make decisions based on what she wanted rather than what she needed. The lifetime where she'd be her own boss—and, someday after that, where there'd be someone who'd look close enough to see *her*.

That lifetime *had* to be waiting for her. Other people had it; she should be able to, too. And she was trying. No doubt about that. Why, she was even writing a novel in the hopes that it'd supplement her cooking income. Anything for financial independence.

And while novel-writing might not seem like an avenue to financial security and eternal happiness, in her hand-to-mouth childhood the one thing she could never seem to beg, borrow, or steal was love, so she'd looked for it in books. Money being scarce—or non-existent—she'd chosen the happy endings in romance novels whenever she could afford a book.

And, now, she figured that if she could fashion a *fictional* happy ending in a book, she could fashion one in reality as well. And if she earned some extra money doing so, all the better.

At least, that was the thought. And Todd here was her ticket to both ends. Her employer to handle the cooking-money end of things and the inspiration for her romance hero for the literary-money. She could learn what made him tick, what had made his relationship work, his emotions for his wife, see what it was about him that made him worthy of being loved and, *voila!* instant romance hero.

Not that she'd tell him. There were limits to what people would put up with and, because of his reticence with publicity since his wife died, she was putting hero-inspiration into that category. If he didn't go for PR to talk about *his* career, he certainly wouldn't want to go for it for hers.

"Hello in there?" Todd tapped the table.

Oops. "Sorry." A blush blazed its way upward, warming her skin. "Um, well, I can whip up pretty much anything you want. What do you have in mind?"

The phone trilled yet again, but Todd ignored it and shrugged. "I'm not really much of a big eater these days. Feel free to try out whatever you want to keep yourself entertained. I usually give most of it to the Grays anyway."

"Grays?"

"Jasmine and Earl. An older couple who've been with us—me—for years. Earl takes care of the outside of the house and Jasmine the inside."

So why exactly was Jolie here collecting an exorbitant salary? He had a housekeeper, a gardener, and an answering machine, all with only one person living in the house.

She didn't mind earning an honest living, but this was starting to feel like a handout. To her. And she didn't do charity.

Unless… it was the company he was paying for? Someone to be here all day?

Hmm. That was understandable, given the circumstances, but still… Didn't he have family? Friends?

"Not very talkative are you?"

Her? "Oh. Sorry. Just thinking what's for dinner." She was not about to call his bluff. She knew *all* about keeping up appearances that everything was going along swimmingly in one's life. If he wanted to pretend, far be it from her to call him on it.

"Come up with anything?"

"I haven't made up my mind yet. I'll have to go food shopping and see what strikes my fancy."

The phone rang again. What was with these people?

Todd glanced toward the den, home of the (obviously) super-large-capacity answering machine. He set his fork down, then wiped his mouth with the cotton napkin.

Nice manners. Nice mouth, too.

She shouldn't be noticing things like that.

"I'll drive you in. I've got to stop by my offi—my brother's office and take care of a few things."

Nice recovery, but she saw that grimace. Self-deception must be the order of the day.

"That's okay. I've got my car."

"No sense wasting gas. I'll take you." He leaned his forearms on the edge of the table and turned those emerald eyes on her. "So, Jolie Gardener, how'd you end up in my kitchen?"

She shrugged, going for nonchalant. "Same way everyone else did. I applied at the agency, put the car in gear, and here I am."

"No. What I meant was, how did you end up in cooking? And are you always this literal?"

She laughed. He *got* her. "Hey, that didn't take you long. Good job."

"What are you talking about?"

She scooched closer to the table and plopped her chin in her hand. "Well, it's this test I do. To see how we'll get along. If it takes someone too long to get me, it's going to be a long assignment. And I don't mean in terms of time. But if people, you for instance, get me— my humor—I can tell we're going to work well together."

"Ah," he nodded, "getting it" all the more. "The litmus test of contractee and contractor. I like it." He pushed his plate aside. "So, what happens if your client doesn't 'get' you? Do you ask to be reassigned or do you just stick it out?"

"I never quit."

"Never?"

"Never." If she'd ever let quitting worm its way into her vocabulary she would've been one of those statistics on the news every night.

"Sometimes quitting is a good thing."

His voice was barely out of whisper range, but she heard it. Heard the words and beneath them too.

But at least he'd said them.

It didn't take a genius to figure out why he'd stopped painting, but maybe those words were a sign he was on the road to recovery. Perhaps that's what her exorbitant salary was all about: having someone with him all day and so he could find some way to open up. Come back to the world of the living.

Paint again.

Oh, if she could somehow help him regain the will to pick up a paintbrush, it'd be worth a shot, because for Todd Best to give up painting was like Michelangelo putting clothes on the statue of David.

Yep, she was back to nudity again.

"Um, well, okay, I'll definitely take that ride, if you're still offering." Inane chatter (or graciously accepting an offer) was a good way to get her mind off nudity—his, David's, or otherwise. "But it's not going to be a quick run. I'll need to meander around the store. An hour at least, maybe more. Or I could just have the stuff delivered and grab a cab if you want to leave before me. If not, I hope your car has a good trunk 'cause I tend to splurge the first time in a new kitchen. To make sure I've got all the necessities. Okay with you?"

He had a really cute, little quirky look going. Like she was speaking some foreign language he knew a little of and he was trying to conjugate the verbs.

"Aren't you exhausted yet?" he asked.

"Huh?"

"Well, if your mouth is moving that fast, I can only imagine your brain has to work twice as hard to coordinate all those thoughts."

His smile had taken the sting from his words, but still, they rankled. Yes, she was a talker. Sometimes it was scads better than silence. Or her thoughts.

"You'd be amazed." She stood to clear the table but Todd beat her to it, picking up his plate and heading to the sink.

Boy, was he tall. She wasn't used to feeling dwarfed around guys, since five-ten was no slouch in the height department, but with him…

It was such a screaming shame that the guy had pretty much every attribute in tall, dark, and gorgeous one could want. Except the dark part was dark blond. But it'd do. If she were wanting.

Which she most definitely was not. She'd learned her lesson. Falling for the guy who paid her salary—and greeted her naked—was not a good idea. Not to mention, a sure-fire way to disrupt the fictional exposé of his life she was working on, thereby derailing the perfectly planned path her life was about to take.

The phone rang again. Jolie glanced at it with raised eyebrows. "Are you sure you don't want me to answer that?"

Todd's steps faltered. *Not again.* He ran a hand through his hair again. He wasn't ready to deal with this. Not yet.

Not today.

Fuck it. He tossed his plate into the sink, half-hoping to hear it shatter. At least it'd give him something to focus on instead of the goddamned phone.

"I'm sure. Let's go, Jolie. I'll take care of the dishes when we get back."

"Um, well, okay. If you're sure. I mean, it is my job—"

"And it's my house. Dishes can sit."

He held out a hand to her. The faster they got out of here, the faster he didn't have to deal.

Then the doorbell chimed. Now what? He dropped his hand and spun on his heel toward the foyer. "I'll get this while you hang up your apron and get your purse."

He yanked on the brass handle, then immediately tried to shut the door when he saw who was on the other side, but Lizette was quick.

Too quick, dammit.

The news anchorwoman shoved a microphone in his face and her foot in the door, the cameraman's red light blinking like a distress signal behind her.

"Mr. Best, if you could give our viewers an idea of what today means—"

"No comment. All publicity is to go through the office." He stepped out of the line of filming and tried to maneuver her foot back through the door. He didn't want to do bodily harm, but he could be persuaded to change his mind.

"They gave me the same response."

"Then that's your answer. No comment." He closed the door enough to trap her foot and let her know he meant business. Luckily, she knew when enough was enough and retreated.

He shut the door, sliding the deadbolt home, then rested his head against the doorframe.

The phone rang again.

He was going to lose it. His stomach was churning, acid backing up into his throat. He wanted to scream, beat his head against the mahogany door, rip down walls…something. Anything to end this charade of normalcy that he was barely hanging on to.

He should have bought a new bottle of Beam last night, not just pulled out the remnants of another night's misery. He could've spent the day in a stupor, fading in and out on his sofa, and letting this whole fucking day just pass him by.

"Are you okay?"

Jolie.

He sighed. He'd forgotten she was here.

He cleared his throat and pushed off the door, turning to face her. The phone rang again.

He had to get out of the house. "Yeah, I'm all right." He took another breath. He would be all right; that was the sad irony of it. "How do you feel about a duck and run?"

"Duck and run?"

"My car's inside the garage. You're going to want to duck your head to avoid making tonight's news."

"I am?"

Poor thing was looking at him like a deer in the headlights. Or maybe like a sane person staring at a crazy one. He grabbed her hand and headed toward the garage door. "You are. Or you'll find yourself the object of intense media scrutiny. That reporter, and others like her, will hound you for information about me."

"What could I possibly tell them?"

Exactly.

He stopped, his grip tightening as she swung around to face him. His fingers clenched around hers. "Nothing, Jolie. You're to tell them absolutely nothing. No matter how much anyone offers you for my life story these days, or any snippets about how I live, don't tell them a damn thing." He opened the garage door.

"The last thing I need or want is for my life to be an open book."

Chapter Three

R eady?" Todd secured his seatbelt in the 560 SL and turned on the ignition.

Sunlight streamed in the beveled windows at the top of the garage door as Jolie bent forward, her mink hair spread over a gauzy top so splashed with color it reminded him of his drop cloths.

Not that he'd seen one of those in two years. Nor would he ever again.

"As I'll ever be." She wrapped her arms around her legs, tucking her purse beneath the seat and her head between her Indian Yellow capris. Todd punched the garage door button, feeling like a racecar driver in the starting gate—only he had more to lose than a driving trophy.

Gunning it, they bounced over the end of the driveway as the newswoman and her cameraman clunked down the walkway. He knew Lizette; he'd been counting on her heels to slow her up.

In the street, he slammed on the brakes, silently apologizing to the Mercedes and Jolie, then shoved the car into drive, and tore off down the street just as Lizette reached the end of his driveway and flung her arms to her sides.

"Can I peek now?" Jolie spit some hair from her mouth as she turned his way from her doubled-over position.

"Sure." He tapped the brakes once the video threat was gone. "Sorry about that."

"What exactly was that?"

"A pain in my a—an invasion of privacy." He glanced over. "I'm sorry about all the phone calls, the doorbell, the high-speed chase. I guess the job description didn't say anything about a media circus."

Jolie sat back and set the torso portion of her seatbelt in place, brushing long hair off her face. "You guess right."

He turned back to the road, slowing his speed to a non-ticketable offense. "I always appreciated the press coverage back, well, before, but now—" He shook his head and stopped at the stop sign. "It's gotten worse as today approached."

"Today?"

"Nothing. Never mind." Not what he wanted to talk about. He leaned an arm on the steering wheel and checked the oncoming traffic.

"Oh, well, um… not a problem," Jolie said with a happy-go-lucky tone he'd give anything to have back in his life. "Kind of exciting, I guess. And you know, the job description didn't mention nudity either, but I seem to have overcome that."

He glanced right and her face filled his line of vision. She had grayish eyes. No, not gray. Something beyond gray. Not blue, not hazel…

"Hello in there?" She waved her hand in front of his face. "Are you okay?"

He found himself responding to her smile. It wasn't her fault he was having a shitty day. "Sorry. Again."

"No biggie. But I have to tell you, if you're in the habit of greeting your employees in the buff—not that I'm complaining, mind you—I think one's the limit for this line of work."

He ran a hand through his hair and massaged the back of his neck. Yeah, that.

He sighed. "I had a, well, rough night."

"I gathered that. Oh, and you missed a spot." She pointed to his chin.

"What?"

"Nothing. Never mind." She waved her hand and sat back. "Go on."

"Like I was saying, it was a tough night and I just kicked back on the sofa." He should have gone up to bed; would have if he'd known the "new girl" would be a witness to his habit of sleeping naked. Not that he'd been thinking of much of anything. Or maybe he'd been thinking too much, hence the hangover. "I was pretty groggy when I heard you moving around. Hangovers and nudity are not normal occurrences, I promise."

"I imagine the Grays would have apoplexy if they were. Where are they anyway?"

A car behind him honked and Todd turned left onto Orchard. The Grays were another thing he hadn't wanted to deal with today—

none of them had wanted to deal with today. Thank God they'd finally taken his advice—he couldn't really order them around—and taken a vacation. "They usually show up around lunch. There's not a lot for them to do, it's all pretty much under control. And it's not like I'm high maintenance. Right now they're visiting their grandson."

"Oh."

He liked this chef. So far. She'd backed off the issue of *today* and wasn't plying him with questions. She might work out.

He almost laughed. Who cared if she didn't? Not him. It'd just be some other woman in his house where his wife should be.

"So—" Her animated hands never stopped moving. "Do you go to your brother's office a lot during the day? Or hang out at home? The links? I mean, I don't want to be invading your space. I can work around whatever schedule you've got going. I just like to know up front so I can plan. That way I won't bother you, yet I can still get your meals ready when you want them."

Hmm, maybe she wouldn't work out. This was the chattiest one yet. Ah well, a few days in his presence would either cure her of it or have her running for the hills. Nothing new there.

He pulled up to a traffic light, then held up his hand to her.

"What?" She tucked a strand of hair behind her ear.

"Do you ever stop to take a breath?"

And in one fell swoop he swiped the refreshingly happy smile from her face and sent the corners of that perfect-bow mouth into a frown.

Way to go, asshole.

He blew out a breath and touched her shoulder.

Which sent her sliding against her door, back to the leather, shoulders squared, eyes like a kicked puppy.

Note to self: Don't touch the chef.

"Hey, I'm sorry." He raised his hands. "And I didn't mean that comment as an insult. I just don't think I've ever met anyone with quite as much energy as you. At least, not in a long while... " Two-fucking-years-long while.

He turned back to the steering wheel. Two fucking years.

The light turned green. Todd cleared his throat and stepped on the gas. The car lurched forward.

He didn't need this. Not today. Not another chef to get used to, another person to make small talk with, someone else who knew his life story, or all the pity that entailed.

He just needed a clean start. He'd thought moving to this new house, one Trista had had nothing to do with, would do it. But he'd brought it all with him. The memories, the pain…Even the art. Oh, that was all hidden in the attic over the garage, but still, it was there, gnawing at him.

He needed to deal with it. Finally, inexorably, deal with it.

***

Jolie smoothed her yellow capris and squidged back into her seat in the proper position. Talk about overreacting. She shouldn't have flinched, but she wasn't used to being touched. Bad mother, yada, yada, yada.

"Well, um, that's okay. No apology necessary." She sat up a little straighter—kinda hard to do in the bucket seat, but, hey, she was a trooper. "I have a thick shell anyhow. And I know you didn't mean it that way. But I do tend to talk a lot. I like to get to know people and have them know me. 'Cause what you see is what you get and some people can't deal with that, know what I mean? Some people are always looking for the hidden agendas and ulterior motives and that's just so not me. I've got too much going on in my life to take the time to do little subplots." She tucked some of her blowing hair behind her ear. She liked the top down—a sense of freedom rushing over her with the wind.

"So, Jolie—can I call you that?" he asked with a smile.

Oh, good. She'd gotten him smiling. "Sure. Why not? It's my name."

Another little chuckle. "About this morning. You were a good sport about the whole thing."

"That's me, Good Sport Jolie."

"Can I finish my sentence?"

She slunk down in her seat, tucking hair behind both ears. Bad habit she had of cutting people's sentences short even though she always tried very hard to adhere to the niceties. Not having had many growing up, niceties were important to her. "Yes."

"Look. Today's… well… " He exhaled heavily and ran his fingers through his hair again. "I need to get out. Tonight. Not be home. How about if we grab some dinner out instead of you cooking? We can call it an apology and a get-to-know-the-new-employee wrapped up in one." He touched her shoulder with his free hand.

Oh, he was one of *those* people. The touchy-feely kind. He probably wasn't even aware he was doing it. God, how lonely he must be since—

She was *so* not going there.

"Look, Mr. Best." She slid to the right, just out of finger-reach. "You don't have to take me out. The apology's fine. I was hired to do a job and I don't mind starting. Really."

He zipped over to the curb, hitting the brakes in front of a brick building that looked more like a church than a grocery store. It even said St. Gabriel's. She braced herself against the dashboard to stay in her seat. What?

"Let's get one thing straight." He was all business, quarter-turned in his seat, his arm leaning on the steering wheel, his other on the back of the seat, that nicely tanned muscular thigh sliding between them—

She *really* needed to stop noticing those things but that Naughty Girl side sometimes wouldn't be denied.

"First of all, my name is Todd, not Mr. Best. Makes me feel like your damn grandfather. Second of all, I haven't eaten out in over two years and I thought *today* it'd be a good idea, and third, I've just given you the night off with pay and a free meal. Are you going to take me up on the offer or not?"

Whoa. So much emotion over dinner. "Okay."

"Okay?" His eyebrows shot up to his hairline. "What? No discourse on the type of restaurant? No dissertation on the correct time for the meal? Just okay?"

"Yep. Just okay. Whatever you say. Boss."

He was quiet for a heartbeat or two, then cocked up an eyebrow and corresponding side of his mouth and chuckled again. Hmmm, maybe she missed the chuckling stipulation in the employment contract and that was what the exorbitant salary was about. She shrugged. Even if it wasn't, it didn't matter; chuckling could only be good for the guy since he'd been through so much. Besides, she wasn't cut out to deal with people who were that sad. Too much down emotion was bad karma, so making people chuckle was kind of her *raison d'être*. (That on-line French course she'd taken to help out with some of the trickier menus she learned in culinary school often came in handy outside the kitchen.)

"Okay. Dinner it is. Any special place you want to go?"

"Well, since you're asking, yes, there is. I've always wanted to try out *The Midnight Maiden*."

"*The Midnight Maiden*?" His voice got all hoarse and raspy as he moved the car back into traffic. Did he swallow a bug?

"Yeah. You know, the boat down on the riverfront landing? It's a floating restaurant, but I'm pretty sure it's docked."

He nodded but seemed to be having trouble swallowing. Must have been a really big bug.

"Uh, Mister, uh, Todd? Maybe you should pull over? Cough that thing out?"

Oh, boy. It was worse than she thought. He *was* choking. His eyes grew wide, but then he coughed and shook his head, the insect seeming to have magically dissolved. "No, I'm fine. I know *The Midnight Maiden*. It's a good choice. We can do that. Sure."

Why did that *sure* sound less sure than the word *sure* implied?

"Here's Arena's Grocery," he said, suddenly all choked out and business-like. "I'll drop you off and run over to see Mike. I'll be back in an hour or two."

He was looking somewhere over her left shoulder and she got the feeling he thought she wasn't in the car anymore. Or maybe he hoped so.

Fine. She grabbed her purse and scooted off the warm leather, thankful she'd chosen capris today instead of a skirt. Much easier to slide with and not expose certain parts that shouldn't be. Though since *he* had exposed—

Not going there.

"Sure," she said in a tone loud enough to garner his attention, bunching her hair behind her neck like a ponytail and flipping it to settle down her back. "If I'm done earlier I'll just head on up to the office. Around that corner and down a few blocks, right?" She pushed off the car door, wiped away the fingertip smudge marks, then slung her purse strap over her shoulder. "Toodles."

And so, she left the man with way too many dark thoughts for a summer day sitting in the bright sunshine.

Chapter Four

Todd pulled into his space in the parking garage, killed the engine and stared at the sign in front of him. *Reserved for T. Best.* Someone had written "he" after the T.

The Best.

Once upon a time that had meant the world to him.

Once upon a time he'd felt a sense of pride when he'd seen that nickname.

Now, he just wanted to throw something. The Best. Yeah, that was laughable. To be the best, you actually had to compete. Had to enter the race—the race he'd dropped out of two years ago and had absolutely no glimmer of desire to get back into. He was done with landscapes. He'd never paint one again.

He couldn't. Trista had inspired those paintings during their first picnic years ago, when he couldn't believe his luck that such a beautiful, vivacious woman had consented to go out with him, a poor artist without two nickels to his name.

He'd tried to be different from all the other guys she could date, guys he could never compete with because they'd been in different social circles. Then he'd taken her on that picnic, his sketchpad always with him, and when he'd drawn her, she'd focused on the scenery he'd depicted behind her, pointing out how he'd captured it, and that had been the start of it all.

Todd sucked in a breath, shutting his eyes against the pain lancing his gut. When would it stop? It'd been two years. He'd said goodbye a thousand times; what more did God want from him?

God—ha. The same God who'd stolen his wife, his life.

God, who'd left him to live an empty existence.

Todd gripped the steering wheel and pushed back, locking his arms.

He couldn't go on like this, drowning in sadness. He'd gone through the motions for the past two years, trying to live a semblance of a normal life. But he never stopped thinking of her. It wasn't healthy; he knew that. He had to move on; he just didn't know how.

He swallowed and swiped a hand over his mouth. He'd missed a few spots shaving.

As if anyone would notice.

Jolie had.

Yeah, she had.

She'd noticed quite a bit, now that he thought of it. She'd noticed his pain and had changed the subject half a dozen times this morning. He didn't know if she was always as chatty as she'd been today, but, ironically, it really hadn't bothered him. He hadn't wanted her to shut up and leave him alone the way he had with every other woman who'd been in to prepare gourmet meals he'd barely tasted.

Yet, with Jolie, he'd actually forgotten for a few minutes. That story about her mother misspelling her name…how could anyone care so little for someone they were supposed to love?

At least his crushing disappointment in the love department hadn't been due to a lack of love, but Jolie…God. That must have been so rough on a kid.

Todd released his grip on the steering wheel. If an innocent kid could pick up her life and move on, he should be able to.

But how?

The parking spot sign wasn't giving him any answers, so Todd clicked off his seatbelt and opened the door. Maybe something would come to him on this improvised trip to the office.

At least there he had Security and receptionists to keep the vultures at bay.

***

Jonathan Griff gripped the rim of his hat and straightened it, willing the twitch by his eye to subside. He could do this. He was ready.

He peeked out from behind Mr. Arena's tower of paper towels. There she was. Now, how to do this? How to do this?

He tugged on the hem of his suit jacket. Maybe he should have

24

worn a tie. No, that'd be too formal. He didn't want her to think he was anything other than what he was supposed to be: a helpful older gentleman. They'd chat and maybe he could invite her to the store.

That was it. Be inconspicuous. Just happen along and start up a conversation. Let a cordial relationship develop.

He could do that.

He straightened his spectacles and stuck his hands into his jacket pockets, trying not to think of his personal stakes that were riding on this assignment. He was the only one of his initiate class who hadn't earned his wings. Sure, some people took longer than others, but when that six-year-old had managed to earn them with one assignment, well, he'd been pretty demoralized. But Raphael seemed to have faith in him, and he wasn't going to let the archangel down.

Nor would he let Jolie down. She deserved a happy ending, poor girl. Dealing with a drunk of a mother, then some of those foster families…

She needed a break and he was just the Guardian to give it to her.

If he could only find her.

"Well, hello there." An elderly, silver-haired woman stopped her cart next to him, the smile hinting at something he had no need of as a celestial being.

Ah, widows. If he were still mortal—

But no. He was here to do a job. He patted her hand, injecting a little Befuddlement into the touch. He could manage Befuddlement without messing it up. She'd never remember having seen him.

Now where did Jolie go?

He hurried to the cleaning products aisle. Not there.

Then the pet food aisle. Not there, either.

He tried the breakfast cereal aisle, but, again, no sign of Jolie.

The twitch picked up the tempo as he rolled around the endcap to the book and greeting card aisle. Not there, either. Funny, he would've thought that'd be an aisle she'd check out, seeing as how much she adored books.

He was so proud of her for trying to write one. And a romance novel at that. That girl certainly deserved some romance in her life.

As did Todd.

Jonathan steepled his fingers against his lips. *Dear Lord, please give me the knowledge to bring these two together.*

He rolled around the endcap again, still praying, and—

"Ow!" Something smacked into him at just the right angle to send him tumbling.

His spectacles fell off, skittering somewhere across the floor, but he couldn't follow their sound as a female voice chimed in with the clattering cart wheels, the ringing in his head from the pain in his knees as they hit the floor—

"Oh my gosh!" Slim arms reached for his. "Are you all right?"

It was her. He'd recognize that voice anywhere.

"Fiddlesticks!" He stood up and brushed off his sleeves, then straightened his hat, trying not to squint too badly at her, the plus side being that the twitch had stopped. "Oh, no. I've crumpled my hat and lost my spectacles."

Now how was he supposed to help her if he couldn't even see her? This was not working out as he'd planned. So much for being inconspicuous.

Jonathan knelt, sweeping his hand along the linoleum floor for his spectacles.

Of course Jolie, God love her (and He did) dropped right beside him to help.

Jonathan's fingers tripped over the wire frames. "Aha!" He toppled over, managing to get his butt on the floor first, his black shoes stretched out in front. Not the most graceful of landings, but better than smacking his schnozz on the linoleum. He affixed the spectacles to the bridge of said body part and smiled into her worried face.

"I am so sorry. I was in a hurry, and not paying attention. I didn't see you."

"Don't beat yourself up over it, miss."

"But I—"

Jonathan clambered to his feet and held out a hand to her. "Are you going to sit there all day, or are you going to join the world of the living, my dear?"

"Honestly, I'm really sorry. Are you okay?" She ignored his hand and scrambled to her feet unaided.

"Now, now, it's over and done with." He straightened his hat. Had to keep up appearances and all. "And it was both our faults. There's nothing more to be said, you hear?" He went to pat her hand, then remembered her dislike of touching. Although… he *had* seen that second shoulder-touch Todd had done in the car and how she hadn't freaked out quite so badly. Something to consider.

"You're okay? No shooting pain down your legs? No sore elbows or anything?" Her eyes turned plum-colored when worried. She had such expressive eyes, the sweet thing. And to be so concerned…

But then, she always had been. Which was just one of the reasons listed on the Heavenly Checks and Balances Accounting Sheet that confirmed the need for his intervention.

"I'm fine," Jonathan answered.

"That's a relief."

He doffed his hat. He'd always liked that word. Seemed so elegant and genteel. Something a Guardian should do when meeting his Charge for the first time in the flesh. So to speak. "Thank you, my dear."

"Thank me? For what? Running you down?" She pointed to her shopping cart where a bright yellow something was caught beneath one of the wheels. "I wasn't paying as much attention as I should've been. I tend to lose myself in the spice section."

"Well, there's no harm done. And thank you for helping an old man." Jonathan looked around. Baking Goods. Yes, that made sense. "An interesting place to lose yourself in."

Her cheeks flushed and it just made her all the prettier. It was true what they said about goodness shining through.

"I know it might sound silly, but I just love Italian grocery stores' spice aisle." She swept her hand around them. "Spices are like the national food of Italy. You can't make good sauce without the right amount of fresh spices. Oh, and sugar." She hefted a five-pound bag of just that off the shelf next to her and headed to her cart. "Of course, that's a trade secret I don't usually share, but if you put a pinch in the sauce with a big onion… yum!"

Jonathan couldn't help but smile. Jolie was exuberance personified, always throwing herself into every venture with such hope and determination. It was up to him to make sure this all worked out for her. The way it should, and the way she deserved.

Yes, there was to be no more heartache for this Charge. Jolie was about to get her Happily-Ever-After, no matter what he had to do to ensure it.

***

She was blabbering. No surprise there.

Jolie couldn't believe she'd run the old guy down. Shame on her. Mooning about her boss and she injured someone. That was just one reason why thinking about Mr. Best in any terms other than professional was a bad idea. She needed to remember that. This poor man was so gracious about the accident, but she felt awful.

Jolie set the sugar into the cart next to her purse and wrenched her kicky yellow flat out from beneath the asphalt-covered wheel. She deserved to have it ruined, but what a pity. They were a really comfortable pair of shoes and went with about half her wardrobe. How was she supposed to pass the remainder of her first day shoeless?

Was it too much to ask that she'd get through the day with her shoes intact? All she wanted to do was help out Mr. Best, earn her paycheck, and keep her life on track.

She looked up at the fluorescent lighting, hoping the roof would somehow open and heavenly wisdom would be imparted. Or that her shoe would magically float down, fully restored. Really, she wasn't picky.

"But how are *you* feeling, my dear?" The little guy adjusted his glasses as he approached her cart.

Ha. He did not want to know how she was feeling.

"I really want to know."

??

"You have a funny little twirl to your mouth, as if there are a million thoughts running through your mind. What's got you so worked up?" He patted her hand.

What was it with men in this town today? She hadn't been patted this much since Mama's fifth—or was it sixth?—boyfriend decided she was cuter than her passed-out mother. Her imagination had saved her then (though it was a good thing the guy wasn't too well-read or the bubonic plague she threatened him with wouldn't have worked).

This patting was different though, but she still didn't need anyone comforting her. She could take care of herself. She'd gotten pretty good at it.

Jolie stepped away and shook her head. "Nothing's getting me all worked up. I'm just relieved that you're okay. But now I've got to finish my shopping and figure out how to save my shoe."

28

The guy snapped to attention, reached into his suit pocket, and removed a business card. He flipped it over to her between his first two fingers.

"Well, I can't help with your shopping, but the shoe's no problem." He wiggled the card.

She took it. "Heavenly Shoes." The address was just down the street. How was that for serendipity?

"My shop," he said. "Stop down when you're finished and I'll fix the shoe quick as a wink." He accompanied that statement with a wink.

Temptation floated before her, but, really, *she* ran over *him*. She should do something nice for him, not the other way around. Of course, if he had to hand out cards to drum up business, maybe he could use her money.

"All right. I'll be there in a few minutes." Besides, now she had an excuse for the grocery delivery thing. She certainly couldn't go running around town with one shoe, now, could she? And she doubted Mr. Best, make that, Todd, would want to run over to her apartment so she could find another pair of shoes to wear to dinner tonight. She might as well do some efficient time management and take this guy up on his offer.

"Oh, I'm Jolie Gardener, by the way."

He nodded as if he already knew. But that wasn't possible since they'd never met. Which was odd, considering how long she'd been in town—

"Jonathan Griff, at your service." He tipped his hat to her. His poor, dented felt hat—yet another casualty.

"Are you new to town, Mr. Griff?"

"Oh no. I've been gone for a bit with other business, but I'm back now." He quarter-turned, then looked back. "Be sure to stop by, okay?"

"I will." She waved and he turned all the way with a little bow, then practically skipped through the check-out lanes without buying anything.

So what was he doing in the grocery store? Not like it was an interesting place to hang out. But then, she was the one who spent her time trying to make happily-ever-afters happen with imaginary people, so who was she to judge?

Chapter Five

A church bell chimed when Jolie entered Heavenly Shoes. Lovely bluish-white carpet covered the floor, making it feel as if she were walking on clouds.

Okay, so *technically* she'd fall through a cloud since a cloud was basically just water vapor, but she was sticking with the whole cottony, springy imagery.

Bright, sunshine-yellow walls led to a ceiling so covered in sparkling lights she could hardly see the tiles. It was one of those old-fashioned shoe stores with rows of seats and slanted bench thingies so Salesperson Prince Charmings could help Customer Cinderellas with their shoe selections.

A large glass case at the back was filled with an array of not-your-run-of-the-mill footwear. Shimmering ruby red slippers, cream-colored Victorian ankle boots complete with hook and eye lacings, a pair of pumps that looked like they were made of glass... Some really outlandish shoes in that case.

The girl behind the counter smiled at her. "Hi. I'm Dawn. Can I help you?"

"Hi." Jolie held up her beleaguered shoe. "Mr. Griff said he'd take care of this for me. It's definitely seen better days."

Dawn commiserated, then took the shoe and disappeared into the stock room. Not a minute passed before she was out again. "It shouldn't be long. Would you like to have a seat?"

"Actually, could I see these?" Jolie pointed to the pumps in the case.

Dawn smiled. "We get a lot of requests for those." She took a key from her chain and opened the cabinet.

"I know. A friend of mine wore them in her wedding."

Dawn smiled. "Mr. Griff does like to lend them out. Especially to brides." She set the shoes on the counter. "Want to try them on?"

Jolie had to touch them. The temptation was too great. "What size are they? I wouldn't want to crack them by trying to shove my foot in something too small."

"You know, I don't know." Dawn looked puzzled, then shrugged. "But don't worry about cracking them. They're made of Lucite, not glass."

"Okay." Jolie was just about to slip the little suckers on when, lo and behold, out popped Mr. Griff from the back, her mangled shoe looking completely new. *Completely.* There weren't even any smudge marks on the inside.

And he had a book with him.

It was pathetic really how Jolie's heart sped at the sight of a book. She would've thought since she could now afford her own books (and she bought them, thankyouverymuch) that the old hunger for the printed word wouldn't plague her any more. But nope. She saw that paperback in his hand and it was all she could do not to salivate.

"Here you go, my dear." He was practically kicking up his serviceable black-clad heels. "All fixed and fit as a fiddle." He handed her the shoe and she had to tear herself away from the book.

"And I thought you might like to have this. To get my new business off the ground, so to speak." He held out the paperback.

Was he kidding? The guy must read minds. She wanted to grab it, stopping only when she saw the shaking of her hand. For Pete's sake, it was just a book.

Yeah, and Todd's abs were just another six-pack.

Not going there.

"Your new business?" she asked because she was interested; it had nothing whatsoever to do with Todd's abs.

Really.

Mr. Griff went to tip his hat, but nodded instead, being that he was unable to remove his hat since it had gotten crushed in their—okay, *her*—little mishap. She really hoped he could get it back into shape as fast as he had her shoe which looked brand spankin' yellow again.

She slipped it on to hide her unbridled curiosity at the book he was offering. "What new business is that?"

"I'm opening Heavenly Books next door. That way, people heading down to the river can pick up some reading material. It's a nice way to pass the time on a pleasant day."

He pushed the book toward her on the counter, right past those Lucite shoes she'd suddenly lost interest in.

All of the happy memories of her childhood were wrapped up in books. Adventure, escape, freedom, family… it was all there, so she simply couldn't refuse the book—as long as it wasn't charity. She didn't do charity. Period, end of story.

"Take this book and mention me to all your friends. Word of mouth is the best advertising."

"Oh, I most definitely will. Thank you so very much, Mr. Griff." She took out her wallet and the little man patted her hand again.

"Now, now, you must call me Jonathan and put that away. These are my gift to you. Have a good day and come back when you need another story or a new pair of shoes."

He was so earnest she couldn't argue with him. And he was right anyway; she'd definitely mention him to her friends. Minus the running over part, of course.

She thanked him and departed with her treasures into a beautiful, if a bit on the hot side, summer day. Luckily, a nice breeze wafted from the river a block away. She loved this neighborhood. It was one of those old-fashioned ones where people took pride in, and care of, their storefronts and sidewalks. Window boxes overflowed with portulaca and geraniums dotted the second floor apartments above the brick storefronts. Nicely pruned trees lining the sidewalks held little twinkling lights during the Christmas season, making it real festive. Just like today with all the people heading to the river, tons of kids and baby carriages in tow.

Halfway down the street she finally gave in to temptation to see the book he'd given her.

It was a Regency. How did he know that, out of every kind of romance novel there was, Regencies were her favorite? There was something about the women in those books. Their society wanted them to be pretty little brainless ornaments, concerned with nothing but the latest fashion and *on-dit*, but those heroines wouldn't stand for it. They worked within their mores to assert their independence and make their own way in the world.

She so admired that. It was what she'd always aspired to: to lose the case managers and social workers and make her own decisions. To be responsible for her own life. But no, what kid ever got that kind of autonomy? Especially one in the system?

That had to be why she was drawn to those books. They'd validated her desire to make a better life for herself during all those years when she'd needed the affirmation.

The breeze kicked up again, ruffling her hair, flouncing the hem of her gauzy shirt, whispering over her skin like the soft brush of a feather, and a songbird warbled in one of the trees as Jolie passed an old-fashioned, wrought-iron bench by Arena's.

She'd love to park her tushy down and read a few chapters, but it probably wouldn't look so hot when Todd pulled up and she'd sent the groceries home, only to be caught reading on the job.

The job. Right. Work first. Hard Work and Persistence, those were the mantras of her life, with a little Hope and Wait thrown in for good measure.

To that end, she hiked her purse strap farther up her shoulder, tucked the book under her arm, decided to bypass her friend Bella's restaurant around the next corner, and headed over to Todd's office— okay, his *brother's* office.

Yeah, like that was the truth.

Jolie crossed Market, waving to Signore Girondi at his newsstand, then came to a stop a third of the way down the next block in front of the mirrored building.

Best Enterprises.

An entire building. An enterprise. He was *that* good. Or he would be if he'd just pick up a brush. Good thing demand was still high for his prints so he could afford his big ol' empty house.

Tall glass doors swooshed open as she approached, and a blast of Freon-coated air rushed by, flipping the hem of her blouse, tickling her tummy like that tickle she got when a good-looking guy stared at her but she didn't want to let him know she'd noticed, but she also didn't want him to think she wasn't interested so she'd shoot him eensy-weensy glances out of the corner of her eye, all the while little flips and twinges danced through her stomach. That kind of tickle.

A guy in rent-a-cop gray with a flashy gold emblem on his shirtsleeve stood up behind a desk when she headed over.

"Hi," she said, putting enough chipper in her voice to merit a smile. "I'm here to see Mr. Best."

"Which one?" The man didn't crack a smile. Not even a little insincere twitch of the lips. Nothing.

She couldn't have that. She'd asked a simple question, not the combination to Fort Knox, for Pete's sake. "Um…Todd?"

He scanned her from head to toe. Now, if Joe Schmoe on the street were to do that she'd be highly insulted—or highly flattered depending where Mr. Schmoe fell on People Magazine's Sexiest Man Alive list. But Sour-Puss made her feel as if she was in a doctor's office. Or a police line-up. Honestly, did the guy think she was packing a gun in this outfit?

So just for kicks and giggles, she did a "ta-da" twirl on her repaired shoe, turning back to face him just in time to see him roll his eyes.

And the faintest glimmer of a smile. *Bingo.*

She only got the glimmer, but it was enough. He tucked his chin onto his security-guard-special collar and lifted a large leather book from somewhere below the chest-high marble security desk. "Sign this."

Nice manners, buddy. She gave him that eyebrow-raising trick.

"Please," he conceded, his smile getting a little bigger.

Now that wasn't so bad, was it? "Sure, okay." She scribbled her name in her best USA-Today-Best-Selling-Author autograph (yes, she'd been practicing; it never hurt to be prepared), and headed to the shiny silver elevator bank.

"Miss? Just a moment, please."

Wow. He'd progressed from two words to five. She did tend to grow on people.

She turned around. "Yes?"

"Mr. Best's office is on the tenth floor, but there's a retirement party on the eighth, so you might want to stop there first."

"Gotcha. Thanks for the info." She tapped the UP button on the elevators. Retirement party? She doubted Todd was in party mode. Not "today."

She'd take her chances in Mike's office.

With a soft little *ding*, the doors opened to a nice, *chi-chi* elevator, all mirrors and muted lighting. And paintings. His paintings. Just like in the lobby.

A soft whir and before she knew it: Top Floor. Of course his office would be on top. Okay, his brother's office. Yeah, she was getting tired of making that distinction. It was *his* office—his brother was just borrowing it. Or keeping it dust-free for him. Whatever.

She took a few steps into the empty elevator foyer. Where was everyone? At the retirement party? Hmm, maybe Todd *had* gone.

No, that just didn't ring true. Not with his mood "today." She'd take a look around.

Steel gray carpet, very plush and sound-absorbing, swallowed her footsteps. Pale gray walls, what few there were, stood as the perfect backdrop for Todd's vivid landscapes. Banks of windows let in almost a three-hundred-and-sixty-degree view of the town. Traffic on the street was light today. Probably because of all the people hanging out at the park on the riverbank. A rainbow of shirts of all sizes and shapes ringed the fountain there. A couple of paddleboats lazed around on the river with a pair of speedboats rippling past them.

She hung a right at the water cooler and headed toward the offices. Probably where the big guns handled all the sales that got Todd's pictures into every prestigious building in the country. From the looks of the furnishings and décor, they did their jobs extremely well.

A huge expanse of cherry wood double doors loomed at the far end of the hall. It must be his office. His brother's—oh, whatever.

A matched set of his paintings graced the doorway. She read the plaques beneath them. Riverwalk South and Riverwalk North.

Ah, yes. There was the fountain. The speedboats. The docks. A perfect depiction of the view from the windows. Man, the man had talent.

She was about to knock when she heard voices. Aha! She was right. He was here. But obviously not finished so she decided to park her butt on the ottoman by the door and wait.

She pulled out Mr. Griff's book—it didn't feel right to call him Jonathan—and read the back blurb.

Hmmm, the heroine refused proposal after proposal, determined that no man would be in charge of her life.

Substitute "no one" for "no man" and Jolie was right there with her.

Yep, this story looked promising. Mr. Griff had picked a good one. She flipped to the inside cover and read the excerpt.

"Destiny is mine," proclaimed Rebecca Featherington.

You go, girl. Time for Chapter One.

"You're taking her to *The Midnight Maiden*?"

Jolie's ears perked up at the question coming from the office. They had to be talking about her since she was the only one she knew who was going to *The Midnight Maiden* with Todd—*and* qualified as a "her."

This was better than any book. She put Miss Featherington down on her leg and shamelessly listened in. Self-preservation was a hard-learned battle and those lessons never left a person.

Someone cleared his throat. Todd, maybe.

"Uh, well, yeah." Another throat clearing.

Bingo. Todd. The men's voices were similar, but Todd's seemed just a bit lower in pitch. Maybe that was because he still had something caught in his throat. She scooched a little closer to the door.

"Really? *The Midnight Maiden*?" asked his brother.

What was with the disbelief? It was just an old boat someone turned into a restaurant. Sheesh. He was making it sound like the Taj Mahal or something.

'Course, the Taj Mahal was a monument to some guy's wife. Like the biggest declaration of love in the world.

"Yeah," Todd answered and whatever it was that was stuck in his throat was obviously gone. And yep, she was right, his voice was deeper. It resonated up her spine in a way his brother's didn't.

"I asked her where she wanted to go and she picked that place. So we're going," said Todd.

"Are you ready for that?"

"For God's sake, Mike. It's just a restaurant. I think I can handle it."

"Well, after Trista—"

"Look, Mike, Trista is gone and I'm not. I realize that. I didn't put any stipulations on Jolie's restaurant choice, so I'll have to live with it. I've had to live with a lot of things since my wife died. I'll get over it."

Why was she not liking where this conversation was headed? What did Trista and *The Midnight Maiden* have to do with each other?

"Well, if you're sure—"

"Let it go, Mike, I'm thirty-four years old. I can handle a restaurant. I'm not an invalid."

True. Those legs and other body parts had been in absolutely perfect working order this morning.

"Okay," his brother continued, "but why are you taking the new chef out? You've never done that before. Is she cute?"

Oooh... Jolie wanted to hear the answer to that one.

"I guess," was the much-awaited, tummy-twiddling response.

Gee, thanks for the vote.

"But what does that matter?" Todd continued. "She works for me."

And has seen you in the buff, buddy.

"That's what concerns me," Mike answered. "She's the first woman you've taken to dinner since Trista. What's going on?"

Something hit a desktop. Sounded like a fist.

"Dammit, Mike. Leave it alone. I told her I'd take her to dinner to get to know her, so she wouldn't have to cook on her first day. That's it."

Yeah? And what about apologizing for the whole naked thing? Where did that fit in, buddy boy? And the whole "I need to get out tonight," hmmm?

Mike's "Are you sure?" was followed by a piece of furniture slamming against something.

"Look, Mike. You might be older, but your claim to bullying went out when we were teenagers. Knock it off. Stop reading things into this. It's dinner. Plain and simple. The fact that I'm taking her to our favorite restaurant has nothing to do with it. She asked, I said fine. End of story. Got it?"

"But on your anniversary?"

His anniversary. Their favorite restaurant. That explained the aspirin and OJ and *today*.

No wonder he weirded out in the car. Why didn't he say something? She would have understood.

"Yeah, well, I... celebrated... last night. Toasted Trista, us, and happily-never-afters. Woke up with one hell of a hangover."

And naked, with a strange woman witness to his binge.

"And what about reporters? They've been calling the office all day."

"Yeah, I know. My house, too. Lizette even showed up on my doorstep, cameraman in tow."

"So what do you think is going to happen if you're seen out and about with a pretty woman, Todd? People are going to talk." Finger-strumming on the desk. "Though it could stir up interest in your paintings again. Hell, maybe we *should* tip off the local papers."

"Bad idea, Mike. That part of my life is over. And it's just a dinner. Let it go, will you?"

Maybe Mike couldn't let it go, but she sure could. Jolie grabbed her purse and her book and tiptoed back to the elevator to wait for Todd in the lobby. Whoever said no one ever heard anything good about themselves while eavesdropping hadn't listened in on that conversation. She now knew she was "I guess" cute and that she had the power to stop Todd's pain.

She'd just cancel dinner tonight. No big deal. That way he wouldn't have to resurrect the memories and she wouldn't have to watch him pine. Winners all around.

She made herself all comfy in the rounded burgundy chair in the lobby with the good wishes of Mr. Sour-Puss-Turned-Pussycat-Security-Guard, and had barely read two pages before Todd stepped from the elevator, looking surprised to find her there.

Or was that embarrassment? Had he heard her upstairs?

Well, she wasn't going to open old wounds. If he wanted to talk about it, he could start the conversation.

"So where's the food?" he asked.

Or not. Self-deception being the word of the day and all.

"Hiya," She jumped up out of the chair with a little ballooning of her gauzy top. "Have a nice meeting? I finished the shopping early and thought I'd save you the stop. I sent the food home with the delivery service. There was quite a bit and I really don't think it would all fit in the trunk of your car."

"So can I still pay my mortgage this month?" A slim smile accompanied the sarcasm.

Gee, what a kidder. But at least he wasn't stressing about his dinner options.

"Probably," she answered. "But don't count on next month. That's when I break out the Lobster Newburg and shallots with escargot."

"I guess I'll just have to cut back on electricity then. But it'll be worth it if your omelet's anything to go by."

"You got that right, mister."

"So, shall we?" He gestured toward those big glass doors.

"Whatever you say, boss." She jammed her book inside her purse and headed out.

"Oh, really? What*ever*?" That slim smile opened just a tad for a glimmer of teeth, and an eyebrow arched.

Oh, so they had some innuendo going, did they? Normally she could double-entendre with the best of them, but somehow, seeing the guy in the buff—and a very buff buff it was—getting all squidgy around him, and the whole cute/dinner-at-the-wife's-favorite-restaurant/hot-guy thing kinda put a damper on her banter. But at least he had his good mood back.

But still, she couldn't let him have the last word. "Yes, what*ever*—as long as it's got whipped cream attached to it."

Oh Lord. What did she just say?

Chapter Six

Back in the Dream Machine, AKA her favorite car ever—his black 560 SL convertible, tan interior, complete with all the bells and whistles and the closest thing to a new car smell on a vintage—Jolie gnawed on the inside of her cheek trying to figure out how to disappear after that little comment back in the lobby. God. Whipped cream. Freud would have a field day with that.

Plus she had to come up with some way to change the venue for the evening's meal. If she cancelled, it could open up a can of worms that would be better off staying closed. After that little episode with Mike, Todd would probably want to prove something, if just to himself. Maybe she should change where they were eating.

"So, what do you have planned for lunch?" he asked into the silence.

She kept waiting for some comeback to her one-upmanship in the lobby, but… nothing. He went right to lunch.

Lunch. Ohmigosh. Lunch. Of course there'd be lunch. She just happened to forget about it between the car and the food shopping, hitting Mr. Griff, then her shoe and the book. And, of course, that conversation. How was a girl supposed to think about food with that conversation roaming around inside her head?

Mind on the job, Jols.

She grabbed her hair, bunching it at the base of her neck, and rested her elbow on the door. "How about ham and cheese on an English muffin with honey mustard? Or I can throw a quick mandarin chicken salad together. Or do you want something on the grill? I bought salmon and tuna steaks. Though, they're best if marinated and that'll take too long. I guess a burger would be quick. Whatever you want, just—"

"Jolie."

Then he started with the touching again, which stopped her from rattling on. Words, that is. Her nerves were a whole other story. She almost wished he wouldn't touch her. Which was a big change from wishing he flat-out wouldn't touch her, *à la* the earlier car ride.

She slid a peek at him. He was grinning.

"Jolie," he said again.

Honest to God, no one ever said her name quite that way, a French slide to the "J" and a bit drawn out on the "ie." She could listen to that sound for the rest of her—

"Yes?" She wasn't dwelling on his voice. Or anything having to do with the rest of her life unless it included the words, "Jolie Gardener, Proprietor."

"Relax. You don't have to impress me with five-star meals. I'm just an average guy and an average sandwich sounds fine." He nodded to the vehicle ahead of them. "If I'm not mistaken, that's the delivery truck. I'll help you unload and then we'll just grab whatever's closest."

Oh, boy. He really shouldn't have said that. Naughty Girl sprang to life, ready to grab what was closest all right.

That would *so* not be good for their collective paycheck.

"Okay. Sure. Fine. Sounds like a plan." *Brilliant conversation, Jols.*

Todd zipped in front of the truck and signed for all the stuff from the delivery guy. Amid the cacophony of something like fifteen phone calls, the three of them wrangled the bags to the kitchen in no time flat. Jolie started emptying the bags while Todd, a couple of grocery items in hand, saw the guy out.

"Sure do appreciate the help, sir," Mr. Delivery said.

Sound reverberated in the house, probably due to all the empty wall space as Todd had yet to hang a picture, his or otherwise, and the front door was directly opposite the kitchen so she could see the man touch the rim of his baseball cap like a salute.

"You and the missus have fun putting all that away, ya hear?" There was a little tongue click at the end of his sentence.

The missus. That was probably a common enough mistake, but how would Todd react?

To her surprise, he chuckled.

"What's so funny?" she asked as he entered the kitchen.

"This." He held up two round white containers.

Whipped topping.

Oh.

The guy thought Todd and she— Mister and missus— Whipped topping—

Just crack open the limestone tiles and bury her beneath them. That's what she got for trying to be a smart aleck.

"God only knows what he thought we'd need two of them for." Todd arched his eyebrow. "So what was it you said earlier about whipped—"

"Okay, okay." She threw a roll of paper towels at him. "It's not nice to tease people."

Todd caught the towels and, in a heartbeat, got all serious. "I'm not teasing you, Jolie. Well, okay, maybe I am, but in a good way. I'm not trying to hurt your feelings or embarrass you. You have to admit, it's a funny coincidence."

He was right, but the kicker was, she *would* actually like to see what the two of them could do with whipped cream. How was that for embarrassing? But no way, no how, would she admit to it. He was finding it funny while she was finding it a turn-on.

"Yes," she said in the most devil-may-care voice she could muster, "it is pretty funny. And pretty messy."

The ironic thing was, if that brand hadn't been listed in his personal dossier the employment agency compiled on its clients, she would have bought real cream—*unwhipped* cream—and this debacle would never have happened. But no. He had to like the commercial stuff enough to mention it on his Favorites list.

The phone rang again, for which she was thankful. Todd? Not so much. He cursed and headed toward the den while she went back to emptying the bags.

"I unplugged the phone." He was back in two seconds flat. "That ought to end the calls."

Ah yes. She still had to address the dinner location tangent. "Uh, Todd?"

"Yes, Jolie?"

She had to bite back a sigh. He really did say her name completely differently than anyone else ever had. And before she analyzed if that was a good thing or not, she dumped a bag of peppers in the vegetable bin and stuck her head around the fridge door. "Um, about tonight—" She poked her head back into the fridge. She couldn't look at him when she said it. She wasn't a good enough liar.

"What about it?"

"Um, well." *Bam, clang*, went the drawers and shelves. "I was thinking that I'm not really dressed for *The Midnight Maiden*. Maybe we should go someplace else. Fast food or something. It really doesn't matter. It's the gesture that counts. So I'm totally fine with someplace other than *The Midnight Maiden*. Or I could cook. Whatever." For the fifth time she moved the butter between the dairy drawer and the little flip compartment on the door.

Silence.

Could be good, could be bad.

"Oh."

Or utter dejection—which was not one of her options.

She peered around the door, ready to duck back in if he was staring at her. She could pretend all right, but flat out lying to him was sort of hard.

Does lying by omission count? Naughty Girl asked. *You know. The love story thing?*

Not now! Jolie shoved Naughty Girl to the depths of Whose-Side-Are-You-On-Anyway while Todd mangled one of the twisty-ties on a produce bag, his shoulders hunched. She banged the drawer a little more so he'd think she was still inside the fridge and not staring at him.

He took a big breath, then threw his shoulders back and raised his chin, dropping the bag on the table. Okay, they'd be eating bruised tomatoes.

He turned and—darn it!—she wasn't quick enough to bury her face back in the fridge. Which was sort of a good thing since her nose was getting cold.

About the only part of her that was.

"I've made the reservations. We have to go," he said as if declaring World War III. "I'll unpack the rest of the things," came out like orders in a military campaign. "You go ahead home and get ready. I'll pick you up at seven."

"But... but... but... "

Really, Jolie, just 'cause the guy has a magnificent one, you don't need to harp on it. Get your mind out of the boxers and into this conversation.

Naughty Girl was lecturing *her*?

"Lunch," Jolie managed to spit out. Finally.

"I'm perfectly capable of throwing a sandwich together."

"Well, um, okay. Of course you are. But the dishes. I can do the dishes."

His shoved his hands into his pockets. "I said I'd get to them. And I will."

First the dinner location, then the whipped cream fiasco. It was probably in her best interests to just agree with him and get the heck out of there.

She side-stepped toward the patio door with an ungraceful lunge to grab her purse off the tabletop where it had fallen over. "Well, if you're sure, then. I mean, if you really want to go to *The Midnight Maiden*, I guess I can't stop you."

His eyes narrowed. "Is there a problem with *The Midnight Maiden*? It's where you said you want to go, right?"

"Problem?" Did she just squeak? That was so not attractive. He nodded. "No. No problem. Seven is fine. I'll be ready."

Of course she couldn't exit gracefully. The darn purse got caught on the French door handle as she closed it and she had to make another exit. How mortifying.

God, she was only trying to do a good deed. She yanked open her car door and sat, banging her knee on the steering wheel of her Bug. The guy didn't have to take her there. There were a zillion restaurants in the city; any one of them would do.

She turned on the ignition, the sputtering *rumble rumble* sounding as agitated as she felt. Why did he have to have his heart set on that one?

She backed out of his driveway and headed out of the cul-de-sac. Well, it wasn't as if she had a say in the matter anymore. She'd tried. Now all she had to do was kill time until dinner. Thank goodness for Mr. Griff's book. That ought to keep her occupied.

At the stop sign, she reached for her purse and opened it.

The book wasn't there.

Oh crud. It was sitting on Todd's kitchen table, right next to the bag of capers and spices.

Great. She was batting a thousand today. First she asked him to take her to his wife's favorite restaurant, then she innuendo-ed all over the place with whipped cream, and then she left a love story sitting out in plain view.

Why didn't she just rip the guy's heart out and be done with it?

***

Todd stared at the bags on his counter after Jolie left.

It was so quiet.

Too quiet.

Funny, he hadn't noticed the silence before today. It'd just *been*. Now, it screamed at him.

He grabbed the closest bag and removed sea salt, garlic, a bunch of parsley.

Get over it, Best. He couldn't use chatter to fill the space in his life. No matter how pretty the chatterer.

He'd lied to Mike earlier. Jolie wasn't cute; she was gorgeous. Tall and lithe with a ballet dancer's frame, Jolie had a beauty he could appreciate with his artist's eyes. Perfect bone structure, creamy skin warmed by a curtain of mink hair, those eyes… He still hadn't figured out what to call that color.

He exhaled and pulled a bunch of fresh basil from the bag. The last thing he should be thinking about was the color of his chef's eyes. For all he knew, she had a boyfriend somewhere who wouldn't appreciate Todd's observations.

And he had no business looking at another woman.

His gut clenched. Damn it all. When would it stop? He wasn't being unfaithful to Trista by finding another woman attractive. He knew that. It just hurt so damned much that he couldn't let go.

A yellow flyer clung to the band around the oregano. St. Gabe's Church was having its annual fundraiser again. He'd participated every year—well, every year that he'd been painting. He'd done one special picture for the art auction, painted just for the church. A one-of-a-kind, never-to-be-done-in-print piece.

Those paintings had brought in enough money to launch a daycare, a shelter, and fully fund the school. It'd been Trista's idea.

He crumpled the flyer in his fist. That was why he hadn't

participated since her death. It brought it all back—the times they'd gone together, his first unveiling of the painting, her excitement like a child on Christmas morning, as if he'd painted it just for her.

Of course, he *had* painted it just for her. Every landscape had been painted for her, through the eyes of his love. He wanted to give her the beauty she'd seen in him, for the faith she'd had in him.

He folded the brown bag and stuck it on top of the others. He should get the food put away and maybe grab a swim. Exercise, a good sweaty workout, always helped to clear his mind, something to do with endorphins. Whatever it was, he'd better get to it. Jolie had had enough to deal with already; he shouldn't bring his troubles to dinner.

Life went on.

And so would he.

Chapter Seven

Jolie heard the *vroom vroom* of Todd's car and grabbed her watch off the bedside table. Six forty. Crud. She had to hurry; no telling what could happen to the Dream Machine outside her less-than-desirable-address apartment complex if she kept him waiting.

She marked her page and headed to the one small window allotted her by Mr. Murphy, the avaricious landlord (which explained how fifteen mostly vacant apartments could fit in a building designed for half that number) and peeked out.

Sure enough, there he was. Man of her dre—her heroine's dreams.

Sheesh, for someone who required thirty minutes max to get ready, she should have been able to squeeze those eighteen hundred seconds somewhere in the last four hours. But no. She had picked up a favorite book and wham! the world disappeared.

Jolie rushed back to the bathroom, grabbed the curling iron for two little flips, brushed some mascara on and, oh what the heck, grabbed the tube of pink sparkly lipstick. Sugar Plum Ice, Sugar Plum Gloss, some sweet fruity name. She was a flurry of flicking hands and twitching hair and then into the sink went the magic wand of hairdos, the magic wand of eyelashes, and the newly acquired magic wand of lips. Yeah, she was definitely destined to write fairytale happily-ever-afters.

His footsteps *ching*-ed against the metal steps in the stairwell. What the heck did she do with her shoe? She'd chosen the turquoise dress and her kicky yellow flats just wouldn't do. Silver sandals would have to suffice. Well, one of them anyway. Where was that other one? She lived in an eighteen by eighteen foot box—how far could one footless shoe go?

Shadows flickered beneath her door. Great, he was there and she was still shoeless.

She kicked a pillow that God-knew-why decided to spend the day on the floor, and luckily found the other one.

She wasn't normally this disorganized, but for some reason she was all thumbs trying to get ready for this date—dinner.

It's a dinner, Jolie. Nothing more.

Tell that to her hormones.

Todd knocked.

"Be right there," she said, trying not to break her neck as she slid Foot into the sandal. Of course, she shoved the little thong thingy between the wrong toes, so she had to do it again.

Shoe on, she took a quick breath and found herself going all 1950's glamour goddess before opening the door, brushing the hair from her forehead and running her hands down the dress. If she'd had a mirror by the door she would've glanced into it and puckered her lips, brushing at the corner with her pinky finger in case any lipstick was smudged. But, no mirror, so Todd would have to take her with smudged lipstick or not.

Oh, take me, take me.

And it was with that thought that she opened the door.

Hellooooo.

Naughty Girl was on the mark with that assessment. The man was looking good. Really good. Sinfully good. The kind of good that could get a good girl into trouble.

And she was so trying to be a good girl.

"Hi," Jolie said, trying to keep the husky glamour goddess from emanating from her throat *à la* Anne Bancroft in "The Graduate." Or Mae West with her "Come up and see me sometime."

Would it be too clichéd to lean back against the door frame? Probably. Not to mention pathetic. He thought she was, quote, "cute, I guess." Not the most inviting reason to do a come-hither.

Plus there was the job she had going with him. And that was *all* she had going with him and as soon as Naughty Girl listened up and paid attention, they'd all have a much better evening.

Well, no, that wasn't true. They'd probably have the best time if she took Nasty's advice, but that couldn't happen.

"You ready?" he asked.

"What? You can't tell? Well, gosh, I didn't think the fifteen minutes I was missing in my normal routine would show that drastically.

See what happens when you get caught up in a good story? Pages fly by and the time even quicker. Before you know it, you're missing dinner—and obviously necessary primping time—because you've got to find out if Lady Hammonton sashays across the crowded ballroom right into the oh-so-dashing Jeremy Godfield's arms and—"

"Jolie?"

Okay, let the floor open up and swallow her whole right now.

"Um… right. Sure. I'm ready. Just let me grab, um… my bag." Luckily, she'd had the forethought to hang her bag on the closet door so she wouldn't have to do the throw-the-clothes-all-over-the-bed/sofa thing in front of him.

Bag in hand, she stepped through the door, pulling it shut behind her. "All ready," she told him.

"You look very nice," was what he told her in return, the upward curve of his lips drawing her attention to the sparkle in his green eyes and those crinkles at the corners.

And there went her knees to mush.

It only took four words. Four words! How did he do that? She'd have to remember that one and throw it in her book somewhere. *Turn heroine's knees to mush in four simple words, by Todd Best.*

"Uh, thanks." *Uh? Uh? Good God, Jolie, your vocabulary is regressing.* "You look pretty spiffy yourself." Khakis with a forest green golf shirt tucked in the waistband showed off his upper body quite nicely. Not that she was supposed to be noticing. That "she was human" excuse was getting a bit thin.

It was a breezy night with the soft wind off the river, perfect for cooling the summer air. The early arrivals to the evening cricket chorus warmed up their "instruments" from the grove of elm trees behind the parking lot, Jolie's heels clicking a soft rhythm along the pock-marked cement walkway. At the top of the steps to the asphalt, she turned to look at Todd and darn if she didn't touch him on the arm. His touchy-feely-ness must be catching. "We're eating outside, aren't we? I hope so. I love to watch the stars come out."

He tested the railing then pulled his hand back as it shook in the loose moorings of crumbling concrete, and lightly gripped her elbow instead. "Sure. We can eat on deck if you want."

"Thank you. Oh, look." She pointed to a flock of birds fluttering in for a landing. "How cute! Pigeons."

"Pigeons are cute? That's a new one," Todd laughed. "Most people I know think they're pests."

"You must hang around city people. They call them rats with wings, but I think pigeons are pretty, with their soft gray feathers and all those jewel tones in their necks. I like to feed them. Appreciative little things, though I have to remember to stay away from parked cars when I bring them leftovers, 'cause my neighbors are not so appreciative."

"You seem to have a penchant for feeding things," he said as he held open the door to the Dream Machine.

That was a first. Never had a man opened a car door for her.

Showed the kind of guys she dated. Not that there'd been too many, anyway, but yes, there had been a few and she'd been "curious," but once she saw what it was all about, she'd decided she was going to better herself so she had a choice of an improved caliber of men. If only her mom had had the same epiphany.

"I guess I just like to feed God's creatures." Plus their begging for scraps ran a little too close to home with memories of her childhood, so, yes, she fed them.

She slid into her seat, swinging her silver sandaled feet into the car, looking for a way to change the subject before becoming lost in the miasma that was her past. "Oh, look how the sky is laced with all those pretty shades of pink and orange and red."

"Um hmmm," Todd said, slipping into his tan leather seat beside her.

"Pretty non-committal for a guy who paints for a living." She pulled the seatbelt across her chest, latching it in place.

"Do you have a music preference?" Todd reached for the radio.

Okay. *Ixnay* on the artistic talk. But music worked. "I enjoy classical."

"Classical," he returned, *sans* emotion, his fingers stilling.

Oh, dear God, she'd done it again. Trista must have been a big classical fan. Restaurant, book, music…

Just shoot her now.

"Todd, really, it doesn't matter." She reached for his hand and a thousand fires started under her skin. The guy was potent, so she ripped her hand away and stuffed it in her lap. How could she feel like that while he was remembering his wife? How could she feel like that at all? It just wasn't a good idea, no matter how she tried to rationalize it. "We don't need music. Or you can put on anything. Rap, hip-hop, Alternative, Top 40, I don't care. Whatever you want."

"What I want is... " He blew out a breath and sat back in his seat, his hands clenching the steering wheel, eyes closed, mouth tightening.

This was so not a moment she wanted to be a part of. She had to leave.

She undid her seatbelt and scrambled for the door handle. She couldn't be witness to this. It was too personal, too intense.

"What I want, is dinner." He turned her way with the barest semblance of something called a grin and nodded at the seatbelt hanging over her shoulder. "Want to buckle up?"

"Um… all right." She re-attached the seatbelt. If he wanted to pretend that flashback didn't happen, she could too, though who were they kidding?

"Oh, here." Todd did a funky sliding/grabbing movement over the seat. "I assume this is yours." He handed her something small, rectangular, and paperback, and she wanted to slink under the seat.

"Unless you ordered *The Dashing Rogue* from the grocery store for dinner tonight?"

If she could order a dashing rogue for dinner, Todd would be her first choice.

Yeah, yeah, bad idea.

"Sorry. It must have fallen out of my purse. Thanks." She shoved it under her thigh. "A new bookstore opened down the street from Arena's Grocery and the owner gave it to me."

"So, do you read those or was he just giving out anything?" Todd started the car and backed out of the parking spot.

This would be the perfect time to tell him she was writing one, but did she really want to do that? She couldn't afford him to ever link himself to her story—not with the whole "I don't want my life to be an open book" comment. He wouldn't be too thrilled to show up in the pages of her manuscript, disguised or not, so she better make sure he had no cause to recognize himself.

"I'm a big fan of romance novels," seemed like a safe answer since he'd caught her reading one on her first day.

He couldn't take exception to that, right?

***

Jonathan Griff stared at the figures on the television screen in his sparse apartment. Guardians didn't need many comforts. He wouldn't even have the television if it weren't absolutely necessary. Having given Bixby his laptop after Bixby had accidentally flung his into the river dodging that dog, and the human economic downturn having inspired tightening of gold-braided belts in the Celestial Realm, Jonathan had had to put in a request for a retro model television to be able to monitor his Charges. Rafael had raised his brow when he'd first seen it, but the archangel was nothing if not supportive.

Though how much longer Rafael would be patient with him, Jonathan didn't know. He wasn't quite sure what the criteria was for earning his wings, but he was going to try his hardest.

Starting with getting these two on the same wavelength.

Eye twitching, he'd cringed when Jolie shoved the book under her leg. He'd thought for sure the romance novel would help, but if she kept forgetting it or hiding it, the notion wouldn't take hold. And Todd had totally dismissed the flyer.

Jonathan tapped his index fingers together then steepled them beneath his chin, resting his elbows on his knees. He needed another angle on this. Those two were in want of some serious help.

***

Todd ran a hand through his hair, then hit the turn signal at the entrance of the complex. Romance novels. That figured. "So, you're one of those."

"Those?"

"Happily-ever-after types." A horn blared as the driver swerved around him. Stupid kids, doing fifty in a thirty-five-mile-an-hour zone. Thought they'd live forever.

If they only realized.

"Well, yes, I do hope for happily-ever-afters." Graceful hand movements accompanied Jolie's words as if the words alone weren't enough to convey her hopefulness. Someone ought to bottle that enthusiasm as an antidote for depression. "Sure beats the alternative. Who wants an unhappily-ever-after? You have to find something good in any bad situation. Otherwise why bother doing anything? So, when life gets a little too real, it's always nice to hop into a book where you know things are going to end up okay, no matter how bad they seem." She dropped her hands into her lap, the fingers interlaced.

He'd been that optimistic once. "Real life's not like that."

"I know, but isn't it cool to hope?" There went her hands again, a ballet of movement as she slicked her hair over her shoulder. "I mean, good things have to happen to people. Look at those who go through absolutely horrible situations then go out and become beacons of hope for others."

"Such as?" He glanced over to see her eyes widen.

Violet. Her eyes were violet.

"Wow. Really? You don't see this? At all? What about that fire on River Road?"

"Tragic." No one would ever forget the largest block fire in the town's history five years ago. He tapped his brakes and came to a stop at the traffic light behind a Salvation Army truck.

"I know. The factory exploded and the whole block went up in flames."

A truck bearing the Red Cross logo crisscrossed the intersection with a Meals-On-Wheels delivery van. "I fail to see the hope in that, Jolie. Many people died, even those who went in after the kids in the daycare center." Oh, yeah. He remembered that fire. And the new daycare his painting at the auction had funded afterward.

"But it's the hope they gave us, Todd. The hope in human nature."

"Hope in human nature? That's your happily-ever-after?" Had she *seen* the news reports of that devastation? Hope in human nature? Oh to be that rose-colored-glasses-hopeful again.

She touched his arm, and Todd pulled his gaze from those violet eyes to where her warm, graceful fingers tightened against his skin.

"Do you remember that day?" she continued. "First the boom, then the smoke. No one knew what had happened before the building was one big gas ball. And then it spread. All those houses just went up in flames, fire racing down the street like a match to gunpowder right toward the daycare center. They couldn't get those kids out fast enough."

Todd let up on the gas as the truck in front of them started moving, and gave Jolie one last glance, the star on the Make-A-Wish

Foundation billboard behind her framing her head like a crown. "You find this story uplifting?"

"Argh!" she huffed, facing front and throwing her hands in the air. Even that was a symphony of movement.

"Not uplifting, Todd. Of course not. But when the neighbors came, and all the factory workers who were running for their lives stopped to help get those kids out, it was amazing. People were coughing and crying, some were bleeding, but they ran into that building to get those kids. Babies were asleep on the upper floors in their cribs. And not one of the children died. If everyone had waited until the firemen arrived, most of the kids would have died from smoke inhalation or worse. That, to me, is heroic. And hopeful. Those injured and scared people chose to help others."

A local bus pulled up, a banner for Habitat-For-Humanity gracing the side. "Some would argue it was instinct."

"Not instinct, Todd. A genuine goodness in the human race. They could have elected to keep on running, got themselves out of harm's way, but they didn't. They chose to stop and help. We always have choices, Todd. It just depends on how we make them."

As they passed Children's Hospital, a car merged in front of them, American Cancer Society bumper stickers across its fender.

What was with all the charity advertising? Some philanthropist come to town? He'd been one of those once— "So, Jolie, do you have any idea where my happily-ever-after comes in, since you're apparently able to see the good side to everything?"

"Well, actually, yes, I do."

He did a double take. He probably should have expected that answer from Little Miss Sunshine, but honestly, she was surprising him at every turn.

"Your happily-ever-after is one day at a time. Seeing the people who care for you. Your brother, for instance. He wouldn't worry himself about your business and welfare if he didn't."

Todd snorted and almost missed the turn-off. "Don't forget the six-figure paycheck."

"Really?" she squeaked. "Now I'm surprised. I wouldn't have pegged you for being so negative. Or so cynical." She shook her head. "You think your brother's only helping you out for the money?"

She was right. Mike wasn't like that. And Todd knew it.

He gauged the merging traffic before joining it. "No, you're right. Mike's a great guy. He jumped right in when I was... floundering, I guess, and has kept the company rolling. I owe him a lot."

He owed him more than a lot. Hell, he didn't know if *he* would've hung around taking the abuse, the constant barrage of "leave me alones" Mike had had to deal with.

But Mike had taken it all and more. Those first few days...

There'd been no hesitation on his brother's part. He'd quit his job to take on the task of overseeing Best Enterprises, the company Todd had built with Trista's encouragement. The company that kept his pictures in the public eye and his bank account full. The company that had proved Trista's faith in him.

And what was he doing about it now? Griping. Being annoyed that it even existed. Wanting it gone.

What did that say about his value of Trista's memory?

Todd reached over and squeezed Jolie's hand. "How do you do that?"

"Do what?"

He didn't think her eyes could get any wider. Even more so than when she'd gotten an eyeful of something she never should have had to deal with this morning. He really did owe her this dinner and a nice time. Enough with the angst.

"Put a person's life in perspective with a few simple words."

She straightened her back. "Okay, number one—simple? I'll have you know I've read and read, and studied, took classes to get my vocabulary out of *simple*."

He bit back the smile. Such indignation. "And number two?"

She crossed her arms. "Number two is none of your business."

And now he really wanted that answer. He cocked an eyebrow and the corresponding corner of his mouth at her, letting a little of his smile through. "Please? With whipped cream on top?"

Her exuberance returned in her smile. What was it she'd said earlier? He got her? Yes, he sure did.

"Okay," she said after the laughter receded. "Number two is just a sunny outlook on life, because it's true, you know. People do have choices. You've got a choice each morning to get out of bed on the right side or the wrong side. I mean, yeah, life's hard. Different people have different definitions of hard, but it's all in your perspective.

"Take me, for example. I could have let the system turn me into another welfare mom at age sixteen like a dozen girls I know, but I chose to get out of it. I wanted more for myself. So I struggled and stayed clean, and got myself into a decent school and learned a trade. I had the perfect excuse to be mad at the world, but I got mad at my circumstances instead and changed them."

"And here you are."

He was wrong. Her eyes could get wider.

"Ye…yes. Here I am."

***

Jonathan sat back in the threadbare BarcaLounger. Had Jolie really said all of that? To Todd?

Jonathan tapped the corner of his mouth. *My, my. Big strides for her.*

He couldn't help smiling.

Oh, yes, this was going to work out. He just *knew* it.

***

Jolie clamped her mouth shut. Had she just said what she thought she had? Had she just laid her entire life on the table for him? What was she thinking? She'd never told anyone that stuff. It made her feel a little weird, kinda open and vulnerable. Naked.

And they were back to that.

"So, Jolie Gardener," Todd said after a few minutes of much-needed silence.

Much needed for her so she could recover from that unplanned therapy session. Not that she needed therapy; she was just fine. Really. Talking about it without breaking down was a positive. Proved she was beyond it all.

She smoothed her dress over her lap and checked her earrings. Proving it to herself just like Todd was with his determination to have dinner at *The Midnight Maiden.* See? They had something in common.

"Yes, Todd Best?" There. Pleasant, solid, no shakiness in her voice. She was fine.

"What does a personal chef do with herself when she's not cooking meals?"

"Plan them?"

He laughed. Good.

"You are really good for me." He squeezed her hand again as he slowed down on the exit ramp of the closest thing to a highway this little burg had to offer. "I'm glad you took this job."

She let the words wash over her as Todd zipped into the parking lot by *The Midnight Maiden*. Other than for her meals, she hadn't received many compliments in her twenty-eight years.

The boat bobbed on the tiny river waves, the ropes creaking against their moorings, a line of white Christmas lights blinking from the upper deck. Yes, she was glad she'd taken this job as well. For a whole host of reasons.

They found an empty parking spot near the gangplank and Todd held out his hand as he, once again, opened the car door for her. "Ready?"

"As I'll ever be." She slid off the seat and something plopped on the pavement just as her feet did.

"Your book." Todd bent to retrieve it. "Here, you better not lose this. How else will you find out if *The Dashing Rogue* lives happily-ever-after?"

He was teasing and she was enjoying.

And, yes, she did want to believe that, somehow, the dashing rogue would have his happily-ever-after.

Chapter Eight

Hurricane glass sconces lined the cherry-paneled walls of the interior dining room of *The Midnight Maiden*, the bulbs flickering like flames as the maitre d' led them through a maze of little cherry wood tables on mauve carpeting, over to the stairs. Todd flourished his hand for her to precede him, so up she went, the wind kicking up as she exited the stairwell.

Purple and orange rays of the waning sun bounced off skyscrapers onto the glittering water like a laser light show. A prop plane skimmed the riverbank, large yellow banner proclaiming the name of the sightseeing company that had recently started air tours of the city.

"Wow. The view is gorgeous." She tried to keep her hair from blowing around, but gave up when a handful ended up clipping her in the eye. "I've never been on a boat before. I like this gentle rocking. Is it always like this? I guess I can see how this upsets some people's tummies. But not mine." At least not tonight. Please.

Not that she was nervous or anything.

"Uh hmmm," said the Man of Suddenly Few Words behind her.

What happened to Mr. Chatty from the car?

The maitre d' unhooked a velvet rope at the bow of the boat and ushered them to the lone table there. Todd's celebrity status came in handy.

Or maybe he just paid a lot for the privacy.

Guilt slithered down her spine, but she squashed it. No one would ever know he was the basis for her romance hero. No one. Why should they?

The d' held out her chair—darn. With Todd doing all the door holding, she'd kind of hoped he would've done it here, too. But beggars couldn't be choosers—*not* that she was a beggar. Nor would she be. In no aspect of her life, job, housing, affection… nothing.

Bringing home (again) the fact that Todd was a respected guest, a couple of elegant menus appeared as if by magic in front of them as the d' himself started rattling off the *spécialités*. But Jolie wasn't in any frame of mind to memorize stuff. The wind was ruffling Todd's hair and the sun reflected off the water into those incredible eyes of his, highlighting the laugh lines at the corners.

Why were they called laugh lines on guys and crow's feet on women? Talk about inequality of the sexes.

"Jolie?"

Could she—just once—stay on topic with the man around? "Yes?"

"Would you like an appetizer?"

Oh. Food. She should be all over that, but found herself thinking about sparkling green eyes instead. Husky laughs and inside jokes. Broad shoulders and nicely-shaped pecs straining against cotton...

And the inside of her mouth getting as dry as that cotton. And incapable of speech, too. Oh, for Pete's sake!

Luckily, there was a goblet of water on the table and she took a quick swallow, stopping just before a gulp. That would so not be attractive. 'Course she had to make a quick grab for the napkin to blot the corner of her mouth where the water wanted to make a reappearance. Honest to God, where was her composure?

Finding it somewhere down near her knees, she pulled herself together and gave Todd a dazzling smile. At least, she hoped it was dazzling and not desperate. Or ditzy.

"You know, Todd, food's my livelihood, so I'd rather not have to think about it. Why don't you go ahead and choose for us."

Off went Mr. Maitre d' with their drink orders and appetizer selections, whatever they were, and she was left with a gorgeous man and a glorious sun just as it hit the water line.

"Is it going to hiss, do you think?" Todd asked.

The scent of him registered before she realized he'd scooted his chair closer. *Grey Flannel*, her favorite cologne. It was subtle, not all cowboy boots and chaps.

There was an image.

What was the question again? Hiss? Right. "I used to think the sun drowned each night when I was a kid," she answered. "Although that could have something to do with Mr. Gaston falling off the top of the dam where he'd been fishing and never making it out of the river."

Now why had she dredged that awful memory up? Seriously, she needed to focus on the conversation.

"You saw someone drown?" Todd touched the back of her hand. "How old were you?"

There was a lot to commend this touchy-feely business. Amazing how much heat there was in fingertips. "I was six and he always used to tell us these incredible stories, how big his catches were and how many he could reel in in his younger days. I know now that they were all fish tales and might've had something to do with re-living his glory days, not to mention the fifth of whiskey he carted around like a newborn, but he could tell a good story." And was in some way responsible for her own story-telling dreams, but she didn't want to clue Todd in on that.

"So, what happened?" He hadn't pulled his hand back.

"Apparently he finally caught something and wasn't prepared. It yanked him over the side and that was the last we ever saw." She shrugged because she should be over a six-year-old's terror. "We don't know if it was a fish or an old log or a piece of furniture, but I like to think that Mr. Gaston went down with the biggest fish of his life."

"Is that your happily-ever-after for Mr. Gaston?"

He remembered. She couldn't help smiling. "Yes. That's Mr. Gaston's."

Todd tapped her hand one last time, then reached for his water and took a sip. He dipped the goblet toward the horizon. "Ssh. Listen. I think it's hissing."

"Do you do this a lot? Sit and listen to the sun?"

He chuckled and set the goblet down, wiping his tanned hands on the beige linen napkin. "No. But I really did try when I was a kid. My grandparents lived on Cape Cod and I'd spend a couple weeks during the summer with them. Every evening, my grandfather and I would set the crab traps and watch the sunset. I think it was that, more than anything, that started my painting."

Well. He mentioned painting. Hmmm. She had to handle this delicately, not scare him off. Kind of like feeding a wild animal. Or one of those rats with wings. Put her hand out gently, slowly. Offering, as it were. "How did the sunset do that?"

He drummed his fingers against the cream tablecloth, a light *thum-thum.*

"I kept studying the sun, watching it, listening to hear that hiss, night after night. I remember how beautiful the sky looked just before it hit the water, all the colors, and the water sparkling as if it were lit from beneath. It mesmerized me."

His laugh was self-conscious and she smiled again. Putting out another figurative hand.

"I didn't realize it at the time, but that was my calling, my talent rising to the surface. By the end of that summer, I found myself grabbing crayons and colored pencils, anything to capture what I was seeing."

"And did you?"

He looked back at the sunset. She looked at him, holding her breath. Would he share it with her? Talk about it? When was the last time he'd spoken about it?

"Eventually I did. It took a while, some experimenting with different media until I was satisfied I could do justice to God's creation."

Don't make a big deal out of his revelation. She swallowed, trying to keep the grin off her face. "You've certainly done that. I've seen your work and it is truly amazing. I feel like the scene is right outside an invisible window I'm looking through. As if I could reach out and touch whatever is in your painting."

"My wife used to say the same thing."

And there went the mood.

But she refused to let that happen. She didn't let "quit" into her life and she wasn't going to allow it into his. Not on her watch. "The critics do, too. They love your work."

"Loved. Past tense."

"No. *Still.* They love your work, Todd. Your paintings sell every day and the demand hasn't abated. Just because you're taking a hiatus doesn't mean people are going to stop wanting your work."

He snatched his hands off the table and shoved them beneath it. "Jolie, I'm not on hiatus. I'm finished. Done. No more artwork."

Right. She'd just watched the guy light up talking about the sunset, for Pete's sake. He had no idea who he was dealing with. He'd let her in a little and she'd gotten hold. Tenaciousness had seen her through some lean times. This was no different.

"Well," she said with a just-enough-under-exaggerated sigh, "that's a shame. I'm sure your wife wouldn't like that."

"Leave my wife out of this."

"Sorry." Not really. It needed to be said. How she knew that, she had no idea. Maybe it had to do with not liking bad karma. "It just seems a shame to let go of her memory like that."

"You don't know what you're talking about. The last thing I'll do is let go of her memory."

Those green eyes, they were a-blazin'.

Well, some emotion was better than none.

"But, Todd, if you stop painting, something your wife admired about you, cared about, inspired in you, you are, in essence, putting her memory away. In a box, locked up tight with a key, never to be seen or felt or experienced or shared again. How do you think she'd feel about that?"

He turned his head, gracing her with the view of his sharp jaw line, the muscles bunching along it. She hoped he wouldn't crack a tooth, but he needed that food for thought. Because she, as an aspiring writer, someone creative and with—she hoped—talent, she understood how the urge to create overtook everything so that it had to emerge or it'd mess with sleep patterns, consume thoughts, and take over a life. Creative expression needed an outlet. If it were bottled up inside, at some point it'd explode. Or die. And that would be such a tragedy for him.

There was another minute—or five—of silence, then he sighed and brought his hands back to the table, reaching for his glass of water again. He didn't take a drink, just kind of swirled the liquid around in the glass.

"I never thought about it like that." His voice was low.

Oh, thank God the words "you're fired" didn't come spewing forth. She'd particularly hate a Donald Trump moment right then. Not that there was ever a good time for a DT moment, but now would have been especially awkward.

Luckily, the maitre d' picked that moment to show up with their appetizers and drinks, and Todd did the wine twirling/sipping thing. She was not a sommelier, nor would she ever aspire to that particular function. She'd done heavy book research about wines for her career instead of actual sampling, due to an instinctual aversion to the stuff. Actually, she wasn't big on any form of alcohol unless it was cooked into a dish. Saw too much of the not-so-pretty side effects of a drinking binge—this morning included.

Though some parts of this morning hadn't been so bad.

Mr. Maitre d' placed the broiled scallops in front of them. Jolie didn't think she'd ever seen a scallop quite that size, about as big as a four-year-old's fist. She spun the plate around to study all sides then took a bite. It was like eating a slice of heaven, the texture of flan, with a dark, almost chocolate, roux with a hint of burgundy—*au jus* for scallops. "I have to get this recipe."

Todd added a few "uh hmmms," but the silence wasn't strained. Always a good thing.

Amid the soft *lap-lap* of the waves, the little *chink* of utensils against china, she took another bite and it was all she could do not to moan. The scallops were to die for.

Or it could be because the last ray of sun hit Todd's profile at just the right angle.

The man was truly beautiful and all five of her senses knew it. Not to mention the seven layers of skin she possessed.

She needed to focus on the food.

"So, where did you get the idea to go to culinary school?" Apparently Todd was on the same wavelength.

"You know *Casteleoni's* downtown?"

He nodded.

"I worked there and Bella, the owner, suggested it."

"So what else do you do with your time?" Todd asked. "I'm sure cooking doesn't occupy your entire day."

Words failed her. What was she supposed to say? That she was in the market for a hero and *oh, by the way, you're my inspiration to a best-selling happily-ever-after*?

Not if she wanted to stay employed.

A sliver of sumptuous scallop slid down her throat again and she waved the fork around. "I keep myself occupied. I take classes at the community college."

And she did. Just because it was a random semester here and there, he didn't need to know the details. "I want to open my own pastry shop someday."

Or write a best-seller with movie rights.

"Your own pastry shop. That's ambitious."

"That's me, Ambitious Jolie."

"I thought you were Good Sport Jolie?" he teased.

He remembered…

"Good sport, ambitious. Take your pick." Jolie cleared her throat and squirmed around in her seat. "So, what do *you* do during the day? We still need to work out a schedule so I'm not in your way."

Todd's eyes narrowed as he stared over her shoulder again.

"Hello? Todd?" She waved her fork tines in his face.

"Hmm. What I do. Well, let's see. I work out, check in with Mike. Correspondence, bills. That sort of thing. Whatever people do in their lives, I guess. Nothing out of the ordinary." He shrugged, then met her gaze.

There was nothing ordinary about the full force of those green eyes. Focused on her, a glint of determination in there—just to come up with his daily schedule?—that, for a second, she forgot her own name. Well, no, not really, but what had they been talking about? Something about ordinary things—

Flash!

A burst of a light pierced the dusky sky, zinging into her eyes, and Todd grabbed her hand—not in a good way—and pulled her down to the deck as if they were being bombed.

"Mr. Best, can you tell us who she is? Does this mean you're painting again? Can I get an interview? A quote—Hey! Get off me! Give that back!"

Now what? Todd could claim being ordinary all he wanted, but she knew differently. The man was still a celebrity, and this little brouhaha proved that the Fates agreed with her.

Chapter Nine

S on of a bitch. How'd they find him?

Todd rubbed his thumb and index finger over his eyes, trying to readjust his vision to the gray violet of the night, the same color as Jolie's widened eyes. He squeezed her hand and stood. "Stay down." He hated subjecting her to this circus more than he hated going through it.

He patted her shoulder and strode over to the two waiters holding a squirming, cursing man between them. The white lights ringing the edge of the boat and the residual from the flash made it tough to see who the man was. Not that it mattered, because *anyone* writing about him was the problem.

"We're sorry about that, Mr. Best," one of the waiters said at his approached.

Todd raised his hand. "You aren't the ones who need to apologize." He glared at the reporter.

"Ken Shaw with *In The Spotlight*." The reporter yanked his arms free from the waiters and stuck out his hand. "I'd like to ask you a few questions about—"

"I know what you'd like, Mr. Shaw." Todd ignored the hand and crossed his arms over his chest. "What I'd like is some privacy. Any idea whose wants I care more about?"

"Yeah, but look, people are curious. You're a story—"

"No, you look, Mr. Shaw. I'm not a story. I'm a person. And the lady with me is a person. Neither of us cares what your readers are curious about. She has nothing to do with the art world. Nor, frankly, do I any longer. That's your story. Period." Todd held out his hand. "I'll take the photo, if you don't mind."

"No way. That's my meal ticket for the month. Maybe I'll see you around this place."

"Mr. Shaw, this area is clearly marked *Private*." One of the reasons he and Trista had frequented it. "That includes the taking of unauthorized photographs. I'm sure management would be more than happy to contact the authorities should I care to press the matter." Todd flared his palm. "The memory card."

The two waiters, who could pass for bouncers at any of the downtown clubs, cracked their knuckles. Todd had to cough to cover his laugh, but the theatrics worked. Shaw glanced between them, then at the railing.

"It's not worth it, Shaw. Hand it over. And while you're at it, you can tell me how you knew where I'd be."

***

Todd returned to the table, batting 500. Shaw hadn't leaked his source—Todd hadn't really expected him to. He'd hoped, but at least he'd gotten the memory card. He ran the slim plastic rectangle between his fingers. Pity it was digital; he'd relish ripping a roll of film from the back of a camera, but this was more civilized.

He didn't feel civilized.

"What was that about?" Jolie looked at him from her chair.

"I thought I told you to stay there." He pointed to the deck behind their table.

"As in literally? I thought you meant at the table." She placed her purse beside her plate. "So what *was* that?"

Todd reclaimed his seat and stretched the napkin across his lap, then leaned toward her. "Look, I'm sorry. This morning, the reporters, everything."

"I'm okay. It's fine. I—"

"No, it's not fine. It's a hassle. It's invasive and callous. I'll understand if you want to reconsider."

"Reconsider?"

Todd sat back in his chair and drew a hand through his hair. "Working for me. Trust me, it's not fun having your life bantered about in the papers. There's always some photographer looking for a quick buck from some national trashmag. You just met one. It's only going to get worse. I shouldn't have brought you out tonight."

"Well I'm glad you did. I wouldn't have seen this place if you hadn't. And that guy was so far away he probably didn't get anything printable anyway."

"Good Sport Jolie to the rescue." Todd tossed the memory card onto the table. "Well, at least I got this, so it doesn't matter what he saw."

"The memory card? What are you going to do with it?"

Todd picked it up. "How about I toss it overboard?"

He cocked his wrist but Jolie wrapped her fingers around his arm. "Wait."

It was the shock of her touch that stopped him. Her fingers were warm, soft. The way she leaned forward, her turquoise dress contrasting with the cream tablecloth, the swell of her breasts being pushed up—

What the hell was he thinking?

He pulled his arm free, an instinctual reaction because he certainly didn't think about it. Hell, all he could think about was how wrong it was to notice her breasts.

"That's not environmentally friendly, Todd," she continued, obviously unaware of the wrong direction of his thoughts since she linked her hands on the table *right beneath* her breasts, pushing them up even more. "You can't just toss it in the river. What if everyone else did? The fish would die of poisoning. Then the bigger fish would die, and so on until you've disrupted the food chain."

She sat back and her dress re-situated itself, thank God. The blood rushed back into his brain as she put things in perspective again with her concerns. Where had she been two years ago when his life had gone to shit? He could have used some unbridled optimism then.

Not that he would have listened.

"You're right. The last thing I need to do is enable that reporter to cause any more damage—to me or the environment."

"I'll just put it in my purse until we get home—uh, back. Then you can dispose of it."

Home. When had he called that place home? It was just a place to sleep, store his clothes, and eat. But yes, she'd been at home in his kitchen. Had moved right in, basically, and made herself a part of the scene.

Wait a minute. Could she be a plant? Shaw's source maybe?

She raked the card toward her purse with her nails, but he stopped her, hating what he was thinking.

"Wait, Jolie." The last two years had really done a number on him, but lessons learned… "I'll hold onto that."

"Uh, okay." She slid the plastic to him, a twist on those pink lips.

"Thanks." He shoved it into his pocket, then picked up his fork, but just as quickly put it down. Was she really here for the chef position or working for someone—*something*—else?

"Really, Jolie, I won't hold it against you if you want out. I'll write you a glowing reference."

"Why would you think I'd want out? It's really no biggie." She speared a forkful of scallop.

If she *was* a plant, she'd want to stay. Of course, if she wanted the job, she'd want to stay, too. He really hated not being able to trust anyone. He fiddled with his fork, then tapped the tines against his plate. "Jolie, about this morning—"

"You already apologized. It's forgotten." She twirled her fork every bit as expressively as she did her hands.

"Not that. You never answered my question. How did you get in my house? And without me hearing you?"

She raised her eyebrow. The fork stopped mid-twirl and she didn't even seem to notice when the scallop dropped to her plate.

Hell, he was going about this all wrong. But still, she'd started today. *Today.* Mike wouldn't have been that callous to send someone out on this day. It was too coincidental and he didn't like coincidences. No one had tried this angle before, but it made sense and the timing was right. "So how'd you get in? Why today?"

Jolie took her time placing her fork on the plate and dabbing the corner of her mouth with the napkin. She smoothed it across her lap, then looked at him, the usual brightness missing from her eyes. "I used the key the agency gave me for the side door. They said to start first thing this morning so I did. Any other questions?"

Todd studied her. Indignation, the requisite glower… She was either a very good actress or telling the truth.

He was sick of worrying about it. She hadn't asked a zillion questions like the reporters, his other chef had left, and it was perfectly reasonable for the agency to send someone over since *today* wasn't anything special on their calendar.

He exhaled, letting it go. Unless she gave him reason to be

suspicious, he'd take her at face value. With those expressive eyes—and those irrepressible hands—he didn't think she was pulling one over on him. "I guess they got the dates wrong, because I thought I wasn't supposed to have anyone here this week."

"Well, that can be easily arranged." She crumpled her napkin and slid sideways off her chair.

He grabbed for her hand. "Jolie. Wait. I'm sorry. I didn't mean to imply—"

"Oh, I think you did."

He exhaled. Snagged. "Okay, maybe I was testing the waters. I know you didn't have anything to do with *that*." He pointed back to where Mr. Shaw had made his less-than-gracious exit. "It happens more than I'd like. I'm sorry."

She perched on the edge of the seat, those violet eyes turning as dark as the night behind her. Without the twinkling stars. He'd done that and he felt like a heel for it. The one person who apparently didn't have an agenda with him today, and he'd insulted her.

He was a real prince. "Please stay."

"Why don't you just give them an interview and have it over and done with?" she asked, re-positioning the napkin after a few seconds' consideration.

"Because I don't think it's anyone's business but mine how I spend my days or what I do with my life. Talking about her isn't going to bring her back."

No, but painting might.

He shoved the thought from his head. Painting wouldn't bring Trista back, it'd bring *it* back. The shock, the anguish, the desolation.

He couldn't go through that again. He just wanted to move on with the rest of his life.

***

Jolie jabbed another forkful of scallop. She plopped it into her mouth, then grabbed her napkin to spit it into. Too cold. Great, she couldn't even enjoy her first—and probably last now that it'd forever be associated with his suspicions —meal at this place. How dare Todd insinuate—

But what about the novel?

That was different. It wasn't as if anyone would know it was him when it got published. *If* it got published; there were no guarantees. By then, she'd be long gone anyway, and this would be just one in a string of assignments. No one would ever know Todd was the inspiration.

Uh huh.

She refused to feel guilty about something she hadn't yet done, so Naughty Girl could just keep quiet.

"Well, hello there!" exclaimed a chipper voice at her side.

Mr. Griff? What was he doing here?

Well, thank goodness for it because the last thing she needed to be doing was wrestling with her conscience about something she might or might not do at some point in the future, cluing Todd in to the fact that she might not be what he thought she was. Or maybe she really was what Todd thought she was, thereby getting herself fired for something she hadn't even done yet.

"Miss Gardener?"

"Hi," she said, turning all perky, as if she hadn't just had one of the heaviest discussions of her life, complete with unwarranted—sort of—guilt complex. "What brings you here, Mr. Griff? Are you meeting someone for dinner?" And how'd he get past the bouncers?

He slapped his leg and laughed as if she'd said the funniest thing he'd ever heard. "Oh, no." He wiped the corner of his eye. "I came to give, er, *get* something I left behind. And there it is."

He scurried over to a bench behind her beneath the pretty white Christmas lights, his serviceable black shoes clicking along the deck, retrieving something large, flat, and rectangular. He stuffed it under his arm then scampered back. He always seemed to be moving about with new verbs she'd never really thought of before. At the grocery store he'd clambered off the floor, now it was scurrying and scampering. What would he try next? Scuttling?

"Who's he?" Todd asked, his eyes narrowed.

Great. Now he was back to wondering if she was involved in some covert spy mission. "Relax. That's Mr. Griff. The one who gave me the book. Not a reporter."

Mr. Griff reached them with his large, rectangular something.

"What on earth is that, Mr. Griff?" Jolie asked.

"Curiosity killed the cat, Cat." He wagged a finger at her.

"Her name is Jolie," Todd corrected.

The little guy had a cat-ate-the-cream grin. "Her middle name is Catherine."

Todd looked at Jolie who could only shrug, clueless how Mr. Griff knew.

"So what is that, Mr. Griff?" She nudged the thing.

"Oh." He swept it from under his arm as if it were a European crown jewel. "It's a book on Hans Holbein."

"Holbein the Younger?" Todd asked.

Who the heck was Hans Holbein the Younger and why did Todd suddenly find this conversation interesting?

"Yes," Mr. Griff answered Todd, turning slightly and flipping the book open. "He's very talented, don't you think?"

She craned her neck to look across the table. A book of paintings—but not landscapes like Todd's. No, these were all portraits. They looked like oils, but since she wasn't a connoisseur, she couldn't be certain.

But Todd was. He studied the faces in the pictures, both pages, then slowly turned to the next page. No one said anything, but Mr. Griff had a secret little Mona Lisa grin going.

"Would you like to keep it for a bit? Since you're finding it so interesting, I mean." Mr. Griff somehow managed to slide the... encyclopedia, for lack of a better word, onto the table without disturbing any of the place settings.

Todd flipped another page, his eyes roaming the picture in a really intensive study. Was he looking for the talent, the mastery, or whatever it was an artist saw when he looked at a painting, like she did when someone served an amazing menu item, like, for instance, broiled scallops?

"I'd love to take a look at it, if you wouldn't mind." Todd finally tore his eyes away from the painted page and arched a brow at Mr. Griff.

Mr. Griff made no effort to hide that enigmatic smile and it made her nervous. What if Todd began thinking along the lines he'd been thinking earlier?

And what was with Mr. Griff showing up here with a book Todd would be interested in? It was eerie how the shopkeeper seemed to read minds.

"You certainly can. Take as much time as you need. Jolie knows where to find me." He tipped his hat, turned with military precision, and scuttled (no surprise there) away.

Todd followed Mr. Griff's departure with narrowed eyes, as if he was trying to figure out why a complete stranger would lend him a book. She just hoped he didn't come to the conclusion she thought he might.

Luckily, the maitre d' chose that moment to interrupt the visual tracking and Todd returned his focus to the table, handling the dinner order with aplomb.

"So, who's Hans Holbein the Younger?" she asked after the d' left.

Todd turned another page. "A portraitist. A courtier to King Henry the Eighth in the sixteenth century who painted many of the royal court."

"Oh. That's impressive." She took a sip from her glass, gazing out over the inky water where a boat whispered by, its deck lights outlining its shape. *The Midnight Maiden* rocked with the wake.

"It is. Especially when you realize this guy lived to his mid-forties. He started out doing religious paintings, then came to the attention of Sir Thomas More. He painted More's portrait and King Henry became a fan. After that, he was the official artist for Henry's wives' portraits, as well as for the search of subsequent wives. Matter of fact—" Todd flipped another page and pointed to a woman in a big black coat with a funny black cap on her head. "He ran into trouble after Jane Seymour's death. Henry sent him to paint Christina of Denmark, who then passed on his offer of marriage."

"Smart girl." Henry wasn't the most forgiving of husbands. Nor the most faithful. Given his track record, Jolie would refuse him, too.

"True." Todd turned the page. "Henry then sent Holbein to paint Anne of Cleves." He cocked the book toward Jolie. "Her."

Anne had a tiny waist and was dressed in a copper-colored outfit, complete with jewels and chains all over it. Those people back then certainly knew the meaning of the word ostentatious. She had a funky little cap on her head with dangly things on the sides, kind of like Princess Leia, though Anne dear might have been bald under it, 'cause not a wisp of hair escaped.

"Henry was quite taken with the portrait and offered for her. She, poor thing, accepted."

"So, what was the problem?"

Todd closed the book with a wry grin. "Holbein was put between a rock and a hard place. Henry had already struck out with Christina, and Anne was not quite the, shall we say, most inspiring of subjects—"

"A bow-wow?"

"That's one way of putting it. But since Holbein was so famous for his portraits, he must have either wanted to portray her well, or Henry's advisers wanted the king married no matter what. Whatever the case, Holbein, um, took some liberties with his subject."

"Aha! I bet Henry was none too thrilled when the beauty in the portrait ended up being more beast-like."

"Considering their marriage was annulled six months later, I'd say that's a safe bet."

"Holbein's lucky Henry didn't behead him or something." Henry's bad temper being somewhat legendary and all.

"True. But Holbein the Younger was one of the outstanding artists of his time. Henry would have been hard pressed to replace him. The man was a great observer of detail in his paintings, had superb handling of color, a compelling realism."

So, Todd went off on a tangent, looking more alive in the last fifteen minutes than he'd been all day. Or any time since his wife died, according to the news coverage she'd seen. Mr. Griff's book could be a good thing for him. Funny how the man knew just which book to give.

Dinner arrived and Todd continued to wax poetic about Hans Junior. It was interesting for about the first ten minutes, but when he went in depth about brush strokes and pigmentation and a whole bunch of other mumbo-jumbo she'd heard before but never really took the time to learn, she got distracted. Not daydreaming, just distracted. Like noticing how his mouth looked really sexy when he said the word "strokes." Made her want him to do that to her.

Well, okay, that wouldn't be the smartest idea she'd ever had, but when the guy was lit up like a Christmas tree, going on and on about something near and dear to his heart, it was kinda hard *not* to go that route, since she'd never been near and dear to anyone's heart.

So, with some daydreaming on her part, and art lessons on his, they made their way through dinner—lobster thermidor and asparagus with hollandaise being some of her personal faves. The maitre d' checked in periodically, but not intrusively, thankfully. She'd always found it to be a bummer to be having this great conversation and right when she was ready to make the point, the big comment that made her seem brilliant and witty, there'd be a, "Would you like coffee with that?" What a dénouement, and not in a good way.

Todd went on about Sir Holbein. Or Mr. Holbein. She couldn't remember if he was knighted or not. It would've been nice for the guy to get that reward, but, hey, with Tudor job positions fluctuating according to the king's whim, it seemed keeping one's head in that period of English history would be reward enough.

"Would you like dessert?" Todd asked, closing the book.

No, she was not going to ask for whipped cream. "No, thank you. Dinner was more than enough."

Todd held her chair as she scooted out of it and it was utterly ridiculous how happy his warm body against her back made her. Yes, so maybe she did scoot slower than necessary, what of it?

He touched her elbow to lead her back toward the stairs, Mr. Griff's book slung under his other arm, and she tried to suppress the shiver his touch evoked.

She gave a little finger wave to the d' who apologized yet again for the intrusion, and within minutes, they were outside the ship, back on terra firma where the wind blew her hair all over the place—again. It figured. A girl could not have a good hair day around a ship.

"Thanks for this, Jolie. For tonight." Todd's voice was husky, which she might not have noticed had she not heard how difficult this would be for him during her little eavesdropping incident at the office earlier.

"No, really," she said. "Thank you. It's the best dinner I've had in a long time." Ever, actually, but she did have some self-preservation.

"Look," he said, leading her to the car, "it's pretty late and Lord knows I've had enough to eat. Why don't you take it easy tomorrow and come around lunchtime? I think I can skip breakfast." He opened her car door again and she fought the swoon.

"But it's my job and high time I started, don't you think? I'd like to earn my paycheck, if you don't mind."

He closed her door with a "If that's what you want," then slid his toned thigh, calves, and firm tushy (and she should know) into his seat. He did that twisty-turny move to put Mr. Griff's book in the space behind the seats, then he glanced at her.

Once again, she fell victim to those eyes. God, they were incredible. His piercing gaze made her feel as if he could see into her very soul.

Here's hoping he can't or he's in for a surprise.

Naughty Girl just *had* to ruin the moment.

"Ready?" he asked.

Uh oh. Maybe he *could.*

"Ready?" she squeaked out.

"To head home?"

Duh. "Yep," she said in an effort to keep the blush and embarrassment off her face. "Anything in particular you want me to make tomorrow? Or should I just wing it?" The engine purred as they headed onto the pseudo-freeway.

"Nah. Surprise me," answered the walking advertisement for fantasy lovers everywhere.

"Okay." She sat back and let the wind muss her hair some more. At this point, it was hopeless anyway, so she might as well enjoy the sensation.

The ride back was nice. Quiet, but nice. There was none of the angst from their earlier conversations and, despite the reporter interruption, Todd was doing okay. Mr. Griff's book helped. Todd had certainly jumped into that with both feet.

All in all, he'd done rather well. He'd talked about painting, had mentioned his wife—albeit briefly—and had remained at the restaurant after the reporter debacle. The night wasn't a disaster. Maybe he was starting to heal.

As they pulled onto her street, Jolie realized that her life, too, seemed to be on the upswing. It was finally at the point where she could say she was pretty happy with it. Not overly ecstatic, but nowhere near the bad places she'd been, and definitely headed down the road to her goals and personal happiness.

But when they rounded the bend toward her apartment complex, her thoughts of a decent life went down the tubes.

Or, rather, up in flames.

Before them—and about twenty fire, police, ambulance and reporter vans—her apartment building was on fire.

Taking everything she owned with it.

Chapter Ten

Her apartment.

Her home.

Her entire life. Gone.

Up in smoke. Flames. *Ohmygod.*

Jolie had the car door open even before Todd stopped, and she hit the ground running toward the line of bystanders, praying that whoever was screaming near her would just shut up already because it was really getting on her nerves.

It wasn't until Todd appeared beside her and yanked her into his arms that she realized the screaming banshee was her.

That shut her up.

"Jolie, Jolie," he said into her ear as her face was jammed into his shoulder.

Any other time she'd relish this moment, but not now. Everything she'd ever owned, bought, treasured was gone.

She clutched the sides of his shirt, vaguely remembering not to grab the skin beneath. She needed this, him, his support, otherwise she'd collapse. The disbelief, the agony was just, well, *crushing*.

Someone official talked into a bullhorn. She tried to dry her tears on Todd's shirt, figuring he'd have to have known what to expect the minute he pulled her into his arms. Hysterical woman equaled tears. Simple arithmetic really.

"Sshh, Jolie." He rubbed little soothing circles on her back. "It'll be all right."

"All right?" She sniffled and pulled back. "All right? How can you possibly say that?" Okay, so maybe that tap on his chest was a little harder than she intended, but, honestly, *all right*? Was the man mad? Out of his mind? "I've lost everything. Everything!"

Said man picked that moment to go all sweet on her, cupping her drenched cheek in his hand and searching her eyes. "No, you haven't lost everything. You're still here. Still alive." He brushed some wild hair off her face and went back to cheek-cupping again. "Remember your happily-ever-after scenario? You need to focus on that now. It could be so much worse. You could be inside that building. Things are replaceable—people aren't."

He did have a point.

So there they stood, surrounded by blaring horns, mist from the dozen or so hoses aimed at the burning pile of brick and mortar she used to call home, hundreds of people milling around, and the world shrunk to one tiny plot of concrete where Todd held her.

"You're right." She leaned back, trying to muster the bravery she'd carried around like a shield since, well, forever. "I could've been in that building. It's after eleven, so I might have been asleep. It could be worse."

No, she couldn't find the bravery. Not yet. She'd never lost *everything* before. Not in one fell swoop. Not like this.

She sunk back into his arms. Since he was offering, she might as well take him up on it as she took inventory of what was left of her life.

Luckily, she'd been in too much of a hurry to get to her reading sojourn that afternoon to fully unpack her car. Her manuscript was still in the back seat of the little German engine that could, and she had her purse, so all means of access to her money were still hers. Oh, and the clothes on her back. Okay, so everything wasn't gone.

Todd was right—it could've been worse, though it could've been oh so much better.

But she'd been through nasty disasters before; she just hadn't been counting on ever having to start over from nothing. But, Lord knew, she was fully capable of re-establishing residency in the blink of an eye. Now if she could only stop those eyes from blinking back tears and clear her vision.

She had to pull herself together. After all, she *was* alive. "Let's make sure everyone got out," she said to Todd, mustering the courage to pull out of his arms.

They skirted the huddled groups of sobbing people and she was about to head toward the front of the pack, when Todd grabbed her hand. Fool that she was, she felt that tingle.

One would've thought losing her entire life's worth of possessions would have deadened her nerve endings, but apparently not where he was concerned. She probably didn't want to know what it'd take to do that.

"Jolie, this is a friend of mine. Detective Phillips."

"A detective? Is it standard procedure for a detective to show up at a fire?" she asked.

Detective Phillips shook his head. "The fire marshal said the origins look suspicious so we're on hand to check it out."

Todd took her hand, intertwining their fingers, and thoughts fled her mind.

"Suspicious?" he asked. "Do you think someone set it on purpose?"

Detective Phillips shrugged. "Too early to tell. But the fire alarm was pulled before anything happened, so, luckily, everyone got out. It was either an incredible coincidence or someone wanted everyone out before they tried to gut the place. We'll go in with the arson team once the fire's out. What's your interest in this place, Todd? I thought you were over in the Mirror Lake Development?"

"I am. Jolie lives, er, lived here," Todd answered.

Detective Phillips flicked his head toward the collapsing pile of rubble. "Sorry about that, miss. You'll need to make other arrangements. The Red Cross should be setting up around here shortly to help you with shelter until you get back on your feet."

Detective Phillips nodded then, with a quick clasp to Todd's arm, headed off.

"It's going to be okay, Jolie."

She sighed. "I know. I'm over the initial shock that my entire old life is gone."

Todd raised his eyebrow and she had to chuckle. "Well, okay, maybe I'm not completely over it, but I'll make it. I always have before. Now it's time for me to stand on my own two feet—in the only pair of shoes I have left, apparently." She couldn't help herself when she reached out to touch his arm. That darn touchy-feely-ness he'd started…

"Thank you, Todd, for helping me through the worst of it. Not really what you expected this evening, I'm sure." God, it felt so good to lean—just a little bit—on someone else.

Remember the last time you did that?

Naughty Girl had a point. Mom hadn't done such a hot job on the support thing and forget about Chucky. He'd been a lost cause even before they'd begun but she hadn't realized it.

Jolie pulled her hand away. "I'll let you get on home while I find the Red Cross and discuss my options. Thanks for a really nice evening. Up 'til now, of course, but then, you didn't have anything to do with that."

"Jolie." And just like that—again—Todd stopped her rambling. "I've got four unused bedrooms in my house. Why don't you crash there until you can find other accommodations? No need to stand in line behind dozens of other people waiting for the overworked volunteers. Plus—" there was a twinkle in his eye— "just think how easy it'll make your morning commute."

Stay in his house? In a bedroom a few dozen feet down the hall from his? He might think nothing of it, but then, he wasn't aware of the little flamenco dance that'd been going on under her skin all evening. And just from being near him. But sleep under the same roof? Her hormones were going to go into the spin cycle for sure.

As if they weren't already.

She opened her mouth to say, "Thanks, but no thanks, you really don't need to rescue me," (but, sure, why not?) and found herself saying instead, "Really? That would be so nice. Thank you very much." *Okay, Naughty Girl, what are you doing butting in?*

Shut up and thank me later.

Naughty Girl and those good points of hers…

So Jolie did a bit of searching among the throng to find her car and caravanned behind Todd's be-all/end-all of cars to his house, her new home.

Home—oh Lord, her apartment.

I will hold it together. She would. No big deal. It was just a few things. Things. Things shouldn't mean so much.

But in the confines of her little car, she could admit to herself—only—that they did mean something.

A lot.

All her books, her clothing, her shoes—goodbye kicky yellow flats—meant something. Things she'd bought, worked for. Earned. Owned. All gone in the blink of a planetary eye. All because of someone's momentary carelessness.

She refused to consider arson. Yeah, it was kind of suspicious that someone emptied the building before it went up in flames, but she was going with coincidence. That someone could have done it on purpose hurt more than she could bear. So she just wouldn't think about it. What was it Scarlett O'Hara said? She'd think about it tomorrow.

Or never. What good would it do anyway? This was the hand she'd been dealt. Same as any other event in her life. She would, however, like to discuss with the Dealer the extraordinarily bad hands being dealt her.

She pulled into Todd's driveway and drove into the bay beside his while he unlocked the door to the covered walkway between the garage and the house and held it open for her. Still chivalrous in the face of tragedy. *Gotta love this guy.*

Whoa. That was just an expression and her subconscious—or Naughty Girl—better ban it from their collective thoughts. Pronto.

"Top of the stairs to the left," Todd said with a nod up the back staircase once they were in the mudroom. "Take any room you'd like. I've got a t-shirt you can borrow to sleep in. I donated my wife's clothes before the move, so unfortunately I don't have anything feminine for you."

She pshaw-ed him with her hand while her brain played catch-up. He mentioned his wife so calmly. She was impressed.

"A t-shirt is fine. Really." They hit the top landing and she hung a left while he went right.

"I'll be right back. Any preference on color?" He smiled and she couldn't help but return it. The guy could be quite charming when he wanted to be.

And even if his charming-ness was just to pick up her spirits after losing all her worldly possessions, she'd take it. Her nerves were a bit frazzled from the whole trying-to-keep-it-together thing. "Whatever color you've got, though pink is my favorite."

"I'll see what I can do."

I'd like to see what he can d—

Enough, Naughty Girl.

Jolie spun around and entered the room. Soft sage walls with crown molding. White-washed furniture. Big ol' four-poster with mounds of pillows. Comfy chair in the corner, window seat with a cushion that matched the muted slate-and-sage plaid bedspread. Understated elegance. Probably came from a decorator because Todd was known for the vibrant colors in his paintings. She doubted he'd had *anything* to do with decorating this place since he had yet to hang anything on the walls except a flat screen TV.

But the quality was there. The pillows were down, the intricacies of the trim meant it wasn't off the rack, and the carpet was the plushest she'd ever felt. She stifled the groan. It was one thing to work in the kitchen then go home to her world. She could appreciate the luxury, but leave it behind. Because she had to. If she weren't able to leave it behind, she'd end up coveting it, and that was just so not healthy for her—or anyone's—self-esteem.

But to stay here, living in this luxury—even for one night—was going to make it pretty tough to leave. But she'd do it. She'd manage.

It was what she did.

Todd returned, and, yep, the t-shirt was pink. Okay, it might have once been red and gone through too many washings, but it was pretty darn near pink. Honest to God, the man should come with a suit of armor.

For more reasons than one.

"Here you go. It's the best I can do." He offered it to her and she put her pesky little hormones on inactive duty. She was not going to brush his fingertips with hers when she took it. She wasn't.

Really.

Of course Naughty Girl overrode that directive and "just happened" to slide her fingers over his.

"Well, goodnight," he said as if a lick of fire didn't traverse his entire nervous system from their "accidental" touch as it did hers.

"Goodnight. See you tomorrow. We aren't going to have a repeat of this morning, are we?" She couldn't resist the dig.

"Nope. Promise. No nudity from here on out."

She could honestly say that was a bummer.

***

Todd closed his bedroom door, crossed to the bed, and sat. He toed off his shoes, then rested his elbows on his knees.

A woman. In his house. Overnight.

81

He scrubbed his face. Yeah, she was in a separate room, but it didn't matter. Her presence filled his house.

It wasn't her perfume, though he'd caught a whiff of something flowery when he'd held the door for her earlier. It wasn't her things, because, let's face it, she had nothing.

God, he knew what that felt like.

Todd pushed his hands off his thighs and headed to the bathroom, stripping his shirt off as he went. He hurled it into the heap in the corner behind the door with the last three days' worth of laundry, walking out of his pants as he went. He should probably pick up the mess.

In the doorway he turned around. At least the mess made the room look lived in.

Lived in.

His stomach clenched. What did it say when his room wouldn't look lived in if it weren't for dirty laundry? There wasn't a stitch of anything personal in the room—no pictures, no newspaper, no magazines, not a knick-knack anywhere. Just a bed, two nightstands, a dresser and a television. Even the remote was tucked into a drawer. Probably next to a Bible and the Yellow Pages.

He snorted. He didn't think he'd put anything in the drawers.

For the first time, he really looked at his room, the place where he spent roughly a third of his life. The decorator had gone minimalist here. Pine furniture with hidden hardware. Straight curtains hung beneath a rectangular valance, beige-on-brown pattern. Tan paint on the walls, muted earth tones on the bed.

He recognized the signs: Soothing. Comforting. Cocooning.

Barren.

He grabbed the doorframe above his head. Where was the color? The brilliant blue of an ocean sky that had filled his and Trista's bedroom with the memories of rolling waves crashing on the beach during their third anniversary trip—the first time they'd been able to afford a real honeymoon. They'd captured those memories with hokey tropical souvenirs and Trista had invaded his supplies to pick paint colors. They'd chosen yacht-white for the crown molding and furniture, hibiscus-red, bird-of-paradise blue, orchid-orange, every color of the tropical flora that had been around their bungalow, reminding them of how much they'd enjoyed the trip and each other—

He gripped the molding. Trista was *gone*. Had been for two years.

And now there was another woman in his house.

Todd shook his head and turned to the sink. It wasn't as if Jolie were in his house to stay. He was just helping her out. Over a hard patch.

He grabbed his toothbrush. Jolie had looked so devastated. Her perpetual smile had disappeared and the sparkle in her violet eyes had shriveled up and died in the flames. Then she'd screamed…

It'd been gut-wrenching to hear.

Gut-wrenching to remember what that much pain felt like.

He stopped brushing, meeting his own eyes in the mirror above the sink. *Remembered* the pain. Not *felt* it.

He set the brush down and swiped a hand across his mouth, his fingers finding that spot he'd missed shaving. The one Jolie had pointed out.

His eyes widened. He could remember the pain without reliving it.

Did that mean he was forgetting? Forgetting Trista?

He closed his eyes. There she was. The first time he'd seen her. The day she'd said yes to his proposal. The first time they'd made love. The happiness in her smile when he'd shown her that first painting…

His legs buckled for a few wobbly seconds and he sat on the toilet lid. He remembered everything, but it hadn't speared him in the gut.

The hurt was replaced with…

Acceptance? Comfort? What was it?

Todd pinched the bridge of his nose. He couldn't put his memories away. Not tonight. He couldn't deal with this tonight.

Because he now had to forget that there was another woman in his house.

***

Jonathan paced outside the archangel's office, clutching his tweed beret, wringing the shape out of it, and wishing his eye twitch would slow it down to a snare drum pace. It always flared up when he was nervous and, oh, Boss, was he in for it now.

How did these things happen? One minute he'd been trying to sneak into Jolie's apartment, and the next, *poof!* the whole thing went up in flames.

Why'd that man have to set that oil on the window ledge? And over an open flame? Jonathan couldn't be blamed for not seeing it in the form he'd been in, but his timing couldn't have been more off.

He wasn't cut out for this job. He knew it. He just didn't know why Raphael didn't know it. The archangel was always giving him another chance, encouraging him. Why, when he'd almost broken that time-travel device in Tudor England, then almost lost those gold coins...

Why couldn't things go right for him? His Charges were the ones to suffer. Look at Jolie. Now she was homeless.

"Jonathan?" Raphael opened the door to his inner sanctum, gold light blazing through the opening. "What are you doing here?"

Jonathan gulped, smoothed a finger over his eyebrow to calm the twitch, then gave the beret one last twist before shoving it in his pocket. Time to face the celestial music.

"Sir, I've...well...I've bungled it. Again."

Raphael smiled. As always. With light and love, and no vestige of sarcasm. Jonathan always felt guilty when he received those unearned smiles.

"Jonathan, it's not possible for you to bungle an assignment. It's merely a change in direction. Now, come in, and let's see if we can steer this project back on course." Raphael beckoned him inside. "When good intentions are at the basis of an angel's actions, nothing bad will happen. Remember that, Jonathan."

Sure, he remembered that. He remembered it from the first time he'd messed up, and the second, and the third...

He just *had* to get it right this time.

Chapter Eleven

Surprisingly, Jolie slept. She hadn't really expected to, but apparently her itinerant childhood made her capable of far greater things than she knew.

She threw back the eight-bazillion count sheets and grabbed a quick shower. She would've loved to have taken the time to float in the swimming pool he called a bathtub, but she was not one to take advantage and she did have the guy's breakfast to prepare. Luckily, she'd bought everything yesterday that she'd need to whip up a feast fit for a king. Or a good-Samaritan landlord.

But, surprise, surprise, she entered the kitchen to find Todd smiling away at the stove.

"Hey," he said, all chipper and perky, his yellow polo matching the sunny disposition.

Wait a minute. That was her role. "What are you doing?"

He smiled. "I'm, how did you put it? 'Burning the butter for your morning omelet.'"

That was her line. "But why? *I'm* supposed to be cooking *your* meals."

He waved a hand toward the breakfast bar and she followed the silent instruction. It was his house after all and he was paying her salary.

"With what you went through last night, the last thing you need is to wait on me. Figured you could use some TLC."

Good thing he turned away or he might've caught the tears that sprang to her eyes. No one had ever thought of her before.

And she needed to ignore the warm fuzzies his concern garnered. She could take care of herself, remember?

"I'm perfectly fine. Really. You were right, they were just things. I'll get more." She sat down. "Has there been any news on the cause?"

He slid a decently fluffy omelet onto a plate and added a piece of toast, then placed the whole thing before her where he'd already poured the o.j. and set out utensils. Had to love a guy who planned ahead.

"The reports say the cause is still under investigation, but nothing conclusive has been found. Luckily, no one was hurt."

Thank goodness for that. As he'd said, things were replaceable.

Todd pulled a plate from the warming drawer and sat next to her. "So, is that the best omelet you've ever had or what?" he mimicked her once more.

She gave him a well-earned smile for the jest. "Second best," she said, mouth full of something that truly was comparable to her own excellent omelet-making skills.

He laughed, getting her again. A bit of silence followed the shared joke, then Todd cleared his throat, glancing away and fiddling with his fork. "I've got to run downtown. Do you want me to drop you anywhere?"

The offer was tempting, but he hadn't hired a new best friend and she had tons of errands to do, re-building her life and all. "That's okay. I've got a zillion things to take care of. Melanie will get me there."

"Melanie?"

Jolie felt her cheeks flame. "Um, yeah. My car."

"You named your car Melanie?"

She nodded. Melanie was the first big purchase she'd made on her own and the car was like a best friend. They'd been through quite a lot together.

Mel was a VW bug—but not the new kind unfortunately. No, she was a classic—though not in quite the shape a classic classic should be in. She was classic in the very essence of the word. The first coat of paint was still on her (well, most of it anyway), and the dent on the driver's side door was from the year she was bolted together. The spare tire still had its original air. Hopefully. But Mel was cheap, though she preferred "affordable," and got Jolie where she needed to go.

"I would've figured you for a Scarlett," Todd returned.

And there he went, getting her again. Almost.

"No. She can't be Scarlett. Scarlett's headstrong, unpredictable, gets things done in her own way. When I buy a used car, I need predictable, steadfast, and loyal."

"Melanie Wilkes."

Jolie nodded. "You got it."

"So you and Melanie have plans then today?"

"We sure do. But don't worry. I'll run a few errands, come back for your lunch, then head out again. I'll be out of your hair all day."

Speaking of hair, he did that hand-raking thing through his again which was so utterly masculine and *très* sexy. Which she shouldn't be noticing.

"Actually," he said, oblivious, "take all the time you want. I probably won't make it back for lunch and I've got dinner at Mike's house tonight. My sister-in-law likes to have me over every so often. Just to make sure I still know how to interact with the human race and keep my manners up to par." He put his fork down and grinned at her. It was nice to see the smile, given that yesterday he'd been just a teensy bit grumpy. And a big bit hung-over. What a difference a day made. "So, take your time. Don't rush back on my account. You've got a key. Come and go as you please."

She loved this job. Two days and she'd only cooked one meal, gotten really nice digs to stay in, and eye candy as a boss. She should probably be paying him.

She insisted on doing the dishes, and after a bit of exasperating reasoning (she was good at that) he gave in and went off to his day.

First order of business once the kitchen was back to its pristine-ness was to get some clothes. The turquoise dress was nice, but not for everyday wear. And she did mean *every* day unless she hightailed it to a store.

Jolie drove Mel—who, thankfully, was cooperating—to the outlet shops where she put her fashion sense in touch with her thrifty side, and they all ended up happy with their purchases. A few shorts and shirts, some capris, jeans, pjs, and a few unmentionables, plus go-with-everything shoes. No more every-color-kicky flats. Until the insurance money showed up, she was no longer Imelda Marcos. A quick trip to the drug store for those essentials a woman couldn't live without, and she was ready to call it a day.

Except she could use a few more notebooks and number two pencils. That was how she wrote, longhand, in spiral-bound, three subject notebooks. She got the feel of the story more, and liked the connection of a sharp point as it rasped across the paper. Not to mention, before her current assignment, she simply couldn't afford a laptop, so any research was done at the internet café on Main Street. With what Todd was paying her, however, she might be able to reconsider her technology options.

But, for now, notebooks in hand, she was set. Well, except for her little library of "keepers," those books she loved to read over and over again. She had almost the entire Bridgerton collection in that apartment. It'd taken a while to amass and there was no way she could afford to re-do it overnight, but she was going to make a start.

A girl needed some avenue of escape when reality got too harsh. Plus, she did need the newspaper to check out the apartment listings, so she decided to head over to Mr. Griff's new store.

A church bell chimed as she entered. He must like the sound to have it in two of his stores. The little man himself balanced atop a step ladder, stacking books.

"Hello, my dear," he said as he climbed down, his black shoes clinking against the metal rungs. "I'm so sorry to hear about your home. Such a shame. I'm sure it was an accident, though. Perhaps someone knocked something over they didn't see that wasn't supposed to be there?" He coughed. "What can I get for you?"

"Thank you, Mr. Griff." She tried to keep her eyes on him rather than straying around the room. He'd sure filled the place in a hurry. "I, um, lost my books in the fire. So, I need to re-stock. But only one or two until the insurance money comes in."

"Absolutely not. You'll take what you want and pay me when you can."

"Oh, but I couldn't—"

"Of course you can. You want to, you know you do. Not another word. Select a few of your favorites."

The temptation was just too strong. And, really, it wasn't as if it was charity. She was good for the money. He knew where she lived. Well, used to live. Heck, even she didn't know where she lived anymore. Which brought her to the next order of business. "Do you have today's newspaper, Mr. Griff?"

He handed one to her.

"Just add it to my tab," she said as she piled a few books—okay slightly more than a few—in front of him.

"Nonsense. What kind of a soul do you think I am if I took advantage of your misfortune to earn an extra fifty cents?" He rang up the books, but the total seemed suspiciously low. How did this guy expect to stay in business? "Take the paper and find yourself a safe place to live, you hear?"

She heard, and she thanked him. And left him to his delusions. 'Cause what she was willing to pay and what constituted "safe" were worlds apart. Besides, it was just a place to put her head and her stuff until she finished her degree and opened her shop. She'd worry about the hominess of her home after that.

But she decided to keep that to herself as she made her way home.

Todd's home.

She really should find another place to stay in the interim. Todd had that big ol' house empty for a reason and it just wasn't right to impose.

She started to call her friend, Bella, then stopped mid-number punching. Who was she kidding? Bella was a newlywed. She was not going to want someone barging in on her at this stage of her marriage.

That option was out.

Option number two was Chloe. Chloe had a boarding house for girls like she and Jolie used to be—wrung through the system and coming out on the other side with no one to care. Chloe was the one who cared. For as many as she could get her hands on.

A quick phone call and Jolie realized Chloe had enough drama going on with some developer trying to take her house, so Jolie didn't even mention her problem.

It looked like she'd be stuck at Todd's. Which wasn't necessarily a bad place to be stuck—as long as she made up for the imposition.

So, after hanging her new clothes in the closet and selecting a pretty pastel, handkerchief-hem camisole and white capris to go with her silver sandals, she headed out to his pool. Seemed a shame not to make use of it. She could read the newspaper poolside as easily as on a park bench. Easier probably.

"I should have bought a bathing suit" crossed her mind before she took a seat at the wrought-iron table amid a beautifully landscaped garden. She opened the paper to scan the classifieds.

Apartments, here we go. Sadly, there didn't seem to be a glut of efficiencies or one-bedrooms, which posed a bit of a problem. She ran her finger down the column as she ticked off those that just wouldn't do. Which left very few that would. Factoring in her budget, it left even fewer options. Then she took a look at the locations and she was even more discouraged. She sighed and put the paper aside, channeling Scarlett again.

She would've liked to read the book Mr. Griff had given her, but in all the drama of last night she'd left it in Todd's car, so she decided to take this time to work on her own. It was a safe option. Todd wasn't around, and she had new supplies and a few hours to plot and plan.

The late afternoon passed in a flurry of characterization. Her hero, Tom, was fleshing out very well. And if there was more than a little of Todd Best in him, well, no one would know. Not unless they spent some serious time with him. The man, not her hero.

Aren't they one and the same?

Not daring to venture down that avenue, Jolie stopped periodically to dip her tootsies in the pool. Sheer bliss. Heavenly. Paradise. Whatever the adjective, it was just too wonderful to have the opportunity to cool off at will.

She grabbed a quick salad for a late lunch or early dinner—Todd did say meals were included—and lit a few of the tiki torches ringing the pool deck. All she needed was a virgin daiquiri, some Jimmy Buffet, and a sexy native island guy.

The French door from the kitchen opened and out walked Todd.

She glanced heavenward with a quick "thank you."

"Having a party and forget to invite me?" He chuckled.

"Sorry, it's just too nice of a night to be indoors. And the pool was calling me." She scrambled to close her notebook. "What are you doing here? I thought you had dinner plans."

Those laugh lines deepened near his eyes. "I do, but I started thinking you might be lonely and let yourself get down about the fire. I didn't like the idea of you here alone. So, would you like to come to dinner with me?"

Where *was* this guy's white horse?

Chapter Twelve

Todd didn't lie. Mike was definitely earning a six-figure salary. His house was as big and gorgeous as Todd's, with the perfectly manicured front lawn with down-lights along the brick walkway and up-lights on the trees. Double etched-glass front doors opened into an impressive marble foyer. Basil and cream wainscoting wound up the curved front staircase where a crystal chandelier glimmered overhead.

Mike's wife was the requisite thin blonde, but any comparisons to the living embodiment of Barbie ended there. Except, darned if she wasn't named Barbie. Well, Barbara, but close enough.

Todd made the intros and Barbara welcomed Jolie graciously into Versailles, er, her home even though she looked a little unsure of who Jolie was supposed to be. Was Todd springing her on them?

Maybe she shouldn't have come. Maybe Todd was just being nice and she should have declined, like last night at *The Midni*—

"Jolie, huh?" Mike entered from a room on the right, drink in one hand, the other outstretched, a big smile across his face. Too late to back out now.

Not that she ever did. No quitting for her. No siree. "That's me."

Mike's hand engulfed hers. As in, absorbed. He was big. Bigger than Todd, who was plenty big. They looked alike too, only Mike had some gray at the temples (another "distinguished" feature on a man that didn't translate to women) and his eyes didn't have Todd's haunted sadness in them. But definitely good-looking. Their parents must have gone swimming in the gene pool at Lourdes to create these two.

"You're the new chef?" Barbara ran a manicured hand over the buttons on her peach blouse and fingered the pearls at her neck.

"Yep. Omelets to bedtime snacks, I do 'em all." Cute little slogan. Or so Jolie thought until Mike almost spit out his drink.

Oh. Probably not a good idea to mention bedtime snacks in conjunction with Todd.

Not that it meant anything. The man was safely ensconced in his memories. Nothing for anyone to worry about.

"Well, my cooking experience isn't in the same realm as yours so I hope dinner is somewhat—" Barbara's fingers creased her crisp linen pants as they slid down the sides then linked in front of her, her shoulders so rigid she looked like there was a curtain rod holding up her dress.

"Please." Jolie put a hand on Barbara's arm. More touchy-feely-ness. What was with that? "Don't worry. I'm sure dinner will be marvelous. Really." She smiled and got an answering one in return. "I don't do critiques or restaurant reviews. And I usually do a pretty good job of clearing my plate."

It was the one thing she didn't like about her job. Everyone thought they needed to hire a five-star chef when inviting her to dinner. No way. She was just happy someone else had planned and cooked the meal. She wasn't fussy. Not after some of what she'd eaten *before* going into the foster system and, sadly, during.

Barbara let go of the tight rein on her shoulder blades and they dropped back into place.

"Would you like a drink?" Mike asked Jolie, his eyes taking her in. Of course, he'd had that little "is she cute" conversation with Todd, so she shouldn't be surprised. It didn't, however, necessarily make her comfortable.

"Soda or iced tea if you've got it would be nice."

"Iced tea's in the kitchen and I have to check on dinner," said Barbara. "I'll be right back."

"Would you like some help?" Jolie asked. The least she could do for her sudden appearance was help out.

"Oh, but you're Todd's—our—guest. You needn't concern yourself with the meal." Barbara still looked flustered.

"I don't mind. Really. It's about time I started earning my pay." And it was the perfect excuse to remove herself from Mike's inquisitorial looks. She'd let Todd deal with those.

***

92

"Earning her pay? What does that mean?" Mike asked after the women left. He took a sip of his drink then headed toward his study.

Todd shoved his hands into the front pockets of his khakis and followed. Not where he wanted to go, but he knew his brother. Mike never let up when he got his hooks into something. It made him a great negotiator for a businessman, a pain in the ass for a brother, and sometimes, now for instance, too damned nosy.

But he followed Mike anyway. He wasn't going to get out of this conversation so he might as well get it over with.

The study's cherry paneling reminded him of a principal's office, more so when Mike chose the seat behind the desk, drew his elbows onto the leather blotter, and linked his fingers with feigned nonchalance.

Todd knew the posture. Had used it himself when bargaining with hotels and whatnot to display his works.

How long ago those days seemed.

But he hadn't forgotten, which was why he only glanced at the padded leather wing chair across from Mike, opting, instead, to rest his hip on the edge of the deep windowsill. "Got another one of those?" He indicated Mike's drink.

"Really? Two nights ago wasn't enough?"

"Are you my keeper or my brother, Mike?"

"I can't be both?"

"Not anymore."

Mike sat back with a wry grin on his face. "Well, well, well. What's gotten into you?"

Todd exhaled. "Nothing's gotten into me, but the other night was an ending of sorts. Maybe a beginning, I don't know. But I'm back. In my head and in my life. You're off duty."

Mike chewed the inside of his lip, fighting the smile—not that he did a good job of it.

"The drink?" Todd reminded him, pointedly.

"Right." Mike slid to his feet and poured a Dewars.

Todd took the tumbler and saluted. "Thanks for everything, Mike."

"Aw, come on, Todd. It's what brothers do. I'm just sad I had to step in. You know Barb and I miss Trista, too."

"I do, and I appreciate everything you've done. Even if it didn't seem that way at the time."

"So does this mean I can go back to my old job?"

Todd swirled the amber liquid in the glass. Did it? "Give me some time. It's been two days and I'm still coming to grips with things."

"Okay. That's fine. Whatever you want." Mike sat behind the desk again, putting his boots on the gleaming polished surface. "So what's with bringing your chef to dinner?"

Todd raised an eyebrow. "I didn't think you'd mind."

"Oh, don't get me wrong, I don't. It just seems a little unusual. I mean, I haven't exactly met any of the other hires before."

The Dewars burned going down, just what Todd needed. "It's a long story."

"Does she have anything to do with my being off duty?"

Did she? Todd shook his head and took another swallow. "Mike, I just met her."

"And Trista sideswiped you with one look. There's precedence, Todd."

"You're out of your mind." He was, right?

Todd studied the liquid in the tumbler. Jolie didn't have anything to do with his decision to wake up. Well, okay, she'd had something to do with it. He hadn't considered the correlation between giving up his art and locking Trista's memory away before it had come from Jolie's lips.

It made sense. But, damn, he couldn't do it again. Couldn't look at an apple tree or a rolling hill with the same eyes because he'd seen them through Trista's. She was his muse. And now she was gone.

But her legacy, that he could address. That he could carry on. He and Trista weren't just about paintings. Weren't just about themselves. They'd given to the community, shared his talent and her inspiration in other ways, and he'd let that stagnate.

She wouldn't want that. *He* didn't want that.

He had Jolie to thank for that. Maybe that was why he'd asked her tonight. The thought of her sitting alone in his house, a new place for her, all of her things gone, she didn't deserve that.

Oh, hell. She also didn't deserve the third degree she was probably getting from Barb as he sat here contemplating the meaning of life.

Todd set the glass on the windowsill. For all Barb's blonde

sweetness, she was a barracuda when it came to family. Especially about him since Trista's death. She'd been the one on the porch fending reporters off with the flick of a wrist. He couldn't imagine what she was doing to Jolie in the kitchen.

"I'll be back, Mike."

***

"So how do you like working for Todd?" Barbara asked as they traversed the marble-lined corridor from the living room to the kitchen. "I'm sure it's quiet compared to what you're used to."

"Uh huh." Jolie was pretty non-committal. Talking about a client definitely wasn't a good policy. Not to mention, she'd hardly worked for the guy. One omelet did not a career make.

Barbara opened the door to the fridge and poured the iced tea, then fluttered around the kitchen with its bazillion—okay, maybe forty, but still—cabinets. Pristine white, with brushed nickel knobs, nothing pretentious, but classy and functional and elegant—just like Barbara and the world she inhabited.

"Can I help with anything?" Despite Todd's efforts, Jolie wasn't used to being waited on. That, and silence, made her edgy.

Barbara glanced over from the double convection ovens set into a fieldstone wall with a cute smile on her face and nodded toward a large bowl and veggie-stuffs on the island. "If you'd like, I was just about to start the salad."

Back in her element, Jolie was feeling comfortable, chopping and dicing away. And of course, garnishing. A little swirl with the carrot peel here, a decorative tomato there, la la la la la.

"Do you work at many homes, or just stay at one for a while?" Barbara asked, setting out the preparations for garlic bread.

"This is my third. I worked for an older couple until they finally had to go into a home. That was sad. They really didn't want to leave their house, but they just couldn't get around anymore." In went some fresh basil and parsley. Adding the basil as part of the salad rather than in the dressing gave it more of a zing.

"My last job was with a family. When their youngest went off to college they didn't really need me anymore. I guess take-out and TV dinners work for the two of them because I know for a fact Mrs.—I mean, the wife—doesn't cook." Jolie shrugged. She'd bet it had more to do with having the house all to themselves. That was probably the real attraction—and who could blame them?—but of course no one would give that as a reason to let go of the hired help.

"And now you're with Todd. It must be lonely after having people around."

"Lonely?" Jolie shook her head. "Not really. He's chatty enough. Plus I've only been there two days."

"Todd? Chatty?" Barbara pointed a knife at her. "Todd Bartholomew Best?"

"Is there another?" *Bartholomew*?

"No." Barbara shook her head. "But Todd hasn't really—" The knife paused mid-twirl. "He hasn't really been himself since… well, I'm sure you know about Trista. His wife."

Jolie nodded. Oh, yeah. She knew.

"They were such a great couple. Perfect for each other. Her death hit him hard. He rarely goes out and we only see him when I force him to come to dinner." Barbara started slathering butter on the bread. A little thicker than necessary, but with the tears welling in her blinking eyes, she probably couldn't tell.

Jolie wasn't about to correct her. "Well, I didn't know him before, but he seems to be doing okay." She tossed the salad now that all the ingredients were in the bowl. It looked rather festive, if she said so herself. "I mean, he was out yesterday and today. I barely saw him." No way was she going to mention that she had actually seen him bare-ly.

Barbara put down the knife with a sharp little slam. "Todd? Out? All day? Where did he go?"

"Um." Okay, now she was in a spot. Her loyalties were with Todd since he was technically her boss. But also *technically*, Mike paid her salary since he ran the company, and Barbie here was his wife, so did she owe that loyalty to them or Todd?

Gosh, this reminded her so much of those years in the system. Where to place her allegiance? Without it coming back to bite her in the butt.

So, she pulled on old experience and went for middle of the road, praying she'd get out of the inquisition with her job and integrity intact.

"He took me to the grocery store yesterday and then he went to Mike's office." So far so good. "Then we went to *The Midnight Maiden*—"

"You're kidding!"

The reaction wasn't unexpected given her eavesdropping incident. See? Came in handy at times. Prepared her for this moment. "Uh, no. Then today, he was out all afternoon. Can't tell you where."

"Can't?" Barbara slanted her eyes. "Is it a secret?"

"Oh, no." Jolie tossed the salad a little higher to show it was finished. She was ready to end the conversation. "I don't know. He didn't tell me and, last I looked, it's not in my job description to keep tabs on the guy." She said it with a smile to take the sting out of the words, but really, this little tattle session needed to be over.

"Of course not." Barbara got the hint.

Couldn't blame her for trying. Barbara loved the guy. Mike, too. And, nope, couldn't blame them for that either.

It would be so nice to have even one person have such feelings for her.

Someday.

"How did you end up at *The Midnight Maiden*?" Barbara asked.

"I asked where she'd like to have dinner, that's how." Todd strolled into the kitchen, minus the white horse he'd definitely earned with that perfectly timed entry. He picked out a sliver of carrot from the salad bowl and Jolie restrained herself from slapping his fingers.

He waved said carrot Barbara's way. "Barb, do not drill my chef. I don't need her quitting because of nosy in-laws. I'd miss her omelets."

He smiled at Jolie, and, silly her, tingles danced all over her body and a ridiculous grin spread across her face. But she wiped that sucker off pretty quickly. No need for eagle-eyed, suspicious Babs catching it.

"And," he continued, "I invited her to *have* dinner, not make it." He took the salad bowl from her hands and winked at her. "Go on into the dining room and have a seat. I'll take care of this."

Just as she cleared the majestically arched doorway, Barbara asked, "Really, Todd. What on earth has gotten into you? *The Midnight Maiden?*"

Hmmm, Jolie would have liked to revive her eavesdropping

experience again, but, sadly, Mike was fast approaching so she'd have to forego the clandestine listening-in. Who knew what she would have found out about Todd's impressions from last night? After the reporter fiasco and his subsequent suspicions, she would've liked to hear the outcome of his mental musings.

"So, Jolie," Mike said, leading her away from the interesting doorway to the table. He pulled out her chair. Chivalry was alive and well and living in the Best family. "How was dinner last night?"

"Good. Great." Did he think it wouldn't be?

"I was surprised to hear you went there."

Nice try, but he knew where they were going beforehand, so all his past tense-ing didn't fool her. But then, she wasn't supposed to know all that, so she'd have to go along with the program. "Oh. Well it was very nice."

Footsteps echoed in the marble corridor, followed by a stern, "Mike." Todd entered the room. "Leave her alone. You've got questions about my dining habits, ask me." Her rescuer parked himself across the table from her and she could honestly say she was thrilled. And *not* because her hormones were up and dancing.

Todd started dishing out the salad, looking more calm and composed than she would've expected with the cross-examination they were getting. "So, dinner was very nice. The weather was perfect, we ate up on deck, and the chef outdid himself. Any other questions?"

Mike clammed up with a smile and poured the wine while Barbara entered and took her seat. "Not a one." Mike raised his glass. "Here's to new friends and dinners together."

Jolie took a sip, just a mite to be polite, and studied Mike over the rim of her glass. Did he mean dinners together as in, the four of them having tonight's dinner together, or dinners together as in, Todd and his new friend dining together? Was that what he wanted for Todd? She'd gotten the impression from Barb that they weren't quite ready for him to move on.

Or she could just be reading something into a perfectly innocuous statement because she wanted to.

***

"So, Todd, what's going on these days?" Barbara asked. "We barely see you, yet you seem to be out and about all over the place."

"Look here, Miss Nosy-Pants." Todd's smile brought a blush to Barbara's face. "I have a life and I'm living it. I'm here at least twice a month. Not too shabby. Plus I've decided to start a project that will keep me busy."

"Project?" Mike and Barb asked in stereo from opposite ends of the table.

"Yes, project." There. He'd said the words. Now he was committed. "I've decided it's time to open the attic above the garage." He held out his hand for Jolie's plate. She was quick to catch on. Part of the "getting" thing they had between them?

He filled her salad plate. "I'm hiring a crew to come out this week."

He hadn't quite expected the dead silence.

"Open the attic?" Again in stereo.

Nor the disbelief. Okay, so two years was a long time, but wasn't this what they wanted? For him to move on?

"Uh, yeah." He took a bite of the salad. Ambrosia. "You made the salad, didn't you?" he asked Jolie. Barb was a good cook, but nothing like Jolie.

"With Barbara's ingredients. How'd you know?"

There she was, Good Sport Jolie, again. "I recognize the little twirl to the vegetables."

Thank God Jolie could carry on a conversation. And since Mike and Barb were looking at him slack-jawed, as if he'd grown a second head, he was really glad he'd brought Jolie along.

For conversation?

Yes for conversation. Great. Now he had to argue with his conscience. He stabbed the arugula.

Barb was the first to recover. "Oh, Todd, that's terrific news! So exciting. How wonderful!"

"Does this mean you'll be showing them?" Mike finally reattached his bottom jaw. "Where do you want to have it? Private or open to the public? Are there enough for an entire show or will you be doing more? When are you planning?"

Hadn't Mike heard a word he'd said? He wasn't going to paint landscapes any more. He was done. That phase was over. He knew it as sure as he was sitting here.

"Mike, I am not showing again. Nor will I add to that collection. You can have them. Hang them in the office, throw them out, donate them to a hospital, I don't care. But no show. I'll never do another one again."

"Oh, but Todd, you can't mean that." Barbara reached over for his hand and he pulled it out of the way.

"I do mean it, Barb. It's time to put the past behind me. And that includes my landscapes." He didn't care if it hurt her feelings. For Christ's sake, he'd just made a huge decision. What more did they want from him?

"Oh, but, but… " Barbara wiped the corner of her eye. "But, Todd, Trista wouldn't want you to do this."

Todd set his knife and fork down carefully beside his plate. He had to do it very slowly, almost jerkily, because he might just break the damned dish. "This has nothing to do with Trista. It's about me and living the rest of my life."

He glanced at Jolie. He'd survived her saying it, but once was all he could manage. Although, it didn't slice him in two as it had last night.

He cleared his throat. Maybe he was making progress.

Then he got a good look at Jolie's face and had to wonder if she'd survive the rest of this meal.

"Jolie, I'm sorry you have to be a part of this. I hadn't expected to go down this road tonight. I shouldn't have mentioned clearing out the attic." He turned toward Barbara. "Let's not go into it any more. I'd like to have a nice dinner and then head home."

"Todd—" Mike began but Todd cut him off.

"Let's leave it at that, Mike. I can always change my mind, you know."

That stopped Mike. Barb grabbed her wine and Jolie stared into her salad.

Great. Good job, Best. Way to set the mood.

Well, it couldn't be helped. Yes, they'd been managing his life for the past two years and he appreciated it, he really did, but it was over. As for showing again, Mike could plead all he wanted, but Todd was not going to go through that circus.

He was emptying the attic to start over. To start fresh.

***

Jolie picked at her salad, wanting to fade into the woodwork, hoping someone would shatter the tension in the room before Mouth said something inappropriate; silence making her edgy and all.

"My apartment burned down so Todd let me move in." Oops. Too late. *Open Mouth, insert kicky yellow flat.* If she still had kicky yellow flat. Unfortunately, she'd lost that in the fire—along with, apparently, her common sense.

"Well, there's a subject change." Todd had his smile back, so apparently inappropriate comments had their purpose.

Why it had to be *her* inappropriate comment, though, God only knew.

"You're living with Todd?" Mike's fork stopped mid-air and he drilled Todd with his stare.

"I think I'll get the rest of the meal." Barbara's mouth scrunched to the side as she went back into the kitchen.

"Wipe the Puritanical look off your face, Mike." Todd resumed eating his salad. "Her apartment burned down last night after dinner. I wasn't about to leave her stranded. I may have been out of touch with people over the past two years, but simple courtesy isn't a social grace you forget."

So now she was a social grace? First cute, now that.

"Burned down? That's awful." Barbara reappeared, all composed, smiling and Barbie once more. "It's lucky you were with Todd."

"It's very nice of him to let me stay until I can find another place. I've started looking but there aren't many places available this week." In her price range and with something other than a pitbull with a choke collar for security.

"There's a lovely apartment complex over on Windy Ayre," Barbara said, placing a tray of lasagna on the table.

Jolie knew the complex she was talking about. Talk about the picket fence/red geranium window box image. And with image came hefty rental fees.

"I'd probably have to talk to my agency about adjusting my rates for that place." Darn, she had the most annoying habit of spouting information that really needn't be spouted at all. And the agency—

and Todd, or Mike, or whoever—paid her just fine, but those college courses weren't cheap and she refused to hand over more of her hard-earned cash than necessary for someone else's tax deduction. She was going to get her own house sooner rather than later if she could help it. After the pastry shop, of course.

"Which agency is that?" Mike asked. He must have had a few on-call to help with the help if he couldn't remember the one he'd just hired her from.

"Domestic Gods & Goddesses? The office is on First Avenue by the river," Jolie answered.

"I don't believe I'm familiar with that one," Barbara said, dishing out some awesome-looking lasagna.

"It's the home of omelet makers extraordinaire. Right, Jolie?" Todd smiled at her, which, of course, garnered him a smile in return.

"Domestic Gods & Goddesses?" Barbara turned to Mike. "We should give them a call, honey. We could use someone to make extraordinary omelets, too."

"Sure, Barb, go ahead. But no one's ever going to be able to make a better breakfast for me than you."

Barbara turned pink and lowered her eyes, but her smile was as wide as the arch on the doorway.

Okay, welcome to a whole new realm of innuendo. Or was it just flat out flirting? And was it still called flirting when it was one's spouse?

Jolie tried not to stare at the two of them, but the air in the room was suddenly super-charged with an energy she'd become all-too familiar with over the last thirty-six hours.

And she was feeling rather envious.

Todd shifted in his seat and suddenly decided to dig for buried treasure in his lasagna.

Which was a pretty good trick. She did the same while Barbara turned an even pinker shade of pink.

"Or maybe I won't call them," she said in a breathy little rush.

Well, duh, the guy was all but shouting he wanted to devour her and they were going to need privacy for that. The last thing these two should want was a third party around the house.

"So," Barbara continued, dabbing at her mouth. "Your apartment, Jolie. I have a friend in real estate I can call if you'd like. I'm sure she'll be able to find you something."

"That's—"

"Unnecessary," Todd cut in and they all spun their heads to him as if it were his serve at Wimbledon.

"Oh?" Mike quirked an eyebrow.

"Jolie can stay as long as she likes. Why should she have to pay rent when I've got four perfectly good empty bedrooms in my house?"

He smiled her way and her insides melted. Just simply melted and turned to mush and got all warm and fuzzy, completely laying waste to her composure. Good Lord, the man had a killer smile.

And she wasn't the only one struck dumb by his offer. Mike and Barbie's mouths were hanging open which was pretty hilarious.

Or would have been if she hadn't suddenly realized they were stunned because he'd invited her to stay. Her. One homeless, family-less, degree-less domestic goddess.

A charity case on two legs with a battered Bug in tow.

Oh *no*. Even though she had a plan and her life was on the upswing, recent fire disaster notwithstanding, she was *not* a charity case. Tough if she didn't fit with their pre-conceived notions of who should share Todd's home.

But he'd asked and it was his home and why shouldn't she stay? As long as it wasn't charity, everything was fine.

But for something not to be charity, payment would have to be involved.

Payment...

They didn't think—

She wasn't—

They weren't—

Oh.

Somehow she'd make it through the rest of the dinner. And find some way to pay Todd for her room.

But *not* in the way Barbara's mind had obviously gone.

***

Oh, dear. Jonathan Griff jumped from his chair and paced the worn floorboards, still keeping an eye on his television screen. One eye. The other one was twitching so much he had to close it or he'd have tears streaming down his cheek. That hadn't gone as well as he'd hoped.

It'd been a great idea of Todd's to take Jolie to dinner to meet his family. Jonathan was so proud of him. Compassionate, that's what the man was. Exactly why he deserved some happiness.

But Michael and Barbara's disbelief could not be tolerated. There were to be no doubts in either Todd's or Jolie's mind. This relationship had to be easy for them, no impediments whatsoever. No family meddling, no more fires, no other people… nothing.

That was his job.

And with that hurt look on Jolie's face, he'd better get to work on Raphael's suggestion of steering the course of true love straight again.

Chapter Thirteen

Morning had broken and Cat Stevens was running rampant in Jolie's head to the accompaniment of a bluebird's warbling outside her window. Or what was soon-to-be her window once she and Todd had a little discussion.

Apron at the ready, she traipsed down to the kitchen to earn her keep. Well, earn her paycheck. For her keep, she had other ideas.

And *not* the ones Barbara had had. She was not that kind of girl. And even if she'd misconstrued Barbara's reaction, there were proprieties to be met, after all.

From the pocket of her yellow-and-blue striped Bermuda shorts, she un-tucked the check for a month's rent. Just like she would for Mr. Murphy, her previous landlord, she was going to pay Todd, no matter what he'd offered.

She placed the check front and center at his place at the table, then set to work whipping up some crêpes with fresh fruit from Arena's. Strawberry crêpes drizzled with orange juice were the perfect summery breakfast when one wished to discuss matters of a financial nature.

The French door to the patio opened, admitting a wet-haired, muscle-glistening man in swim trunks that were plastered to his hips.

"Hey," said the water god, "you're up. Sleep well?"

She had to pull the tongue off the roof of her mouth. Chipper and gorgeous. And half-dressed. What a difference a day made.

"Um, yes, slept very well, thank you. You?" She turned back to the stove 'cause the crêpes were going to start burning.

They could get in line behind her hormones.

The chair scraped along the tiled floor. Whoa daddy. They were having breakfast in the near-buff. She was going to have to clarify exactly what constituted proper morning attire or he'd have to settle for burned meals if he kept showing up half-dressed. Or undressed. Whatever.

"What's this?" asked Semi-Naked Guy.

"Rent." She didn't have to turn around to know what he was holding.

Or, rather, what he was shredding.

"Jolie, I told you, you're welcome to stay here. You don't have to pay me."

"But I'd pay my landlord and, for now, that's you."

"I don't need the money."

She spun around, her backside resting against the edge of the countertop. "I, however, do need to keep my self-respect. I can't just take from you without giving something back."

Oh, I know what you could give—

Shut up, Naughty Girl.

Todd's green-eyed gaze searched her face like pirates searched a treasure map. "Okay. You want to give back?"

She nodded, all the while shoving Naughty Girl out of her head.

"Fine. But instead of money, I want something else."

Here we go. Naughty Girl wrung her hands in glee.

"Cookies."

Jolie did a double-take. "Um, what?"

Say what?

"Cookies. Chocolate chip, to be precise."

Jolie did the finger-in-the-ear thing. "I'm sorry. I thought you said 'cookies.'"

"I did. Chocolate chips." The corners of his mouth headed northward and the sun chose that moment to dip into the room and find his eyes.

"May I, um, ask why?"

"The Best Enterprises Foundation sponsors events for kids in crisis and I know those kids would love to have homemade chocolate chip cookies."

It was all she could do not to throw herself all over him and rain kisses on every inch of his tanned skin. Well, for more reasons than one, but—oh! Where had he been when she'd been in the system?

"So… is that okay with you?"

She nodded. Like a crazy woman. If she even thought about trying to open her mouth to thank him, he'd think she *was* a crazy woman because she was trying really hard not to burst into Hoover Dam-like tears.

Even Naughty Girl shut up, and Jolie thought she caught a sniffle or two from her.

"Okay then. That's settled." He dumped the shredded check into the trashcan, then sidled close enough to peer over her shoulder. "Are those crêpes?"

Chlorine and *essence du Todd* tickled her nose and the little fine hairs on the back of her neck started doing the "Todd Lambada" dance, which had the added benefit of heating her from the inside out so her tears sizzled out of existence.

"Yep. One of my specialties." She turned around and, smart boy, he scooted out of her way. Trying to regain whatever composure she had left, she spooned some of the fruit into the center, rolled the crêpe and drizzled more of the strawberry/orange juice over it. She handed him the plate and he took a seat.

"How about whipped cream with this?" he asked.

Whipped cream. She stifled a groan as she opened the fridge and grabbed one oh-so-innocent-looking white container. Somehow she was going to have to spoon the little pre-fabbed temptation over his crêpe, but, by God, her imagination went steaming into overdrive and Naughty Girl came back to life with a vengeance.

Images of spooning it over *him* flashed in her brain, followed shortly thereafter by images of licking it off.

She grabbed a theoretical stranglehold on Naughty Girl's throat and told her to knock it off. *That is* not *a good idea.*

Though, that tanned shoulder would look supremely scrumptious slathered in white, fluffy—

"Jolie?"

Face flaming, she tossed him the container. She was *not* going near the guy.

Chicken.

"Nice catch," she mumbled in an effort to appear somewhat normal and not like an incredibly grateful, overly-horny, under-sexed, sorry excuse for an employee.

"Are you joining me?" asked Mr. I-have-no-idea-my-chef-is-a-quivering-mass-of-hormones.

"Uh, okay. Let me flip this and I'll be right over." And she'd sit at the far end of the table.

"So what do you have planned today?" asked Mr. Chipper. "I'm going to be pretty occupied in the attic, so, if you don't mind, you can just leave me a sandwich. I'll grab it when I take a break."

Dab, dab with the fruit, roll, roll with the crêpe, and she was ready to brave breakfast with Brawny. Darn if the guy didn't pull out the chair next to him.

So much for avoidance tactics.

"If you're sure… I do have some pages to write—I mean, some notes to organize." Oops.

"Pages? What are you writing? A cookbook?" His tongue gathered the whipped cream from the corner of his mouth.

Mind back on the task at hand, Jols. Which would be pulling her sandaled foot out of her mouth. Pages to write. Sheesh.

"Yes. I'm working on a book. For the pastry shop I want to open." Sure, she could throw some recipes in her manuscript. She'd seen people do that, where they began a chapter with a family recipe. She wasn't quite sure how she'd work it into the story, but if she did, she wouldn't be lying.

"Be sure to include these crêpes. They're great."

"Thanks."

"Are there any more?"

"In the warming drawer."

He walked to the drawer, bent over to open it, and, man! What a view. His back was muscle-slick, a slight rise on either side of his spine, flaring in at his waist. His butt tightened, his thighs tightened, his calves tightened, and a few body parts of her own did some tightening—which sent one riotous bundle of flames from her heart, through several key points nearby—literally—down through her belly to dance along one very tingly area between her legs.

She really needed to stop noticing those things.

"These are very good," he said as he sat at the table again.

Could she *not* get a break? Heck, her nipples were welcoming him back, for Pete's sake. Could she have *some* time for them to calm down before he had 'em up and dancing?

"Thanks," she mumbled, shoveling the rest of her crêpe in. She was out of there as soon as she finished one last bit of juice. *Pseudo-cookbook, here I come.*

That was her story and she was sticking to it.

***

Todd closed the French door behind him, the slate patio warm beneath his bare feet. He breathed in the first scent of gardenias in the garden outside the study. The landscapers had been busy the other day. Freshly planted rose bushes filled the hollow beneath the study's bow window. He wondered what color they'd be when they bloomed. Probably white. For some reason the homeowners' association had a thing for white flowers, but he didn't know why. Maybe he'd call the contractors and get them to substitute some of the more colorful varieties.

If he cared enough. It was, after all, just a house.

He caught a glimpse of Jolie through the study window as she rounded the corner to head upstairs, her long dark hair flowing after her like a horse's tail streaming down the homestretch. Great; her exuberance was back.

He couldn't figure out what had happened during breakfast. One minute she'd been all smiles, her eyes sparkling like amethysts at the thought of baking cookies for the kids; the next, the light-heartedness had vanished and she'd become withdrawn. Almost unsure.

He replayed the scene as he climbed the outside stairs to the garage attic.

The whipped cream. That was when she'd gotten that funny look on her face.

Oh, hell. Did she think he was making fun of her?

He paused on the landing to pull the key from his swimsuit. He'd been surprised at himself when he'd taunted her with the "whatever" in the lobby of his offices, but then she'd shot back the whipped cream comment and it'd taken on joke status between them. At least, he'd thought so.

Hell, he was so out of this male/female thing. With Trista, it'd been as natural as breathing. There'd never been the coyness, the doubts, the should-he/shouldn't-he questions.

Not that he was going down that route with Jolie, no matter how pretty she was, but he'd felt that same repartee with her.

Obviously, she hadn't.

As the moving company van pulled into the driveway, Todd unlocked the door and slid it open. Dust particles danced in the sunlight as he took in the stacks of white-sheeted canvases lining the walls of the stark white room.

He was sick of the blandness. His house was full of non-colors, his garden was a tribute to white, now this place.

Trista's death had leached the color from his life.

He wanted it back.

Chapter Fourteen

At lunchtime, a still-shirtless Todd in a pair of low-hanging, faded-almost-white denim shorts joined Jolie poolside where she was working on her book.

"Mind if I join you?" he asked.

She slammed the notebook shut. Darn. Her hero, Tom, had finally started flowing from her pencil—some angst, a character flaw, and just a hint of the stubbornness that was going to keep him from realizing true love when he saw it.

She'd been having trouble getting Tom and the heroine together, so she'd decided to use what had brought her and Todd together—not that she was in any way comparing the two. One, of course, was fiction and the other, quite out of her league. But now, halfway through that scene, Todd stepped into view and—

"Jolie?"

"Huh? Oh, um, sure. Go ahead." She swept her hand over the chair.

He took the seat, parking his platter and iced tea glass on the white wrought-iron with a soft *clink*.

"Cookbook?" he asked as he swallowed a bite of the roast beef and Swiss sandwich she'd left for him, the muscles in his strong, corded neck flexing.

She nodded, sliding the notebook off to the side.

"Secret cookbook?"

Funny boy. "No."

"Secret recipes then? Or don't you want me to see how much butter you used for the crêpes?" The killer smile was back and her thighs quivered.

Her thighs *quivered*? *Really*? She never would have thought thighs could quiver. She'd read those words in a romance novel—

probably a Regency since heroines were notably shy and virginal—and found quivering thighs to be a bit overdone. But apparently it really was possible.

"No secrets," she said. That he need know about anyhow. "I just don't like anyone looking at my stuff until it's done." She rested the pencil on top of the notebook. "Is your sandwich okay?"

With another bite in there, he nodded.

"Good. How's the clean-out coming?"

He and the three workmen had been ensconced in the attic since right after breakfast. From her bathroom window, she'd seen Todd pause before entering the place where he stored his paintings. It must have been really hard to go in there.

"It's... coming." He cleared his throat. "It had to be done, I guess."

"So what are you going to do with all the space up there?"

Darn if he didn't get a little sprightly. "The light's good. I was thinking—"

"Of painting again?"

"I'm not sure. I might put a chair or two there, maybe an easel and see if I can—"

He looked away, beyond the pool toward the canopy of green at the back of the property with its wooden bench and some bird feeders. The fountain in the pond on the path from the driveway gurgled as a dragonfly buzzed past.

"If you can what?"

"If I can get any of the magic to come out of my fingers again."

Having been on the receiving end of Mr. Touch-Feeley's fingers, she could assure him there was, indeed, magic there.

Probably something else that wasn't a good idea to notice.

"Well, you won't know 'til you try." She swiped the manuscript off the table while his attention was focused on the dark green lawn. Mr. Gray did a good job with the yard. "Just get all your supplies out, make yourself comfy, and I bet in no time you'll be whipping out those canvases so fast you'll wonder if you'll ever be able to stop."

He laughed and she was thankful for the sound. He wouldn't be able to pick up a brush if his heart was in his shoes.

She glanced down. No shoes. Of course.

"I hope you're right, Jolie, but we'll see. First thing, though, I'm going to paint the walls. White is too sterile." He gathered his plate and glass. "And, God knows, I've had enough sterile to last a lifetime." He stood and pushed in his chair. "Thanks for lunch. It's nice having you here."

And away he went. With her thighs quivering after him. She was such a sucker for the tragic hero.

But she had to remember he wasn't a character in a book. That, no matter how inspirational he was for her writing, he was still carrying around a boatload of love for Trista which left about as much room in his heart for someone else as a fortune cookie wrapped around Confucius had for more words of wisdom.

***

Hours later, Jolie was trying her hand at a good ol' Americana dinner, when Todd poked his sweaty self into the kitchen.

"Something smells good in here."

I'll tell him what smells good—

"It's the herbed stuffing I add to the burgers," she said, flipping said burgers on the indoor grill. "Or maybe the buttery corn-on-the-cob."

"They both sound good. Do I have time for a shower?"

Only if I can watch.

Oh, please God, don't let Naughty Girl have said that out loud.

"Uh, sure. Yes, there's time." Her hands were shaking and it had nothing to do with the ice water she plunged the boiled potatoes and eggs into. Matter of fact, she should probably dunk her entire head in that glacial pool to shock her libido into proper behavior.

"Do you have enough for the guys?" he hollered from the steps. "I should have said something earlier, but I was occupied."

With sweeping the last remnants of his previous life out of his attic. As if she'd expect him to remember something as mundane as eating. "Yes, I've made enough. I figured you guys would be hungry."

"You're a godsend, Jolie," came wafting through the vast emptiness of the foyer as he crossed the hallway above her head, marching into that sanctuary he called a master suite, and she wanted to tell him he was the heavenly apparition she needed in her life.

But that would be so overly dramatic.

Though true.

She managed to get through the rest of the meal's preparation by focusing on the workmen carting some furniture and plants up the attic stairs and loads of paintings back down. All that work Todd had done and no one to enjoy it. Gosh, she really hoped he would start painting again. It didn't have to be those beautiful pictures. Maybe he could try abstracts. Charcoal. Stick figures. The *what* didn't matter, it was the doing it that did. She just wanted him to find his passion again.

And then he entered the kitchen and she found hers.

The khaki shorts, royal blue button-down, and canvas deck shoes were such a good look on him. Very Suburban-Man-Chic which normally would make her heart speed up, but it stopped. Possibly literally. There was a little pain right in the center of her chest when she breathed.

Then he smiled and the pain dissipated. And her heart rate went back to normal. And then ratcheted up a notch.

"Here, let me get that," he said and she could only nod. If he said her name she was going to melt.

She held the plate out, his fingers brushed hers, and she sucked in a breath, skin sizzling.

He stopped.

Beneath the plate, his hands halted on hers.

He sucked in a breath every bit as big as the one she did.

Whoa boy.

His gaze shot to hers, his brows reaching for the heavens, and darned if she didn't feel the flickering tendrils of want curling in her belly.

"Jolie."

"Hmm?"

"I'm… hungry."

"Me, too."

"Um, perhaps we better, um… " Todd tugged on her hand and she snapped out of that whirling vortex of chemical hormonal combustion.

"Right," She shifted her weight between the re-quivering thighs. "The food. Outside. Let's."

"Yes. Outside."

So eloquent, both of them.

She relinquished the burger plate, scooped up the fixings and trotted after him into the purple twilight as well as quivering thighs permitted.

The workmen were on their way back up the stairs, their banter breaking the mood. Whatever the mood was. Was it her imagination or had she and Todd been on the same hunger plane back there? She sure as heck hadn't been talking burgers.

"Come and get it, guys," Todd called out as he left the burgers on the table and set to lighting the tiki torches.

Come and get it. Now there was a command her traitorous heart leapt for.

***

Hands on his hips, Todd stared at the flame on the tiki torch and tried to draw more oxygen into his lungs. *What* had happened back in the kitchen? If he didn't know better, he'd swear he'd felt attraction. To Jolie.

Oh, shit. He did know better and that was attraction.

Now what the hell was he supposed to do?

The guys were helping themselves to the meal and he couldn't seem to muster enough effort to turn around. How could he face her?

How could he not?

Had she felt it?

He swallowed his laugh and ran a hand through his hair and around the back of his neck, kneading it. Of course she'd felt it. He'd known the moment she had. Which had been about two seconds after he had.

Attraction.

Desire.

For a woman other than Trista.

One who worked for him.

Oh, yeah. That was brilliant.

Todd sucked in another breath and willed himself to turn around. He shouldn't be surprised; Jolie was gorgeous. And funny. And fun. And bright and sunny—everything that had been missing from his life these last two years.

115

"Todd? You said you were hungry?"

Hungry? Was he?

He shook the double meaning from his mind and turned around, rolling his shoulders as he walked back to the table. It was too much too soon to make any decisions. He needed to digest this sudden shift.

"Yeah, I am." His gaze skimmed her face, then, after the briefest of pauses, he helped himself to the hamburgers. "These smell good," he said.

At least his voice sounded normal.

That'd be one thing that was.

***

Jolie's face felt as if it was on fire, her breathing was shallow, and her hands were trembling. Not exactly her normal state of being. Before meeting Todd Best, that was. Now? Who knew? It seemed trembling appendages were to be a daily occurrence *chez* Best.

Somehow she managed to direct the tremblages (her just-coined term) to a chair and plunked herself in it across from Todd. Let the feasting begin. Of the palate… and the eyes.

"Where are we taking the paintings?" one of the workmen asked, thankfully yanking her musings from the place they had no business going.

"To the office. Mike will let you know what he wants where." Todd helped himself to the fixings for his burger, cocking an eyebrow her way at the scored rind on the pickle. "More garnishing? Cute."

"It's what I do best."

"Now there's a damn shame," one of the other guys mocked with a suggestive waggle of eyebrows. "Garnishing ain't high on the list of priorities for my women."

"Jolie works for me," Todd snapped back.

"Oooo-kay." Scumm-o snickered.

"Look here—" Todd leaned forward in his chair.

"Luigi." The foreman smacked the table. "Knock it off, will ya? Keep yer trap shut or you're fired. Don't go insulting the boss, ya moron." He looked at Jolie and tipped a non-existent hat. "My apologies, ma'am."

"That's okay." It actually wasn't, but with Todd defending her honor, she didn't really need to make a big deal out of it.

Him defending her on the other hand... Naughty Girl was all over that.

Scumbucket scowled and the foreman jumped to his feet. "Guys, let's take these with us and finish up. We'll be out of your hair then, Mr. Best. Ma'am."

The other guy also whipped to his feet, while Luigi Scumbucket took his sweet time schlepping to his, then the three of them headed back to the Land of Attic.

"They didn't need to leave," Jolie said to Todd. "I guess Luigi just thought he was being funny. In a chauvinistic, condescending sort of way."

"There's no excuse for that sort of innuendo." Todd balled up his napkin and tossed it onto the table.

"True. But you didn't have to say anything. I was okay." Jolie unrolled an ear of corn, the sweet smell of melted butter rising in the air.

"Why? Why is it reasonable to assume a woman who cooks dinner is fair game for snide comments and insinuations? Maybe where you come from, but I've always been taught to say 'please' and 'thank you' when someone does something nice for me. That jerk—" Todd thumbed back in the direction of the garage—"doesn't have a clue."

It was the "where you come from" line that snagged her. Actually, yeah, where she came from she couldn't expect much better than a Luigi Scumbucket. But Todd didn't need to know that. And she really didn't want to think about the differences in their worlds at the moment.

"So, good hamburger?" she asked, trying to keep it business-like and not notice that they were all alone with the twilight wrapping around them, soft, flickering lights playing over the planes of his face and those broad shoulders while nature's cricket orchestra serenaded them.

"Huh? Oh. Yeah." He took a bite and she tried not to stare at his mouth.

But, man, was it hard not to. She'd never particularly noticed men's mouths before, but his had a nice shape to it, the bottom lip fuller than the top, slight up-curve to the ends. His teeth were straight and white and then there was his tongue—

"Good!" She cleared her throat and refolded her napkin, then swept it back over her lap. "I, uh, made a ton of them." She set her knife and fork square to the plate. "More than we'll ever need." She readjusted her glass of iced tea. "Lots. We can freeze some for another day and I thought I might give some to—"

"Go ahead, Jolie. Feel free to donate them to the foundation. You don't need my permission. The kids will love them." A long swallow of iced tea went down his throat and she couldn't tear her eyes away from the column of muscle.

Until he lowered the glass; then self-preservation kicked in.

"I've got a question for you." He placed the glass on the table, his fingers mere inches from hers.

She reined in her digits. No meandering pinkies for her. "Shoot."

"You mentioned something the other day about sixteen-year-old unwed mothers? Kids like you? What did you mean?"

"Oh, you don't really want to hear that." She flipped her ponytail back over her shoulder and turned her head.

"Actually, I do. I can't reconcile the image of you homeless and you now."

"Now?" She slid a glance back at him.

"Yes, now. You've got a career, you're smart, funny, adaptable."

"Adaptable?" That had her turning back to face him full-on.

"You handled that uncomfortable scene at Barb and Mike's last night. What else would you call it?"

She shrugged. "Desperate?"

He laughed and she loved that sound, deep and joyous and masculine, and it touched every cell in her body. She could listen to him laugh forever.

Uh oh. She did *not* just say the "F" word.

She couldn't have. There was no such thing as *forever*. She knew. Firsthand. Nothing lasted "F," except in the pages of a book.

"Funny," Todd interjected—thank goodness—into her path down Misery Lane. "But seriously, Jolie, were you homeless?"

Mr. Dog-With-A-Bone was obviously not going to let it go. She'd go for the short and not-so-pitiful version—the one that answered the questions and moved the conversation on. She'd developed it early in her house-hopping career.

"Depends on what you mean by homeless." She shrugged to

show it wasn't such a big deal. Eighteen years ago, yeah, big deal. Now? Not so much. "I had a home, just not my own. Actually, I had a lot of homes."

"Foster care?"

She nodded and wrapped her hands around her iced tea, the sweat on the glass sliding under her palms. "It wasn't so bad." If you liked loneliness, being an outsider, and not having a family to call your own. But she was over it. Really.

"What about your parents?"

God, it was like pulling teeth. "Dad's a question mark and Mom made some ill-advised choices. Gone, both of them. Probably for the best if those first ten years were anything to go by."

"How did you make it out of the system?" He touched her, just one fingertip to the fine hairs on the back of her hand, but she felt it. All the way to her toes.

He had to stop. She could get through this without crying as long as she said it flat out. Have him show compassion and she'd be a mush puddle.

So she took a drink of the iced tea and sat back in the chair, far from fine hairs and tempting fingers. "I decided I was not going to repeat the mistake of my genetics. I studied, worked hard and the rest, as they say, is history."

"That's an admirable story."

"That's me, Admirable Jolie." She tipped her glass to him in salute.

His eyes narrowed. "You've certainly got a lot of attributes, Good-sport Jolie, Ambitious Jolie, Admirable Jolie. What about Happy Jolie?"

Okay, enough psychoanalysis there, Dr. Phil. "Well, sure. I mean, where I am now sure as heck beats where I started. There was nowhere to go but up anyhow. Life is good."

"So that's why you took me up on my offer to bake for the kids. You've been there."

She nodded. "But even if I hadn't, I'd still want to help. It's a great cause. Those kids need more people like you."

Those *kids? You were one of them, at one time.*

Out of my head, Naughty Girl.

"That's good to hear because your chocolate chip cookies are going to be in demand."

Oh, he was smooth. She slid a sideways glance his way. "Care to define 'in demand'? Just how many cookies am I going to be making?"

"A couple hundred—"

"Oh, well, that's not so bad—"

"—dozen."

"A couple hundred *dozen*?" Mr. Jolly was getting his jollies on this one. Okay, smart guy, two could play that game. "Boy, I'm going to be able to stay here until the next millennium for that amount of work."

"Hey, you're welcome to stay as long as you like. You know that."

"But what happens if my life expectancy doesn't match my cookie-credit ratio?" She bit her lip, enjoying the teasing. It reminded her of Mike and Barbara.

Todd's sigh was oh-so-dramatic and he rubbed his hand across his chin. She couldn't look away as his palm rasped against the five o'clock shadow just below the surface and she could only imagine what that would feel like against her cheek.

That's right, Jolie. Only imagine it, 'cause that's as close to his skin as your cheek's going to get.

"You're right." He tapped that full bottom lip. "It's not possible to balance the scale of work versus cookie credits. You're going to need help."

"Help?"

"Of course. I can't expect you to spend all your waking time baking, so why not? I've made cookies before."

Hmm, had she been angling for that? She wasn't supposed to make up ways to spend time with him, but apparently Heart had stopped listening to Brain and decided to work on autopilot.

Of course, Brain, not one to be left out, then directed Mouth to say, "Okay then. I'll go out tomorrow and get enough ingredients to make the puffiest, most chocolate-y chips you've ever tasted."

"Somehow I had a feeling you'd say that."

Hey, the guy really did get her after all.

And, yeah, Naughty Girl chimed in, *he could get her anytime.*

Chapter Fifteen

R aphael clicked off the state-of-the-art monitor in his office and tapped the intercom. "Please send Jonathan in, Angela. Thank you."

He rose from the throne and stretched his wings behind him. So busy these days. So many people to help. *He* needed help. If Jonathan could gain the confidence he needed, he'd be the perfect assistant.

Raphael's feathers, softer than any bird's down, whispered along his hands. Such magnificent appendages. Great for convincing non-believers he was who he said he was, but more importantly, inspiring awe in those who had duties to fulfill.

The door to his inner sanctum opened and Jonathan, all four-feet-ten-inches of him, entered. Poor guy had never had any self-confidence from the moment of his birth. Born among a family of six-footers, Jonathan had been the brunt of many jokes. Good-natured or not, they'd taken their toll on him. But Jonathan had never lost the goodness in his soul because of it.

Raphael had had his eye on him ever since Jonathan had rescued one of his childhood tormenters from a rabid dog by finding the small opening that was the only other way into the room and distracting the animal so the bully could escape.

What neither Jonathan nor the bully had appreciated was that he'd been the only one who could have fit through that opening. His sized had served the Purpose for which it'd been bestowed.

"Sir?" Jonathan crumpled his hat between his fingers.

"Jonathan, please, take a seat." Raphael levitated one of the sky blue chairs. He'd decided to employ his powers during this interview because Jonathan needed to feel valued.

"Thank you, sir." Jonathan hopped onto the chair and rubbed at the telltale twitch by his eye before settling the mangled hat in his lap, the fingers of one hand tapping the brim while Raphael floated the chair over to the desk.

"Would you like something to drink?" Raphael materialized a glass of the lemonade he knew Jonathan was fond of. That should ease some of Jonathan's worries.

"Thank you, sir."

Raphael pretended not to notice the shaking in the initiate's hand as he took the glass. "So, Jonathan, how are Todd and Jolie doing? Any movement toward the final goal?"

Jonathan told him about Todd clearing out the attic—at last!—of Michael and Barbara's reception of Jolie—not quite what Raphael would have hoped for from those two, but, still, understandable given their love for Todd and everything they'd done for him—and the upcoming picnic.

"So, Todd is moving on. I'm glad to hear that. What about Jolie?" Raphael leaned against the edge of his marble desk rather than take the seat behind it. The throne was intimidating, though it did have its purposes.

"Jolie, sir?" Jonathan stopped sipping his drink, his eyes wide above the rim of the glass. The twitch, which had slowed during the recitation of events, now kicked back into gear.

"Yes. Has she made any strides in overcoming her feelings of inadequacy?"

"Strides, sir?"

"Yes, strides. You've seen Todd grow and emerge from his despair. Jolie needs to do the same." Raphael waved his hand and Jolie's chart floated from the file drawer. "Her mother never appreciated her. Of course, the poor woman had her own demons to deal with, but still, she did damage all the same. Jolie needs to heal."

"Yes, sir." Jonathan set the glass on the edge of the desk.

"I'd rather there not be any bumps in this road, Jonathan. Todd seems open to the idea of exploring what he's feeling for her, which is where we want him headed. But Jolie's so used to things not working out for her that she needs to feel worthy of his love. We need this to go smoothly for them. They've been hurt enough."

"Yes, sir." Jonathan nodded solemnly.

Raphael tapped the file. "I think you might want to appear among them, Jonathan, in a manner where you can affect events as they happen. Your merchant character nudged them onto this journey, but I'm thinking something more drastic. Something on a more daily basis. Without them knowing, of course."

"Um… okay. I'll think of something, sir."

Raphael held out his hand. "I'm sure you will, Jonathan."

Jonathan's eyes widened and he clutched the felt hat so tightly his knuckles turned white as he considered Raphael's outstretched hand. Gulping, he slid to stand before the chair and placed the hat on the cushion.

Raising his eyes—the twitch now completely gone—Jonathan took Raphael's hand. "I won't let you down."

"Of course you won't, Jonathan. That's why you were chosen to help Todd and Jolie. I have every faith in you."

Chapter Sixteen

Jolie drove the chugging Melanie into Todd's driveway the next afternoon. Todd hadn't been kidding yesterday when he'd said the picnic was next week. It was now Sunday, i.e. "next week," the picnic was in three days, and Arena's was officially out of baking supplies. Poor Signore Arena, she'd thought he was going to have apoplexy when she asked him for the last batch of the butter, but he'd calmed down when she'd told him it was for the foundation.

Jolie pulled into the garage, hoping Todd was around. For no reason other than to help her unload the groceries, so Naughty Girl could stick *that* in her innuendos. Chances were, though, that he was in the west wing, as she'd taken to calling the garage attic where he'd holed himself up in last night after dinner and all this morning. Just as well. With Heart still not firmly under control of Brain, she could end up doing the libido tango again if he was around.

Once she'd gotten the necessary ingredients into the kitchen, she set all the measuring cups, bowls, and baking sheets she'd need, thanking God, the builder, and the decorator that Todd had a dining room table big enough for the cookies to cool on. She'd bought enough plastic storage bags to make a landfill shriek, and a whole lot of chickens were probably walking around in pain, but it was all about the kids, so she'd set her tree-hugger-ness aside and focus on that.

Since chocolate chip cookies baked better if the dough spent the night in the fridge, the day's agenda consisted of making enough dough for twenty-four hundred cookies. Thankfully, there was an industrial-sized mixer that some previous chef must have finagled, so she might make it through this with her mixing arm intact, which was always a plus.

She turned on the Bose stereo and be-bopped along to old Madonna. Not her all-time favorite, but old Madonna was better than new Madonna. Yeah, it was bubble-gum music, but good to be-bop to. Then came Shania and she was dancing some more. It was all good.

She was into some heavy-duty belting out of "That Don't Impress Me Much," when she heard, "Hey, Shania!"

She spun, spatula/microphone in hand, and plunked down her foot to stop the twirl. The image in the doorway, now *that* impressed her much.

"Uh, hey?" she said oh-so-eloquently into the spatula.

"I was coming in to help." Todd surveyed the room, whistling. "Wow. I didn't realize this much went into making cookies."

She nodded and put the spatula down. "These are easy to bake. It just takes organization."

"Don't tell me, let me guess." He cocked that expressive eyebrow of his again. "Organizational Jolie?"

Now that was funny. And they laughed, a shared moment sort of thing.

"That'd be me. So, you really want to help?"

"Point me to an apron."

"Wow. You get points just for saying that."

"Yeah, wouldn't want to ruin these." He flourished his hand over his dusty old shorts, Bermuda-long and faded army green, a rip here, a tear there. Comfy shorts… that just so happened to hug his hips at just the right spot to cause her salivary glands to rev into action. The mustard yellow t-shirt clinging to some flexing pecs as he tied the apron behind him didn't hurt either.

She better make sure to keep the drool out of the cookie dough.

He washed his hands, drying them on that inch-thick cotton, loin-cloth-wannabe towel, and saluted her. "Ready for orders, ma'am."

He was cute like that and she couldn't help chuckling, all the while shoving Naughty Girl out of the picture who was squealing as she went, *Give him some orders already*!

"Okay." Jolie turned off lusting mode and went into baking mode. "I'm making a quadruple batch at a time. You can go ahead of me and measure out the ingredients. I'll sift the dry ones together then add the rest in the mixer. Once we've got everything done, we'll move it to a bowl and stick it in the fridge. Then on to the next batch. Sound good to you?"

He nodded. "Anything to do with chocolate chips sounds good to me."

Was that like whipped cream?

Not going there.

The radio station segued to some really bad stuff from the eighties, so "Hungry Like the Wolf" was grating across her nerves (though she could relate) as she and Todd stepped around each other. For such a big kitchen, it'd gotten extremely small. She was by his shoulder when he reached for the box of brown sugar and she got a whiff of fresh paint and sweat—not normally scents to get her hormones up and dancing, but on him, they worked.

Which she, *again*, shouldn't be noticing.

"So, how're the walls coming?" Jolie picked up the closest thing, which turned out to be a sifter. She started to—what else?—sift while Todd moved on to the liquid ingredients. The guy could crack a mean egg.

"Decent. I almost have the first coat of paint finished. I'll get to the second tomorrow and let it dry until after the picnic."

"So." Did she dare broach the subject? "Have you decided if you're going to paint again?"

He kept his eyes on the measuring cup while answering. He was either a very conscientious cook or didn't want to have the discussion. She'd bet the latter, but she was going to continue as if it were the former. That no-quitting thing of hers and all.

"You don't *decide* to paint, Jolie. It just happens. You *have* to. I'll see. I've got a few ideas in mind." He glanced over and smiled. "Who knows if they'll pan out?"

"And if they do?"

He shrugged. "We'll see. I'm not planning anything further than just trying out a few things."

"Okay. I guess that's good. Kind of trying to let your muse do its own thing."

"My muse. Yeah." His voice drifted away.

Okay, kick her for being an idiot, but that was about to change. Right now. "So, how many people do you think will come to the picnic?"

He mustered a smile and it was bigger than she'd hoped for. "I don't know. There's usually a good turnout. With all this you're making, people should have at least a couple of cookies."

"Good. Because I want the kids to be able to take as many as they want. Cookies are such a nice treat."

"And these kids need them."

"Don't I know it." Oh, crud. Had she said that out loud?

"That's right. I keep forgetting you *do* know. I have to say, Jolie, I'm having trouble seeing you that way. You haven't let life get you down."

Yeah, well, he hadn't seen her at her first foster home, curled into a ball on that lumpy old mattress. "The best way I've found to deal with my past is to put it away. It's over, I'm here and let's move on. Who was it that said 'the best revenge is living well'? That's my outlook."

"That takes a lot of inner strength."

Ha. She could tell him it was more self-preservation and abject terror of being sucked back into that swirling morass of self-pity and loathing, but why go there? "Do or die, I always say. Now, you can start on the next batch while I mix this one up."

He nodded and she turned on the mixer. Something to break up their conversation—and regain her composure.

Not to mention, aside from the occasional stir to get the batter off the side of the bowl, there wasn't too much to do while the mixer did its thing. So she had the chance to watch him.

There was just something about a man in an apron in the kitchen. Especially if the man was *only* in an apron in the kitchen, which, okay, he wasn't, but she had seen him in only the kitchen and nothing else and, boy, was that a sight to remember. So she tripped down sensory lane while he reached and stretched and bent as he measured out the ingredients. Who'd have thought baking was so much exercise?

"You know," he said when the mixer went silent, "the last time I did this was with my mom. I was twelve, I think." His eyes twinkled. "It's fun."

He had no idea.

"Let's see if you're still saying that three hours from now." Jolie maneuvered the mixing bowl to the table and scooped batch number one into another bowl, ready to start again. The mouthwatering aroma of brown sugar and vanilla surrounded her and she couldn't resist a dip into the dough with a spoon.

"I saw that." Todd's mock self-righteousness was hysterical.

"Want some?" She grabbed another spoon and another spoonful, and offered it to him.

With him holding a measuring cup in one hand and a five pound bag of sugar in the other, she had no other option when he said, "Sure," than to hold the spoon to his mouth.

Really. No other option.

His lips closed around the spoon, just a hint of his tongue before it closed, and she could almost feel the heat travel up the stainless steel into her fingers.

There was a little tug as he sucked the dough off and she felt a little tug of her own. Right in her nether regions.

She slid the spoon out and he licked his upper lip. "You're good," he said and there went her mind right to a bed with a roaring fire at the foot of it, a bottle of champagne, maybe some rose petals, and, of course, whipped cream.

"I am?" She pulled her gaze from his mouth, now drawn to his eyes. Warm and intense—just like her.

"Yes."

He put the flour and measuring cup down in one fluid motion and took a step toward her, his gaze holding hers. Her heart started hammering as he reached out, and she stifled a moan as she waited for his embrace.

She closed her eyes as he neared. There was just too much rioting through her body as his chest brushed her arm. She waited for the feel of his lips on hers, completely willing to overlook what surely was complete insanity since they worked—and lived—together, yet it was his hair she felt brushing her shoulder.

Not exactly the image she had going.

She opened her eyes—

And wanted to die.

He had his finger in the batter bowl behind her, scooping out the remains of batch number one.

Thank God no one else was around to witness her humiliation. What was she thinking? As if someone like him would be interested in kissing someone like her; someone without a real name or family to call her own. Just because she came with no baggage whatsoever—no relatives, no nasty in-laws, no history, just her—didn't mean his "you're good" had anything to do with something other than cookies.

"Want some?" said Cookie Monster, now back in her line of sight and holding out a finger full of cookie dough.

She did want some. She really, really did. And she wanted it right off that finger he was waving in her face. Wanted it so badly she had to say no because if she gave in to the impulse of licking his finger, she'd rip apart at the seams.

"Ah, come on. It's good." Wag, wag went the tempting digit.

She was amazed at her inner strength, as he'd called it. Truly.

She shook her head again and stepped back. "If we do this for every batch we are going to be some sick puppies." She prayed the bravado hid the quaking of her knees. He didn't need to know his chef was reading all sorts of innuendos into his words.

Cookie dough. Imagine that.

***

An hour and a half later, they were only halfway done. But Jolie? She was done. Over-cooked, over-heated, and way over-aroused. Todd was not only hot on the outside, he was completely sexy on the inside. Their little baking party had brought out all his childhood memories and he'd wanted to share.

Normally, she'd love to hear those things. Birthday parties, camping trips, whatever. But seeing as how her nerves were still rattled by the near-miss of a kiss, not to mention the mortification of said near-miss, she tuned out the narrative and tuned in to him. Todd Best, the man.

After all, it was in this very spot where she beheld the splendor that was Todd only yesterday. And traitorous Heart wanted to behold it again.

But Brain put her foot down. (Could a brain do that?) They, her collective self, were finished with wandering thoughts and a roaring libido. All Naughty Girl desires were hereby shoved into the closet with Naughty Girl herself and Jolie was going to enjoy the rest of her time in the kitchen.

As they finally finished cleaning up after the last batch, Todd removed his apron, treating her once again to the glorious sight of flexing pecs. "Thanks for doing this for the kids, Jolie." He folded the apron and set it on the counter beside the sink.

"Really, you don't need to thank me." She turned on the faucet.

He turned it off. "I know. You're a special person to do all of this, Jolie. The kids and I really appreciate it."

And then, joy of joys, wonder of wonders, whatever Hallmark expression of happiness she could conjure, he leaned over and pecked her cheek. Now, it was so small it could barely be called a peck. But she could call it that so she would. A peck. There. On her cheek. His lips on her skin and she was so not going to wash that cheek ever again.

Somehow she managed to breathe out "You're welcome" from her suddenly tight throat while he walked around her to the foyer. He could have walked over her and she wouldn't have minded.

The man just made her week.

His thundering up the stairs to the second floor pulled her mind back to reality—

No it didn't. Who was she kidding? Her mind went right to the fantasy: an image of Todd's long legs flexing as he took those stairs—maybe two at a time? Striding across the carpeting to his room, pulling his t-shirt over his head from the back the way guys could. Sloughing his shorts and boxers—nah, it was her fantasy and he was going commando—his *shorts* off as he hit the bathroom, kicking them perfectly into his hamper (again, it was her fantasy so no clothes on the bathroom floor), and stepping under a steaming shower.

Okay, it was eighty-eight degrees out, he'd been sweating, and the last thing he was likely to do was take a hot shower, but, again, it was her fantasy and if she wanted lots of smoky steam surrounding his cut muscles and angled planes, she'd opt for the steaming shower.

And suddenly it was more than a little hot in the kitchen. She ran her wrists under a cool stream of water, then leaned back against the counter.

She really had to get her hormones under control. She should start dating more.

More. Ha. More like, start over. Chucky had been years ago and it'd been so long since her last date she could barely remember it. Steve Somebody. Steve with the slobber lips and cow tongue and ewww, it was just not a good memory.

So she ran through the pitiful short list of guys who'd be date-worthy and every one of them came up short next to Todd. And not necessarily literally, though, yeah, a few of them were on the small side.

No, she meant on the masculine side. The I-really-want-to-get-to-know-them scale. Heck, Todd had proven himself capable of fidelity and deep love, he helped out little kids, was kind to older people, baked cookies with his mom, and teased his sister-in-law. Add to that the packaging, the chivalry, and the way he made her feel, and she was pretty sure no one else of her acquaintance could measure up.

Which was so not a good thing.

Because this guy, this symbol of manly almost-perfection, had one huge, glaring, fatal flaw.

He was still in love with his wife.

And what, even if he didn't have that huge, glaring, fatal flaw, made her think he'd ever be interested in looking her way?

And why did she care?

Because—

...

She did.

Whoa.

Jolie's knees gave way so she braced her hands on the counter. She couldn't care. She *couldn't.* Not any more than she'd care about, say, a lost puppy or child. It had to be all about helping him find his way, getting him to live again. It couldn't be anything more.

She wouldn't let it be.

She'd cared about someone once—her mom—and where did that get her? Alone, destitute, hungry, more than a little scared and, oh yeah, alone. Lonely, by herself. Left.

And that from a woman who was supposed to love her. Therefore, she could not allow herself to care about someone who had no genetic predisposition to care about her, no burning reason to *want* to care about her. That'd be just plain emotional suicide. And she was so much smarter than that.

Keep saying that, mocked Naughty Girl, *and you might start to believe it.*

Chapter Seventeen

Todd showed up half-naked the next morning.

Again.

At least it was the upper half, as his swim trunks were dripping a good portion of the pool on the kitchen floor and he had a towel wrapped around his waist. Not that that did much, seeing as how his gloriously tanned expanse of chest and stomach were on display, but the towel did cover his knees.

When had she ever noticed knees before?

"Good morning," said the man.

"Hi." One-Word Jolie this morning, obviously.

"Since we're going to be slaving over hot ovens today why don't we do cereal for breakfast?"

"I've already made scones." Wow. Four words. Mouth must have decided to cooperate today.

"Oh. Okay. But Wheaties would have sufficed."

Of course, breakfast of champions. He'd been hers with Luigi Scumbucket.

"Well, it *is* my job." Not to mention a way to justify the room upstairs. And, yeah, maybe, just maybe, it had something to do with yesterday's revelation that she wasn't going to give any importance to. "Um, do you want to shower first?"

"Nah. Might as well keep the cool from the pool since the temperature's going to be up in the kitchen. Maybe I'll hop outside for a dip whenever it's too hot in here."

Back to hearing double-entendres where surely none existed, Jolie nodded, grabbed the scones and poached pears in a raspberry sauce, and plunked them, and her butt, down at the island, o.j. between them.

"So, how is this going to work, Organizational Jolie?"

He had the best smile. All white teeth and twinkling green eyes and those laugh lines that crinkled in such an enticing way. She had to work really hard to keep the sigh from her voice as she laid out her baking battle plan.

And then they were off, dropping fifteen dollops of dough on each of four baking sheets in twelve and a half minutes, then switching them out with the new ones and cooling the finished product. No time for worrisome hormone dances whatsoever.

By lunchtime, they were more than halfway through the dough but had run out of cooling rack space.

"Let's do something simple for lunch," Todd suggested.

"I prepped ingredients for a honey mustard chicken salad while you were swimming this morning. I just need to throw that together."

"Okay, but no little curlicue things."

"You don't like my curlicues?" And, here, she'd worked so hard to try to impress him.

"I like them very much. But you don't need any extra work. Matter of fact—" He grabbed the bags of pre-cut veggies from the fridge. "I'll do the salad, you do that thing you do with the iced tea, and I'll meet you at the pool."

"Yes sir, boss." She mock-saluted him, then she took ice from the freezer and gathered up the iced tea and other lunch paraphernalia. He awarded her cheekiness with a smile.

If she forgot how gorgeous and funny and sweet he was, she could have a good time without all those "what if" thoughts intruding.

Too late.

Jolie sighed. Maybe she should just take the iced tea out by the pool and fling herself into the deep end. If she hadn't done so already.

God, she needed to get her emotions under control. She had to stop—

Wait. *Emotions*?

She couldn't have *emotions* for him. Couldn't really be feeling something like this. Something real. Something *emotional*. No, this feeling had to be hormones. Okay, so, sure, she had a crush on him, but rational people did not go from celebrity crushes to *emotions* in such a short amount of time.

She was reading way too much into this… whatever. This attraction. This constant thinking about him. It had to be the temperature, both in the kitchen and out here, frying her brain.

Yes, that was it. Just overactive imagination combined with proximity and the fact that, hello? He was gorgeous and sexy, and liked to play knight chivalric, and she hadn't been on the receiving end of that hat trick in like… well… never.

A shiver ran down her back that had nothing to do with the breeze that was trying its hardest to cool her heated skin, but she refused to acknowledge it. This whole thing was just hormones. Lack of dating. Compassion because she really did feel for him, what he'd been going through. It could have nothing whatsoever to do with emotions or she'd have a whole lot more at risk than just this job and the down payment on her pastry shop.

"Hey there, bathing beauty," said the man of her thoughts, sliding through the sliders at a most inopportune moment. "Lunch is served."

"Tell me why you need me here again?" she asked, choosing the seat across the table from him, hoping, this time, it'd be only their knees that would touch—those knees she'd noticed earlier below the towel he'd left somewhere in the house. "You seem to do perfectly fine on your own when it comes to food."

Todd sat down with a slash of pain across his face, and studiously turned his attention to serving the salad so much that she was almost sorry she'd asked. She was intimately acquainted with that avoidance tactic.

He took a deep breath and set the tongs down. "There was a time when food was the least of my problems. I'd just lost Trista, my wife—" as if she didn't know who Trista was—"and I felt absolutely nothing. Not hunger, not worry, not even pain. I felt… nothing."

He looked at her then, the pain in his eyes softening when she nodded. She'd been there. Been where it was so bad you had to be numb to survive.

He lifted a forkful of salad, staring at the endive and cranberry covered in sweet honey mustard dressing. "I didn't do anything. I didn't get out of bed, I didn't shower, didn't eat. Mike let me go for about three days and then barged in and took over." He shrugged, taking that first brave bite. "I needed it, though I hated him at the time. I hated that he made me face life. Face the fact that Trista was gone and my life wasn't ever going to be the same."

She wanted to cry from the sadness in his eyes.

"I hated him for a while. Him and Barbara. They moved me out of my home, got me up and around, and then the guy moved into my office. I didn't really care that the place was going to go under and my thought was, if I didn't care, why should he? Just let it go. Let it all go." He was back to staring at the endive again.

"But now you're doing better."

With a soft smile on his face and an even softer look in his eyes, he faced her. "Yeah. I'm doing much better now. I don't need someone in to cook for me. I'm perfectly capable of doing so. I just hadn't realized it until we had dinner the other night."

Way to go, Jols. Questioned yourself out of a job. Brilliant.

"But I still want you to stay," he said.

"You do?"

"Yeah. I do. It's nice having you around and I figure you can use the job. Not to mention the place to stay."

"Hey, I do just fine on my own. I can find another place to stay. I don't need your charity." She stood up, not sure if she was too proud or angry or humiliated.

Or hurt beyond words.

She'd thought… Oh what did it matter what she'd thought? This was just like every other time. Every other place.

God, how could she have let herself think—hope—

"Jolie, wait." Todd touched her arm. "Please. Sit. That didn't come out right."

Her wobbly knees weren't giving her much choice. Nor was the fact that she could barely breathe with the pain in her chest, so she sank into the chair, her back ramrod. "What?"

"I like being around you and that's not something I've felt in a very long time. Two years to be exact. I haven't liked being around anyone, including my brother, yet here you are, and I find myself glad to have a chance to chat, glad to have you here to share my meals. I like having someone else in the house with me." His hand flexed on her arm and she stared at it. Her skin knew it was there, but Brain was just now processing that information. "Plus, you're an amazing cook. I'd appreciate it if you'd stay. Keep me company. And make all the curlicues you want. Please?"

She was such a sucker for *please*. Not to mention, being needed. By him.

"Well, put like that, I guess I have to."

"Thank you."

There went that smile again, melting her composure like candle wax that had had a flame on it for too long. She was even more of a sucker for *thank you.*

"And the kids thank you," he said.

She shook her head. "No way. You don't get to bring the kids into this. I'd finish the cookies and do your picnic even without the begging."

"I know you would. And that's why I like you so much, Jolie Gardener." Then he gave her a little arm rub, à la "Way to go, Sport."

That'd be her, Good Sport Jolie.

***

"So," Todd said when they were once more dropping cookie dough dollops onto trays, "how'd you learn to cook if you moved around a lot?"

Now there was a nice way of putting it. *Moved around a lot.* Made her sound like an Army brat instead of a homeless one.

"I lived with the Carlesons for an entire school year and Mrs. Carleson was a stay-at-home mom." Jolie pulled up another baking sheet. "I think she just really liked trying to make things nice for those of us who didn't have such a great lot in life. There were three of us staying with them in addition to her four kids. Her husband traveled on business a lot. I think he was some big-wig in a computer company. Anyway, she'd always have freshly-baked cookies or brownies for us when we got home from school."

Todd started on his second tray. "That must have been nice. I loved when my mom made brownies."

Okay, she'd add brownies to her list of To-Dos.

"It was." She opened the top oven for her two trays then the bottom one for Todd's. "One rainy weekend, her husband was away, her kids were off on some church outing, and the three of us were there with her. One of the kids asked if she could teach her to bake and we all jumped on the bandwagon."

Actually, the "her" had been her. So desperate for something— *anything*—normal in her life. Toll House cookies had fit the bill.

"She sounds like a nice woman." Todd handed her the second tray and she set the oven timer.

"She was. Still is, I guess."

"So what happened? Why couldn't you stay there longer?"

The very same question she'd asked herself all those years ago. "Her husband got transferred so we did, too." She shrugged as if it weren't a big deal, but yeah, it'd been a big deal. Big. Huge. She'd cried herself into dehydration the day she'd found out.

"Do you ever keep in touch with the people you met?"

"No." She brushed some cookie dough crumbs from the edge of the counter into her palm. "What's the point? We never knew how long we had at a house, how long we wanted to stay or were wanted to stay, so what was the point of getting attached?"

"Well, Mrs. Carleson sure knew how to make a great cookie."

"Yeah, she did. And it actually helped me because if I could convince my other foster moms to buy the ingredients, I'd make cookies for the family. Once that happened, I was usually a big hit."

Todd stopped dolloping and pointed his scoop at her. "Is that why you became a chef?"

"No. I became a chef because I have a knack for it. Because it's a job and it pays decently and—"

...

Oh crud. Was he— Could he be onto something?

...

Oh man. She'd picked her career to make people like her.

Obviously that was why she baked for her foster families. If she could make the world's best cookies, they'd want her to stay.

And now her adult life was mimicking her childhood, going from house to house, cooking for people and staying with them until their lives changed, while hers just kept repeating itself. She stood there a moment, hands still, the kitchen quiet around her. He'd named it so easily. The thing she'd spent twenty-eight years doing without ever once calling it what it was.

She'd never seen this?

Apparently not and now she felt like she'd just been clobbered by the tallest redwood tree in the Pacific Northwest.

And if a giant redwood tree hypothetically fell on you and you didn't see it coming, could you still make a sound?

Again, apparently not, because there was nothing—not even air—able to get past the lump in her throat.

Todd dropped his cookie scoop and rushed around the island, taking her by the shoulders. "Jolie? Are you okay? You look a little pale."

She nodded, though words were beyond her.

He backed her up to a chair and guided her into it.

She knew what was going on, but for some reason it didn't feel like it was happening to her. It was as if she were watching herself over her own shoulder, detached from her very own sucker-punch of realization.

Todd thrust a glass of water into her hands. She knew she was supposed to do something with it, but for the life of her, she didn't have a clue.

He guided the glass and her hands to her mouth. "Drink. You'll feel better."

If he said so.

The cool water passed her lips and suddenly she was back in her body and she gasped at the sharp stab in her stomach that she recognized immediately.

Pure, unadulterated pain.

But gasping in a mouthful of water had the immediate effect of dousing the pain in hacking coughs. Todd smacked her on the back and even though it wasn't the touch she'd like from him, his body contacting with hers was enough to stem the pain and focus her on the here and now.

Here and now. Not *done and gone. Get over it and yourself, Jols. Move on.*

Right. That was all in her past and if she chose a career because of her needs as a child then it was up to her to make certain she became a success at it.

Jolie waved him away and stopped coughing. Her throat was a little raw from the water going down the wrong pipe, but she was okay. Back in control. Knowing where she was going, and what she was doing in her life.

She was.

Really.

"Thanks." She took another sip of water to ease the soreness in her throat.

Todd's eyes scanned her face. "Jolie—"

She shook her head and did the "talk to the hand" thing.

He nodded. "You're welcome."

Thank goodness the man could take a hint.

The timer chose that moment to ding and it was a good choice.

"We better get back to our schedule," Todd said.

Honestly, she could kiss the man for the normalcy.

Among other reasons.

***

From the shadows of his patio, the night sounds whispering around the soft ripples of the pond fountain, Todd watched through the kitchen window as Jolie puttered around his kitchen once the baking was completed. She hadn't wanted his help for the cleanup and, while he felt like a heel for leaving her the mess, he also understood her need for space.

That'd been a tough revelation for her. He hadn't realized at the time what he was saying, what effect it would have on her, that her career choice might be a subconscious fulfillment of a basic principal of life, until he'd seen that look on her face.

He couldn't imagine what her childhood had been like for her. Years of her life. Formative years.

He rubbed the side of his jaw, catching remnants of cookie dough in the stubble there. Brown sugar, cinnamon, apples... The little comforts of home. Things he'd always had growing up and had missed since Trista's death.

But Jolie, she'd been through it her entire life. He'd had a great childhood, a wonderful marriage and, though he missed Trista like hell, he'd never doubted she'd loved him.

He'd also never anticipated that their happiness would suddenly be torn away.

Unlike Jolie, he hadn't expected the worst. Maybe that was why it had hit so hard and blindsided him.

But look at her. Dancing again to some song he couldn't hear— albeit less exuberantly than the Shania he'd encountered earlier—her lips mouthing the words, expressions flitting across her face, she was back to her normal self.

But where did that "normal self" hold the pain so no one could see? And how had she, as a child, found the wherewithal to construct such walls? How had she maintained the will to live, to go on, with no one? To make something of herself and fulfill her dreams?

He didn't have no one. He had Mike and Barbara. The people he employed. Friends who still called even after two years of silence from him.

Who did she have?

She snuck a cookie off the cooling rack, her shoulders hunched as if waiting to be condemned for that action. The fact that she felt she had to sneak it broke his heart. What was it like to not feel comfortable helping yourself to a cookie? One she'd slaved over for two days?

Hers was a strength he'd never seen before. Piercing eyes, a determined set to her mouth, a sharp jaw that rounded in softness when she smiled, Jolie was a hell of a lot stronger than she gave herself credit for.

And that strength inspired him.

She inspired him.

***

Whoever said introspection was good for the soul never had a past they wanted to run away from.

And, apparently, she wasn't the only one. Todd had made darned sure to stay in that west wing until way past a reasonable dinnertime. Which made the roast chicken go cold, so Jolie chopped it up, tossed it with some honey-mustard-flavored mayo, red grapes, and almonds, put it on a bed of endive on a *batard*, added a tomato rose and parsley garnish to the side, and left him a note on the counter. Past nine o'clock, she called it a night and headed up to bed, Mr. Griff's book in hand.

Witnessing Miss Rebecca Featherington's parasol dilemma (her parasol, his body part, their collision) was much more appealing than delving into the dark closets of her own mind.

Just as she was about to turn off the light, Todd ascended the staircase. And sure enough, her nerves got all jumpy and she barely moved in her bed so she could listen.

Why? God only knew. Maybe Miss Rebecca Featherington's

Victorian ideals had rubbed off on her. Maybe she should be clutching her very lacy, very starched white nightrail to her neck so the wicked lord wouldn't take advantage of her innocence.

And maybe she should abandon Miss Rebecca Featherington and her parasol to over-acting purgatory.

When Todd's footsteps reached the top of the stairs, a quandary struck. Should she call out "goodnight"? Go to her door to say it? Ignore him and pretend she was asleep? With the light on? Uh oh. What if he came in to turn it off?

Yeah, right. He probably wanted to avoid her as much as she wanted to—

"Jolie? Are you awake?" he asked outside her door.

"Um, yes?"

The doorknob clicked but didn't open.

"Thanks. For the sandwich."

"You're welcome."

"It was good."

"Um… okay?"

With a heavy breath, a little *plunk* thudded on the other side of the door like his head was resting there. "About this afternoon… "

Oh, God. She couldn't re-do this. She simply couldn't.

His knuckles rapped the door. He, apparently, could. "Do we have to talk through this?"

That low, husky question was not good for her equilibrium. "I'm… um… not really dressed." She couldn't stifle the groan once the words were out. Good Lord. She *used* to be able to think straight. Used to be able keep her wits about her, but that capability had flown the coop ever since she set eyes on one unbelievably sexy naked man in his kitchen.

Who now stood outside her bedroom door chuckling at her supposed state of undress. "Well, I guess turnabout is fair play. I just wanted to say thanks for staying."

"You're welcome." *He* was thanking *her*?

Todd cleared his throat and the doorknob clicked again, but still didn't open. "Well, goodnight."

"Goodnight."

She flipped off the light, scrunched down beneath the eight-bazillion count sheets, and smiled herself into Slumber Land.

So this was what it was like to feel wanted.

Chapter Eighteen

Picnic day arrived after a pretty decent, non-emotion-laden second baking day full of snappy tunes, good vibes, and totally surface-level conversation. Todd still did his disappearing act up to the west wing in the evening, but that was okay. All the cookies had been baked, the mess cleaned up, and her gut hadn't taken any more rapier jabs. Things were looking up.

"You ready?" Todd was looking rather sporty in his navy shorts and red-with-a-gray stripe rugby. White running shoes and sharp sunglasses completed the ensemble.

Jolie elected to go with a yellow sundress (darn, no matching kicky flats), tan sandals, and her own sun-reflective gear. "I'm ready and so is breakfast."

"Thanks. Mike will be here any minute to help with the cookies."

They threw back banana chocolate chip pancakes—he did say anything to do with chocolate chips was fine with him—rinsed the dishes and loaded the cookies.

Once Melanie's passenger seat had the last bag it could hold, Jolie flipped her hair over her shoulder as she stood, a few stragglers adhering to her neck from the slight sheen (she did *not* sweat) the exertion left on her skin. "We are definitely going to need Mike's car. It's going to be pure torture driving with *eau de* chocolate chip wafting around me."

"I know what you mean." Todd closed Mel's door. "I feel like I should bring a glass of milk, but there probably wouldn't be any cookies left by the time I got there. Here. Let me."

She was swiping at those darn wayward hairs when Todd's finger whispered over her cheek, capturing the strands and tucking them behind her ear.

Such an innocent gesture, really. Nothing to it, right?

Then why did a line of fire shoot straight from her cheek back to the ear he touched—and was still touching?

His finger was just barely grazing, hovering there, but she could feel his warmth like a flambé torch. And it was suddenly very quiet around them, as if the birds took an intermission break. No one drove down his street, there was absolutely no wind to rustle, not a single leaf or errant newspaper, and she was hopeless to do anything but stare up into his mesmerizing green eyes and hold her breath.

He seemed to be into not breathing, too.

Then, softly, almost like a feather, his fingertips glided behind her ear and down her nape, chills and goose bumps following along, and her breathing jump-started into shallow little half-breaths doing the salsa.

Todd broke eye contact and his gaze followed the path of his hand. His golden lashes flickered as his thumb brushed her cheek and lightly stroked her bottom lip.

She was helpless to do anything but watch him and try to keep air going into her lungs.

He didn't have laughing eyes anymore or a smiling tilt to his mouth. It was as if he were trying to figure out exactly who she was and what she was doing so close to him.

She'd like to know that herself.

His hand slid beneath her hair, his palm scorching the back of her neck, and she was suddenly very hot. Dry-mouthed.

She moistened her lips and he sucked in a breath.

His piercing gaze were back and she couldn't look away.

His eyes got closer.

Todd got closer.

And suddenly it was his lips that had gotten closer, and a tide of hot burning need swept over her as his mouth covered hers. Someone groaned and she wasn't sure who.

Todd slid his other hand beneath her hair, cupping her face, and leaned her back against the sun-warmed metal of the car, no room for even air between them. Her arms found their way around that rock-solid abdomen and she was hanging on for dear life, plastered up against that chest she'd seen glistening in sweat, dripping from the pool, and covered in body-hugging clothing, and her knees were threatening a walk-out.

She clasped his back to keep from going boneless and he growled. That was definitely him and she was definitely doing something right to get that reaction. Her heart jumped and she couldn't help herself, she had to trace the sinewy muscles of his back with the tips of her fingers.

Todd pulled her tighter to him, though how that was even possible she didn't know, but, honest-to-God there was nothing so thrilling as a lean, muscled man using his power for good.

And this was so good.

But wrong.

So wrong.

How could he do this?

How could *she* do this?

As his tongue did a sexy, bone-melting, swirly dance on her lips—and traitors that they were, they opened to let him in—Brain picked that moment to get a conscience.

What are you doing, Jolie? asked Brain.

Well, duh. Kissing the hunky guy?

Why?

Because he's kissing me? Was Brain even in her body? How could it not know this?

And what are you expecting to come from this? You work here, remember? What do you honestly expect to come from this? This isn't a fairy tale, you know. No guaranteed happily-ever-after. Think you can handle that?

...

And there would be the words of wisdom.

Brain was right. Heart needed protection. Heart had taken some pretty nasty knocks in their collective life and couldn't bear many more.

She needed the job; he was still in love with his wife. Whatever this was, it wasn't what she wanted it to be.

So somehow—she wasn't quite sure how—she managed to pull back from the Todd/Jolie sandwich. Yes, there were a lot of shaky, heavy breaths and connecting body parts, but at least Lips unlocked and Tongues receded to the correct mouths. It was possible Heart could come away from this unscathed.

She nibbled on her lip. Swollen. She shouldn't do that again.

Although, Todd's harsh, indrawn breath could entice her to do it one more time.

Just once.

Yep, same harsh breath.

"Jolie." His fingers feathered her neck again and her feet began to melt onto the driveway at the way he said her name, his voice warm and smooth, wrapping around every letter like caramel on a Halloween apple.

And when he leaned in to go for round two of the knee-trembling, thigh-quivering, stomach-twisting kiss, with yet another warm-as-melted-butter, "Jolie," she swayed just the slightest bit his way with an answering, "hmmmm?"

"I'm sorry."

"Mmmm." That was nice—

Sorry?

He said he was *sorry*? For kissing her? As in apologizing, never-should-have-done-it-won't-happen-again-because-it-shouldn't-have-happened-in-the-first-place sorry?

Alrighty then.

She stepped back to find herself battling Melanie's door for space, so she put both hands on Todd's chest—and not in a good way—and shoved. Enough to show him she meant business.

"Whatever." She turned around and fumbled with the car door.

"Jolie—"

"Forget it. Let's just go."

Why wouldn't the darn thing open? She jiggled the handle again.

"What about the rest of the cookies?" Todd's voice was tight, restrained. A bit hoarse.

Oh yeah. Cookies. She leaned her forehead on Mel's roof. Now she was stuck here waiting for Mike to show.

With someone she wasn't about to turn around and face.

"Jolie—"

Mike roared up in his black, shiny Navigator as if it were a racecar, ending the moment.

"Mike's here." *Thank God.* "I'll get the rest of the cookies and you help him make room." Jolie stepped sideways from her car, leaving Todd to explain the sudden chill in the air to his brother because she just couldn't.

***

Todd raked a hand through his hair. *Smooth move, Best.* God, he was an idiot. What the hell had he been thinking?

"Did I interrupt something?" Mike's car door slammed.

Obviously, he hadn't been thinking.

He'd been feeling.

Feeling.

He hadn't felt in… so long. And… God. It'd felt so good. *She'd* felt so good.

She'd made him feel so good. So alive.

"Todd?"

"Huh? What?" Todd turned around to find Mike too close for comfort. The bond between them that had served him when he was at his lowest was not what he needed now. Mike could read him like a book. "Uh, no. We were, uh, just deciding if we needed your help."

"And?" Damn Mike for that smile hovering around his mouth. "And?"

"*Do* you need my help? Or do you have things under control?" The smartass didn't even bother to hide the grin now.

"Everything's fine, Mike. But, yeah, we need your help. Let's put the seat down so we can get the rest of the cookies in your car." He bypassed his brother's smirk and headed to the back of the SUV.

"Todd, seriously. What did I interrupt?"

"Nothing, Mike. You interrupted nothing."

"A lot of words for nothing."

"You want to open this trunk? Jolie's going to be back with the cookies any minute now."

"For what it's worth, Barb and I really liked her."

"For what it's worth, that's nice. Now how do you work this thing?"

"You know, Todd, you couldn't run from the truth two years ago and you can't do it now."

"Just shut up, Mike, and open the damn door." He didn't need any great revelations from Mike. He was having enough of his own.

One being that Jolie had run from his kiss.

Another, that it bothered him she'd run. More than he had a right to be bothered.

Oh hell. He didn't have any rights. Not for kissing Jolie; not even for *wanting* to kiss her.

He was sorry he'd done it. Well, not for the actual kiss, because, honestly, he couldn't regret it. He should, knowing how he'd felt about Trista, but kissing Jolie had been the first burst of real sunshine in his drab existence of the past two years.

No, he wasn't sorry for the kiss itself. He was sorry for using her: her zest for life, her exuberance, her generous spirit. Of taking some of that for himself. To absorb some of her positive, sunny energy inside him and allow life and, perhaps, hope, to sprout.

Jolie was life personified, every breath she took filled with such expectation. She was the first person to make him feel alive in two years. The first one to bring him back to himself; the sexual energy was just something extra. Something all her own.

But for her smiles, her laughter, even her singing, he owed it to her to make this right.

And he owed it to himself to not run away from it.

***

Jonathan Griff could barely contain himself. They'd kissed! Oh, he was so happy. It would only be a little while longer; he could *feel* it.

And soon he'd feel those wings on his back.

But he had to make sure. He didn't want things going wrong now. Raphael had specifically said no bumps in the road and the emotions were so raw at this point. So new.

He rubbed his chin. No bumps…

He didn't want to leave this up to chance. No, he'd have to get more involved as the archangel had suggested. Of course, with what had happened the last time he'd gotten physically involved—

But no matter. The fire had worked out for the best for Todd and Jolie. And this time he'd be more careful. No more accidental slippages causing any more damage to their growing relationship.

Chapter Nineteen

Can I have another cookie?" A cute little girl with braids all over her head batted her big brown eyes at Todd by the dessert table. So young and already so wily. Jolie remembered it well.

"Sure you can, honey." Todd handed her not one, but two.

"Thankth, mithter," the girl lisped as she skipped away with her treasure. "You're the betht!"

Jolie couldn't stop her chuckle. That girl had no idea who she was talking to, just some nice man with cookies, but yeah, he was the best. Literally and figuratively.

And Jolie really shouldn't be thinking like that.

Todd looked over, catching her eye, and his smile faded just a bit. He was probably wondering if she was going to get angry over some perceived sexual harassment—with the nudity and the lip-lock, maybe she had grounds.

But, no. He hadn't made anything a condition of her employment and until that happened, she was going with normal hormonal combustion. And Luck. Whether it was good or bad remained to be seen, but Luck had a lot to answer for in her life anyway—what was one more thing?

Or, maybe he was wondering if she'd get all mushy about the kiss. No worries there. That'd be the last thing she'd do. Matter of fact, she'd ordered Brain and Heart to throw it out of memory. A one-time event; that was it. Not worth the agony of remembering.

But Skin and Mouth remembered and they were shivering.

Traitors.

"Jolie!" Her friend, Chloe White, approached the table. "I didn't know you'd be here."

"I work for Todd, er, Mr. Best." She nodded in Todd's direction without taking advantage of the opportunity to steal another look at him. Score one for her.

"Hey, Todd." Chloe waved and took a cookie. "You made these, Jols?"

"Yep."

"Hi, Chloe." Todd stood next to Jolie. "Are the girls having a good time?"

"Always." Chloe, another system survivor, took in foster kids herself. "You know how they look forward to this picnic. It's been a count-down on our calendar for months."

"I'm glad. You should bring them by the house to swim sometime. The pool barely gets used."

"I'll keep that in mind. You know, Todd, you're pretty lucky to have Jolie working for you." Chloe munched away with a curious gleam in her eye.

"I know." Todd's soft voice did awful/wonderful things to Jolie's insides.

"She's an awesome cook."

"I know."

"Hello? I'm standing right here?" Chloe's method was so transparent and Jolie really wished she wouldn't do what she was obviously trying to do.

"Not to mention, very helpful with my girls." Chloe blathered on as if she hadn't heard the censure in Jolie's voice.

"Really?" Todd asked.

"Yes. She takes them shopping or, if I need to run a few errands, she'll stop by." If Jolie still had her kicky yellow flat it'd be protruding from Chloe's mouth at that moment. "She always has the girls in the kitchen helping her. Some of their best memories are going to be decorating cookies on rainy afternoons."

"Rainy afternoons. You don't say."

Jolie chose to ignore Todd's gaze as it rested on her—or rather, she let him think she was ignoring it—by adding more cookies to the doily-covered trays in a vain attempt at blending into the background. How did one ask one's friend to shut her trap in public? Perhaps a well-aimed glare?

"Yep. And every Christmas we have enough gingerbread men to form an army." The glare hadn't worked, but luckily for Chloe, a whistle sounded from the field.

"Time for the kickball tournament," she announced, grabbing another cookie. "I've got to get my team set up. Catch up with you two later. Jolie, if you can come by a week from Monday, I'd appreciate it. I've got another appointment about the house."

Jolie nodded and Chloe ran off, and, oh, the awkward silence she left behind.

"So," Todd said, "gingerbread men?"

"Yep. With chocolate chip buttons, licorice scarves—"

"Whipped cream fur on their hats?"

Okay, that earned a smile from her. She shook her head and finally looked up. Those crinkles around his eyes she liked so much were back. "I refuse to introduce impressionable children to the hazards of whipped cream. We use icing."

"Ah, icing. Definitely much less hazardous." For a moment they smiled, and then… it just happened. One little chuckle, then another, and they were back to the easy camaraderie of before. Before The Kiss.

"Looks like you've got a lot in common with Mrs. Carleson." Todd pulled out another aluminum tray and covered it with doilies. Only a real man could handle doilies and maintain his masculinity. "Chloe's girls are going to remember you later on in life with good memories."

"I hope so. The good memories, I mean. They are so lucky to be living with Chloe." Jolie retrieved another bag of cookies and loaded the tray, trying to ignore Todd's shoulder mere inches from hers. "She's trying to adopt them, but it's pretty hard for a single woman, and she's got a problem with some builder so all her money's tied up in that legal battle. It's a bit of a strain on all of them since nothing's permanent in the girls' lives. I try to help out where I can." She folded the empty plastic bags. "If, God forbid, any of the girls gets moved, at least she'll have our time together to remember."

"And maybe she'll become a baker or chef someday, too."

Boy, did the guy get her or what? "At least she'll have a direction in her life, a career goal. I know it helped me stay focused. I knew what I wanted in life, where I was going. It kept me on the straight and narrow."

Todd took the folded bags from her and their fingers brushed. Not much, and not deliberately, just enough to remind her there'd been a *reason* for The Kiss.

"I guess there are opportunities aplenty for them to stray from that path," he said as if his skin wasn't scorched.

"Yeah, desperation and despair are the Pied Pipers of scared and lonely kids."

"I admire you, Jolie." His voice went all soft and her legs started with that wobbly-knee syndrome again.

"You… you do?"

"Yes. You're not about to let life get you down."

"I've only got one life. Might as well make the best of it."

"When life hands you lemons—"

"I make some pretty awesome lemonade."

"I'd like to try it sometime."

They were talking about a drink, right?

"Hey, Todd!" Mike jogged up to the table. "The games are about to start and we need a few words from our CEO."

Todd's eyes flickered once more over her face. "Can we talk about… lemonade later?"

She gulped. "Sure."

He wrapped his un-scorched fingers around her upper arm and gave it a little squeeze. "Thanks. I'll look forward to it." He jogged after Mike to the podium on the field.

What a view. Gluteus Toddius all the way.

***

Jonathan Griff popped up at the cookie table, heavy satchel in hand, intent on putting his latest plan into action. This Guardian stuff was not for the faint of heart or the lazy. So many variables, it was like conducting an orchestra. And he was determined to get it right. "How are you doing, my dear?"

"Hi, Mr. Griff. I'm doing well. Yourself?" Jolie looked like a beautiful spring day in her sunny dress and even sunnier smile.

"Good, thanks. I'm doing just fine. It's good to see you so cheerful. Not like the first time when you were having a bit of a bad day with your shoe."

"I know. And then both my shoe *and* I went on to have an even worse night."

Guilt wicked its way down his back. "Ah, yes, the fire. Have you found a safe place to live yet?" Of course, he already knew how well it'd worked out, but she couldn't know he knew. It'd be so much easier if Guardians could share their job description with their Charges, but with so many non-believers these days, not to mention dissection-happy scientists and government agencies, that wasn't a good idea.

"Actually, Mr. Best has let me use one of his rooms until I can find a place in my price range."

"He's a good man, that Todd Best. You should stick with that one because you could do a lot worse than him." But certainly not any better; he was one of the best, no pun intended. There was a reason his family had that last name. Generations before him had earned it.

Jolie's face reddened and she shuffled the cookies around on the platter before her. "What brings you here today, Mr. Griff?"

"Oh, er, I've had my eye on this picnic for a while." He leaned against the table, crossing one ankle in front of the other and settling in for those Heavenly words of wisdom it was his duty to impart. She was a smart girl; she'd take the message to heart.

"I was thinking that the children would like a few books of their own, and since books are my business, I'd like to donate some. Nothing like losing yourself in a good story, I always say." He nodded, waiting for her to agree, as he knew she would—and did. "And how are you doing with the one I gave you? *The Dashing Rogue*, I believe?"

"I love it, thank you. Regencies are my favorite."

Of course he'd known that. That'd be why he'd chosen it. Full of hope and dreams and, of course, happy endings. All wrapped in a package she'd like.

"They were simpler times then, weren't they? Nowadays there are all sorts of rules to follow, approvals to be gotten… It's much harder. But back then, a girl's Guardian only needed to tell her who she was to marry and she'd go along with it." Ah, for the good ol' days.

"That's simpler? I'd call it indentured servitude of the worst kind."

That wasn't supposed to be her conclusion. Indentured servitude? How did people come up with these things?

Jonathan uncrossed his legs and raised himself to his full height, which The Boss had assured him was considerable when righteousness backed it. "As long as the Guardian had the girl's best interests at heart, it'd be a good thing, right? Most young people can't tell who'd be perfect for them, so who better to see things clearly than the one who cares for them?"

She… *snorted*? "Yeah, but if we let the older generations decide everything we'd never have technology or rock music or the right to vote."

"Ah, but with age comes wisdom, don't you think?" Goodness, she was a tough sell. He wouldn't have thought it. Of course, there was her upbringing.

"In some cases, sure," she argued. "But for a spouse? I don't think so. How well did all those arranged marriages work out? Were the people happy?"

"And the divorce rate nowadays is such a good indication of the choices your generation has made?"

"But at least they have the choice."

"So, if someone, say a Guard, er, *good* friend, drops the perfect man in your lap, you'd walk away from him simply because you weren't the one doing the choosing?"

"Are you trying to fix me up, Mr. Griff?"

Fiddlesticks. He hadn't meant to be so transparent.

"Oh no, my dear. I don' play matchmaker. That's best left up to those who know better." Though how much better, he was beginning to wonder.

He glanced skyward. Hopefully The Boss hadn't heard that. It couldn't be good to doubt Him or an archangel, but with Jolie's reticence on the subject, Jonathan had to wonder if Todd truly was the correct choice for her. "I, er, just like giving out some food for thought, that's all."

Well, regardless of what he thought, The Boss knew what was best. It was not Jonathan's place to question—unlike Jolie's. And he'd better not stay any longer; she'd already guessed too close to the truth. Besides, he had his plan to put into action. "Speaking of giving out food for thought, I'd better get this brain food out to the kids." He reached into his satchel for a few books and put them on the table, careful not to crush any of the cookies. "I'll see you again, my dear. Have a blessed day."

"You too, Mr. Griff. Here, would you like a cookie?"

"Thank you. Why, I knew the sweetest woman once, who could make the best cookies. The woman had a heart of gold."

Yes, Marybeth Carleson had a heart of gold. One, it seemed, she'd passed on to Jolie, along with the recipe.

***

The picnic was pretty spectacular in Jolie's opinion. Todd, er, his company went all out for the kids. The picnic was more a fair than an ordinary picnic. Dunking booth, carnival games, the kickball tournament, a watermelon seed- spitting contest, pie-eating contest, and more food than teenagers and their younger counterparts could possibly consume. But Jolie knew these kids; they were hungry in more ways than one. Food was simply the physical manifestation of that hunger, so there wasn't much left to clean up when the day ended.

And, yes, she was both gratified and proud that every child got at least three cookies and not a single crumb remained.

"My work here is done," she muttered, rounding up the trays.

"Spoken like a true superhero."

She spun around to find Todd right behind her and her face took on the temperature of liquid chocolate, warm and melting. "Uh… Hi?"

"Hi." He laughed and helped toss doilies into the trashcan. "Have fun?"

"It was wonderful. This is a great event."

"It's one of my favorites. We've been doing it for about six years now."

He leaned over to wipe the table and she struggled not to watch—that whole "sorry" episode earlier rearing her self-preservation instincts. "The kids seemed to get a lot out of it."

"They used to get more out of it." He was still wiping away.

"What do you mean?"

"We used to have an auction in the evening for the community. A lot of corporate sponsors, Best Enterprises, included." He'd wiped that spot on the table at least six times. "But I haven't organized it in the last few years."

Few—or two?

Jolie found her own spot to wipe. "Well, the picnic's a wonderful thing to do for them. I'm sure they appreciated it."

"Just like they appreciated your cookies." The tone in his voice made her look at him. Sure enough, a soft smile graced his lips.

And she had to stop remembering what those lips had felt like.

She turned back to her wiping. "Glad to help."

"Really?"

That got her attention. No one should ever doubt her sincerity about helping kids in crisis. "You don't believe me?"

"It's not that, no. But I'm thinking of doing something else and could use your help."

Oh, well that was different. She abandoned her cleaning frenzy and stood, resting her hand and the dishtowel against her hip. "That sounds mysterious."

His eyes twinkled. "No James Bond, I promise." *Pity.* "Did you see your friend Mr. Griff here today?"

Of course. Covered in a suit so that she'd worried about heatstroke in the midst of their chattel discussion. "Yes. He was giving out books to the kids."

"I know. What a great idea, and the kids loved it." Todd reached past her to lift the stacked aluminum trays and she was treated to those flexing pecs and biceps again.

"Anyway, seeing him solidified an idea I've had."

Hmmm, Doily Man was shuffling his feet. "And that is… ?"

Todd took a deep breath as if her were about to plunge from a platform dive. "That book he gave me about Holbein?"

"The Younger."

A smile. "Yes, the Younger. The portraitist."

She waited.

"He painted portraits."

"Got that."

"Oh, right. Anyway, I, um, thought, that is, I'm thinking about giving it a shot. Painting. Portraits."

Glory hallelujah! She knew he could do it, she just *knew* it! "That's great, Todd! You'll be painting again. How wonderful! I'm sure Mike will be thrilled."

And he was back to shuffling, which was quite endearing—not that she needed any help in finding him endearing.

"The thing is… " He did that hand-raking thing through his hair.

"Go on."

"I haven't concentrated on portraits in the past and I'd like you to… " He shoved both hands into the front pockets of his shorts.

"To… ?"

He cleared his throat and stopped the shuffling, throwing back his shoulders and looking her in the eye. "To pose for me."

Okay, where'd her tongue go?

She swallowed (twice) and it reappeared. "Pose? Me? For you?" Though it seemed to have lost its capacity for more than the most basic elements of speech.

"Yes. I need a subject and you're around, and, well, I can pay you."

Whoa. Wait. She got to spend hours on end in his company *and* got paid for it while he studied every angle of her face? Was there a downside to this?

It was perfect. A chance to help him and lord knew, she wouldn't find it a hardshi—

Hold on. Didn't most artists' models pose in the—

"How *exactly* would you want me to, um, pose for you, Todd?" And where did that "sorry" issue come into play?

He got her meaning in an instant. Well, goody, she could make him blush every bit as much as he could her.

"I just want to paint your *face*, Jolie. I told you that your name fits you, and I'd like to capture it on canvas. You've got beautifully expressive eyes, gorgeous high cheekbones, a classically sculpted nose, perfect angles and hollows to practice portraiture. Nothing more." The blush was gone as he met her eyes, hand over his heart. "I promise."

"Okay." She wasn't giving him any chance to back out. She could do this. For him. For his art. "But on one condition."

"What is it?"

"Well, first of all, you don't need to pay me. I'm staying in your house on your charity, so now we can call it even."

"It's not charity, but fine. Done."

"And second—"

"You said one condition."

She gave him her best version of his eyebrow-quirking maneuver. "And secondly, while I'd love for you to start showing again, I don't want my face plastered all over some art gallery."

She'd been on a local agency's flyer for the foster program one year and the ribbing from it made her shy from that type of publicity ever since. Plus, there'd been something about the whole world seeing her at her most vulnerable, and she just didn't want to ever feel like that again.

And no, there was absolutely no correlation whatsoever between her wanting her privacy and invading his by using him for inspiration for her story. If it ever did see the light of day, no one—including the man himself—would know who'd inspired it. But a painting, especially a portrait… people would have to be blind not to see it was her in that frame.

"Don't worry about it, Jolie. I'm not planning to show again. This will be for me. I'd like to give it a go for the sheer pleasure of painting. Nothing more."

"Okay. So, that's what all the painting and whatnot was with the attic?"

Just remember, Jols, you're basically a science experiment. Don't forget it.

Thanks, Naughty Girl, for putting it all in perspective. As if the "sorry" incident wasn't enough.

"Yes, though the idea actually started when we were talking about the sunset on *The Midnight Maiden.* As I was reliving how I got started painting, the urge kind of nudged me. Mr. Griff's book did more nudging."

"You were pretty interested in it. And I got a whole lesson on Junior."

"Sorry if I droned on about him."

"Not a problem." She shrugged. "I'm glad I could help. And it was kind of interesting, in a medieval sort of way."

"Tudor, but that's not important. Anyway, the attic seems like the perfect place to set up a studio, hence—"

"The project."

"The project."

"But you told Mike you weren't going to paint anymore."

He put both hands on his hips and the movement stretched his shirt across his own set of well-defined angles and hollows. "Of course I did. If he hears I'm even thinking about picking up a brush, he'll be all over me. You saw what happened when I gave him the last of my landscapes." He shook his head. "I don't want him bugging me. This is for me. To see if I can re-discover the joy of the process."

"And I'm part of the process?"

"You're part of the process. An essential part."

"A convenient part. You could have a bevy of fans banging down your door to sit for you for free."

His fingers reached out to stroke her arm. Mr. Touchy-Feely didn't seem to be aware he was doing it. "But I feel comfortable around you, Jolie. You won't ask a dozen questions about my work or my life, or go blabbing to the media. You treat me like a real person, not a celebrity, or worse, someone to be pitied. I don't have to rehash every painful moment of the past two years. You're my friend, Jolie, and I can really use one."

And there went another sucker-punch to the gut. Or somewhere suspiciously close to her heart. The guy had an incredible way with words. He really should try writing.

"Put that way, you've got a deal." Jolie held out her hand.

Todd took a deep breath and looked at her outstretched hand.

He was really going to do this. He was going to paint again.

He could do this with Jolie.

He took another breath and shook her hand and the contact seared up his arm, infusing his body with her vitality. No one was like Jolie.

What about your wife?

Oh hell. He hadn't thought that. Trista, with her light auburn hair, those amber eyes, her laugh, her smile… She was one of a kind.

Just like Jolie. In her own, different, special way.

Trista was gone. She'd loved him and wouldn't want him to mourn her forever.

She'd actually want him to move on. Go forward in his life. Maybe even—

Maybe even care for someone else.

He'd never thought he could care for another woman, but the woman in front of him, so bright and optimistic and generous and full of hope, so vibrant and alive…

So damaged from her past yet brave and strong and determined to go on.

No, Trista wouldn't have a problem with him being attracted to Jolie.

The question was, would Jolie?

Chapter Twenty

Want to take a dip to cool off?" Todd asked her as they returned home—er, to the house.

His house. Not her house, not *their* house. Big difference.

"No thanks." She closed Mel's door with a crunch that could only mean the seatbelt had made another ding in the doorframe. Just one more dent in Mel's exterior. Comparisons to herself not allowed.

"That's a pretty definite no."

"What I mean is, I want to grab a shower and then I've got some more work to do on my, um, you know, book. I haven't had a chance to add in the crêpes and I might as well do a chocolate chip cookie recipe notation on exactly how much of each ingredient goes into making twenty-four hundred cookies while it's still fresh in my mind. Plus, I had some other ideas that I'd like to write down and then maybe give them a whirl in the kitchen. If you don't mind, that is."

"There you go again."

"What?"

"Your brain on warp speed." He tucked a strand of her hair behind her ear. "And before you get all uppity about it, I meant it as a compliment. Your mom should have named you *Joie de Vivre.*"

Joy of living? Happy, carefree? That's how he saw her?

Wow. She could definitely live with that. "No offense taken." Especially since he was tucking yet another wayward strand behind her ear. Oh, for a windblown "do" again.

"How about eight o'clock tomorrow?"

"Eight o'clock?" She was still stuck on his fingers in her hair. Maybe his "sorry" earlier wasn't for kissing her. Just maybe.

"Tomorrow morning? Attic? Remember?" He dropped his hand and thought rushed in.

"Oh. Sure. Eight's fine. What would you like for breakfast?"

He waved his hand. "Really, I'm fine with cereal."

"And, really, I'm fine with cooking. It's what I was hired for, after all. I've got a great recipe for a ham and Swiss puff pastry quiche."

"That's fine. Whatever works." Todd did the hands in his pockets thing and the crickets chirped around them. A soft breeze from the river rustled the tree near the driveway while a frog dove into the ornamental pond with a *plop*. The scent of Todd's warm skin and that Grey Flannel she liked so much added to the ambiance in a way that could only be described as wonderful.

And then Todd took a step inside her personal space and things went from wonderful to spectacular, what with the moon electing to train its beams on Todd's golden hair while his gorgeous eyes held hers captive, and memories of The Kiss filling her mind.

Would he or wouldn't he?

Did she want him to?

Uh, duh...

"Jolie... "

"Todd... "

Nervous laughter broke the spell.

"I guess I'll see you in the morning." His voice was husky and this time she knew for sure that nothing was stuck in his throat.

"Yes. In the morning." Her articulateness was astounding.

"Well, goodnight then." He didn't step back.

"Goodnight." Neither did she.

"Meow."

Meow?

It took another "meow" before she realized Todd wasn't imitating a cat, but, rather, a white kitten with four black paws wound around and between their ankles like a Celtic knot.

"Oh, look how cute." She picked the little guy up. He purred, butting her cheek with his head. "Is he yours?"

"Never saw it before."

"Do you think he belongs to someone?"

"Probably one of the neighbor kids."

"It's a little late to go door-to-door, don't you think?" And, yep, she did have an inkling what a girl with big violet eyes and a cute little kitten nestled against her cheek could do to a big tough guy's resolve.

Todd sighed but with a little smile going on beneath that tough exterior as he crossed his arms on his chest. "Okay, you can keep him until someone claims him. I guess we can print up some Found posters."

"Thanks, Todd." She gave the kitten a little kiss and he purred even louder. The kitten, not Todd. But she wouldn't mind Todd doing some purring—"I'll keep him in my room."

"Lucky for the both of you I use kitty litter on my driveway in the winter instead of salt, so there's a bag of it in the garage." Todd petted their new friend.

Yep. If guys could get a girl's attention with a puppy, why couldn't girls do the same with a kitty? The question then begged to be asked about why was she vying for Todd's attention, but she'd ignore it for a while.

"I bet he's hungry. I'll make him some eggs. Unless you've got cat food around for some other winter predicament?" Jolie rubbed Mr. Kitty's cheek with hers, that soft rumble of his tickling.

"Funny." Todd tapped her nose. The kitten's, too, before heading for the litter.

Jolie watched him go with a sigh. *Could* there be something happening between them? Or was she just imagining it? Mom had thought so countless times and those guys had never worked out. What if she had the same tendencies?

That put a damper on the residual goodness of the day, and since the kitten couldn't answer that question and standing here in the moonlight mooning over Todd definitely wouldn't, Jolie headed inside to take care of the newest addition to the fami—

To the *household. Not* the family. There was no family.

"So what are you going to name him?" Todd asked carrying a plastic box filled with kitty litter through the kitchen door.

"Mr. Kitty?" She shrugged, cracking an egg for the kitten who'd decided to take up residence on top of her new sandal.

"Jolie, I can't go around calling him Mr. Kitty. And how do you know it's a boy?"

"Didn't anyone ever teach you about the birds and the bees, Todd?" She almost choked on the words, as the image of The Kiss loomed large on her mental horizon.

Todd got a wicked, wicked grin on his face. "Trust me, Jolie, I know all about the birds and the bees."

"I believe you." Oh, yeah. No doubt there. Her face was like a thousand degrees, and she spun around to hide that fact, dislodging the kitten who meowed as his bed turned into a carnival ride.

She whisked the eggs a bit harder than necessary. "As to your question, male cats look like a colon under their tail and females look like upside down exclamation marks."

"Punctuation? That's how you tell? Thank God humans are different."

You got that right, buddy. Way different.

"So, is there another choice for a name? I'll lose all sense of masculinity if I have to call him Mr. Kitty."

"Do you have a better idea?" Into the pan went the overly-scrambled eggs.

"Killer."

She snorted. "Puhleaze. Does he look like he's dangerous?"

They looked down where the kitten had curled up between her feet again. His little pink tongue lolled out the side of his mouth and he snored softly.

"Sleepy."

The kitten's tail twitched.

"I don't think he likes that one, Todd."

Todd's eyebrows arched. "How about Socks then?"

"Or Boots. As in Puss-in." As a writer, she was familiar with this process, kind of stream-of-consciousness rambling to get what she needed.

"Fine. It's late, I'm sweaty, and you're naming the newest punctuation mark to join the household Boots. Shoes, Sandals, Sneakers… any kind of footwear is better than Mr. Kitty. I'll see you both in the morning."

And there he went, taking all thoughts of what if with him—which was probably for the best anyway. He was just coming out of his self-imposed emotional hibernation; it probably wasn't the best idea to read anything more into *anything* other than he was rejoining the world of the living and she just happened to be handy.

Right. That was what she needed to remember.

Jolie hunkered down to pet Boots while he slurped up his eggs—her own little "just so happened to be handy" friend. Nothing wrong with being the "handy" friend, as long as you weren't looking for professions of undying love and everlasting commitment, though if no one claimed Boots, he could expect just that from her.

What could she expect from Todd?

Jolie couldn't go there. So she chose to go to her room instead. She settled Boots on the pillow next to her, and he, sweet thing, licked her knee with his sandpaper tongue, then wrapped his tail around his body, flicking it softly against her thigh, his black paws such a contrast against his snow-white fur. He purred himself to sleep while she struggled away on her manuscript. With Todd pulling at her heartstrings, she wanted to imbue Tom with all that emotion. At least it'd be good for something.

An hour or so later, her pencil was a nub and her brain numb, so she put the notebook aside. Tom was working very well now. Perfectly ready to let a woman into his life.

And she wasn't even going to touch that thought.

Chapter Twenty-One

J olie, you need to put the damn cat outside."

"I can't. He might run away."

"Stop moving. He's distracting me, damn it. Every time I move he's swatting my shoe laces."

"So take off your shoes." Did she just suggest Todd remove an article of clothing?

"Fine." Todd exhaled and removed them. "Why didn't you leave him in your room? He's going to start in on the paintbrushes soon."

"So give him one. What's it going to hurt? You have yet to pick up a brush."

"That's because I'm sketching you first. Turn your head to the right. There, that's it. Now tilt your eyes up toward the top of the window. Just like that. Good. Hold it. Don't move."

There she sat, staring at a piece of window trim in the west wing the Morning After. *Not* that this was a Morning After worthy of being called a Morning After, given that the time she was spending with him was relegated to discussions about light, positioning, and, of course, the diatribe against the kitten. An artist's model's life was definitely not glamorous. Quite odious, actually. They'd been there for a good two-and-a-half hours so far and Todd had said all of six words which weren't cat-related: "Good morning," "Sit here," and the ever-present "Don't move."

Yep, that was about it. She was hoping it was simply that he'd gotten up on the wrong side of the bed that morning and that this wasn't his normal artistic temperament. Because, if it was, she might push for an end to his re-instituted career before he'd even had a chance to get started. Or at least suggest he find a new model because she didn't care how cute and sweet and caring and sexy and funny and friendly and nerve-shivering he was, this was not worth it.

"You know, Jolie, you really are a beautiful woman."

Well, okay, maybe it was. "Um, thanks?"

"Don't move."

And there went that moment.

"I just hope I can do your bone structure justice. The way your lashes brush beneath your eyebrows—they're incredibly long, but natural-looking. Not come-hither. More… inviting. Yes, that's the word. A window dressing for your soul. I've got to get the curve of them right."

Wow. He could say that without dissolving into a puddle of mush on the floor? She, on the other hand, was getting quite boneless. "Todd—"

"Ssh. Don't move your mouth. I've got to get the tip of your lip right where it vees into the middle."

Yeah, well, he'd better get the droplets of moisture (not sweat because she didn't) beading above said lip before they cascaded all over the place.

"I've got an itch."

His sigh was loud enough to wake the neighbors. "Fine. Take a break."

She scratched the itch on her hand, rolled her head, worked the kinks out of her shoulders, did a few arm swings. At least she had a pillow on the stool so Tush was in decent shape, but her right calf felt as if it'd fallen asleep. She did some toe-pulls to stave off a charley horse and a minute or two of run-in-place.

"What are you doing?"

"Stretching?" Novel concept.

"You need to stop. You're shaking the floor and your lip line is going to bleed charcoal as if you don't know how to use lipstick." He rubbed the canvas with his little finger and his brows scrunched down until his eyes were almost invisible. And there he went with that hand through the hair again.

"Are you always this chatty when you paint?" She couldn't help the nudge. It was like some little imp got inside of her and wanted to push Todd's buttons.

I know some buttons I'd like to—

Be quiet, Naughty Girl.

Spoilsport.

"Huh? What?" Todd took the stick of charcoal from his teeth, leaving a gray smear beside his mouth.

"I said, don't you think you should take a break? Your hair is sticking up from where you've run your fingers through it too many times, you've got a streak of charcoal across your cheek, and your personality is as sparkling as a flat bottle of old cider."

"What?" He sighed. "Sorry. I guess I got involved."

"A bit."

"I just want to get this right. It's much different trying to convey the intelligence and beauty of a face than depicting nature. Portraits are so, well, personal. I've got to capture the essence of my subject in a way I've never done before."

Forget those quivering thighs. Face, portrait, subject—she was just a facial subject on a piece of canvas and she really had to concentrate on remembering that.

And not let Heart slip into Stomach at the realization.

"Can I see it?" She did a little hop-step over to the easel.

"No."

"You're kidding."

"No, actually I'm not."

"But it's a picture of me."

"And I'm the one painting it, therefore, I call the shots. No one sees my work until it's ready for presentation."

The half-grin on his face told her he knew it was bugging her not to see it, and that he was enjoying bugging her, but no way was he going to let her see it.

"Fine." Two could play that game. "Then you can't see my book until it's finished." Oh lord oh lord oh lord. Open mouth, insert kicky yellow flat-less foot.

"Fair enough. Now are you finished stretching?"

Shoot. He won that round. She glared at him as she re-took her perch on the boring stool, readjusting her purple t-shirt. "What time's lunch? As the chef, I need to get started."

"Have you really worked up an appetite sitting there?"

Truly, he had no idea. "Actually, I thought *you* might have, seeing as how you're working so hard."

"Why, Jolie, is that sarcasm I hear?" He raised his eyebrow, which raised her body temperature, and she had to look somewhere else. "Let me finish your cheek while the sun is at this angle and then we can call it quits for the day. Okay?"

Smooth, warm-as-honey, conciliatory words did wonders in an argument. "Okay."

***

Just how long did the sun remain in one angle? Didn't it travel across the sky in something like sixty minute intervals until high noon, at which point the sun was, well, high? As in, straight up in the sky? As in, it couldn't possibly be casting any shadows because it wasn't on an angle?

Apparently such knowledge was beyond her hero over there, who was *still* sketching away. She must have an awfully big cheek if he was working on it for over an hour. Talk about unflattering.

The charley horse was coming; she could feel it. It was about the only thing she *could* feel. Her feet were asleep, her legs were cramping, and her tush had high-tailed it to China about twenty minutes ago.

"I'm sorry to be a nudge about this, Todd," she said in the sweetest voice petrified lips and a dry throat could muster, "but is there any chance we can stop? If nothing else, Mother Nature needs a visit."

He was really into the sketch, arm extended, swishing across the canvas in quick little strokes. His lips were a thin line and he was biting the top one a bit. Too cute. A lock of that gorgeous hair was flung sideways across his forehead, just begging to be smoothed back. Well, in her imagination anyway.

"Yoo-hoo. Todd?"

"Give me a minute," he gritted out between his teeth.

She was so tempted to do the *Jeopardy* theme, but that might really bug him. And, even though he bugged her with not letting her see the piece, she didn't want to put any onuses on his painting. Instead, she elected to pass the time quietly—a rarity for her since silence made her edgy, which only underscored her determination to help him out.

Besides, she'd been staring at that darn window trim for so long she hadn't really noticed the rest of the place. He'd painted three walls a bright yellow and the other a sky blue, as if he wanted to bring sunny days inside. And he must have actually done that, opening every window in the joint (of which there were many) for the last two days because there was only the faintest trace of new paint smell. But it was closed up today, so it was a good thing he'd installed a wall A/C unit because any more heat in this place could melt a glacier or two.

A plump white sofa sat in the corner, a comfy chair also in white near it, a couple of orange throws flung over the arm rests, and a geometric-design rug under the grouping on the hardwood floor. One lone chrome floor lamp rose up and over the seating area and colorful tropical plants in beautiful clay pots dotted the set-up. The guy definitely had an eye for color.

Finally, he sighed and gave one last two-handed rake through his hair, hiking his faded royal blue t-shirt up a bit over his waist. Between the glimpse of naked abs and him working out his own kinks, her traitorous fingers were itching to do some walking, and she didn't mean through the Yellow Pages.

"Thanks." He stretched his palms outward, fingers interlaced. "That—" he indicated the canvas, the brushes, and his whole studio in general—"felt good."

"I'm glad." There was a moment of silence, expectant, eager, while their eyes did some heavy-duty communicating. She wasn't quite sure what they were saying to each other, but if the smiles were anything to go by, it was all good.

"Ready to grab a bite?"

The man did have a way with words.

Chapter Twenty-Two

After four hours of sketching, Todd had a new appreciation for the human form, but that appreciation took on new meaning as he followed Jolie back to the kitchen along the flagstone path. Long, toned legs, rounded butt, the silky fall of her hair…

Staring at her for so long today, tracing the curves of her face with his eyes, then doing it on paper—he was only human. And there was that kiss between them that just wouldn't leave him alone.

"So is it almost done?" Sunshine bubbled over Jolie's shoulder with her smile when she looked back.

"Done? No, not yet. There are so many nuances. Take the nose, for example. It has so many contours, the shadows, the bridge. It can take a while to capture it perfectly. And a cheek—just a curve, right? Not really. The tightness of the skin, the imperfections, the texture… What a challenge to—"

"Imperfections? My cheek?" Jolie stopped in front of one of the French doors and ran her fingertips over her cheek. "Where?"

Todd stood behind her and their eyes connected in the glass pane.

Time stopped.

Which it shouldn't. Not if he wanted to be able to finish the painting. Not if he didn't want her to quit because of inappropriate advances. She was his employee and that kiss should never have happened—not that he could have stopped it. Just like he couldn't stop staring at her. Couldn't stop wanting to touch her.

Todd swallowed. "Not your cheek, Jolie. Yours is flawless. You… your skin is flawless."

"It is?"

"Jolie, I told you. You're a—" His voice deepened and he

couldn't stop that either. Hell, he was having a hard time breathing. "A beautiful woman."

She turned around. To face him. Up close.

"I am?" she whispered.

"You are."

He should take a step back. Turn around. Something. It was too intimate. They were too intimate. He had to stop noticing the warmth in her violet eyes, that slight curve of her mouth—hope or happiness? Maybe both. She hadn't taken this job to have him maul her. He had to put out of his mind how she was the perfect height for him. How her head would fit beneath his chin if he were to embrace her, how the fall of her hair would brush his stomach, how her breasts would press against his chest—

His fingers strayed to that flawless cheek, a breath away from her skin and—

"Boots!" Jolie yelled, jostling the suddenly squirming little bugger in her arms, who was, if Todd read it right, digging his claws into her skin.

Foiled by a cat.

He should probably thank the little furball. He needed distance from Jolie. Professional distance.

And emotional.

***

Phew! That was close. Jonathan wrapped all four of his paws around Jolie's arm and hung on, not daring to take one off to smooth out the twitch by his eye. He hadn't meant to dig his claws in so hard, but being squished between the two of them in the approaching kiss hadn't been part of his plan.

Not that he didn't want them to kiss again; he just didn't want to be such an intimate part of it. Besides which—

"We're back." The sing-songy voice was just what Jonathan had been expecting.

Thank goodness Jasmine Gray had finally shown up. It was about time. She had a part in this whole thing, and her gallivanting around someplace else was not going to help these two. Still, one couldn't stop Mother Nature when the will to procreate was upon

Her, and Jasmine did deserve to see her grandbaby. It was just unfortunate timing that the baby had arrived when Jolie was set to meet Todd.

"Jasmine." Todd's greeting was about as short as one could get. Probably because he realized how close he'd come to embarrassing all of them if he'd acted on that kiss. But Jonathan had plans for that.

Raphael had been right; this being-part-of-the-action was a good thing. Todd and Jolie needed to come together and do so seamlessly. Each had been too hurt, through too much. It was their time now. With no bumps, no dings, not even a swerve.

A kitten was the perfect, inconspicuous cover and he was going to make sure everything that needed to happen, happened. With Jasmine's help. After all, it'd been her idea in the first place to lead Todd back to the land of the living.

"Oh, Todd, it's so good to be back. I, of course, loved seeing our grandson, but there's no place like home." Jasmine stepped from the kitchen and Jonathan raised his head, thankful for once for the twitch. Jasmine would recognize it. And him.

He hid a smile when her eyes narrowed. She'd figured out exactly what his presence meant, even though he hadn't warned her Jolie was The One. Every other chef the agency had sent over had been in preparation, but Jasmine, a mortal, was not permitted to know the Ultimate Plan before it unfurled.

Jasmine smiled one of her biggest smiles. "You must be the new chef."

"Yes, I am." Jolie stuck out her hand. "Jolie Gardener."

Jonathan waited. Jasmine was nothing if not predictable.

He was proven right again as Jasmine shook Jolie's hand for a mere second before pulling her into an embrace. Plump and round, with gardenia perfume and a gray topknot on her head, Jasmine was everyone's idea of motherly, something and someone Jolie sorely needed in her life, and the only reason Todd hadn't been able to give in completely to his despair.

It was because of this woman's unselfish love that her prayers for a new wife for Todd were about to be answered. *If* Jonathan could ensure their path was smooth.

"Welcome, Jolie!" Jasmine tucked Jolie's arm under hers and pulled her close—just as Jonathan knew she would. "We're going to have such a lovely time. I'll go over Todd's schedule with you and tell you what he likes to eat and—"

"Jasmine," Todd interrupted, "Jolie's been here almost a week."

"A week? But you weren't supposed to have anyone—"

"I know, but somewhere the lines got crossed."

Jonathan wondered if those crossed lines were part of The Plan. Apparently Guardians didn't get to know the entire Plan either. The Boss did like to work in mysterious ways.

"She started a little early," Todd continued. "Good thing, too. She made cookies for the annual picnic. The kids gobbled them up."

"How wonderful. Those kids need some treats in their lives." Jasmine released Jolie and, going along with Jonathan's charade, plucked him from Jolie's arms and held him beneath his "armpits." Dangling was not fun. "And what have we here?"

"Oh, well, he found us, and Todd said—"

"How precious! Does he have a name?"

"Boots," Todd and Jolie answered together, one with a smile, the other with a snort.

He wasn't too thrilled with the name either, but since "Boots" was the first "pet" Jolie had ever named, he'd deal. And they had come up with the name together, so there was that.

"Boots?" Jasmine's tone went along with Todd's derision. "What kind of name is that for a kitty?"

Todd cleared his throat. He was definitely a kind man, not wanting to hurt Jolie's feelings about the stupid name. "Trust me, Jasmine, it's better than what he started out with. I hope he won't bother you, but he sort of adopted Jolie, so until someone claims him, he's ours."

Definitely a kind man, letting Jolie care for a stray. The man was compassion personified. These two would make wonderful parents.

"Of course he won't bother me, Todd." Jasmine positioned him in the crook of her arm. "Well then, *Boots*, let's see about getting all of you some lunch."

"I was just about to—" Jolie said.

"Oh *p-shaw*." Jasmine frittered her fingers. "It's already started. Grilled chicken and asiago cheese on focaccia. Piece of cake."

Jonathan could relate to the surprised look on Jolie's face. Jasmine certainly wasn't one to let moss grow under her feet.

Which was why she'd called on her own Guardian after Trista died. Jasmine had been Jonathan's first solo venture at caring for a Charge and a relatively easy one at that since she'd been born with a charm on her shoulder. She'd made all the right choices in life, loved and was loved; nothing for him to do, really, though he'd had to save her from a terrible scooter spill when she was ten. He'd inadvertently revealed himself, which was the basis for both the delay in earning his wings and these interim challenges. But it had forged a bond between them so when she'd implored him to help Todd, well, he'd taken the request to The Boss and the rest, as they say, was history.

Now on to the future. Their future.

Chapter Twenty-Three

Jolie followed Mrs. Gray into the kitchen. She'd never met anyone like her. Commandeering but endearing. Bossy but empathetic. Sweet, loving, and an awesome hugger. Everything a mother should be.

"Earl, this is Jolie, the new girl," Mrs. Gray said to a man seated at the table. "So you see, Todd wasn't alone and starving while we were gone." She directed Jolie and Todd to the table while Boots got the laundry basket treatment and a slice of cheese.

Earl stood and shook Jolie's hand. "Pleased to meet you, miss."

This was Todd's gardener? The guy looked ninety years old and as frail as a puff of air. Why was she thinking there was a top-secret landscape company involved somewhere?

"You must tell me all about yourself, Jolie." Mrs. Gray placed their sandwiches on the table. "The last girl? Michelle? She was a dear, though she had the worst luck with her alarm clocks. Never could get here early enough."

"Now, Jasmine, you know I told her not to come in so early," Todd broke in, which was pretty impressive with the way Mrs. Gray never took a breath. And he thought *she* talked a lot?

"*Pish.* I was the one who ended up making your breakfast. Not that I minded, but still, it was one of her duties. She just wasn't right for you, Todd."

Who was she trying to kid with that mock severity? The love she felt for Todd was just beaming through every pore.

"Well, you won't have to worry with me," Jolie added. "If I oversleep, Todd can just knock on my door."

Or any time he wants—

"Beg pardon?"

And again with the inappropriate comments, but Todd came to

the rescue. "Jolie's apartment burned down her first day here, so I offered her one of the empty rooms. You know, one of the ones I offered you and Earl, but you refused to take?"

Mrs. Gray's skin pinkened but her indefatigable-ness re-surfaced as she bustled more about the kitchen, tossing some chicken scraps to Boots. That was going to be one very happy kitten. "How very sad for you, my dear. And so gallant of you, Todd." She sent an approving smile his way.

Mrs. Gray's sandwiches were very good and if Jolie were actually writing a cookbook she'd include them. Mrs. Gray was chatty in a curious sort of way, but not intrusive. Jolie liked her—especially since the love the housekeeper had for Todd was so obvious. It was a good thing he'd had her in his life to help him through those tough years.

Earl, seemingly content for his wife to monopolize the conversation, was a shadow next to her, but affection ran between them as she spared a glance his way every so often with a smile just for him or re-arranged his napkin or refilled his iced tea, that sort of thing. Just like she did for Todd. And for her. As if they were family.

Jolie sputtered into her iced tea.

"Are you okay, dear?" Mrs. Gray asked, her eyes all warm and concerned.

Jolie nodded , but couldn't get a word out, half afraid to answer because of what might come out.

A family. The one thing she wanted above all else in this world.

But one kiss did not a fairytale ending make and she had to remind herself of that. Of what it felt like to hope, only to have those hopes crash and burn.

She'd survived it once—barely. And bare or not, she didn't think she'd survive Todd.

***

"So, my dear, tell me how you've found working for Todd." Mrs. Gray pounced on Jolie not two seconds after the men departed the kitchen—and in no way was that a surprise.

"He's pretty easy to please food-wise."

"I know. That's why this is such a perfect job for a young girl like you, though I've told him time and again I'm perfectly capable of feeding him." She stacked the plates in the sink and made a big production of scrubbing them.

"Perhaps he doesn't want to take advantage of you?"

Mrs. Gray shone a grateful smile to Jolie, complete with little sparkling drops in her eyes, and clutched the dishtowel to her chest. "Oh, that's so sweet. And he is, you know. Sweet."

Jolie nodded, pretty much in agreement there, though she would've added hot and sexy too, but she'd go with sweet for now.

"You do know about his wife?"

"Yes."

Mrs. Gray clicked her tongue. "We practically raised Trista, you know. Parents always traveling so someone needed to be at home when the dear thing came home on break from boarding school. She didn't have much of a family. All those trappings and ritzy vacations and high-end schools added up to one lonely life. I felt so bad for her. You can imagine how happy we were when she met Todd."

Jolie nodded, but why was Mrs. Gray telling her this?

"Her parents weren't, though. He was a poor, starving artist. Not someone worthy of a Pennington in her parent's estimation." Mrs. Gray sniffed. "Hogwash. Why, he was perfect for her."

Jolie's stomach thudded. Just rip her heart out right now, why didn't she? Todd was perfect for Trista, ergo, he couldn't be for Jolie. Why the torture? Though, if she were honest with herself, this was just what she needed to hear to banish those aforementioned hopes— but honesty wasn't ranking high on her list of wants and needs at the moment.

"And the two of them, they proved her parents wrong. Beautifully wrong. I was so proud." Mrs. Gray sniffed and Jolie was right there with her. "And then for her to… to… "

She covered her face with the dishtowel for a moment, composed herself then continued, "Well, you can see why we're so protective of Todd. He's family, and family's important."

Ah. *Protective.* Got it.

Jolie stood. "Mrs. Gray, really, I have no designs on replacing Trista in Todd's life. Honestly, I just want to do a good job and—"

"Oh, no, my dear." The plump little lady had some muscle under that skin when she grabbed Jolie's wrist. "That's not what I meant at all." She tugged Jolie back into her chair and covered Jolie's hands with her own. "Where is Todd right now?"

"The west wing. I mean, in the garage attic."

"And what's he doing?"

"Painting. Well, sketching actually. I think the painting part comes next."

Mrs. Gray smiled, squeezing Jolie's hand. "You're the first person to get him to even mention the word 'painting' again without a growl, let alone pick up a brush. I cannot thank you enough."

"Really, it has nothing to do with me."

Mrs. Gray raised her eyebrows.

"Honestly. He said it's been percolating in his head for a while. I think it was Mr. Griff's book about portraits that really did the trick."

The housekeeper did the hand-patting thing again and nudged Boots's laundry basket with her foot, which woke the little puffball up, causing him to leap to the kitchen floor like the devil was on his tail. "Mr. Griff, was it? If you say so, dear."

Chapter Twenty-Four

Jolie wasn't sure what it was she and Mrs. Gray accomplished with their girl-talk, but apparently she'd gotten a seal of approval on something so farfetched it'd be laughable if it weren't so desirable. But just because Todd was painting again—and it was her he was painting—and they had some chemistry (Mrs. Gray surely didn't know *that*), did not mean there was anything more to it than painting. But just in case…

"Todd?" Jolie opened the door to the west wing, kitty in hand, er, crook of her arm.

Todd was deep in concentration with another charcoal stick between his teeth and hair mussed again, but his arm was moving furiously over the canvas. More canvases were stacked on the floor beside the running shoes he had yet to re-don, with one canvas leaning against a leg of the easel.

Wow. When he said he was going to start painting again, he wasn't kidding. It looked like he had enough canvas prepped for a marathon session.

She should go. This probably wasn't a good idea, whether or not Mrs. Gray condoned it.

She was just about to close the door when Boots jumped from her arms with a "meow."

Todd looked up, his eyes all deer-in-the-headlights.

"Um… hi?" Jolie did a little finger twiddle.

Todd whipped the charcoal out from between his teeth. "What's up?"

"I, uh… never mind." Darn cat. She tiptoed in. "Sorry to have bothered you. I'll just get Boots and be out in a jiffy."

He sighed and sent her pulse streaking through her veins as he did the hand-through-hair move again. "What do you need, Jolie?"

"Need?" She could think of quite a few things, but none were appropriate at the moment.

"The reason you're here?"

"Oh. That." *Wanted to see you in action*? No, that didn't sound right. *Missed you*? Definitely not. "Um, just wanted to see how it's coming?"

"Jolie, I told you no one sees these. Not even you, okay?" Todd stood with a soft smile on his lips.

"I guess." But she really did want to see that picture. Or, did he say *these*? There were more than one? How was that possible? She was with him the whole four hours—and she knew four hours of stool-perching when she did them—and he had not changed canvasses at all. "Will I ever get to see them?"

He shrugged. "Maybe. If I'm satisfied. Otherwise I'll just paint over them and start over."

"So, *are* you satisfied?" Jolie gulped. Count on Naughty Girl to show up for that comment. "With them, I mean. Are you satisfied with them?"

"Not yet." He looked back at the canvas, his arms crossed over his chest, a charcoal slash on the faded t-shirt, the sun highlighting the blond hair on his forearms.

Forearms? First knees, now arm hair. She was noticing a lot more detail these days. Perhaps *she* should take up painting.

"It is my first day, after all," Todd continued, oblivious to the minutiae that so fascinated her. "I'm working on form, perspective. Plus there's an essence to you I want to capture. I haven't gotten it yet."

"An essence?" That ended the minutiae pondering.

"Something. I can't put my finger on it. I can't get it to come out of the charcoal, but whatever it is, it's you. Who you are. I can see it in you, just below the surface, but I can't replicate it on canvas."

He walked toward her, the gray painter's shorts hanging low on his hips, and he stopped a hair's breadth too far away. His finger traced her cheekbone. "As if you're a rose just waiting to bloom, the moment before the petals unfurl. One touch of the sun and you'll burst into beauty."

Oh my.

His fingers traveled softly down to her jaw line, just dancing on the surface of her skin, but every soft touch swirled her tummy like a waltz and she was powerless to say anything.

Speech might have left, but Touch and Smell were alive and well and working overtime. He was so close she could almost taste the warmth of his skin, the slightest hint of perspiration, that maddening Grey Flannel that wrapped its own essence around her like a warm mist from a hot spring. She could drown in the scent of Todd and die a happy woman.

His fingers slid under her chin and with very little urging she tilted her head back. He closed the distance between them and his height was just perfect to stand over her, to thrill but not intimidate.

Which was fine because her feelings were doing their own intimidating.

Jolie took a deep breath, both to infuse her mind with *essence du Todd* and also gather her bearings because if she was ever going to have a prayer of a happily-ever-after, she had to risk her feelings at some point.

His eyes swirled with every different shade of green there was, a stormy ring of dark gray around the pupils, and she was caught in their snare. Here, too, she could drown in those depths and not mind at all.

Todd invoked one churning sea of roiling emotions in every fiber of her being and she swayed into him, as natural as breathing.

"Jolie," he whispered, doing some swaying of his own.

It didn't take much before they were within each other's sway, and arms became involved. And lips. Man, did lips become involved, and this kiss was every bit as spectacular as yesterday's.

And she was in so much trouble.

It wasn't just a kiss in the general sense of the word. It was another Kiss. One she'd never forget.

And would probably never duplicate with anyone but him.

It was that thought which gave her the strength to pull back. Well, that and maybe just a tad bit of abject terror of getting hurt.

"Todd, I… " What? Needed his kiss for her very breath? Would never kiss another man as long as she lived? What? "I… wonder where Boots is." Oh boy, was that lame.

"Boots?"

She could so identify with his disbelief.

"Um, yes. My kitten?" She tucked some un-tucked hair behind her ears and looked away. "He's here somewhere."

"Boots."

"Yes, Boots."

Todd took a big breath and ran a hand through his hair.

At some point she really needed to ask him to stop doing that or she might be back in a clinch with him again, this one of her own doing.

"Jolie, you're not worried about Boots."

"I'm not?"

"No."

"But I am."

"No." He took her hand. "You're not." He tugged her over to the sofa. "You're avoiding what just happened."

"I am?"

That got a smile out of him. Good. That made one of them.

"Yes, you are." He sat and patted the seat next to him. "Sit."

Any other time she would have said, "Woof," or "Yes, master," but not now. Instead, she re-tucked that un-tucked hair then put her hands beneath her thighs and sat.

"Jolie."

She bit back the sigh at her name and, instead, bit her lip as she faced him. "Yes?"

"I'm not sorry I kissed you." His eyes were all solemn.

"You're not?"

"No, I'm not. Today or before the picnic." He tugged on her hand, and reluctantly—okay, not *that* reluctantly—she gave it to him. The man *had* just said he wasn't sorry he kissed her. That could only be good.

Hopefully.

"But you said—"

"I know what I said, but that was because, well, I was surprised that it had happened. But I'm definitely not sorry."

"Surprised?" She was sounding more like a parrot by the minute.

"I haven't kissed anyone in two years."

"Then why did you? Kiss me, I mean?" Oops, Naughty Girl jumped out of her hiding place.

"Because it felt right."

Okay, Legs were melting.

"And because I wanted to."

And there went Tummy.

"You did?" Sheesh, what was next? *Polly want a cracker?*

"Yes. And you wanted to, too."

And there was the tidal wave of a blush. Of course she'd wanted to. He had to know that, so why was she acting like a teenager with her first crush?

Because he truly was her first crush.

And she was more than a little worried that it might end differently than how she'd like. When she allowed herself to think about what she'd like, that was.

So she wouldn't. Think about it. Scarlett did okay in the end and she would, too.

"Jolie? You did want to?"

Lying by omission was one thing, but to his face? Not quite. "Yes, you're right. I did. I'm sorry."

"Sorry? What for?" He laced his fingers with hers. "I'm flattered."

She was hoping for more than *flattered*. Turned-on, unable to live without you, thinking of forever, take your pick. *Flattered* fell way down on her list. "Well, that is, I, um, work here and—"

"This has nothing to do with our working arrangement. Nothing at all. It's not like I've kissed every woman who's cooked for me in the last two years."

"You haven't?"

He brushed something from her forehead. "No. I haven't. Not a one. But with you, I may want to again."

There went Heart. "You will?"

He nodded with a twinkle in his eye. "Any objections? And no strings attached, no matter what your answer. Promise. Your job is secure, regardless."

Now there was an offer. Full of possibilities. One of them being heartache.

What would the heroine of her story do?

That probably wasn't the best question to ask since everything always worked out in romance novels and this was her life she was talking about, but Todd wasn't like any of Mom's losers, so she'd be foolish to not take the chance. Of course, she might be foolish for doing so, but nothing ventured, nothing gained and all that. "Nope. No objections."

He un-tucked her other hand and linked all four of them together. "I'm not sure where this will lead, I want you to understand that. But since yesterday morning, I've had a hard time concentrating on anything besides what it felt like to hold you in my arms. Sketching you today was that much harder, I think, because I was trying to capture what I felt when we kissed."

She wanted to ask him what exactly he had felt, but would she like the answer? What if it didn't measure up to what she felt? She couldn't be the one to feel more. She just couldn't. She'd done that too many times in her life and, while she'd survived the crushing disappointment up to this point, she wasn't sure she'd be able to this time.

"*Will* you be able to capture it, Todd?"

His smile was soft and melted-bones inducing. "I'm sure going to try." He wrapped his big strong hands around hers and her skin sizzled and tingled in every good way. He placed a soft kiss to the back of each hand. "But I may need you to sit for me some more."

"You will?" She wasn't all that enthused about the idea. Charley Horse Leg twinged in agonized remembrance.

"I promise to give you something more comfortable than the stool, okay?"

"Okay."

"That's it? No twenty-questions on what we'll use? No dissertation on the merits of cotton fiber versus wooden furniture?"

He *got* her. Totally. And managed to make her laugh so easily. "Anything has to be better than that stool."

"Hey, I gave you a pillow." Oh, so now he was doing insulted.

She could, too. "And, for that, Tush thanks you. The rest of me, however, is pretty jealous of Tush, so you'll have to make all of me happy next time."

There was a heartbeat—or seven—of silence.

But Naughty Girl was fist-pumping all over the inside of Jolie's brain.

Todd unlaced his fingers and cupped her cheek. "I'll try."

Whoa.

So, they were leaning in, lips just about to make contact, when who should appear? And she wasn't talking eight tiny reindeer.

"Meow."

"Boots," they said in unison, laughing as a whiskered white face appeared between them. Kitty-boy was doing his own leaning in—off the back of the sofa to get his muzzle between them. Now the *cat* had an agenda, too?

Boots might want to talk with Mrs. Gray because apparently his agenda was in direct opposition to hers.

Todd picked the kitten up. "And where have you been? Kind of interesting you choose this moment to interrupt." He plopped Boots onto her lap and the little moment-ruiner did a few circles with some finely honed claws before curling himself into a powder puff, staring at the two of them, his tail flicking her leg, one black paw forward, almost drumming his kitty fingers on her skin.

"I've heard of guard dogs, but a guard cat?" Todd laughed.

"Do I need guarding?" Naughty Girl just couldn't mind her own business.

"I—" Todd reached out for her hand and Boots swatted it. Chuckles escaped from both of them as Boots pulled his paw back to lick it.

"I guess he thinks so." Todd nudged her chin up to look in her eyes. "But I have no idea. This is all new to me, Jolie. I haven't found myself wanting to kiss anyone since I met Trista. I can't promise anything, because I have no idea what's happening."

"No idea?" There was Naughty Girl again, but Jolie was with her on this one. He certainly had some idea because his body parts were all in perfect alignment with hers a few moments ago.

"Other than I want to kiss you again and I like being around you, no. I never thought I'd want to feel even that again. And now I do."

"And now you do." His lips were beautifully shaped, the fuller bottom one just right for taking between her teeth and give a little tug before—

"What are you thinking?"

"Thinking?" Please don't let that be her Anne Bancroft voice.

"Yeah, what were you just thinking?" He had his own Barry White going, mesmerizing her. Honestly, she could just stare at his mouth all day.

"Your mouth," she answered.

"My mouth?" He groaned. "You're not making this easy."

"Easy?"

"You know, I don't think I've ever heard you so monosyllabic before."

He started to reach for her hand again and Boots shifted on her lap, his raised paw fending off approaching fingers.

Todd did the "hands-up" stance. "Okay, Boots, I give up. She's your property. Got it." He looked at her. "But I'm going to be trespassing whether that cat likes it or not."

She couldn't stifle the shiver that raced down her spine until Boots dug his claws in her leg, ending that delicious moment.

"So." Todd sat back and folded his hands on his (flat, sculpted, toned, hard, six-pack) abdomen. "Guard cat aside, what was it you came in here for in the first place?"

"Um… " Yeah, what exactly had been her motivation? At this point she was lucky she remembered her own name, let alone motivation. "Oh, I was wondering what I should make for dinner tonight since Mr. and Mrs. Gray are here. Is there anything special they like?"

"Anything you want to serve is fine. I doubt if they'll even stay. They just got back and they're not as spry as they once were. My bet is they're probably already on their way home to recover from their trip and get to bed early."

Truly he did not understand women. That whole Venus/Mars dichotomy. After that conversation she'd had earlier with Mrs. Gray, she was betting the Grays wouldn't be out of Todd's house until their stay was bordering on rude.

"Humor me." She set Boots on the floor and stood.

Todd followed her up, giving Boots a nudge with his toe. "She's a big fan of Italian food."

"Okay, I'll do manicotti."

"Isn't it late in the day for spaghetti sauce?" He traced her arm from wrist to shoulder.

"Trade secret." Boots was doing figure eights around her ankles. All sorts of touchy-feely stuff she was suddenly finding more than bearable.

"Honestly, Jolie, don't bother. I'm sure they're gone. And, really, I'm not picky about dinner."

"Trust me, okay? I have a feeling they're staying so I want to make a nice dinner for them. Besides, cooking is what I do. Why I'm here, remember?"

His hand stilled on her shoulder and he searched her eyes. "You're right. Jasmine will probably have a ton of pictures she wants to show me of her new grandson. It's her fourth, but she treats each one as if it were the first. Family's important to her."

"I know. She told me."

"She did?"

"Yep. And she considers you family. That's why she'll stay."

Todd dropped his hand, shoving both in the back pockets of his shorts, and turned toward the easel. "Actually, Trista was more her family."

"I know, she told me."

He stopped. "That, too?"

"Yes. She told me how she pretty much raised Trista and how you—"

He turned around, eyes narrowed. "How I what?"

Oh darn. She didn't mean to bring up his and Trista's early years together. "Um, how much she cares about you?"

Todd shook his head and walked back toward her. "I'm not buying that. What'd she say?"

Okay, what happened to cajoling? His growl would rival a deadly panther's on the prowl. And, yeah, maybe she was feeling just a bit hunted. And not in a good way.

She stepped around the corner of the sofa. "I don't really remember." And she didn't—not verbatim. General gist? Yeah, got it. Word for word? Slipped her mind.

He followed her. "Jolie." Definitely not cajoling.

"Oh, well, she might have mentioned how you weren't exactly Trista's parents' first choice for a son-in-law," she said, gripping the back of the sofa.

"I see." The seconds ticked by, each one marked by a tic in his cheek. His jaw was clenched and, while that increased the masculinity aspect of his face, it wasn't a good thing at the moment.

"I would prefer if you wouldn't discuss my private life with Mrs. Gray. Or anyone, for that matter." He rubbed his eyes with the finger and thumb of one hand, exhaling.

Really, he didn't have to ask her twice. As if she'd go chatting him up with everyone—

Oh. Her manuscript.

Well, okay, *maybe*—in a way—he might see it as such. If he saw it, that was. But he wouldn't.

Besides, it wasn't *really* about him. It was more about his emotions and how Tom felt and acted. Todd was just the inspiration. Her muse, you could say.

She took a step back from him. "Look, Todd, it was just a conversation between me and Mrs. Gray. A lady, I might add, who cares for you a great deal. We weren't carrying tales or gossiping. She just wanted me to know how special you are." Not that she'd needed to be told.

Silence stretched from terse to bearable, but it was a long agonizing journey to get there. Especially because he kept his gaze on her the whole time and she was beginning to squirm under it.

That's what a guilty conscience did for you. Interesting how Naughty Girl chose not to comment on any of this.

"I'm sorry," he said at last. "It's just that when Trista died there was so much press coverage. Like the other day with the phone calls and reporter on my doorstep. Everyone wanting to know how I felt, if I'd paint again." He laughed and it wasn't kind. "You know, that's my favorite line. Your wife dies or your dream falls apart, or whatever tragedy has just smacked you in the face, and there's a reporter with a microphone inches from your nose and he's asking you how you feel. What's he want, an I'm-going-to-Disney-World response? I'm all for giving people the news, human interest stories, but for chrissake, can't a man grieve in peace?

"Um—" Honestly, *what* should she say?

"Sorry. I overreacted. I realize Jasmine was just staking her claim. She tends to do that with anyone new around here."

Somehow Jolie doubted Mrs. Gray had *quite* those same words to say to just any chef who worked there, but he didn't need to know that.

"It's just that any threat to my privacy touches a nerve. A few, actually." He did the hand-raking thing and for once she was unmoved.

Maybe she ought to toss her manuscript.

But that was ridiculous. No one would ever know she based the emotions on his. It wasn't like he was ever going to read the darn thing, so, not a problem. Right? Right.

"Well, Todd, it's not as if Mrs. Gray is—"

"MEOWWWWW!"

Kitty terror grabbed their attention fast. Poor little Boots was tangled up in a drop cloth and running around in circles, which made the straightjacket he was working himself into even tighter.

Todd and Jolie did some pretty fancy dance steps to cut off the kitten's access to more of the cloth, then they sat on it to untangle him without losing a finger or an eye. Terrorized kitties were a touch manic.

Finally, with a bit of laughter, some catching of breaths, and avoidance of Kitty Scissor-Paws, they managed to calm the little guy down just as the attic door swung open.

"Oh, Todd." There beamed Mrs. Gray, a vase of pink roses in her hand.

"Hi, Jasmine." They stood, managing to kick the drop cloth out of the way as Mrs. Gray sashayed into the room. "What brings you here?"

Boots dug his claws into Jolie's forearm and when she looked down at him, she could have sworn the cat was gloating. She wouldn't blame him, actually, because this was the second time he'd saved her from a potentially embarrassing situation. Well, three if she counted that moment on the sofa, but she'd consider that scenario more exciting than embarrassing had it been allowed to play out, but maybe it was a good thing it hadn't; they'd had the chance to talk some more. Get to know each other better.

She did want to get to know him better. And if that wasn't more than a little scary, she didn't know what was.

"I brought these roses for the kitchen," said Mrs. Gray, holding up the flowers, "and thought you might like some to brighten up your studio. Although, it is pretty bright already." She spun around. "You've been busy, I see."

"I better start dinner." Jolie wanted to extricate herself from the impending little *tête-a-tête*. One was her limit for an emotion-laden day like this was turning out to be.

Back in the house, she secured Boots in her room because, even though he might have saved her pride, kittens and spaghetti sauce were not a match made in heaven. And she had a lot to do to get the manicotti in the oven in time.

She also had a lot to think about.

Jolie replayed the scene from the attic in her head. Todd liked kissing her, wasn't sorry he had, and would probably want to again. How'd she feel about that?

Honestly, part of her wanted to hope. Wanted to take a chance. The part of her that had lived without hope for so long was feeling like a drowning person grabbing for a life preserver. But was that a good thing? Was Todd her life preserver?

And why did she need one? Why wasn't she happy with her life as it was? Stick to her plan?

She slid the dish into the oven and set the timer. She *was* happy with her life as it was.

But she wasn't going to deny that it could be better. Yes, she had her plan and would continue to study and save for her pastry shop, *and* finish her story, but why couldn't she throw a relationship into the mix? Just because Mom's love affairs (not that any of them had been based on love) had been disastrous, with men parading in and out, knocking the two of them around a few times, and Mom turning to booze to drown the pain and sorrow, but Jolie was an adult. She knew the dysfunction of those types of relationships. Recognized it for what it was and knew she didn't want it. Even Chucky… For as disappointed as she'd been, she'd known their relationship wasn't the for-real one she'd wanted. He wasn't the type of man she wanted.

Todd, however, might be.

And that was the big question mark. Was he worth risking her heart for? Her barely-held-together psyche? She'd overcome a lot, but the family thing… The love everlasting, the til-death-do-us-part, that was what her soul ached for. The security of knowing someone was in her corner. Someone would be there to care for her. Love her. That's what she wanted in the deepest, darkest part of every lonely night she'd ever had.

It also scared the heck out of her.

There'd been a time when not having a family had really bothered her. But then she'd realized it could be useful. When you had no one around who really knew you, you could be anyone you wanted to be. So she'd decided it was up to her to be responsible for every aspect of her life: financial, professional, emotional. She'd knew what could happen when she tried to depend on others who weren't dependable, and had decided, at the ripe old age of eleven, that she wanted more.

But she knew, eventually, she'd want her own family, someone to love who'd love her back. So why *not* now? Was there a law that said she couldn't work toward *all* her goals simultaneously?

Other people did it. Even though Mom had taken the wrong train to Happyville with any one of a host of male counterparts, it didn't mean *she* had to.

Todd wasn't pushing her away. He'd purposely—on *several* occasions—reiterated his desire for her to stay, had said she was good for him, liked kissing her, *wanted* to kiss her. Plus, she had Mrs. Gray's seal of approval. He wanted her, she wanted him; when was the last time that had happened?

So, okay, it was risky. She got that. But with the first of her paychecks leaving a hefty sum in her bank account and the promise of more to come, if she had to pick up and start over, it wasn't as if she'd be destitute. And it wasn't like she'd never done it before.

And, heck, she was even light on the personal property front due to the fire. It seemed the planets were aligned for her shot at the brass ring. With such indicators, she'd have to be the ultimate pessimist not to take the chance.

She'd take baby steps with this "thing" with Todd. Allow a relationship to happen if it was going to. They'd already passed the "like" stage. He got her and they laughed at the same things. God knew they certainly found each other attractive.

So what if nothing had lasted "F" before in her life? Other people had it all—why couldn't she?

Chapter Twenty-Five

Seven a.m. came way too early after last night's dinner where, much to Jolie's delight, she'd been proven right. The Grays had stayed. With a little cheating on her part (Signore Arena's already-made homemade sauce and manicotti), she managed to whip up a nice meal. She added her own tasty loaf of garlic bread and a pretty salad—curlicues included. And with ice cream sundaes—whipped cream included—for dessert, Mrs. Gray had the perfect excuse to haul out those baby pictures.

Todd had played with the carrot strips while Mrs. Gray waxed on and on about her son, Charles, and their new grandson, but luckily, she steered clear of The Trista Years, though the possibility had been there. But they managed to escape that, and Todd had had a huge look of relief on his face when they'd left.

Which had been late. Later than folks their age should be out, but they wouldn't consider staying—as Mrs. Gray made sure to tell Jolie on the sly.

The implication had made for a pretty interesting dream. Unfortunately, with the alarm singing the latest Top 40 hits, she didn't have the luxury of lounging around in bed replaying it, so she made her way to the kitchen to answer the call of Eggs Benedict.

Todd walked in from the pool, mid egg-poaching, all dripping wet again, and she stared. She couldn't help it because now she knew exactly how that chest felt against her breasts, the strength in those nicely defined biceps and exactly how she fit against the whole set of gloriousness.

"Where's the cat?" he asked.

Not exactly the greeting from her dream, but whatever floated his boat. "In my room. Apparently ice cream acts like a sleeping pill. He snored all night long."

"Good."

She had about two seconds to register the "good" before Todd swooped in and planted one on her. Really planted. That kiss grew roots which wound around her heart then branched into all four limbs.

She did some winding of her own. Her arms went around his neck and, yeah, his muscles were rock solid and his stomach twitched whenever her breasts made contact. Tongues renewed their acquaintance and, if it weren't for the humming of the blood through her body, she'd swear she'd died and gone to Heaven.

He slid his hands from her waist to cup her face and he pulled back just inches, his mossy green eyes full of warmth and maybe, just maybe, something more. "Good morning," he said, nudging her nose with his.

"Is it? I think I might still be dreaming."

"If this is a dream, I don't want to wake up."

He kissed her again, a soft one this time. He tickled her lips and she felt that tickle in her tummy, all fluttery and jittery. Then her knees went to mush again.

"Wow," she said once she could breathe again.

"Wow works." Yeah, that was arrogance in his smile, but who cared? The man was entitled to it.

And since it was her kiss that put the smile there, she was entitled to some of her own.

"I've forgotten how nice it is to get a greeting like that in the morning." He linked his hands behind her waist.

"It is?"

"Honestly, Jolie, is that all I had to do to render you speechless? Kiss you? You should have told me that at the beginning and it would have been quieter around here a lot faster."

"Are you saying I talk too much?"

He kissed her nose. "No. I'm saying you talk a lot. There's a difference. And—"he resettled his lower body against hers and she took a trip into outer space for a moment because there wasn't much left to her imagination with wet swim trunks plastered against her nether regions—"even though I like the kissing part, I'm missing the chatter. So I think I'm going to have to curb some of the kissing."

"Oh no you don't." She yanked his hair to bring their faces within smooching distance. "I'll talk your ear off all you want, but you don't get to quit the kissing thing until all parties involved agree."

"Oh, so we're involved, are we?"

Good question—and not one she was going to be the first to answer. "Well, if you're not involved, then who the heck am I kissing? I could swear it's you."

"It most definitely is." Which he again proved quite nicely.

Until the Canadian bacon started to smell funny. Great. He really was going to sexy himself into starvation.

"Oh, no!" Jolie pulled out of his arms to turn off the flame and catch the hollandaise right before it scorched. Didn't matter though. Lightly scorched or burned, once hollandaise went bad there was no redeeming it.

So now she had rubbery poached eggs, burned bacon, and hellacious hollandaise. What a day this was shaping up to be. Oven mitts, clanking pans, banging oven door, their quiet interlude was shattered. And then the smoke detector kicked in.

"It's never a dull moment with you, is it, Jolie?" Todd laughed as he grabbed a dishtowel and swatted the smoky bacon air away from the detector. "Don't tell me. Excitement Jolie?"

"Ha ha, very funny. I wanted breakfast to be perfect."

The alarm went silent and Todd flung the towel over one shoulder. He took the pan out of her hand, removing the mitts with it, then tilted her chin up. "It is."

The heck with scorched hollandaise. Her skin was on fire, her bones were melting all over again and pretty quickly they were in another lip lock that could've gone on forever, if not for the little pitter-patter of petite paws. Well, actually, claws on limestone tiles. And said claws pouncing on her sandal-clad foot and Todd's naked one. (The man did like naked in the kitchen.)

"Boots!" they yelled in unison as they jumped apart.

Boots, the little meddler, catapulted into the air, executing a perfect full-twisting inward somersault, and landed on all four of his black, claw-bearing paws as if nothing had happened.

"I think that cat's got it in for me," Todd mumbled, rubbing the naked foot.

"Or perhaps he thinks our time would be better spent with you at the easel and me on the… sofa?"

"Fine, you can have the sofa. But you've got to promise not to fall asleep. It's a pretty comfortable sofa."

"Cross my heart, witches' honor, Girl Scout promise, take your pick." She made the accompanying hand motions and got him laughing again.

"I pick getting changed out of these wet clothes. I'll be right down."

She wasn't going to think about him stripping off his clothes. Nope. Not her. "I'll whip up some French toast in the interim."

"Really, Jolie, Whe—"

"I know, Wheaties would be fine. But sorry, buck-o, you're stuck with a hot breakfast."

A moment—or maybe an eternity—of silence before his wicked, wicked grin reappeared. "A *hot* breakfast. Ah, how well you know me." And on that note, he sauntered out the doorway.

Did she know him well? She knew he kissed like nobody's business—and that she'd like to keep it nobody's business but her own. She knew he was a decent guy who had a bad thing happen to him. She knew he had reached a turning point in his life and she admired that he wasn't afraid to move forward.

And… she knew that she'd fallen in love with him.

***

Todd took the stairs two at a time. He hadn't had this much energy for as long as he could remember. Well, in the last two years, anyhow.

He stripped off his bathing suit in the shower, marveling that he hadn't made a conscious decision to not leave it in a wet heap on the floor as he usually did, but had just done it. Jasmine had nagged him all last summer, but back then, he couldn't seem to remember even the simplest of things.

But now, with Jolie here, it was like he'd gotten a new lease on life.

He grabbed the shampoo and worked it into a lather. Oh, he knew it was his attraction to her that had woken him from two years of just existing. He wasn't going to kid himself that it was something he'd done, some decision on his part. There was just something about her. She was so wide-eyed in spite of how shitty the world had treated her, so hopeful, so ready to believe, that his psyche couldn't help but tap into those emotions.

Today, for the first time in too long, he'd woken with a smile on his face. It'd been all he could do not to open her door and wish her a good morning, but they weren't at that point yet.

He ran the soap down his body and had to re-think that. A certain part of him was *there*, but that was just a physical response—although, he wasn't going to knock it. Jolie had brought on the first physical response he'd had since the funeral. Another thing to thank her for.

He had a lot to thank her for, though it wasn't the reason he'd kissed her. No, he'd kissed her because he'd *had* to. Because he'd wanted to—nothing more, or less, than that. Which said a lot.

But, hell, he didn't want to blow this. She wasn't a light affair kind of woman and he wasn't in any emotional shape to examine forever; he'd been up front with her about not knowing where this "thing" between them was heading.

But did anyone ever really know where it was heading? With Trista, he'd been pleasantly surprised that a woman of her background would go out with him; he'd asked her mainly to give himself incentive to "show her" when he made it big—someone from the other side of the tracks.

But then she'd been real to him. She'd been her own person and had given him a chance.

The same kind he wanted to give Jolie.

Todd leaned his shoulder against the tiled wall and let the water sluice over him, cleaning the chlorine residue from his skin.

That it also felt like a cleansing of his soul wasn't something he could ignore. He'd carried the pain with him for so long, had wrapped it around himself to keep out the world. Yet somehow, with her smart phrases and her soft admissions, and that incredibly upbeat outlook of hers, Jolie had found a tiny gap in the pain and wormed her way in.

He wasn't going to let her get away.

Chapter Twenty-Six

Staring at the man she'd suddenly discovered she was in love with put a whole new spin on posing for him. There she was, staring at him while he concentrated so intently on the canvas and not on her, and all she could think about was what she was going to do about her new-found feeling.

First and foremost, she couldn't tell him. It was one thing to risk her heart in the privacy of her own body and soul, but to put it out there for public trampling, well, she wasn't that brave. No matter the reward.

For all she—and he—knew, she could be Rebound Girl: the girl a guy went out with right after the love of his life broke up with him and he had to prove to himself he still had "it," whatever "it" was, and that Old Girlfriend didn't know what she was missing and he'd show her. That would be Rebound Girl and Jolie so did not want to be her. Since all the parameters were right for rebounding, she'd just stay mum on the whole subject and see where it led.

Especially since he was willing to let it lead where it may. She couldn't expect any more positivity out of him at this stage in his recovery. She could always hope, of course, but Jolie, she was a realist. A newly optimistic realist, but a realist just the same.

So there she was, lounging on the sofa, once again posing for more long hours, staring at the cute lock of hair that fell in his eyes (when she was supposed to be staring at the window), doing the eye-averting scenario whenever he looked like he was going to glance up from the canvas.

"Jolie, can you please stop moving your eyes? It changes the lines under them."

She had *lines*? She huffed. She did not have lines.

"And don't huff. It puffs out your lips. Angelina Jolie is over-rated anyway. Hey, Angelina Jolie, you Jolie... "

Laugh it up, yuck-*ball*. She was still hung up on those lines.

"What's with the frown?" He sighed and put the charcoal down. "Something bothering you?"

"I have lines. Under my eyes."

"Oh, that." He shook his head, as if to say "women." "Light filtering in through the window creates streaks of shadow and light on your skin. Like lines. I want to capture them before the sun changes."

"Oh."

He left his easel and sat on the sofa next to her. The not-very-wide sofa.

"Don't you remember me telling you that your skin is flawless?"

She nodded.

"It is. Peaches and cream." His voice got deeper. "Honey smooth." Honey smooth all right. "I'm hungry again."

He leaned in and *voila*! another clinch. She couldn't help herself, and, apparently, neither could he.

What a difference to the kiss when the man she was kissing was the one she could do it with for the rest of her life. She savored every nuance of his mouth, the play of muscles beneath her fingertips, the scent of his shampoo as his hair brushed her cheek. Her body strained toward him and, God, the relief when he leaned over her, pressing her into the softness of the sofa. He shifted, almost on top of her and, oh, it felt so right. So different from any guy before.

This man was The One.

He angled his head, his tongue stroking hers, and she groaned. Then his hand caressed her breast and she almost exploded with relief. She hadn't even realized she'd wanted him to touch her there.

Of course, if she'd thought about it she probably would have realized she did, but thinking was not happening at the moment. Feeling was. Majorly.

She leaned into his caress, her nipple front and center in the middle of his palm, just begging for attention and, sweet man that he was, he obliged. His other hand combed through her hair, twirling the strands around his fist and holding her head in just the right place for maximum effect.

Her hands slid under his shirt, brushing the fine hair there and stroking his sides. He groaned, his stomach muscles clenching as she feathered her fingers near his navel. Then she was sliding them up his chest to do some of her own obliging—

Todd ripped himself off of her with a howl.

"What the hell?" He turned and there clung a white Boots on Todd's red t-shirt. Ouch. That had to hurt.

"Get the damn thing off me, Jolie!" He reached over his shoulder, spinning, but it was futile. Boots had picked the exact spot where Todd couldn't reach him.

"Hold on." Jolie pulled herself off the sofa and the moment her hands touched Boots, the little hell-cat let go and plopped into her palm.

Todd glared at the cat who was now purring contentedly in her arms. "We need to get some Found posters out. I want that menace out of here."

Boots snorted.

Todd glared at him. "I'm the only person I know with an attack cat. How ridiculous is that?"

She reached out to rub his back just as the studio door opened and in walked Mrs. Gray.

Jolie shot Boots a glance. The cat just smiled at her.

Wait. He *smiled* at her?

"Good morning, all. I thought I'd bring some brownies up today."

Brownies. Of course. Todd loved brownies. Jolie knew that.

And so, apparently, did Mrs. Gray.

Jolie would've thought—and actually did—that after their little gabfest, Mrs. Gray would want Jolie to be the one to butter the guy up—or brownie him up as the case may be. 'Course Mrs. Gray couldn't have known Jolie was doing just that before she thought to arrive with said brownies, but still, wasn't the way to a man's heart through his stomach?

Which just put a whole other spin on her reasons for becoming a chef.

She'd let Mrs. Gray do the brownies today.

"I'm just so thrilled you're painting again, Todd," Mrs. Gray waved those brownies like a red flag at a bull, all the while working her way oh-so-nonchalantly toward the easel. "I thought we should celebrate."

The woman was good, Jolie had to give her that. She might actually succeed in seeing what Todd was working on because his eyes were glued to that plate of chocolate.

"Take one more step, Jasmine, and those brownies won't taste very good when we scoop them off the floor."

Or so Jolie had thought. *Nice try.*

Mrs. Gray conceded gracefully. "Well, you can't blame me for trying. I have been with you almost since the beginning, you know."

He took a brownie. "I know and you didn't get to see them until they were finished then either. Nothing's changed."

"Oh, but I think it has, dear." She offered Jolie the tray with a very pointed look.

What'd I do? Jolie was, after all, following the woman's implied orders.

Maybe she'd misunderstood.

Not wanting to face that possibility, Jolie located her sandals and slid them on. "It's almost lunch time. I better head into the kitchen to get started."

"Oh but I wouldn't mind, dear—"

"I know, Mrs. Gray, but after four hours of sitting here, it's past time for my muscles to earn their keep." Scooping up Boots, Jolie made a beeline for the door.

She'd let Todd explain to Mrs. Gray exactly why it was her hair looked like a tornado had blown through the studio, and why his shirt was hiked in the back.

Chapter Twenty-Seven

Bright and early—too early—Monday morning, Jolie was in her usual pose staring at the window trim, a repeat of the weekend. Seemed that the Grays liked to spend a bit of every day with Todd. It could be because their son lived farther away than an easy driving distance and they were lonely, but Jolie was betting Mrs. Gray was working on keeping the new chef out of the kitchen and in Todd's line of vision as much as possible.

Sadly, while she might be in his line of vision, it was with a canvas between them. At least the tedium of modeling allowed her to plot out the rest of her manuscript. If only she could bring her notebook and pencils, but he'd get suspicious. *As if* anyone had cookbook ideas burning in their mind with such intensity that they had to get them on paper before the ideas crumbled.

Unfortunately, she couldn't explain a burning desire to write without blowing her cover. But when they were finished for the day, she was fully intending to put Annie, her heroine, and Tom in some pretty interesting conflicts, maybe even—

"Jolie, can you push your shirt off your shoulder?"

Remove clothing? Now there was a new twist.

"Um, why?" Not that she was opposed to the idea, but just to get all the information upfront before she made a complete boob of herself. Or *showed* a complete boob.

"I've got your neckline curving just right, but I want to include your collarbone and I need the perspective as it relates to your shoulder."

So clinical, yet she was melting again. Him, her, body parts, disrobing… This would be so good in her manuscript—if her brain cells didn't fry before she got to the notebook.

She pulled the little cap sleeve down her shoulder, but the neckline started choking her.

"Perfect," said Todd.

Not if she wanted to breathe it wasn't.

"Todd," she gasped, "it's choking me."

Really, the man could look more concerned as she gasped her last breath on this earth.

"Can you hold it for just a minute or two please? I've almost got it."

Obliging Jolie tried.

"You're turning blue."

Obviously not successfully.

"Breathe, Jolie."

She shimmied the cap sleeve back into place, allowing the neckline to reclaim its position and Lungs inhaled.

"Did you get it?" She rubbed where the neckline had chafed her throat.

"No," he sighed and it was a heartbreaker. "I didn't have enough time."

"Can't you just draw a line with a little hook on the end?"

He quirked that eyebrow again and her tummy shifted. "How about if you stick to cooking and I'll stick to painting? Of course I can't draw a line with a little hook on the end. Your body's not a roadmap."

Though it could lead to some interesting places.

But she was mum on the subject. Which could be because she was incapable of speech at the thought of him discovering those interesting places.

"No, I need the image. Maybe if I were used to painting the human form, but it's been a long time." He looked around the studio. "Maybe if we... " He left the easel to rummage in a pile of drop cloths by the sofa. "Aha." He flourished a—gee, what a surprise— drop cloth her way.

She arced an eyebrow at him. (Hmmm, she'd picked up that little trick of his.)

"For you." He gave the cloth a little fling like he was shaking water from it.

"Obviously. The reason is unclear, though."

"To wear."

"Sorry, Todd, but I believe my budget allows for something slightly more expensive and with more coverage than a towel. I may have lost everything in the fire, but I believe clothing can be purchased."

He exhaled. "Jolie, for today. Right now. Take off your shirt and wrap this around you. Then I can see your collarbone, the shadows there, and get the proper perspective to your shoulder."

He was looking pretty pleased with himself, but Jolie was still at "take off your shirt." Somehow she'd hoped if this day ever came that there'd be a few murmured words, perhaps a kiss or two, maybe even some *help* with said shirt, but apparently not. She got the doctor's orders version. *Take off your shirt and cough.*

Did wonderful things for her libido.

Not.

"Is this really necessary?" she grumbled as she rose from the sofa.

"Yes, it is. Now where's Good Sport Jolie today?" He teased a reluctant smile to her face.

"She wants to go shopping with Spendthrift Jolie and make sure they have enough of a wardrobe to never need to wear a drop cloth again." She yanked her new apparel out of his hands. "Turn around."

Boots was asleep on the comfy chair—apparently Mr. Meddler didn't find nudity a reason to interrupt them. That cat's priorities were a bit skewed.

She shrugged out of her shirt, whipped the bra off and the towel around her in one motion so quick it'd make Boots's head spin if he were even watching. But the little turncoat was snoring.

"Okay, I'm ready." She resumed her position on the sofa.

Todd turned around. "Grea—"

He stopped mid-word and she stopped mid-breath at the heat burning in his eyes. She knew that look. Had seen it up close and personal.

The silence in the room was booming.

Todd recovered first, though the state of that recovery was in serious question. He snapped his jaw shut, ran a hand over his mouth, then puffed out a long breath. "Okay, then. That should do it."

Do it? Do what? Naughty Girl could conjure a whole lot "it"s to do.

"Now, *ahem*, Jolie." Todd settled on his stool. "Can you, um, lower your left shoulder a little? That's it. Now roll it forward, yeah, like that. Tilt your chin up and back. No, a little lower. There. Um, could you, um, drape a few strands of your hair over your shoulder? Not that many. Okay, that's good." He shifted, resting a heel on the rung of the stool. "Could you, that is, could you have it, move it a little to the right? You know, sort of resting across your, um, breast, rather than alongside it?"

He picked a good spot for her hair. It could cover the nipple poking through the thin fabric. The nipple he'd fondled—

"Like this?" She willed Naughty Girl away.

He swallowed hard. "Yeah," he rasped out, "that'll do."

It sure did "do." She was a mass of fluttering nerve endings about to combust. And if his blazing green eyes were anything to go by, he was right there with her.

And she did wish he were there with her. But he was ten feet away behind a tripod of wood and canvas and charcoal. An amazing barrier when she thought about it. So flimsy physically, but metaphorically as strong as a castle wall.

Castle walls have been breached before.

She wasn't going there.

The temperature was up in the studio, though cold air blasted from the air conditioner. A fine sheen graced Todd's forehead and her body was damp in some pretty provocative places, her skin and his eyes separated by one very thin, very flimsy piece of cotton. Talk about a turn-on.

If only she knew where she stood with him. Obviously he was attracted to her, and she knew he liked kissing her, knew he liked her, but did he like her like *that*? Or was she just the woman in the right place when his hormones came out of hibernation?

"Todd?"

"Hmm?" The charcoal rasped over the canvas.

"What will you do with these pictures once you get them the way you want them?"

"I don't know. I'll probably just end up painting over them." He rubbed a finger on the sketch.

"Do you think… that is… could I have one?" That got his attention. "It's just that no one's ever painted me before and I think it'd be kind of cool to have one."

"A Todd Best original?"

"Well, sure, since you're painting it, but no, that's not why. I've just never had a portrait done and it's something all mine that I can take with me when I get a new apartment."

"Jolie, I told you. You don't need to get a new apartment. The room's yours." He looked back at the canvas, smudging something else. Why couldn't she at least take a peek?

"But what about when I get another job?"

His arm stopped and he leaned back, poking his head around, his brows vee-ing inward. "Are you quitting?"

"Of course not. I never quit, remember? I'm talking about when you, you know, don't need me here anymore. You said yourself you don't need someone to cook for you. Once I've overstayed my welcome, I'll need my own apartment and a new job. I'd like to have one of these pictures as a souvenir. To remember this by." She almost said, "remember you," but caught herself at the last minute. It wasn't like she'd ever forget him.

He put down the charcoal and stood. "Jolie, I can't see you wearing out your welcome for quite a while. And I've also told you I like having you around, and that I have four unused bedrooms and my house needs some life in it. You have enough life in you for ten people. And have you forgotten what I said when I kissed you? Why would you insist on thinking I'm going to want you to leave?"

Maybe because in her world good things were always too good to be true. But he didn't see that in her so no way was she going to point it out. "I don't know. Maybe it's, well, that is…"

"What?" He walked around the easel.

"Well, what if you find… you know… someone? You're not going to want me around. And she, um, she's sure as heck not going to want me around."

"Ah." He sat next to her on the sofa, the not-very-wide sofa, and traced her cheek with his fingertips. "Jolie, I'm not going to find someone. Not now."

"You can't know that."

"But I'm not looking, so I can know it."

She shook her head. "But that's when it happens, Todd. The minute you stop looking is when you find them."

The words sat between them and Todd's fingers stilled as he replayed her words.

Once again, she'd put his life into perspective.

Her violet eyes darkened to plum as they widened, her lips forming a small "O" and he realized—

She was right. He *had* found someone. Without even looking.

The revelation settled on him like oils on canvas, smooth and rich with vibrant color.

He traced her mouth. "Jolie. I told you I have no idea where this thing between us is going, but if it is going anywhere, I'm not going to be looking for someone else." Her eyes widened. He hadn't read this wrong. She was as attracted to him as he was her. He knew that. But was she thinking along the lines he was? Hell, he'd been out of this new-relationship dance for too long.

But if he had to take the dance floor, there was no one else he'd rather waltz with than her. "For all intents and purposes, Jolie, you're the one. That's all I can promise right now. That and the fact that I don't want to find another woman. Okay?"

Her smile burst into the room, radiating her warmth through every part of it. Trista had never lived in this house, had never visited this studio. With that one smile, with the acceptance and joy in it, Jolie forever imprinted her essence, that thing he wanted to capture, in this room and in his home.

And his heart.

"Meow."

And now the cat decided to wake up.

Chapter Twenty-Eight

J onathan Griff yawned and stretched his paws out in front of him, kneading the pungent earth beneath the rose bushes as the sun hit the garden the next morning. Life was good. Jolie and Todd were on the road to a forever after, Jasmine was aware her prayers had been answered, and if he didn't quite feel his wing buds starting to grow, at least his eye twitch had stopped.

All in all, everything was going according to plan.

Well, he'd had to improvise a bit. Jolie and Todd had been getting a little too hot and heavy before they'd delved into the deeper issues facing them. Sure, making love could move things along, but it'd also make things more tenuous. More complicated. The old does-she/doesn't-he dilemma. He didn't want them to have to face those questions just yet. Best they figure out where they stood, *then* take that big step.

Then there was the fact that Jasmine was a little *too* helpful, always showing up at just the wrong moment, and he'd had to intervene before she saw something she really hadn't needed to see. He'd been planning to have a discussion with her about her "helpfulness" last night, but by the time she and Earl had left, it'd almost been today and everyone had sacked out immediately. *Separately.* They'd sacked out separately. Jonathan had been a little disappointed, but, then again, those two needed to move at their own pace. They both had so much to overcome.

In the meantime, since his chaperon services were only necessary to run interference with Jasmine now, he decided to just hang out here and enjoy the sunshine and let Mother Nature take her course where Jolie and Todd were concerned. After all, Mother Nature *had* kept the human race in existence for all these years.

***

"Where's the kitty from hell today?" Todd asked as Jolie settled herself on the sofa for the morning.

"Actually, I think he's more heaven-sent."

"And what, pray tell, has given you that idea? He's carrying his own pitchfork around with him—four of them, actually." Todd swiped at his shoulder in memory.

She wagged a finger Todd's way, enjoying the new depth between them, the new camaraderie and understanding. And kisses. Definitely the kisses. "If it weren't for his interruptions we'd probably be visiting Mrs. Gray in the cardiac unit. She has walked in at some pretty momentous moments if you recall."

"Oh I recall all right." His smile was as broad as his shoulders.

"Stop that." She tossed a pillow at him. "Or you're not going to get your sketching quota done today. Besides, aren't you finished yet? When does the paint go on?"

"Jolie, this isn't paint-by-numbers." He tossed the pillow back and she executed a one-arm catch that'd make a quarterback proud. "I can't put a timetable on it. I won't start with color until I'm ready."

"Fine, fine. I'll just turn into an old maid on your sofa."

"Hardly. Now, enough with the drama. Hold still."

And so it went. She never had the chance to tell Todd that Boots wasn't with her for the simple fact that she couldn't find him when she was heading out to the studio. Of course, she didn't get to tell Todd much of anything because of that no-talk rule.

And she really wanted to talk. Well, that wasn't what she *really* wanted to do, but what she really wanted to do wasn't quite appropriate at this stage in their relationship.

Relationship. There, she'd said it. They had a relationship. A fledgling one, yes, and perhaps a bit tentative, but she was "the one" for him (even if it was just for this moment in time), and he was most definitely "The One" for her, the caps saying it all. If she could just get this stuff on paper, it'd make the perfect poignant moment for her hero and heroine.

"Todd?" He hadn't looked at her in recent memory and, really, he had to know what she looked like by now. "Do you mind if I call it quits? You haven't looked up in the last half hour and I've got a few things to do. You don't need me here, do you?"

207

It was to her eternal chagrin that he didn't get the innuendo at all in that question and waved her from the room. Fine. She tied up the straps to her halter top (no longer needing to use a drop cloth since this style of top performed the same function though in a more socially acceptable way), slipped her feet back into her tan sandals, and closed the door behind her.

Now, before yesterday, she might have been in a bit of a dump since he'd elected to barely respond, but with what he'd said yesterday in that very same spot, well, she couldn't ask for more than that.

Okay, actually, she *could* ask for more, but it wouldn't be the right time. He was still healing and she, well, she was still leery. But willing to risk it.

Because the reward was so worth it.

Which was why she wanted to get it on paper in her story. No longer was she going to try to publish Annie and Tom's story—oh who was she kidding? It was hers and Todd's, thinly veiled, and she was going to watch that happy ending come true.

She opened the door to the kitchen.

"Now, Jonathan," Mrs. Gray was saying, "I really can't see—oh hello, dear." Mrs. Gray gathered… Boots? off the kitchen table and spun around.

"Mrs. Gray? The cat's name is Boots." Jolie removed the kitty from her arms. "And where have you been, you little monster?"

"Oh dear, that's no way to talk to your… er… *cat*." Mrs. Gray's hands were all flippy. "Besides, um, *Boots* was just keeping me company."

"I'm glad to hear it. I thought he might have run away."

Mrs. Gray laughed as if it was the funniest idea she'd ever heard. "Oh, I highly doubt that." She poured out a bowl of milk and added a touch of vanilla.

"I don't know that the vanilla is such a good idea, Mrs. Gray."

She went to pick Boots up to keep him away from it, but Mrs. Gray shook her head. "Nonsense, dear, that's how he likes it."

Boots made a beeline for the bowl, proving her right.

All the same, Jolie was glad she'd bought the glycerin-based version, otherwise they'd be making an emergency trip to the vet since any other kind could be kitty hemlock.

"You're here early today, Mrs. Gray." Jolie leaned back on her elbows on the granite surface, crossing one ankle over the other.

"I have some catching up to do." Mrs. Gray refolded the dishtowels on the countertop.

"Catching up on what? The house is spotless." No doubt due to the bi-monthly cleaning company Jolie had recently found the receipt for.

"Oh, a few things around the house, that's all." She placed all but one of the dishtowels in a drawer by the sink then turned to Jolie. "And what are you doing back so soon? You two aren't usually finished in there until just before lunch."

Jolie pushed off the island and walked around it, absently straightening the barstools. "Oh, I got bored. And restless. It's so blah in there, staring at the window."

"The window? Why on earth would you stare at the window when you've got a perfectly good specimen of a man in front of you?" Mrs. Gray huffed and grabbed the remaining dishtowel, shaking it like she was cleaning an area rug. "Honestly! What is the world coming to today when two attractive young people, together for hours on end, studiously ignore one another? What do I have to do? Lock you in a broom closet together?"

Jolie was halfway to the fridge when those words had her spinning back around and plunking her butt on a barstool. "What?"

Mrs. Gray shoved her hand to her hip and wiped some wisps of hair off her face. "What what?"

"What you just said. What did you mean?"

Mrs. Gray patted her bun and her eyes got all squinty. "Oh, nothing, dear. Just the ramblings of an old woman. Don't pay me any mind." She frittered her fingers. "Just go about what you were doing. Doesn't mean anything at all. Really." She whirled around, refolding the dishtowel again.

"I'm not buying that, Mrs. Gray."

Mrs. Gray's shoulders slumped as she rested her hands on the edge of the sink. "Fine. It's just—" she took a deep breath—"it's just that it's been over two years. And he's so… I don't know, alone? No—lonely." She looked over her shoulder. "There's a difference you know, alone and lonely."

Jolie knew. Firsthand.

Mrs. Gray turned all the way around. "And, well, you were available and alone, too. The two of you could use someone like each other in your lives."

"Wait a minute. I've never met you before, Mrs. Gray. How do you know this about me?"

And there Mrs. Gray went, spinning back to the sink. "Oh, well, you know, from your employment application at Domestic Gods & Goddesses."

"How do you know I work there?" Jolie was pretty sure that'd never come up in conversation. She recalled mentioning it only to Mike and Barbie.

"Because I'm the one who hired you."

"Wait. I thought Mike did?"

Mrs. Gray shook her head. "No. They left it up to me."

"But why? Todd really doesn't need anyone to cook for him."

It was a sad older lady who cared an awful lot for Todd Best who now faced her. "Not now he doesn't. He did before. Now he just needs someone in his life and I thought… "

"You mean you've been personally selecting chefs to set him up with?"

"Terribly silly, I know. But a way to a man's heart is through his stomach, you know, plus I thought the proximity… " Sad little puppy dog eyes implored, "You won't tell him, will you?"

Guilt scissored up Jolie's spine. She had her own secrets—who was she to criticize? Plus, Mrs. Gray obviously loved him and Jolie was such a sucker for that kind of familial love. "I'm not going to lie, Mrs. Gray." Unless it was by omission. That, she could do. Especially when the omission had such wonderful motivation behind it. And she was the direct beneficiary of it. "But I won't say anything unless he asks."

"Thank you, dear. I knew you'd be perfect for this, er, job." She reached down to pat Boots's head, sending loud purrs rumbling from the kitty's belly.

"Mrs. Gray, what's with calling Boots Jonathan?"

"Oh, that." Mrs. Gray stood and patted her bun again, then wiped the countertop with the folded dishtowel. "I must have slipped up and called him the name of my old kitty. Yes, that's it. My old kitty, Jonathan, who's no longer with us." She took off her apron. "Now, I have a few things to tidy up in the other rooms, so I'll leave you be." She patted Boots once more. "I'll see *you* later."

Jolie might have believed her if Mrs. Gray hadn't removed the apron. Who cleaned in their good clothes?

She stared at Boots, who was sitting on the tile floor, licking milk from his whiskers and swatting dust bunnies with his tail. Or cat-fur bunnies, because the place was too clean for dust.

"Why do you suppose it is, Boots, that I think there's more to your little furry face than meets the eye?"

"Meow."

Jolie's cell phone rang. Jolie studied Boots's blank stare a moment or two longer while the phone trilled again.

"Saved by the bell," she muttered, glancing at caller ID. She recognized that number. "Hi, Bella."

"Jolie! Thank God. I need your help."

"What's up? You sound worried sick."

"I'm understaffed for that big gig I was telling you about. Bruno's out of commission and Giuseppe didn't get clearance from his doctor to come back to work. Reese said he'd help out, but you know what happens when he shows up at events."

Bella's husband was a famous ex-professional football player. He usually *became* the event through no fault of his own. Yeah, low key didn't exactly happen around him. "What happened to Bruno?"

"He broke both his legs chasing a cat out of the kitchen, if that doesn't sound weird," Bella answered.

"You don't say." Jolie glanced at Boots. Mr. Innocent was playing with cat-fur bunnies.

"Yes, and Drew's taking care of him, so she's out."

"Drew? I thought Drew was dating Jimmy DeLeo? What's he have to say about that?"

"Not much I'm guessing. She said it's hard to have a relationship when Jimmy's studying abroad. So, is there any chance you could help me out?"

As if she'd turn Bella down. When there'd been nowhere for her to turn, Bella had opened her door. And given her more than a boost to where she was today.

Jolie glanced out the kitchen window, a perfect view of the gorgeous swimming pool—and a catty-corner view of the west wing. Where Todd was.

Yep, this was a pretty darned nice place to be.

"Of course I'll help, Bel. When is it?"

Boots seemed to have tired of bunnies and was working on sheep. He wound his tail around his body and fell asleep faster than humanly—or cat-ly as the case might be—possible with some serious Zs coming from that itty bitty kitty mouth.

"Friday. I know it's last minute—"

"Hey, no problem. I don't have any plans. Do you need help with the food, too?"

"Oh, God, really?" Bella sounded more than a little relieved. "You're a godsend, Jolie."

Not what dear old mama had had to say, but whatever. "Of course I'll help you, Bella. You want me to come by on Thursday for prep?"

They agreed on one o'clock and Jolie fluffed off Bella's profusion of thanks as she hung up. She owed her friend more than she'd ever be able to repay, what with the job she'd given her years ago, the encouragement to go to culinary school—not to mention the loan—plus a bed when there hadn't been enough money for a place to sleep.

Speaking of sleep… "Is there some reason you're ignoring me, Boots?"

Nothing—not even a whisker flicker. That cat was good. Or she was out of her mind. He hadn't really caused Bruno's accident—had he?

"Was that Bella Casteleoni, dear? Earl and I so enjoy her restaurant. " Mrs. Gray walked back in the kitchen and Jolie shook of the ridiculous thought. Boots was a kitten, not some imp in disguise.

She turned her attention to Mrs. Gray and explained about Bella's dilemma.

"This Friday?" Mrs. Gray wrung her hands. "Oh dear."

"Why? What's wrong?"

"Well, you see, Charles wanted us to come back this weekend and babysit so he and his wife could go away for a few days. The new baby and all, you know. And, well, since you're here, I called him yesterday and said that it wouldn't be a problem. But now Todd will be all alone."

"You mean Todd hasn't been alone in two whole years?" That might be a bit obsessive for everyone concerned. "Wait a minute. Yes, he was. The morning I got here. You'd left already." She stopped—the condition he'd been in when she'd gotten here didn't bolster her argument.

Perhaps leaving him alone wasn't such a good idea.

"It's not that, dear. But Earl and I won't be around and you could both be here, all alone, over the whole weekend… "

"Mrs. Gray, I'm not sure that's such a good idea." It was one thing to be in the moment with Todd, to wish and think what-if thoughts, but to actively pursue something she wasn't sure was in her best interests—

Mrs. Gray wrung her hands. "Oh, but Jolie, one can hope, you know."

Oh, Jolie knew all about hoping and Todd.

"Mrs. Gray, really. I'm here to do a job and that's it. Regardless of who hired me. It's awfully nice that you consider me worthy of Todd—" and, gosh, it truly was—"but I just don't think he's at that point yet." Though, apparently his body was on the mend quite nicely. But Mrs. Gray didn't need to know that.

I notice you didn't say a thing about you not being ready for the match, Naughty Girl mocked.

Go away. Maybe that's because I am ready.

You did not *just say that!*

It wasn't often she could pull one over on Naughty Girl.

"Please, Mrs. Gray, go to your son's house. Let him and his wife have their weekend. Think of it as matchmaking for them. Who knows? Maybe you'll get another grandchild out of the bargain."

Mrs. Gray smiled. "Now wouldn't that be nice."

"I've got it!" Todd shoved open the French door to the kitchen behind her, almost sending it—and Mrs. Gray—careening into the wall.

Jolie cringed, expecting to hear the shatter of glass at any moment.

"Got what, dear?" asked Mrs. Gray.

He strode in, picked up the older woman, spun her around, gave her a kiss on the cheek, then repeated the whole exercise with Jolie.

"I've got it," he said again, smiling away.

"Got what?" Mrs. Gray repeated.

"It," he said as if "it" were a common everyday occurrence one got.

"It?" Poor lady was so confused.

"It," he repeated.

"Oh, I get it," Jolie jumped into the "it" fray. "*It.*"

Todd smiled her way and crossed his arms in front of him. "It."

She beamed back, happy for him.

"Would one of you kindly explain to me what 'it' is? All sorts of horrible medical possibilities are running through my head." Mrs. Gray leaned against the granite counter with a hand over her heart.

They laughed as Todd gave her another hug. "Not to worry, Jasmine. Nothing deadly. I've simply gotten that elusive something I've been trying for when I'm sketching Jolie."

Mrs. Gray looked at him as if he were speaking a foreign language. "And what exactly is that, Todd?"

"Can't explain it. It's an essence about her. Part of her. And I couldn't get it. Until—" he wagged a finger at Jolie—"I added the paint. Oil, in this case."

"Oh really? So I'm right, am I?" She was entitled to her moment of triumph.

"Go ahead and gloat. I feel like I'm on top of the world." His fingers traced up her arm. "Just like I did the day I painted my first sunset and the colors blossomed before my eyes and I could feel the heat of the waning sun."

"Oh, that's wonderful, Todd." Mrs. Gray clasped her hands together, her eyes darting between the two of them.

With her honing in on the location of his hand, Jolie was wondering what *exactly* the "that's wonderful" was about.

"It does feel pretty wonderful," he said, his pearly whites gleaming. "So wonderful, that I'm just going to grab a sandwich and head back into my studio. I probably won't make it out for dinner."

"We'll send a tray up then." Mrs. Gray looked at Jolie, pointedly. "Jolie can bring it up."

Nah, she wasn't matchmaking much, was she?

Chapter Twenty-Nine

With Todd at work in the attic and Mrs. Gray doing whatever she was doing ("catching up"—yeah, right), Jolie sat down to give Annie and Tom some of Mrs. Gray' words of wisdom.

One can hope.

Well, sure. One could. But hope alone wasn't going to work everything out, not without some help from "one." In order for Annie to have her happily-ever-after, she was going to have to metaphorically straighten her backbone and tell Tom what she wanted out of life and where he fit in. Proactive instead of reactive. No more waiting for life to hand her the lemonade—she was going to make her own.

Hmmm. *Make lemonade.* She'd heard that analogy before.

Well, heck, she could "make lemonade," too. Or, if she chose not to, she could let the ingredients sit and rot.

One can hope.

Hope hadn't done anything all by itself at any point in her life. Hope had always needed a nudge. And if she was going to write Annie with determination, she darn well better take her own advice. It was all well and good for Todd not to be sure, to "take it as it goes," but she was done being buffeted by others' wishes. It was time she stood up for hers.

"Mrs. Gray." She strode into the den where Mrs. Gray had situated herself for an afternoon of lust, lies and improbable plot lines—AKA the afternoon soap lineup. "Would you mind watching Boots for me?"

"Who? Oh, *Boots.*" Mrs. Gray slid in the recliner, straining her eyes from TV's top vixen who held a gun on yet another unsuspecting husband. Couldn't the woman be more inventive? "Well, certainly, dear, but why don't you join me?"

"Thanks, but I don't think so." Jolie had had enough with improbable plot lines in her own reality to want to watch them on television. Besides, she had lemonade to make. "I have errands to run. I'll be back in time to take Todd's tray in to him."

"All right. Just plop Jonathan on my lap, then. Have a nice time, dear." It was probably the fact that the vixen decided to pull the trigger that had Mrs. Gray so distracted to call Boots after her old cat. She must really miss him.

***

Melanie zoomed Jolie on over to the local mall in search of figurative lemonade. With Todd's house as sterile and empty as it was, her first step if she wanted to envision herself in his life (and she did), was to be able to envision herself in his home. But at present, it wasn't really a home. Just a shell where he bided his time. So, as an investment in her future, albeit small (to be in line with her budget), she was setting out to make his house a home.

In a fine arts store she found a nice selection of discounted art deco pictures, two of which would go in Todd's den, another for the dining room, and another for her bedroom. His landscapes were understandably off-limits, but surely all pictures couldn't be.

Just as she was leaving, she found a group of decorative plates with a French bistro theme that would be perfect in the kitchen.

A fabric store down the way had some pre-made tab curtains in a bold splashy material that would look really cute in the studio. Not feminine at all and certainly busy enough to hold her attention during four hours (*groan*) of sitting.

Next door to that was a bath store. She loved scented candles and potpourri. Niceties she never had growing up, which was why she'd had a large selection in her apartment before the fire, so she picked up some lavender candles for her bathroom, some sandalwood ones for Todd's (not that she'd been in there, but, as Mrs. Gray said, one could always hope) and some vanilla ones for the kitchen. Boots should like those.

She returned in time for the dinner preparation. She looked in on Mrs. Gray (a familiar theme song blaring away on the telly), and found that the older woman and Boots had decided to take a nap. Mr.

Gray was in there on the sofa, too. No wonder Todd offered them a room. Picture-hanging was out for the moment, though the candles did make it to their respective rooms, which was more than she could say for the three sleeping in the den.

She threw together a light and fluffy dinner of a Spanish potato omelet, tomato/cucumber salad, and focaccia with pesto.

"It smells wonderful, dear," Mrs. Gray said, rubbing her eyes, waking at just the right moment. "Is there anything you need me to do?"

"Nope. We just have to wait for the omelet to cool to room temperature. That's how it's best. In the meantime, I'm going to hang the pictures I bought."

"Earl, go help the girl."

"That's okay, really. I can do it."

"Nonsense, Jolie. We want to help."

Jolie shared a smile with her. She knew all about the help Mrs. Gray wanted to give.

"Perhaps I could use a step ladder," Jolie conceded.

Mr. Gray went on his merry way to get a ladder while Mrs. Gray gave her a hug. "Thank you," she whispered.

"For what?" Jolie really did not want the hug to end.

"For trying to make this house a home."

"Oh, well, they're just a few things, nothing—"

"I'm not talking about the pictures, Jolie, though they are a nice touch."

"You're not?"

"No." Mrs. Gray smiled and stepped back, linking their hands. "I'm thanking you for loving him, of course."

"How… how do you know?" Was it written on her face? *Jolie hearts Todd*?

Mrs. Gray cupped her cheek just as her breath hitched and her throat closed with something suspiciously like tears.

"It's perfectly obvious and perfectly understandable, dear. And perfectly acceptable." Boots twined around their ankles as Jolie's insides went all warm and mushy. "Even your gua—er, kitty here can tell." Mrs. Gray picked him up. "Right, Boots?"

Boots stretched out to lick Jolie's nose. There was something weird with this animal.

"So." Mrs. Gray handed the kitten to Jolie then assembled a dinner tray for Todd. "Why don't you take this up to him? Earl and I can handle hanging the pictures."

Somehow the woman made the switch of kitten for tray all the while ushering Jolie toward the door which, conveniently was opened by Mr. Gray at just the right moment.

"Have fun," he said with a wink.

***

Jolie opened the door to the attic and saw Todd's face shadowed like a black and white photograph in the light cast by the chrome floor lamp. He was bent over the canvas, one paintbrush between his teeth, another whipping over the canvas, a palette in his other hand, deep lines of concentration crisscrossing his forehead. He dabbed at the palette, then back at the canvas, and that lock of hair fell forward again. He flicked his head to move it out of his way.

His eyes met hers.

Wine sloshed over the edge of the glass as the tray trembled in her hands. "Dinner."

Eloquence personified.

"Gweat." He slid the brush from his mouth. "I mean, great." Down went the palette and brushes onto the stool, and he headed toward her.

She held out the tray like an offering at church, and, yeah, worship came to mind. She couldn't help it. He looked so darn yummy all rumpled like that, with a rainbow of paint slashes on his t-shirt, mussed hair, and another pair of brushes sticking out of his shorts pocket. But most of all, there was peace in his eyes. The haunted look she'd first met was gone.

"I didn't realize it was that late." He took the food, his fingers brushing hers. "Thanks. This looks delicious. Want to join me?" He looked around, then smiled sheepishly. "I guess I need to get a table. Sorry, I hadn't thought about eating in here."

"No, no, that's fine. I'll, um, eat later. I've got some writing to do."

He raised the tray, tomato salad corner a tad higher than the rest. "This?"

"What?"

"Are you including this in the cookbook?"

Yeah, guilt razored down her spine. "The cookbook. Right. Yes."

He squinted at her, all six-foot-four of him hunkering down to meet her gaze. "Are you okay?"

Define okay. "Certainly. Fine. Why do you ask?"

"You're not your usual foaming-at-the-mouth self. And I mean that in the best possible way." A dimple glimmered in his cheek.

Of course she smiled. She liked that he teased her. She liked that he liked to tease her.

Oh, heck. She liked that he liked her.

"Now there's my Jol… ie." He lowered the tray and the smile faded from his face.

Was that a good thing or a bad thing?

And *was* she his?

It was one thing to make lemonade out of her own lemons, but what if his were sour?

"Actually, I am fine. Just have a lot on my mind." And there went Mouth off and running. "I just remembered I'm supposed to go to Bella's Thursday afternoon to help her prepare for Friday night's party. Mrs. Gray said they're going away for the weekend, but I'll be sure to have your dinner ready before I go, and— "

"Jolie."

Her lips clamped shut.

He took a sip of his wine. "Do whatever you need to. I'll be fine."

"You're sure?"

A soft smile flickered across his lips. "I'm sure."

Now that "sure" sounded sure.

Chapter Thirty

After a busy two days helping Bella, Jolie dragged her tired toes across the driveway into Todd's house. Thankfully, he'd moved on to the painting portion of his career comeback, so he hadn't needed her in the studio, but Bella sure had.

The hostess of the big party called Bella with the last-minute news that the guest of honor was allergic to shrimp, so Bella and Jolie had no sooner had everything prepared than they had to do it all over again. The honoree couldn't touch anything that had even breathed the same air as the shrimp, so to be safe, they'd scrubbed down the kitchen and utensils and donated everything they'd already prepared. Chloe's girls and the people in a few homeless shelters were going to go to bed on very full tummies.

And while the hostess admitted her error and agreed to reimburse Bella, it was still an amazing feat to come up with more menus, more food, and more time to put it all together.

But they had, and they'd done it well. However, it had done Jolie in. She was so tired she could barely stand when she entered the side door.

Boots stretched on the kitchen chair, then pounced down to rub around her ankles.

"Hey, buddy," she whispered, picking him up. He purred, settling beneath her chin. "Did you get dinner or was Todd too busy to feed you?" She checked the fridge. Sure enough, half a can of cat food remained. She put it on a plate, warmed it in the microwave, and was just about to set it down by the kitchen sink when she looked out the window. Light shone from the studio.

She checked the clock. It was after midnight. Had he been in there all night? Maybe he'd fallen asleep—the sofa was inviting enough. She should go check on him, turn out the light, lock the door, that kind of thing.

She gave Boots his belated dinner. "You stay here. I'll be back in a bit." She locked the door behind her and followed the path to the studio.

It was a beautiful night, a full moon shining brilliantly white in the star-lit sky. The gurgle of the waterfall in the pool whispered along the path and that frog plopped into the pond again. The crickets were quiet, merely a low hum on the air, and the faintest of breezes rustled the leaves. A hibiscus blossom had fallen onto the path and Jolie picked it up. They had such a beautiful scent, even when their one day of life was over. She sniffed it, then tossed it back onto the garden. Maybe it'd be the start of a new hibiscus plant tomorrow.

She tiptoed up the wooden stairs and pushed the door open. There he was, asleep in the chair, an empty plate on the floor next to him, a beer bottle on its side beside it. Mrs. Gray must have sent dinner up before she left.

Jolie carried one of the orange throws over to him. He looked so peaceful. His face was relaxed, even the laugh lines by his eyes were almost gone. She bit back a laugh, remembering how indignant she'd been that she didn't have any lines. His certainly added something to his face. Character? Wisdom? She wasn't sure, but she did know she'd like to see those lines deepen over the years.

That lock of hair was finally out of his face, curled above his forehead, sitting there, just waiting for Todd to change position so it could fall down again. His arms rested in his lap and she had to stop herself from picking up his hand. Such talented fingers, so finely muscled and strong, yet so gentle on her skin.

His legs flared, heels touching. The man even had nice feet. Naked, of course, but that was to be expected.

She smiled. Thank goodness he was asleep because she was sure everything she felt for him was visible in her eyes at this moment.

She took one last lingering look—and a slightly unsteady breath—then draped the blanket over him. He murmured something and she froze in place.

"What?" was out of her mouth before she could stop it.

"My Jolie," he murmured again. This time there was no mistake.

The blanket slipped from her fingers and Todd nestled into it.

The man was dreaming of her?

***

Jolie tried to rein in the bounce to her step as she skipped up the stairs to the studio the next morning. It was entirely possible he wasn't awake yet, but her? She'd been awake for what seemed like hours, after a tough time falling asleep. Heart kept wanting to re-examine the meaning and ramifications of him talking in his sleep about her. And that oh-so-significant "my" before her name. Even though she'd ordered every hormone, every emotion, every nerve cell in her body not to overreact, Heart was break-dancing in her chest like it was Valentine's Day.

She looked in the window. He was just starting to stir. She knocked.

Green eyes lit up when he lifted his head. And so did her heart. It had to have been a good dream for him last night.

He shuffled to the door, all rumpled and sleepy-eyed, and that curl was back on his forehead. He ran both hands through his hair, then brushed the shadow on his jaw and gave her a one-sided grin as he opened the door. "You really haven't seen me at my best in the mornings."

"*That* is a matter of opinion," said Jolie, not Naughty Girl. She brandished the plate she'd brought. "Breakfast is served."

"Are you and Jasmine trying to keep me locked in my tower? I swear, I think I've had the last five meals in here." The supposed lock-down didn't seem to have any effect on his appetite, shoveling in the fried-eggs-over-easy, Canadian bacon, and whole-wheat toast as he was.

"Perhaps you should think about coming up for air, then." She locked her hands behind her back and rocked on her heels.

The eyebrow went up again. "Are you kidding? It's flowing, Jolie. It's working. All of it. Light, perspective, shadows, depth, you… It's as if I've never stopped, yet I've never painted like this before."

"That's a good thing, right?"

He scooped up another piece of egg, downed the entire glass of o.j., used the napkin she'd provided and nodded. "Better than a good thing. I didn't really think it'd happen like this. I started this to see if I could do it. Now, I'm inspired. I want to try all sorts of things, super-imposed images, sepia tones, black and white, profiles, the list is endless."

"So I've outlived my usefulness, then?" She was glad for him. Truly, but if he was so inspired, he could paint anyone.

He set the plate on the floor and when he stood, he was six inches closer and had hold of her hands. "Outlived it? I don't think so." He took another step closer. "If anything, you're more important than ever."

She tamped down the surge of hope. "More important?"

His eyes caressed her face. "Definitely."

A silence so fraught with unspoken words swirled around them, stealing her breath.

Todd squeezed her hands. "Which is why I was thinking… " He exhaled.

"Of?"

He closed his eyes for a second, then shook his head. "I want to paint all of you."

"Um, how much 'all' are we talking about?" She snaked her hands from his into her pockets.

"Not a nude, Jolie."

She wasn't sure if she was happy with that or not. "What do you have in mind?"

He slid one of her hands from her pocket and cradled it in both of his, running those long strong fingers across the tips of hers. "Just you, as you have been these last few days. The essence of you, your grace and energy, the fire just beneath the surface. All of this I've found in your face, but there's so much more. I want to capture the you I've seen on the sofa. Dreamy, soft, enticing, someone a man can dream of, would die to call his. I want to do justice to all of you." He pulled her un-protesting body against his.

Someone a man could dream of. An essence, grace and energy. Fire beneath the surface. And Todd holding her.

There she went melting again.

***

He stared down into that face he'd come to know so well over the last few days. It wasn't much effort to see past the skin to the woman beneath.

Todd's throat tightened, amazed that this was happening. Amazed he could feel again, feel *this* again. Desire for her, and for his craft; two things he would've bet he'd never want or need in his life again.

But Jolie had changed all that.

And now he couldn't stop the feeling. Didn't want to. He wanted to be with her and look at her, and yes, paint her. There was magic between them, just as there'd been with Trista.

Jolie inspired him in so many ways.

But today was all about the painting, so he stepped back. "Can we do the drop cloth again? I want to drape it over you as if you're not wearing anything."

"You want me to take off my top again?"

In more ways than one. But this was about his art. But about them, on the other hand… Well, the truth was, his body was letting him know loud and clear he was ready to move forward. Just the thought of her taking off her top was enough to make him hard. But this was about the painting. It had to be. "I promise I won't look."

"I'm leaving my shorts on."

"Are you saying that for your benefit or mine?"

She stuck out her tongue. "Turn around and I'll strip down."

He groaned and headed back to the canvas, loving that she was comfortable enough to tease, but it didn't help when he was trying to see her through an artist's eyes yet all he could see was a desirable woman.

But he tried. Over and over again, he drew the curve of her jaw, then smudged it out and tried again. He tried to detach himself from seeing the soft blush on her cheek as anything other than another color he had to capture. To not notice how dilated her pupils were from any perspective other than having to recreate them with a brush.

Or how the light rippled over her skin, smooth and unmarred, bathing it in warmth, the scent of her soap reaching him—

"I can't do it." Todd threw down the charcoal.

"Do what?" Jolie sat up, clutching the drop cloth to her chest like the heroine on the cover of some romance novel.

Yeah, don't start thinking about that, Best.

"Um, your hip. There's something wrong with it."

"There's nothing wrong with my hip. Is this like the lines?"

"What?"

"The lines. Beneath my eyes? Remember?"

Ah. He chuckled. "Yeah, I remember the lines, but, no, this isn't like that. I wanted those lines. Your hip has bumps and I can't figure out where the actual curve of it is." But his fingers were more than up for the chance.

Oh, hell. How was he going to get through this? Maybe painting her like this wasn't such a good idea since he couldn't seem to get beyond the physical. *Her* physical.

"First of all, my hip does not have bumps. It's probably just this stupid drop cloth." She pulled it tight.

Double hell. It outlined her breasts and followed where her waist dipped and her hips curved, and his salivary glands went into action.

"Oh, pooh. You're right. There are bumps, but they're from my shorts."

He raised his eyebrows, incapable of speech at the moment.

"I'm taking those off too, aren't I?" She sighed.

"You'll remember later that it was your suggestion?" Whose benefit that question was for was a toss-up.

Speaking of... she tossed a pillow at him. "Trust me, I'll remember."

"It was not my idea." That was *definitely* a reminder for him.

"I know, though it's not as if I can resist a temperamental artist flinging his charcoal to the floor in disgust. Turn around."

He was more than happy to. While she did some adjusting with the cloth and her shorts—*don't think about them hitting the floor and what that means*—he did some adjusting of his own, amazed his libido had recovered so quickly when he'd thought that part of his life was over.

"Ready," she said.

He almost groaned. The word took on new meaning with his new thoughts.

He turned around. Oh, yeah. She was ready.

And so was he. "Ahem, yes, well, that's better."

"Glad you approve."

He grabbed the charcoal and set to work. Line, curve, shadow...

"So, Todd... "

"Hmmm?"

"What was it like when you sold your first painting?"

A good memory. "Unbelievable. We were so poor."

"You were?"

"Well, I guess poor is a relative term. Trista came from money, but when she married me her parents cut her off, hoping to spite her into running home." He remembered those days only too well.

"Obviously she didn't."

"No, she didn't. But we had to really watch our money. I remember we used to have thirty-five dollars every other Friday for groceries. Luckily, a buddy of mine worked in a butcher shop and could help himself—with the owner's permission—to a few of the lesser-quality cuts. He'd drop some off every now and then so we didn't have to buy that. But we really had to stretch those thirty-five dollars and do some major coupon shopping." Especially when they'd spend ten percent of that paltry budget on a cheap bottle of champagne. Ah, the memories of those nights—when they'd lived on love and not much else.

"One of Trista's girlfriends came to visit and you should have seen the disgust on her face at our apartment. It wasn't the Ritz, but it was clean and well-cared for and we tried to make it homey. But Sheila was used to better; used to seeing Trista in better. So when Sheila saw my paintings and found out that I was trying to break into the art scene, she insisted on having one. I knew right away, of course, what she was doing and I refused to take any money from her. Charity was the last thing I wanted."

A flash of something crossed Jolie's face, pain perhaps. Ah, yes, she didn't "do" charity. He understood.

"Anyway, thank God for Sheila because she was a true friend. Still is, though I only get the requisite Christmas card from her now. She and I kept each other propped up at the funeral and I think it's just too hard for us to see each other without the memories."

Usually it was even hard for him to remember Sheila without the memories flooding back, but now, today... Nothing. A quiet remembrance, but no gut-wrenching sadness.

"Anyway, she shopped that picture around behind my back until the manager of one of the galleries downtown saw it and contacted me."

"And you sold your first one. Todd, that's fabulous. How nice it is to have such a good friend."

"Yeah. She's a special lady. And, oh the celebration we had that night, Trista and I. A fancy dinner at The Mid—at our favorite restaurant, champagne, I bought her flowers and she went shopping for a new dress... " He smiled, remembering her excitement. And his.

"The best part was watching Trista's parents eat crow. And not for my sake. They owed her an apology big time. And she deserved it because she…" The memories were soft and sweet. For the first time in two years. "She never gave up on me."

She never had. She'd believed in him and had given him the courage and strength to take a shot at it. All his success had been because of her. All his drive had been because of that faith she'd had in him.

That was why he'd thought he'd never paint again.

But along came Jolie, with her chatter and her optimism and her sunshine—things she'd be fully excused for not feeling with her hard life—and she'd shared that with him. Made him remember how it could be. Let him see the possibility in the future.

Dear God. Could it be… was he was falling in l—

"I always thought it'd be cool to be famous. To have everyone know who you are and make lots of money." Jolie hiked the drop cloth and adjusted her seat on the sofa.

No. He couldn't be falling. It was too soon. Too fast.

Physical. That was it. That was all. And the need to rise above his sadness that she did so well.

"Fame's not all it's cracked up to be, Jolie." How well he knew that. He captured the play of her forearm as her fingers flexed on the cloth with the charcoal. "The money is nice, sure, and my in-laws suddenly found me worthy, but when Trista died it was hell. All the cameras, the reporters, the invasion of my privacy—I just wanted everyone to leave me alone, let me heal in peace. I don't think I can ever go back to that."

"But you're painting again now."

"I know. Because of you."

"Me?" She looked utterly adorable.

"Yes, you. You pushed me just enough—"

"I didn't push."

"Okay, nudged then. Painting's a part of me, of who I am, how I see the world. Always has been. A compulsion that made me feel alive. That's why I couldn't paint after Trista died. I wanted to die, too."

"But now that you are painting again, does that—"she licked her lips—"does that mean you want to live again?"

Oh, hell yeah, he wanted to live again. And he was kidding himself sitting here trying to sketch her. He didn't want to sketch her.

He wanted to kiss her.

"Yes, Jolie, I do want to live again. And I have you to thank for it."

He set down the charcoal and walked over to her.

"Me?" Her eyes, big and violet and—yes—hopeful followed him all the way over as she scooted against the back of the sofa to give him room.

"Yes, you, Jolie." He sat next to her. "It was your happily-ever-after speech that first day, mentioning sixteen-year-old unwed mothers and the mother who couldn't spell your name right, and I saw *you*."

"Me?"

"You." He tucked a strand of her soft silky hair behind her ear, trailing his fingers over the rest of it, imagining it caressing him. "There's so much life in you, so much fire, the desire to not let anything bring you down. And I thought to myself, how amazing it is that this woman who claims nothing and no one, goes on, driving ahead to carve out her place in this world, the past be damned. Nothing's going to stop you from getting what you want, Jolie, and that invigorated me. It inspired me. And it awed me. It does that still. *You* do that still."

"I do?"

He smiled, recognizing that it was all true. "You're parroting me again." He traced her lips. "I know one way to stop that."

"You do?"

"Uh hmmm."

He had to kiss her. Just had to. One soft kiss to capture this tenderness, this new, raw emotion. He cradled her head and brushed the barest of kisses on her soft lips.

She returned it tentatively. He understood. She'd been let down in the past; he'd been hurt. Two scared, battered people coming together.

He slid his fingers into that curtain of hair by her temples, angling her mouth to fit against his and he tasted the seam of her lips.

Desire shot straight to his groin, hot and fierce. She gasped against his mouth, opening, her tongue meeting his with the same intensity, and, in a second, the kiss changed.

Heat flooded him, his blood pounding in his ears, his cock standing to attention, and suddenly he had to get closer. He pulled her against him, but pain sliced down his spine.

"Jolie." He pulled away. "My back. It doesn't want to angle this way. Hold on." He shifted on the narrow sofa, trying to pull her onto his legs without dislodging the drop cloth—more for her modesty than anything else—when Jolie put a hand on his.

"Todd." Her voice, low and throaty, conjured pictures of her naked and sated.

"Yes?"

Jolie licked her lips. Quickly, unconsciously, her eyes staring into his, the tempo of her breathing matching his, her fingers trembling against the thin barrier between them.

It could have been an hour that they stared at each other; it could have been a lifetime. He'd never know. But it was as if they stood on a precipice, wind howling around them, a band of angry thieves rushing toward them, then—

Jolie lowered the drop cloth.

Chapter Thirty-One

She was beautiful. But then he'd known she would be physically because she was in every other way. "Jolie, are you sure?"

"I'm in l—I'm sure, Todd. The question is, are you?"

A gift. He'd been given a gift.

For the second time in his life.

He turned around on the sofa, his hip next to hers, and stretched out beside her, his eyes never leaving hers. He slid one hand beneath her to caress the soft skin at her waist; his other hand found her cheek, his thumb brushing the corner of her mouth. Her breath caught just as he leaned in to kiss her eyes closed. "I'm sure," he whispered against her lashes.

That was all it took.

Her arm went around his neck and he pressed her to him, her breasts crushed against his chest, their lips finding each other. Tongues meeting, stroking, Jolie groaned, the sound reverberating along his nerves and suddenly he couldn't get enough of her mouth. He couldn't get enough of her. It was as if a dam had burst. All this long-denied feeling, the desire for her, came pouring out of him, and he wanted to wrap her in a cocoon of aching need and want.

He threaded his fingers through her hair, fanning it over them, feeling the soft strands on his arms, imagining it raining down on his chest. He fisted some of it, tugging her head back, allowing him to trail kisses from her mouth over her jaw and down the long, graceful line of her neck. Her pulse fluttered against his lips; he could feel her shallow breathing as her breasts rose against his chest, and he wished he'd had the forethought to rip off his stupid t-shirt.

He cupped her, grazing the nipple with his thumb, desire tightening his balls as it pebbled for him. Her head fell back more, this time through no effort on his part, and he traced her collarbone with his tongue, kissing the soft hollow at the center. Her skin smelled of lavender, a soft sheen gliding against his cheek as his lips sought her.

"Jolie… " He breathed in her scent, kissing every inch of her breast, mouthing the soft flesh down to the nipple. Rock hard, it perked upwards as if begging for his attention. He groaned, taking it into his mouth, and Jolie called out his name.

Desire licked through him as he circled her nipple with his tongue. She speared her hands through his hair, holding him close and he sucked, each of her breaths pulsing her further into his mouth.

"Your breasts are spectacular," he murmured against them.

"And by the way, they're real."

The line from a *Seinfeld* episode made him laugh. He pulled back. "God, Jolie, there's no one like you."

"I certainly hope not, because you might mistake her for me."

"Never, Jolie. No one can ever be you."

***

Todd's eyes were the dark forest green she remembered from the last time he'd kissed her. His golden hair, tousled—by *her* fingers this time—fell forward, framing his eyes, making them seem like the only thing in the room, and Jolie sank into their depths.

He wanted her.

She was almost afraid to believe it. But when she glanced down to see his tanned fingers against her breast, her nipple moist from the warmth of his mouth, the rise and fall of his chest, she believed.

And she *wanted*. She *needed*.

She desired.

And was desired.

It gave her courage. It gave her validity.

And it gave her the right to want him.

"I need to feel your skin." She tugged on his shirt. Wanted to feel it against her, around her… *in* her.

Time had no meaning. One minute there was a shirt between them and the next, it was all smooth, golden bronze skin lightly dusted with more golden hair, and Todd was kissing her again.

The kiss claimed her. It wasn't sexual in any foreplay way, but a "you are mine and there's no one else here between us" thing and it was her undoing.

She ended up beneath him and they pulled and tugged the drop cloth from between them, all the while somehow keeping their lips and bodies in constant contact. Somehow Todd shed his shorts and, dear Lord, the man *did* go commando.

His fingers skimmed down her body from the sides of her breasts, around to her tush to dance along the band of her thong. "You've got a thong on."

"Yes." Way to state the obvious, both of them.

"Do you know how sexy that is?" His breathing kicked up more notches than she even knew there were.

"Why don't you show me?" Naughty Girl left residual effects, apparently.

But Todd didn't seem to mind. He growled and her insides got all quivery, then his very big, very hard, thrusting bit of evidence pulsed against her thigh and her melting insides flowed out between her legs. She had no defenses left against him, against this feeling—yes, this *love*—she had for him.

"Oh, God, Jolie." He stopped.

Stopped?

"What?" He *stopped*? Her mind was trying to process this series of events while her eyes searched his.

"Protection. I don't have any."

Well, there was a mood-kill.

"Um." Gosh, she'd never thought about that in any of her imaginings. "Well, I haven't been with anyone in—" she did some quick mental calculations—"six years, and even then we used, um, protection. And I'm on the pill."

"You are?"

She nodded. "Feminine reasons."

He smiled. "Well, that's good, I guess. For this. Now." He swept some hair from her face. "I haven't been with anyone but Trista since I met her, so I should be fine." His eyes brushed over her lips again. "Should we, that is, do we risk it?"

Interesting how her pitiful dating life actually came in handy. As for the risk... no way was she stopping now. This might be her one and only shot at something that constituted happy in her life. "Yes. We do."

"Oh, God, Jolie. What have I done to deserve this? You?"

She could give him a whole list, but he didn't give her the chance before she was swept up in the artistry that was Todd. He touched her, caressed her, kissed her as if she was the only woman in the world and he couldn't get enough of her.

His knee nudged hers apart. *Not* that they needed further encouragement. But the darned sofa was too narrow, so she lifted one leg along the back of it. Which had its recommendations, as his fingers danced along her inner thigh and her hips rolled against them.

His lips re-sought her breasts and she had a hard time breathing. His fingers traced the piping on her thong and she wanted to rip the darned thing off. For such a flimsy piece of material it sure could get in the way.

She couldn't hold back the groan when he slipped inside the thong, finding the very heart of her desire. The man had dexterous fingers, which should come as no surprise considering his skill with a paintbrush. Truth to tell, she was beyond considering anything but the scent of him as she buried her face in his neck, the salty taste of his skin akin to ambrosia. She nipped the corded muscle there and it was his turn to groan.

"Jolie, you feel so good." The words escaped his mouth as she licked her way up to his ear, twirling her tongue around the outer shell. His fingers circled and stroked, one slipping inside, continuing the circling and stroking, and she ground her hips against him, drawing his earlobe into her mouth.

His guttural moan set her heart pounding. "Todd." She reached between them to stroke him. He pulsed against her hand and she had her own satisfaction growl happening. *She'd* done this to him. She and the person she was. The one worthy of being dreamt about.

She closed her fingers around him and he groaned again, his fingers stilling in and on her. "Like that?" she asked against his throat.

He nodded, then slowly slid his finger from her, her inner muscles protesting, clenching around him. Then she felt him smile against her as he thrust back in.

Ahhhh.

Her hand mimicked his and soon there was no telling whose heavy breaths were whose, which groans and sighs of pleasure belonged to which of them. They were both there together.

And it felt completely right.

So right it would scare her if she stopped to think about it.

But no way was she stopping. Thankfully, he seemed to be on the same wavelength.

His finger slid out of her to work the thong off and then she was as naked as he was.

Oh, did it feel glorious.

It felt right.

"Todd, please." She couldn't stop the whisper as his erection throbbed against her when he slipped between her thighs.

"I aim to do just that." Strained laughter was in his voice.

"I hope your aim is true," she joked back.

He pulled back and his eyes blazed into her, serious, ardent. "Very true."

She couldn't speak.

What was amazing wasn't that he'd said it—though that was amazing enough—but what, a month ago, would have sent her screaming from the room, was now so natural, so right, it was like breathing.

She lifted her hips, giving Heart and Body over to Todd.

He nudged her mouth with the tip of his nose and she opened her eyes just as he claimed every part of her with a firm yet gentle filling completion.

"Todd… it's never been like this, I've never—"

"I know, Jolie."

He knew? What did he know?

"It's perfect," he answered her unspoken question. "You're perfect."

She could do perfect. But what about love?

Or was she asking too much?

"I never thought I could care for someone else like this again." His eyes bored into hers while the rhythm he set put her insides on high alert. "Jolie, you are truly aptly named. Beauty. Both inside and out." He placed a kiss above her heart and she melted all over again.

Melted literally, as there were tears leaking from her eyes. Todd kissed them softly and she wrapped her arms around his neck.

She considered saying something flippant, like "and away we go," but she couldn't. It was the most beautiful experience of her life as his skin stroked hers and their breathing kicked up to almost unbearable levels, their bodies moving in perfect unison.

Slick with sweat—yes, this time she was sweating; for him, she would sweat—and they glided against each other, every tantalizing hair on his chest doing wonderful things to her nerve endings. Murmurs and sighs and groans signaled each new height. Moving together faster, gripping each other tighter, suddenly, it was upon them. The wonderful flash of pleasure, the soaring feeling as if her soul had taken wing, rocketing through the heavens.

And she'd rather be on this trip with him than anyone else in the world.

***

Finally, the world settled around them, sounds came back, the musky smell of lovemaking mixed with the oil paints that would forever remind her of this night and she smiled into his chest.

She'd found a home.

Finally.

Chapter Thirty-Two

"Good evening, Beautiful."

There was no better way to wake up than with Todd's smiling face mere inches from hers. "Evening?" She shook the cobwebs from her brain. "It's that late?"

Smiling, he bore not a trace of *haunted* in those eyes. "Well, early evening, but close enough. What are you worried for? You don't have anywhere to be, do you? Though I have heard your boss is a tyrant."

"Yeah, a real brute. Likes to take charge, be in control, *on top* of things."

"Things? Or you?" Oh, he was right there with her on the teasing and it felt so good.

She shrugged, doing a little come-hither from beneath her come-hither-less eyelashes. "Take your pick."

"All right, I will." He surprised her with a quick tongue attack to the left breast. "I pick this one."

She threw her head back in sheer ecstasy. "You don't play fair."

"Ah, but who wants to play fair when one can just play?"

Good point.

Which he proved quite nicely over the next hour or so.

***

It was definitely on the long side of evening and heading straight into night when she stirred again. He twirled a piece of her hair through his fingers and she stretched like a cat after a long nap in the afternoon sun.

"Hi." He tickled her lips with the ends of her hair.

She shook her head. "Hi yourself."

"Hungry?"

"Is that a trick question?"

"Ha." He sat up and the drop cloth barely kept him presentable. Well, for public viewing. For private, it was covering way too much.

His fingers flexed on her hip. "How does Chinese take-out sound to you, Miss Gourmet?"

"Heavenly."

"Okay, then." He grabbed his shorts off the floor and stepped into them. "Let's drag ourselves down to the pool and we can eat there."

That glimpse of glutes nailed her to the sofa for a moment until she got her breathing under control.

"Jolie?"

"Um, okay. I'll be right there. And I have to feed Boots."

"Must you?"

"Of course I do! The poor little guy is probably starving." She sat up and tucked the cloth beneath her arms, not that the modesty was needed. The guy had seen—and nibbled on—pretty much everything she had hidden.

He did a mock sigh. "Fine, if you must. I'll grab a quick shower and run down to the restaurant. What do you want?"

Was a "side of Todd" on the menu? "Hunan Chicken, pork or chicken fried rice, lo mein. Really, anything's fine."

"Anything? And here—" he leaned over to place another bone-melting kiss on her lips—"I thought you had discerning tastes."

"Hey, I do. I only go for the *best*."

He tweaked her nose. Wow. Playful and happy. There should be a big fluffy Cloud Nine under their feet right now.

"Clever girl. You should think about writing a novel instead of that cookbook." He walked out the door. "I bet it'd be a *best* seller."

She groaned—both at his play on words and the actual truth behind his statement. Suddenly her little non-disclosure was looming large on the horizon.

So while Naughty Girl was away, Scarlett would come out to play—and worry about all of that tomorrow.

Boots stretched when she went into the kitchen. Honestly, in her next life she was coming back as a cat. Chase a few mice, cough up a hairball or two, take a nap, have someone feed you, and all you had to do was rub up against them and purr in their ear. Yeah, that'd be the life.

Kitty was eating, Todd was out getting dinner, and she was desperately trying to decide proper poolside attire. She still hadn't bought a bathing suit. The magenta halter would have to do with a cute, black, flouncy skirt.

She heard the dream machine pull into the driveway as she stepped into her hot pink flats. Okay, she needed some kind of fun shoes in her new wardrobe and the store was fresh out of kicky yellow ones. A girl had to have a vice or two.

"Jolie, I'm back." And there'd be one of hers.

"Be right down. I'll meet you at the pool." And she was—*right down*. She was not about to lose one more minute in his presence. If it wouldn't have seemed too weird, she would've tried to finagle a double shower and gone with him for the meal, but she had to have some kind of self-control. Not to mention, there'd be the question of when they'd eat if there'd been the shower-*a-deux*.

She skidded through the kitchen (*note to self: scuff up soles of new magenta flats*) and managed a pirouette stop that looked as if she'd actually meant to do it.

"Hey," she said, all breathy. Not the image she had in mind, but it seemed to work for him as his mouth snapped shut. But she saw the hanging open part. Little tummy flutters duly noted.

"Wow."

Okay, *big* tummy flutters.

He stopped lighting the vanilla candle on the table—aww, he was lighting candles—and came over to her. "Jolie, you look beautiful."

"Coming from an artist of such renown, I'll take that as a compliment." The words and tone were light, but there was nothing light about the thudding of her heart.

"Don't take it from the artist. Take it from the man. You're stunning." He picked up her hands and kissed her knuckles. "*Chère Jolie, voulez-vous diner avec moi ce soir?*"

"*Oui, mon chère.*" If he could ask "dear Jolie" to have dinner with him, she could certainly call him "my dear" when she said yes.

That, and because it was true.

Did she dare hope he felt the same? So it was a bit too early for him to consider the "L" word, but that was okay. She had enough for both of them. She was just happy with being beautiful in his eyes.

"Where," he asked as he scooched her chair beneath her, "did you learn to speak French? Some exotic little bistro on the French Riviera?"

She snorted then covered her mouth. Not an attractive sound. "Hardly. Try 'Languages R Us.'" At his puzzled look, she explained, "A computer program. You?" She took a bite of the spicy Hunan chicken. Yum, they used just enough peppers for some kick, but not enough to overpower the veggies.

"A year, poor and starving, in Paris learning the ropes."

She almost choked on a shitake mushroom. "Paris? You've been to Paris? That's my dream."

"Is it?" He swirled his glass of wine. "Why haven't you ever gone? You've said there was no one keeping you here, right?"

"Money," was the first thing she blurted out, unsure if the nonchalance beneath his question was feigned or not. "Well, that and I think Paris is the kind of place you should go with a lov—lover." Yeah, she could use that word. *Now*.

"A lover, huh?" He was still swirling. "And the guy from—six years ago, was it? He didn't want to take you?"

Again with the snort. She really needed to stop doing that. "Chucky? Are you kidding?"

"Not the Paris type, I take it." A long swallow went down that long, taut throat of his.

Snort again. "Hardly. If it wasn't some place you could get to and back during half-time, forget it. He wouldn't even want to know where it was."

Now the glass came down and Todd was looking right at her. "Then why were you with him?"

Another sucker-punch to the gut. She would've thought her abs would be rock hard from all the blows in her life.

But no. She took her time swallowing the food, which had suddenly lost its flavor. Why were they doing this? She didn't want to revisit her past this way. She'd tried too hard to forget.

"Jolie?" He reached out to stroke her fingers. "Tell me."

"Why?"

"Because I want to know. I want to know why someone as bright and funny and talented and smart as you would lower yourself to go out with a guy who wouldn't at least share your dreams of Paris. Who earns not one, but *two* snorts from you when he's mentioned."

"Maybe because he's the only one who asked who didn't mention money and a motel?"

Well *there* was a zinger to brighten the moment.

"Really?"

If he said one more word in that soft, understanding tone, she was going to lose it.

"Why?" He picked her hand up, but she turned back to the sawdust that was her dinner. She couldn't do this. "Jolie, you're smart, beautiful, fun. Why didn't guys see this?"

It was no use. She put down her chopsticks. "Todd, I can't do this. Can we just let it go? I had a rotten past and I'd like to forget it."

He laced their fingers, reaching for her other hand. "You yanked me out of the depression I'd been wallowing in, trying hard not to forget, and it wasn't easy. But it's for the better. I want to help you, Jolie. You deserve someone to care about you. Someone who thinks you're worth something. Why won't you talk about it?"

She pulled her hands away and clenched them in her lap. Maybe if she squeezed hard enough that pain would remove her focus from the pain tearing through her insides.

"Jolie, I care about you. I can see your pain. I *know* your pain. I've been there. Tell me."

She shook her head, pressing her lips together. The words wanted to come. They were right there on the tip of her tongue.

But she couldn't let them. Twenty some years of anguish, loneliness, hurt, betrayal… If she let it out, he'd be running for the hills and she'd be left alone.

Again.

"Jolie, talk to me. I know you're thinking something, I can see your brain moving at warp speed in those beautiful eyes of yours. But you need to talk to me."

She turned her head. "I can't."

He cupped her cheek, making her face him. "Why not?"

Oh, please, he wasn't going to make her do this, was he?

"Jolie."

Yeah, he was. So she took a big breath. Maybe if she just got it out there in one big rush without thinking about the words it wouldn't be so bad.

"Because, Todd, if I start, I may not stop. I just might have a complete breakdown and I can't do that. I don't know if I'll be able to stop, control it. The emotions, the feelings, the abandonment, the… *hurt*."

Damn, it was that bad.

But he'd opened the floodgates so he was going to get drowned.

"Fine. Here you go. My mother was a drunk, and that was on a good day. She thought she could narrow down my father to three guys, which is always a refreshing thing to find out when you're eight." She gripped the edge of her chair, looking somewhere over his right shoulder. "You already know the name thing. And then, one day, she just walked. Out to a bar and the next time I saw her she was in a box in a church. And then the fun really started. Let's see, shall I start with the foster father who thought it'd be fun to chase a teenager around the dining room table when no one else was home for a little touchy-feely? Or maybe you'd like to hear about the bread and water rations I got when the corners of my bed weren't tucked in properly? Or, I know, how about—"

"What about Mrs. Carleson?" He handed her a napkin.

Damn. He turned on her spigot with that one. Mrs. Carleson, the brightest spot in her adolescent universe. "Mrs. Carleson was an anomaly. The kind of woman every foster kid dreams of. I was terrified to let myself hope. But she made it so darn easy. So I did. I hoped and I prayed and I believed. And then Mr. Carleson got transferred. And while I knew it was nothing I had done, it was one more person I cared about, believed in, who was leaving me. So, yeah, when Chucky offered me a home and monogamy it looked pretty damn good. At that point I was just glad to have someone who remembered my name."

She was slobbering all over the darned napkin.

"I'm sorry," Todd whispered.

But she broke down anyway. Somehow he managed to coax her wiped-out body from her chair and onto his lap, tucking her head beneath his chin, his strong arms wrapped around hers and he wasn't letting go.

But she was. The tears were flowing into hiccups. Her stomach hurt from holding back the racking sobs.

Why was she doing this? At any moment, Todd could have enough and get up, put her in the chair, and walk into the house. Hell, she almost expected it.

But he didn't. He just linked his hand that much tighter to his other arm and stroked her skin. Soothing little circles. The crickets were serenading them and the irony was deadly.

The agonizing words burned her throat raw with salty tears. All she wanted to do was crawl inside the safe haven his arms offered and forget the world.

"I'm sorry," he said against her temple. "I had no idea how bad it really was."

She shrugged. He probably wasn't buying the nonchalance of that; he was a smart guy. Which was why he should've been running in the opposite direction.

But he wasn't.

Instead, he rubbed her arms and kissed the top of her head, his heart thudding in her ear.

"Jolie, do you realize how strong you are? How much of a survivor?"

"What?"

He tipped her chin up until her mouth was a whisper away from his. He stared into her eyes, those green eyes all swirly, and her insides followed suit.

"What it must have taken for you to remain strong, independent, clean. I'm in awe of you."

"You are?"

He nodded, sweeping a hand down her back. "Yes. Do you know how many people would have folded under those circumstances? Turned to drugs, alcohol, other means of escaping?"

She nodded. Yeah, she knew. Could probably name quite a few of them.

"But not you. Look at you. Successful, smart, a good head on your shoulders, trustworthy." The tilt to his lips started one on hers. "You should be proud of yourself, Jolie. Really proud. To know you, no one would think you've seen the things you have, lived the life you have. You're so wonderfully normal."

"What?"

"Um hmmm. But you're not just normal. You're above it. You're empathetic and that's a special quality to find in a person."

"I am?"

He smiled. "You're going monosyllabic on me again. And, yes, you are empathetic. And kind. And optimistic and sunny. That's how you got through to me. How you reached me beneath my pain. How you brought me back to myself."

"I did all that?"

He brushed the hair back from her forehead. "That and so much more." His fingers swept her brow. "You've made me care for you, Jolie."

Care. She could do care.

Suddenly, the look in his eyes swept the past and its pain away. She was here, pretty whole if one didn't look too closely into her psyche, and she'd helped this marvelous man back into life. And he cared for her.

No one except Chloe, Bella, and Mrs. Carleson had ever cared for her. Certainly no one of the male persuasion. Not in any way that mattered.

But he did and he was here and she was here and her emotions were so wild at the moment that she didn't know if she was coming or going, but she did know she couldn't wait one minute longer to grab this man's face and mesh it with hers, to turn in his arms so she was front to front with him, plastered together, their hearts beating as one.

And apparently he was with her on this, because his hands went around her, rocking her closer to him, traveling up and down her spine as if he was trying to commit her figure to memory.

"Todd," she gasped when his mouth scraped across her cheek to nuzzle her ear. "Show me. Here. Now. Show me you care. Make the bad memories go away, Todd. Give me new ones."

And, Lord, did he.

Chapter Thirty-Three

Jolie was sore in places she didn't know it was possible to be sore. But one place that wasn't was her heart. Todd had taken that deep aching chasm inside of her that she covered with every conceivable excuse, rationalization, and hopeful "what if," and filled it in.

She was *not* Rebound Girl. No, he hadn't used the "L" word, but pretty much everything else. As they attempted to regain the professionalism needed for Todd's artistic sessions in the attic, Jolie realized that, for the first time in longer than she could remember—if ever—she had hope. Real hope.

The modeling session ended up being full of heated blushes, silly grins, and way too many kisses and hugs to encourage good artistry skills, so they gave up any pretense of Todd painting her on canvas. There were, however, some interesting moments with him, her, a palette of beautiful colors, and a paintbrush.

Actually, when they were "finished," the drop cloth looked more like a work of art than a means of keeping paint off the floor. Not that they'd been too successful with that either.

Who knew? Maybe drop cloth art could be his next medium.

She'd volunteer to help him with that for, like, the next fifty years or so.

"Let's go out to dinner," he said as they studied the patterns the waning sun made on the ceiling of the studio.

"Fine with me. Where do you want to go?"

"Some place new. Some place all our own."

Some place all their own. She liked that. Liked that he wanted to have memories with her. That she didn't have to play second fiddle to Trista.

"How about your friend Bella's place?" He ran his hands over her stomach.

Her belly tightened and fluttered, the nerves twitching under the heat. Good thing the paint was dry or there'd be a smear there. Well, another one.

"Casteleoni's is nice. Very homey."

"Will it seem strange since you worked there?"

She rolled over to face him. "No. That's the last place that seems strange to me. It's one of the few places I think of as home."

He rolled toward her. "I hope this is another one."

Her breath got sucked all the way into her toes with that. "You do?"

He tilted her chin up with the tip of his finger. "Crazy, isn't it? We've known each other for what? Two weeks? But who cares? Time is irrelevant. So, yes, I do want you to consider this home. And we'll go with a little longer than temporary, okay? I can't promise forever, but for now and a little longer. Can you do that, Jolie?"

Uh, yeah? Hello?

Her "you betcha" got a big grin from him.

And yet another when she answered his, "Casteleoni's, then?" the same way.

***

It was like a family reunion at Bella's. They'd pulled up in the dream machine and Bella had drippy candles lit on the outdoor tables which were covered in red-and-white-checked tablecloths. The street trees' twinkling lights were now year-round, the sky was that last shade of purple before it goes dark, and the ambiance was all *Lady-and-The-Tramp*-spaghetti-scene-romantic.

The whole crew had been there: Bella; her husband Reese; Giacomo and Giuseppe, the life-partner waiters who'd been there for like ever; Bella's stepsister Staci and her fiancé; Bruno with the broken leg and Bella's other stepsister, Drew. She'd known them all so long and so well they could've been her family. And she was there with Todd. Somehow everything just fit.

And now, sitting on the window seat in her room, with Boots snoring away smack dab in the middle of her four-poster, she was putting the finishing touches on Annie and Tom's happily-ever-after. Amazing how easy it was to write theirs when she could feel her own coming together.

Her pencil rasped in the silence of the room, words flowing. She was going to finish this. She didn't need to see how it ended since she already knew, but she'd worked so long on the story, had poured all her hopes and dreams into Annie and Tom, that she wanted them to find their happy ending before she put it aside. She had no intention whatsoever of trying to find a publisher. This was for her.

She never really needed to become published, she realized. Most authors didn't become rich overnight with their writing, and, really, it was the hope she'd needed. The hope in a happily-ever-after in life. To see it was possible, and to know that she could craft one on paper, so she should be able to in her own life as well. And to do that, to begin her happy ending, she needed to finish theirs.

Just like Todd. He was in the studio without her. He had some kind of compulsion to finish the painting that had been consuming him ever since they'd woken up.

So they were both dealing with their compulsions, and Jolie could see the end in sight. Literally. All she had to do was finish the last scene, then tuck the manuscript back under her mattress to be taken out someday to share with her grandkids.

That she was even thinking about grandkids said a whole lot on the subject of Todd and her.

A few more sentences and *voila*! Annie and Tom were on the bow of a floating restaurant, two champagne flutes clinking together in the sparkle of the setting sun, a bottle of lemonade on the floor between them.

The End.

She studied the words. Maybe she should have written *The Beginning.*

Nah. It was Annie and Tom's ending, but now off she was for her beginning.

She started to stash the notebook, but a whiney growl from Sleeping Beauty in the middle of the bed made her reconsider. She put it on the shelf of the bedside table so Kitty Boy could finish his nap while she ran over to Chloe's to help with the girls.

She grabbed her cute little magenta purse—it'd been *right* next to the shoes at the store—and hollered up to Todd in the studio from the driveway.

"I'll be a few more hours," he called. "Think you can entertain yourself?"

"Sure thing. I'm going to run over to Chloe's and take those leftovers Bella gave me. Then I'll do some food shopping. Anything special you want for dinner tonight?"

He stuck his head out the second floor window, his hair falling around his ears in a bohemian, artistic sort of way. "You mean besides you?"

"Ssh, Todd. The neighbors will hear." Not that that'd bother her too much, but she didn't want to jinx any of this.

"Fine." He brushed the hair back to no avail. "You did mention Lobster Newburg a while ago, didn't you? Throw in a few oysters and a bottle of champagne, while you're at it." There was that wicked, wicked grin again.

"You don't need 'em, trust me." A spring sprang into her step on her way to Melanie.

"I do, Jolie."

Something in his tone was awfully serious, causing the spring to fizzle to a stub-toed stumble. She turned around and stared at him. "Need them? Are you nuts? The last thing you need is an aphrodisiac."

He shook that gloriously sexy hair. "Not that. I meant that I trust you."

Forget quivery thighs—it was a good thing he popped back in that window or he might've seen her knees give way. Trust? He trusted her?

Those were words she'd never even dared to hope to hear from anyone before because no one had ever cared enough to give a damn whether or not she was worthy of their trust.

She would do everything in her power to prove she was worthy of his.

***

"So how's life with Todd?" Chloe asked as Jolie stacked the last tray of food in the industrial-sized fridge.

That Jolie kept her face in the cool air had absolutely nothing to do with the question. Really. She just had to make sure the trays weren't crushing each other.

"Jolie?"

Chloe had known her too long.

Jolie shut the door, trying to keep the silly grin off her face. From the one on Chloe's, she guessed she hadn't succeeded. "It's good."

"Just good?"

"Okay, it's pretty great."

"From what Bella said, it looked a bit more than great. Pretty amazing and homey, I believe were her words." Chloe cleared half a dozen cereal bowls from the butcher-block island.

"Homey?" That had a nice sound to it. "Hey, wait a minute. What were you two doing talking about me anyway?"

Chloe snorted. "Come on. Like we didn't gab ourselves silly during Bella and Reese's courtship."

"If you can call it that with her stepmother causing such havoc." Jolie handed her seven glasses with residual amounts of orange juice in them.

"Whatever. You're changing the subject." She wagged one of the glasses at Jolie like a club. "So, what gives?"

Jolie raised her hands in surrender. "What gives is that he's wonderful, and, well, I think he's ready to move beyond Trista."

"With you?"

"Well, if not me, then someone else is in the kitchen making some pretty awesome meals." And in his studio and bedroom making some pretty awesome memories, but those were Jolie's and she wasn't about to share.

"And you? I thought you were all about starting your own shop, giving yourself some financial freedom and control over your life?" Chloe closed the dishwasher, leaning against it.

"Loving him doesn't stop me from doing that." Jolie leaned against the island.

"*Loving* him?"

Wow. She could keep her head up when she said it and there were no twinges of trepidation in her tummy. "Yes. Love. I love him, Chloe."

"And he loves you?"

"Well, he hasn't said the words, but I think the sentiment is there. If not just yet, the possibility certainly isn't sending him running for the hills."

Chloe pushed off the dishwasher and leaned her hip on the island next to Jolie. "Are you okay with that, Jols? I mean, I know all about wishes and dreams. And how they don't always work out."

"What are you talking about? You've got this home, the girls. It's what you've always wanted." Jolie waved her hand in the general direction of the gingham-cushioned, ladder-back chairs.

"You're forgetting the pain-in-my-butt developer who's trying to take it out from under me, which would then throw the girls back into the system." She shook her head and gave Jolie a hug. "I just don't want you to get hurt, that's all."

"I thought you liked Todd?"

"I do." Chloe straightened the placements on one side of the farm-style table. "I also remember him when his wife was alive. How much he loved her. I don't know that he's ever going to be able to feel that way about anyone else again and you deserve to have someone feel that way about you."

Jolie fixed the placemats on the other side. "I'm not asking him to feel that way about me. Heck, I'm not asking him to feel anything about me. He did it on his own. And even if it's different from what he felt for her, I can't begrudge him the memories, those feelings. As long as his for me are true, I'm fine with that."

They met at the head of the table. "But will it be enough?"

Jolie gripped the side rails of the chair. "Enough? Hello? If the man loves me, it'll be more than I've ever expected. I'd thought what I'd read in books was an idealized version, but I see now, with him, it's possible. I know I love him enough to want to give it a shot."

"What happens if it falls apart on you?"

"Are you trying to make me sad?"

Chloe pulled out a chair, motioning to the one Jolie still had in a death grip.

Jolie pulled it out and sat down.

"No, Jols, I'm not trying to make you sad. But you have to admit, past experience does count for something. It's not like we have some guardian angel hovering over us, making things right in our lives. I mean, if there'd ever been such a thing, I would've hoped it would've happened when we were kids when we needed that sort of thing, not as adults. I just don't want you to get your hopes up."

Jolie shook her head. "Too late, Chlo. My hopes are up and soaring right now. And the reason is Todd."

Chloe studied her, care and love and worry in her eyes. But then she smiled and held Jolie's hands. "Then I'm happy for you, Jols. I really am. I want it to work out for the two of you. There's not another set of people I'd like more to see it happen to."

"And you, Chloe. You'll find your happily-ever-after someday."

Chloe shrugged, her grin wry. "Yeah, we'll see."

Just then the girls walked in and the mood lightened as they regaled Chloe and Jolie with rope-swing incidents involving an oak tree, a creek, and a bank of mud with so much hilarity that Jolie was almost jealous of their childhood.

Almost, but not quite, because where she came from had led her here. And ending up with Todd was worth all the pain, loneliness, and heartache she'd endured.

*****

After a couple hours at the grocery store, Jolie pulled into Todd's driveway, picturing herself coming home to it—and him—for the rest of her life.

Oh, darn. That's what she should've done with Annie and Tom. Not had them drift off with the tide into the sunset, but put them on the porch of their own home. A big farmhouse like Chloe's with room for kids to run around, a big ol' gnarled apple tree with a zillion branches to climb or hang a rope swing from or build a tree fort in. A fireplace big enough to stand in and roast marshmallows. And enough bedrooms for a full-size family of their own—and perhaps a few extras.

That was it. That was the ending they should have. She'd have to re-do the last part for Annie and Tom before she put it to rest permanently. And permanently it was because she'd learned what she needed to know. Found out what love was all about.

She bypassed the studio. She'd catch up with Todd once she fixed those last few pages. It was going to be great, just perfect. All she had to do was get it on paper.

She unloaded the groceries, putting only the cold stuff and champagne away, then bounded up the stairs to her room, running the ending scene through her mind. What they'd say, how they'd touch each other, the whole thing.

She skipped up to the landing, fingertips trailing off the railing onto the wall, tap-dancing with twitchy energy. She had to get this on paper. Her muse was bursting with it. She did a little hop-step to her room. One or two more, then she'd get the manuscript out and put the words that would finally finish her dream—

"Todd!"

In her room. *On her bed...*

But with an expression that was not the happy, I-can't-wait-to-see-her look she would have loved to have seen.

He just sat there, looking at her without saying a word, and her chipper mood evaporated in the amount of time it took her to see—

Her notebook in his lap.

Oh.

No.

" 'A rose just waiting to bloom, the moment before the petals unfurl, one touch of the sun and you'll burst into beauty,' " he read from the pages.

Her heart rate tripled.

He flipped to the last page. " 'You never gave up on me,' said Tom. "

Todd looked up with haunted eyes and threw the notebook to the floor.

" 'I always wondered what it would be like to be famous.' " His lips curled as he threw her words in her face. "Is that it, Jolie? Is that what you did this for? Did you think you could take my story—my *life*—and make it fodder for the tabloids? Earn your own fifteen minutes? A big fat bonus from some tabloid?"

He pushed himself off the bed and strode to the window.

Away from her.

"Was that what the photographer at *The Midnight Maiden* was all about? Did you call him? Tell him you managed to do what no one else had—got me to go out in public? Tell him where we'd be?"

His reflection in the window glowered at her.

She couldn't even shake her head. Not in the face of what he'd just read. Anything she'd say now would look like a lie.

He turned around. "My God. I trusted you. I opened up parts of me I didn't even know existed. Laid myself bare before you. All my pain." He raked his hands through his hair, then jammed them to his hips. He exhaled and it resonated with disillusionment, pain. "You're good, Jolie. You knew just how to do it. A cookbook. Ha. I can't believe I suggested you write a book."

"Todd, I…" She didn't know what to say.

Not that he waited for her to say anything. "I want you to leave."

The words… She should say something.

But she couldn't.

"I want you to leave now, Jolie."

Chapter Thirty-Four

S he wanted to—
　　And then—
　　But—

　...

Chapter Thirty-Five

She would have liked to have left his house with dignity and grace, but she didn't.

She would've liked to have come up with a beautiful speech about how he'd inspired her and she was so in awe of him and respected him and would never use him—that she loved him—but she didn't.

She would've liked to have come up with something serene and pithy and mature to explain the pages he'd held, but, again, she didn't. She'd given up explaining herself a long time ago and old habits not only died hard, they sometimes didn't die at all.

What she *did* do was something she was very good at. She'd clamped the tears behind her clenched teeth, straightened her rigid shoulders, taken all her clothes—few though they were—out of the closet and shoveled them into her bag, picked up the manuscript off the floor, and walked out the door and out of that life.

That fantasy life.

Because the man was utterly and truly right. Who did she think she was to take his most private pain and lay it out there for the world to see? Whether or not she was actually going to carry through with trying to publish it was irrelevant. His life and his love story were his, and if he chose to share them with her, she should have taken them for the gift they were and left it at that.

She pounded Melanie's steering wheel and the car coughed and sputtered. Great. Someone else she was losing in her life. She pulled over to the side of the road and rested her head on the wheel.

How could she have been so stupid? So utterly blind to what it would do to him? It wasn't like she hadn't had a clue. "I trust you." Hello? What did she think he meant? "I trust you to do a good job of portraying me as a grieving emotional wreck?"

God, she'd even left her apron and Boots there.

And once again she'd been proven right. Nothing lasted forever. She'd always known it and should have started believing it could.

The car got a little less sputtery and she was able to make it back to Chloe's, the only place she could think to go within sputtering distance. Good thing, too, 'cause poor Melanie ended up coughing her last at the end of Chloe's driveway.

Jolie dragged herself to the front door and Dakota, one of the girls, opened it.

"You okay, Jolie?" she asked.

Jolie didn't even bother to hide the truth. The kid was fifteen and could spot a lie a mile off. "No. I need to borrow a couch for a while."

It was a damned shame that a fifteen-year-old had an instant understanding of complete devastation and the wherewithal to point her to the closest sofa, no questions asked. But then, Jolie would have at her age as well.

None of the girls asked why she was back for the second time in less than two hours and, for that, she was grateful. They just went about their normal Sunday, taking care of their home, helping Chloe when she returned from food shopping.

Food shopping. Oh crud. She'd left all the groceries on Todd's counter. Well, she'd put the cold stuff away. He wouldn't have a problem—

Forget it.

Right. She had no business worrying about him anymore.

"Jolie," Chloe called out from the kitchen, "you want to warm up one of those dinner trays Bella sent? We're going to have one band of hungry workers once we get all this stuff put away."

"Sure," Jolie answered. Typical of Chloe. If she didn't acknowledge the pain it'd go away.

Typical of all of them who'd dealt with shattered dreams on a daily basis. And it usually worked.

But not now. Because she was responsible for this pain. If only she'd thrown the damned thing away!

That said, she pulled herself off the sofa, rummaged through her bag for the notebook, and tossed it into the kitchen trashcan. The "Best" phase of her life was now over. Time to move on.

As she'd done a hundred times before.

***

Jonathan paced inside Raphael's office, the twitch alive and not so well and thrumming on the side of his head. Oh dear, oh dear, oh dear. He'd only been trying to help, but he'd ended up messing up worse than when he'd burned down Jolie's apartment.

If only he'd let Jolie put the notebook away, but he'd known the ending wasn't right.

If only he hadn't kept pretending to nap to get Todd to leave the room. Who would have thought Todd would've tried to make friends with a "pitchfork wielding" cat?

If only he hadn't knocked the manuscript when he'd leapt from the bed.

If only… if only… It seemed his career was one big series of "if only"s. And now Todd and Jolie were both alone and hurting because of him. Maybe he should ask for a transfer to the paperwork section of Heaven. He couldn't screw that up.

"So, Jonathan, Angela tells me there's a problem?" Raphael entered the room so silently Jonathan hadn't had time to compose himself.

But he really needed the archangel's guidance now. It didn't matter how this looked on his personal record; he had to make this right for Jolie and Todd.

He removed his felt hat, clutching it to his chest. "Yes, sir. I, er, I ruined it for them, sir."

"You?" Raphael took a seat by the window and motioned for Jonathan to do the same. "How could you do that? The only way would be with malice in your heart. Do you have that for them, Jonathan?"

"Oh, no, sir. Not at all. Why, I love all my Charges."

"Then there is no problem, Jonathan, only obstacles."

"But it's a big obstacle, sir. You see, I—"

"No, Jonathan." Raphael held up his hand. "No obstacle is too big for a Guardian. You have the goodness of the Spirit in you. You'll find some way to make it right."

"But how, sir? I've split them apart. I've ruined their trust in each other."

"Jonathan, no one can ruin another's trust in someone else. The doubt had to have already been there. What you must do is foster their belief in each other."

"But how, sir?"

Raphael smiled and Jonathan felt the stress leave him. Raphael was always so good about instilling faith. Why, if he were everyone's Guardian, there'd be no war in the mortal world. But such a job was too great a challenge even for an archangel.

"Trust your instincts, Jonathan. You brought them together once, I know you can do it again. Go back to the basics. Use what you know about them to help them see the real person in each other."

"The real person in each other?"

"Yes. Who they fell in love with. What they saw in that other person that fulfilled a need in them. Show them again what they've already seen and let their hearts guide them. That's all any Guardian can do, Jonathan. We don't make things happen. We facilitate them."

Raphael rose, his magnificent presence such a comfort to an insecure initiate-in-training. "Come, Jonathan. I know you can bring them together once more."

Jonathan stood. If the archangel believed in him then he'd be foolish to doubt his capabilities. If Raphael thought Jonathan could fix it, then he could.

He just had to figure out how.

"Thank you, sir, for your faith in me." He settled his hat upon his head and straightened his shoulders. "I'll make it right, sir."

Raphael patted him on the back, leading him to the office door. "Of course you will, Jonathan. I never had any doubt."

***

Raphael couldn't keep the smile from his face after Jonathan left. The man was coming along well; he just needed some confidence.

Raphael waved his hand over his desk and Todd and Jolie's file appeared. Thumbing through the notes, he saw the notation about "Boots" scrambling from the bed, accidentally knocking Jolie's notebook to the floor.

He read Todd's reaction to seeing his own words there.

Well, yes, Jonathan did have his work ahead of him, but the experience would be worth it in the end. It wasn't often they had such hurting people to heal—two on one assignment, no less—but when Jonathan pulled this off, he'd feel so much better about himself.

Raphael tucked the notes back into the file and whisked them to the file room with another wave of his hand. He needed to consult with Angela for any upcoming cases to see which one would best showcase Jonathan's talents and his soon-to-emerge self-confidence when he was finished with this assignment.

Chapter Thirty-Six

He couldn't believe he'd been so gullible. So damned stupid. Todd stared out the kitchen window toward the garage attic. Two weeks. Two fucking weeks since his life had gone to hell. *Again*. Only this time it'd been his own fault.

He'd *known* not to get involved with anyone. He'd known it. People didn't get a second chance like that. Not in the same lifetime. He'd gotten greedy and let it blind him to the truth. But he'd been so certain she'd been for real.

He gripped the edge of the countertop. She was good. Too fucking good. Had strung him along, even giving him good sex in the deal.

He swiped a hand over his face. That was an extra-special shitty part. The sex had been great. The sad part was, he'd thought it'd been making love, not sex. And now her story cheapened it. Cheapened him, what he'd felt.

God, could he ever trust anyone again?

Even Jasmine had turned on him. She'd been hiring the chefs, when all along, he'd thought it'd been Mike. She'd been hiring them to *fix him up* with them! As if he was some basket-case who needed a woman to make him whole. The utter gall of the woman still stung.

Well he was done with it. With everything.

Including painting. He'd tried to after he'd kicked Jolie out. Tried having the neighbor sit for him, Barbara, anyone but Jolie, but he couldn't do it.

Even that was gone for him now. She'd taken it along with everything else.

The back of his eyes burned. No, damn it! He'd had enough pain. Todd pounded the granite countertop. Who cared if he broke his hand? Wasn't like he'd need it anymore now that he wouldn't—couldn't—paint.

He raised his fist again, almost relishing the pain, when he heard the doorbell. Now what?

Too bad Earl and Jasmine weren't here anymore to run interference, but he had asked them to leave. Jasmine's heartfelt apology hadn't changed anything. She'd betrayed him and his trust. She, of all people, had known how he'd felt about Trista. How could she have thought just anyone could replace her?

The doorbell rang again and Todd walked into the foyer. A quick word from him and whatever Girl Scout or newspaper salesman on the other side would get the picture.

He yanked open the door.

"Hello, my boy."

The bookstore guy. What was his name again?

"Jonathan Griff. With the Holbein book?"

"Right. The book. I'll get it." He left the door open, took two steps, then turned around. "Actually, it's in my studio. Why don't you meet me there? Around the drive to the back."

Mr. Griff tipped his hat. "Sounds good."

Now he had to go into that studio. The one with half a dozen portraits of Jolie in various stages of completion. With Jolie in various states of undress. He should've stacked them all in a corner, or, better yet, burned them.

Todd's running shoe caught on the tile grout and he almost stumbled. He couldn't burn them. Who was he kidding?

Jolie might have disillusioned him—no *might* about it, actually—but she'd been the perfect model. Her portrait had flowed from his fingers as if he'd been tracing her—

He met Mr. Griff in the driveway. "If you wait here, I'll bring it down."

"Oh, that's all right. The exercise will be good for me." Mr. Griff plodded along after him up the steps.

Todd unlocked the room, keeping his eyes high on the walls, skirting the stacks of other canvases he'd tried and failed to paint. The ones of Jolie were lining the far wall. The Holbein book was back by the sofa. The sofa where they'd—

"What a lovely picture," Mr. Griff said.

Todd didn't have to look back to know where Mr. Griff was standing. The one finished portrait of Jolie was fourth down the line.

"I see you have a lot more of them."

Todd grabbed the book from beneath a paint-spattered drop cloth.

The paint-spattered drop cloth.

Which he then kicked beneath the sofa.

"Here you go, Mr. Griff. Thank you."

Mr. Griff's bushy white eyebrows furrowed as he took it. "Did you find it helpful?"

Helpful? Todd snorted. Depended on what you called helpful.

"It was… interesting." Todd headed back to the door. He didn't want to spend one more minute here than was necessary.

"Eh, my boy? Todd?"

Todd turned around. Mr. Griff hadn't moved from his spot.

"Yes?"

"These paintings—"

"Are going into a dumpster."

"That'd be a shame. Pretty drastic, too, especially since St. Gabriel's is having their auction. One of your pictures could fetch a nice sum for the church and its families. They did in the past, I remember."

"I know, Mr. Griff, but these aren't finished. The auction's too close, and, frankly, I'm not inclined to finish these. Nor paint any others."

"Well, like I said, it's a shame." Mr. Griff walked down the line of sketches and Todd bit back a groan. The man wasn't going to let it rest.

When he got to the last, Mr. Griff turned around, those bushy eyebrows now raised. "Seems to me, it wouldn't be much work to get a few more ready for the auction. The church could use the money, and so could the kids. They have so little as it is."

Just like Jolie had had.

Yeah, well now she'd have a hell of a lot once she sold her book. *Cookbook.* Hell. He was an idiot.

"I'll think about it."

"Wonderful! And here—" Mr. Griff held something out with the auction flyer. "Promise me you'll take a look at this. You might find it very interesting."

"Fine, Mr. Griff." Anything to get the man out of here so *he* could get out of here. And on with the rest of his life.

Alone.

Again.

***

Four and a half weeks after her life as she knew it (and wanted it to be) collapsed, Hark *The Herald Angels Sing* greeted Jolie as she opened the stained-glass door to the *uber*-plush office of Domestic Gods & Goddesses. She'd been helping out at Bella's while Bruno was recuperating, but he was going to be back and she was now on a mission to get her degree done in record time, so it was time to become employed again.

But not, God willing, for very long. Once she got her degree, she was going full steam ahead with her pastry shop. No more of this chef-for-hire business. No more hoping to earn her way into someone's life by providing meals for them. No more being on the outside looking in.

It was time for her to begin her life on her terms, no questions asked. And hopefully there wouldn't be any questions asked.

Unless Todd had reported her? That'd been merely *one* of the reasons it'd taken her four and half weeks to show back up here.

Jolie straightened her shoulders. Time to face the music—Christmas carols notwithstanding—and take charge of her life.

"Yes, dear?" The little old lady—honestly, bluish tinge to the white hair, stooped and frail, wrinkles to rival a Shar Pei's—greeted her from behind a polished cherry desk. The cream, satin-striped walls around them screamed Upper Crust, as did the Tiffany lighting and the bay window large enough to drive a truck through, with its draped golden window treatments and bird-luring crystal-clearness.

"Hi. I'm Jolie Gardener. I finished my last assignment and am looking for another one."

"Oh. Well, yes, I mean, no, I mean… Oh, dear." The lady—Angela, Jolie remembered—rose from her chair, hands trembling as she pushed it under the desk. "Just a moment, please."

Angela patted the little bun on the back of her head, adjusted her lavender sweater over her shoulders and the slight hump on her back, then scurried toward an office in her orthotics, glancing back once before disappearing inside the room.

What on earth was going on? Had Todd actually told them what had happened? After all his privacy issues, he'd aired this dirty laundry? Was there going to be a lawsuit?

Oh, no. She hadn't thought about that. Jolie tugged on the hem of the white blouse she'd paired with a functional gray skirt and matching pumps. What if he was suing her and she had to pay back all the money? And what if the agency didn't want to send her on any more assignments? She'd never get tuition money then.

Jolie ran her fingers over her hair, slicking the strands back to the clasp at the nape of her neck. Maybe she should find another line of work. One where no one would know about the book or sleeping with the client or whatever other rules she'd broken with this assignment. God, when she screwed up, she really screwed up. Something she'd obviously inherited from her mother.

She was considering cutting her losses and leaving when the door on the right clicked and, to the accompaniment of soft *Muzak*—harp it sounded like—a gray orthotic emerged, followed closely thereafter by the rest of Angela. No surprise there. What *was* a surprise was the guy who followed her.

First off, he was huge. Arms-that'd-do-a-lumberjack-proud huge. Blond and built like Atlas. Or Hercules. She never could keep all those Greek myths straight, but whichever celestial being was the big, muscular guy, this one was him personified, down to the most beautiful face a man had ever sported this side of pretty. Was he the inspiration for the "Gods" part of the agency's name?

Of course there was the smile to match, two slashes of dimples on each side, and blue eyes the color of heaven on a spring day. Boy, if someone stuck him on the cover of a romance novel, he could've sold more books than Fabio ever did.

But she wasn't here to notice the hotness factor of the man who employed her. She'd tried that once and it hadn't worked out so well.

Second, she hadn't had a meeting with the manager when she'd taken the assignment with Todd, so why was she meeting him now?

"Hello." A mammoth hand clasped hers, enveloping it like a warm blanket. "Ms. Gardener, is it?"

"Yes. Jolie Gardener."

"Please, have a seat." He pulled out a chair for her at the conference table in front of the bay window.

"Thanks, uh, Mr… ?"

"Please call me Raphael." He smiled and steepled his hands in front of him after taking the seat next to her, his linen pants brushing her bare calf like a feather. "So, what can I help you with?"

That didn't sound accusatory. Maybe this was SOP when finishing an assignment. "I'm here for a new job. My last one is finished."

"Is it? Which assignment was that?"

"Um, Todd Best." Just saying his name was torture.

"Angela, can you bring me the file, please?"

Angela pulled a file folder from the cherry credenza and handed it to him. Raphael scanned a few of the pages while Jolie tried not to glance over the top.

Raphael glanced up. "We have no record from the client saying you've completed the job."

So Todd hadn't reported what happened. "But I did. The job's finished. He doesn't need a personal chef."

Raphael closed the file and handed it back to Angela. He shook his head. "I'm sorry, but we can't place you on another assignment until the client has signed off that he no longer needs you."

Some of her sinking-heart feeling must have shown on her face because he studied her a minute longer before glancing back at Angela. "The form, please, Angela?"

He took the form, then slid it across the table. "Really, it's not terrible. Simply have the client sign this, stating that he no longer needs you, and we'll close the file. It should set you back only a day or two, no longer. Then we can have you off on a new adventure just like that. Piece of cake." He snapped his fingers.

She wanted to tell him it wasn't going to be that easy. First she had to find the courage to see Todd, then humble herself to ask him to sign the paper, and then pull her shattered psyche back together. Yeah. Right. Piece of cake.

She tried one last plea. "Can't you make an exception just this once? Please? The man doesn't need anyone to cook for him, most especially not me."

Raphael shook his head. "I'm sorry, but we can't. Those are the rules."

"Please? Sometimes rules are meant to be broken. It's not like they're etched in stone, right?"

"Actually, yes, some of them are." He coughed. "I'm sorry, Jolie, but until we get that form signed by Mr. Best, we are unable to place you anywhere else."

She mumbled a "Thank you," dragged the form off the table, and left, all the while contemplating how to accomplish the feat with minimal re-opening of the scar tissue around her heart.

She still hadn't figured it out when she reached Melanie, who, like Scarlett's faithful friend, was back up and running, albeit with some heavy-duty damage to her bank account. Which meant she had no choice. It was either Todd or poverty. Or going through another round of background/reference-check-time-suck with another agency and hoping they didn't contact this one for references.

She was still considering poverty.

A large, yellow flyer flapped beneath Mel's windshield wiper. Jolie hated those things. *Lose ninety pounds in ninety days*, or *Earn fifteen hundred bucks in fifteen minutes*. Yeah, right. If life were that easy, everyone would be thin, rich, and Paris Hilton. Talk about a shame.

But this flyer, however, wasn't about any of that stuff. It was—
Oh.

An art-show benefit for St. Gabriel's Church and the main contributor was going to be—

Todd Best.

Todd was doing a show.

In public. Tomorrow night.

She glanced between the two pieces of paper in her hands. One Todd needed to sign and the other showed her where he was going to be—in public so there didn't need to be any gut-wrenching explanations or confrontations. Just a simple, "Hello, Todd, would you mind signing this so I can get on with my life as you obviously have with yours?" That shouldn't be too difficult, right?

One could hope.

Though she hadn't really been having such great luck in the hope department lately.

Or ever.

***

"I'm not going." Jolie held the dress against her chest and studied her image in the mirror.

Yes, you are.

Great. Naughty Girl was back from vacation.

You definitely should go.

Jolie checked out the dress again. Conservative black. Simple. *Safe.*

"Go away." The dress had been a post-Todd-days pick-me-up. She'd just never thought she'd wear it to see him.

Todd.

Oh, God. She had to go.

That's my girl.

Jolie tried to ignore Naughty Girl, because, really, this had nothing to do with Naughty Girl and everything to do with Jolie and who she was. Who she'd always wanted to be.

From the moment she was old enough to realize her mother was calling the shots and they were all near-misses, she'd known she'd wanted to make her own decisions, wanted the chance to forge her own trail through life.

Well, she'd had that chance and look where it'd gotten her. She hadn't made the best (no pun intended, but somehow it fit) decision with the manuscript. Yeah, her mom's loser genes had shone through, but she couldn't blame everything on her mother. She'd known what it'd do to him if he ever found out, even if the story wasn't supposed to be for anyone but her.

Damn it! He needed to know that. Then, if he still opted out of what they'd had, it was on him. But she wasn't going to try to sell that manuscript and he had to know that. She needed to explain it to him.

She'd *make* him let her explain it to him.

Just like those Regency heroines, it was time for her to take her fate into her own two hands.

And make that lemonade she was so fond of.

Chapter Thirty-Seven

Normally, Jolie wasn't a stand-in-line kinda girl. She had too many other things to do than wait for things when they'd be on eBay soon enough. But for Todd, for him, she would stand in line.

Many people had come out to see Todd's work. She would have hoped the buzz in line would have been for St. Gabe's, but it was all about him. A few young ladies even had the audacity to question if he had a new woman in his life.

If only.

Finally, it was her turn to enter the church hall. White fabric hung from the ceiling—perfect backdrops to showcase Todd's use of vibrant colors. It was one of the things he'd been known for. If the colors on his palette—and then on her and the drop cloth—were anything to go by, he was still using them.

She caught snippets as she wound her way through the maze of tables set up to take donations. She'd write a check later because she was too close and too curious to stop.

Simply beautiful, elegant and winsome, great depth, and *elemental* were the descriptors being bandied about. He'd probably had a slew of models traipsing through his studio to earn those kinds of accolades. Though, really, he could've painted a sack of potatoes and made it look elegant and winsome.

Or grapes. Sour ones.

Someone offered her a glass of champagne and she took it, needing the fortification with the paper from Domestic Gods & Goddesses burning a hole in her black clutch—except it brought to mind the bottle she'd left with the groceries that last day.

She set the glass down.

"Have you seen him yet, Marsha?" One of society's matrons giggled in a girlish stage-whisper to her equally matron-ish friend.

"No, Babette, I haven't. There's quite a crush around him. And who can blame all those young women? The man has returned to the land of the living looking vibrantly alive and well. If I were thirty years younger I'd be in that pack of she-wolves myself."

Words Jolie did not need to hear.

Finally the corridor opened into the hall. Canvases hung in front of the white fabric, some on easels sprinkled throughout the crowd. He must've been painting non-stop since she'd last seen him. There had to be more than a dozen, each with a group of people ringing it.

The throng in the center of the hall told her all she needed to know. Todd was holding court center stage. Her heart sped up and she had to catch her breath.

He was here. She was here. Oh, lord.

She couldn't face him. Not yet. She patted her upswept hair. Maybe she'd coast near the pictures and see who, or rather, *what* he painted, then work her way in from the edges to talk to him. Build her nerve up.

And to plan what she was going to say. "Hi Todd, I love you and never meant to hurt you" was kind of a big left hook to hit someone with.

A pianist tickled the ivories in the corner; champagne flutes clinked amid the little tinkling of artificial laughter as someone said something so *witty and droll* (insert heavy English accent.) All very *chi-chi* and hip. Upper Crust all the way.

"So vulnerable," one lady murmured as she sipped her champagne, turning from the closest picture. "Quite lovely, really," her date added.

Jolie stood on her tiptoes to see over everyone's head. Nothing but frame.

"A wealth of feeling."

"Better than he was before."

"Who is his model?"

Well, the guy was back with a buzz. He was going to have a hard time keeping Mike off his case if the crowd's reaction was anything to go by.

Jolie had no luck whatsoever getting close to the picture and the one little sip of champagne she'd had was bubbling in her stomach, making the butterflies there a little tipsy. She needed to get this over with. She'd catch the portraits on her way out.

She wormed her way into the groupies around Todd, her knees threatening to go on strike when she heard his chuckle. God, she'd forgotten how it vibrated through every nerve she possessed, lodging directly in the middle of her heart.

She reached into her clutch with shaky fingers and pulled out the crinkled Domestic Gods & Goddesses form, needing the tangible reminder of why she was putting herself through this pleasure/pain.

"The model's lovely, Best," an older man said with a whiskey-deepened voice. "Anyone I might know?"

"Now Jefferson, that's part of the mystique. You know I never explain the nuances to my work."

Except to her, but Jolie didn't say it.

"She's not real," a woman by her elbow said. "That's why, right, Todd? She's your ideal woman, the one you're searching for?"

Way to be sensitive, lady.

There was a curt silence. Jolie was hoping Ms. Foot-In-Mouth recognized her enormous *faux pas*.

"I could tell you, Margaret, but then I'd have to kill you." Chuckles all around saved Todd's heartache from becoming public and Margaret's gaffe from dampening the mood. "But yes, she's real."

"So tell us, Todd." That female voice was laced with way too many innuendos and husky come-ons than Jolie cared to count. "How do you capture that feeling? It's intangible, yet you make her vulnerability a physical presence in the painting."

Honestly, it sounded like she was sliding her phone number into his pocket as she spoke.

"Unfortunately, Buffy, I can't answer that."

Oh puh-leaze. The name sooooo fit Miss Come-On.

"I have no idea how I do it. One minute I'm trying to capture something about the subject, and the next, it's there. I've simply got it."

Why did this conversation sound familiar?

Jolie had no time to consider this as, all of a sudden, the crowd shifted and she was there, face to face with Todd.

He was dressed head-to-toe in black, and, oh how it made his green eyes shine like beacons from his face, calling her in. He'd lost some of his tan, probably from painting like a fiend to get these ready, but those shoulders were still as broad as ever and his hair had finally had a date with a pair of scissors. She was rather partial to the earlier "do," though.

Everyone else was carrying on their conversations as if nothing out of the ordinary had happened, but Jolie, she felt like she was Alice down the proverbial rabbit hole.

"Jolie." Apparently Todd felt the same way. He took a step back, blocking the picture near him.

"Uh, hi, Todd." She started The Big Apology, then was jostled by some overweight, over-champagned, be-ringed, art connoisseur wannabe. Todd reached out to catch her elbow, stepping away from the canvas.

Oh.

My.

God.

It was her.

She was the woman in the portrait.

"Jolie."

He was talking to her, but she couldn't pull her gaze from the painting. There was a strange buzzing in her head as it registered that it was *her* back to the artist, *her* long dark tendrils of hair clinging damply to her spine, the swell of *her* hip peeking out from a white cloth covered in different colored slashes of paint, the curve of *her* breast visible beneath her arm. A swath of hair covered her face, but she'd recognize the tip of her nose anywhere. Pink rose petals covered her fingers.

He'd painted her and now he was showing that painting to everyone.

Just as he'd said he wouldn't do.

Just as he'd *promised* he wouldn't do.

"Jolie," he whispered in her ear urgently as, suddenly, she was next to Todd and he had a vice grip on her wrist. "I can explain."

Nothing. Not a single word escaped. Could be because she couldn't breathe. She shook her head and pulled her hand to her mouth—the hand holding the form. It slashed her cheek and she welcomed the pain. It cut through the haze, making her realize she had to get out of there fast.

"Jolie, please. You've got to—"

"No!" Luckily, her breath was still AWOL or she was pretty sure she would've screamed it.

As it was, her voice came out raspy and stage-whisper-y. "Here." She thrust the DG&G form at him and when he reached out to take it, she yanked her wrist back, turned, and pushed through the crowd.

She heard one "Jolie!" before she broke free.

Chapter Thirty-Eight

She ran. Again.

Out the opposite end of the exhibition hall and through a set of dark wood double doors, yanking on the old ornate brass handles with all her strength.

How could he have done that? How could he have put her out there for everyone to see?

The door closed behind her with a soft *whoosh* and she found herself in a moonlit courtyard ringed by a wrought-iron fence dressed in tiny white lights. A fountain gurgled to her left, an ornamental bamboo garden behind it. Two stone benches curved in front of the stone basin where a cherub poured fountain water. A café set of wrought-iron table and chairs filled the far side, another bench to her right. Across the courtyard, a set of stained glass doors led into St. Gabriel's Church and next to it, a wall of ivy, honeysuckle and climbing roses, also draped in tiny lights. The gate was just visible beneath years' worth of growth.

She headed that way, wanting the quickest way out. Of so many things.

She was almost there when she realized what she was doing. Again.

Running. Hiding. Pretending it would go away.

It wouldn't. And therefore, she couldn't. If she didn't face him now, end this, she'd always be the one who ducked and ran. The one who'd be asking what-if questions for the rest of her life. She couldn't do that anymore.

She was in charge of her life. Her. Not a social worker, not Mommie Dearest, not Naughty Girl, and most certainly not Todd Best.

She'd wanted him to be *in* her life, not *in charge* of it and he owed her an explanation every bit as much as she owed him.

She squared her shoulders and turned around, reaching for the back of one of the chairs as the heel of her new kicky yellow pump got stuck in a groove between the terra cotta tiles.

The door she'd come through slammed outward.

"Thank God. You're still here." Todd's hair was mussed, those laugh lines at his eyes were decidedly frowning, and he pulled a big, paper-covered something in front of his heaving chest.

"Yes, I'm still here."

"Give me a chance to explain, Jolie."

"Like you gave me?" Sorry Todd. She might still love him, but she loved herself, too. And she'd never be heart-whole if she didn't stand up for herself.

His eyes closed for a second, then opened, all emerald and pained.

It hurt her to intentionally hurt him. Almost as much as he'd hurt her. "I'm sorry. I guess that was a low blow."

He leaned the object against one of the curved benches. "No, it wasn't. It was well-deserved, actually." He straightened, shoving his hands into his pants pockets. "Can we talk?"

There were two arguments there. She could A) say No and that'd be the end of anything—pain, hope, love, et cetera—or B) say Yes and see what happened.

Was there really any question?

She nodded and he swept a hand toward the bench and sat at one end.

Now, common sense would dictate she sit as far away from him as possible in, say, Nova Scotia, but nope, not her. She chose the other end of his bench.

She felt his gaze on her, yet hers was anywhere but on him. The *fleur-de-lis* top of the fence, the prism of color dancing through the cascading water, a cricket peeking out from the bamboo as it serenaded them—anywhere.

Unfortunately though, she'd gotten rather adept at her peripheral vision honing in on Todd while he'd painted her, so she saw every fidget and pant-leg-brushing he was doing.

"Jolie, I want to explain."

As much as she wanted him to, now that the moment was here, her new bravado faded. What if it was just another relationship blown in her life? Again. Did she really want to take that chance? *What-ifs* were nice because she didn't have to face the reality of a situation. *What-ifs* allowed the possibility to live on. The hope.

"You know what, Todd? It's not necessary. I get it."

"I don't think you do, Jolie. I want you to understand why."

She walked over to the stained-glass doors. The image beyond was distorted, but she saw a soft light shining somewhere inside. "Really, it's okay. I get it. It's a charity benefit and you had all of those paintings just hanging around, reminding you of the liar you lived with. I'd get rid of them, too."

She turned, plastering some kind of a smile on her face as the cricket quieted down. She was going for a light-and-breezy, no-hard-feelings type of thing. "Don't worry about it. I was surprised at first, but it makes sense." Moonlight shone on his face and she turned back because she couldn't keep up the pretense when those eyes that had burned into hers while they'd made love were burning still. "I'm over it. No big deal. I hope the church makes a lot of money from them."

If she'd actually been looking in the door's reflection as she was pretending to, she would've seen him approach. As it was, she jumped when she heard him behind her and looked up to see his eyes in the amber piece of glass.

"Don't you ever stop being flippant? How can you just rattle off these little quips, Jolie? Don't you feel anything?"

She spun around before better judgment kicked in. "*Feel* anything? I don't *feel*? Are you out of your mind?" She put up her hand to ward him off. "I've always felt everything. Every little slight that's ever come my way, every lonely night, every agony of a skinned knee with no one there to kiss it to make it better. Of course I feel. I am human, you know. But I can't let it get to me. I'd be a mass of quivering flesh wrapped around a bruised and battered heart and I'd never get anywhere."

She choked on the tears she refused to let fall. "And, yeah, I feel a lot about tonight. I have so much damn feeling it's threatening to strangle me. But I've got to survive somehow. So don't stand there and ask me if I feel anything, because let me tell you, mister, I feel everything so much it could overwhelm me. And if I let it, I might never recover."

They stared at each other, and, Oh God, her heart felt like it was stopping. Something was squeezing her chest and she couldn't breathe.

She had to get away from him. Put some distance. Gain some clarity.

She took a step around him back the way they'd come, but he grabbed hold of her arms and hauled her up against him. His mouth covered hers and, suddenly, she was breathing in the scent of him and she knew she was going to live.

Oh God, she shouldn't do this, she shouldn't, but she just couldn't seem to help herself. She slipped her arms around his waist and hung on, literally for dear life, drowning in her own insecurities and fears and he was the one thing holding her afloat and safe.

And then he was holding her, all of her. She was swept up in his arms and he carried her back to the bench and somehow they were there together.

"God, Jolie, I couldn't believe it when I saw you in there. I wanted to tell you beforehand, but I was finishing the pictures, framing them, arranging the details, and time got away from me. I was going to come see you yesterday, tell you, invite you, but I didn't know where to find you. I even called Chloe but she wouldn't tell me where you were."

Because Chloe knew exactly what disenchantment did to a person. Jolie loved her friend for trying to protect her. "But you promised, Todd."

His hand was shaky as he swept her hair from her face. The cricket serenade started again, softly this time, as if the moment was being orchestrated. "I know I did. And I regret that more than anything. I regret not discussing it with you."

She shook her head. "You knew how I'd feel."

He cocked his head. "Did I? You were the one who thought it'd be neat to be famous, to have everyone know who you are."

"No. You don't get to blame me."

"You're right. I don't. And I'm not. But you've got to believe me. I didn't do this to hurt you."

She looked into his green eyes, which were open and honest and blazing. He meant what he said. It was who he was; every word was the truth.

Which was what he deserved as well.

"And I didn't want to hurt you either, Todd, which is why I wasn't going to get that book published."

His eyebrow lifted. "Really."

"Yes, really."

His eyebrow didn't settle back into place.

"Fine. Don't believe me." She squirmed, but he refused to let go.

"No way. You're not walking away from me until we get this settled, Jolie."

She stopped squirming.

She glared, but she stopped trying to get free. Running wasn't going to solve anything. Not talking wouldn't either. "Fine."

His grip loosened. "So, if you had no intention of publishing the book, why did you? To spite me? To get your money's worth after you left?"

"What are you talking about? I didn't publish the book."

"Really."

"We've been through this."

"Then what—" he pulled something from his back pocket—"is this?"

He handed her a thin paperback bearing the picture of a man with his arms around a woman on the cover. A golden haired man and a long-haired brunette. The title was *The Best Man*. The author was—

Her.

Her mouth dropped and she pushed to a sitting position next to him on the bench. Sure enough, the copyright page listed Jolie Gardener as the author.

She thumbed to the first page and wanted to die as she recognized every single word in the opening paragraph. Annie and Tom.

She flipped through more of the pages and scenes jumped out at her. Scenes she'd invented, wrote. There was Tom/Todd's speech about a rose about to bloom, his "she never gave up on me," and that big ol' gnarled apple tree with the tree fort and rope swing.

She flipped the book over to read the blurb on the back, but then she opened it back again to that scene with the rope swing.

She'd never added that last part. She'd thrown the manuscript out without moving Annie and Tom off the bow of the boat.

"I don't understand this." She looked at him.

"That's not your story?"

"Well, yes, I guess it is, but I didn't do this, Todd."

His eyebrow went sky-high.

"Really, Todd. I didn't. I threw the manuscript in the trash that afternoon after I left."

"So you're saying a garbage collector went through the trash, found your manuscript, submitted it to a publisher, listed you as the author, and let you get the credit and royalty payments?"

"That's what must have happened because I haven't seen this since then. Honest." It was as if she were in the Twilight Zone. "And, the ending is different."

"That's not the one you wrote?"

"No, and here's something even more bizarre. This is the ending I was *going to* write. When I came up to my room and found you reading it, I was on my way to change the ending to this. But I never did." She flipped a few more pages and shook her head. "I can't figure this out."

"So if what you're saying is true—"

"It is."

"Then how did it happen?"

"I have no idea." She touched the cover. Totally surreal. Incredibly so. "Where'd you get it?"

"Your friend, Mr. Griff, gave it to me when I returned the Holbein book."

"*Mr. Griff* gave you this?"

"Yes. Why?"

She tapped the spine against her mouth. Something wasn't right. "I'm not sure, but I promise you I did not do this. I knew how you'd feel." She set the book on the bench beside her, because, really, the physical book wasn't what was important. "I knew, Todd, before I ever wrote that resolution between Annie and Tom. I knew you'd hate for me to use you as the model, but I had to finish the story."

"But why, Jolie? Why did you use *me*? Us?" His eyes were full of hurt and she couldn't let him think she did it out of spite.

"Because of how much in love you and Trista were. I wanted that kind of love in my life."

A waft of honeysuckle drifted past them and his eyes widened. "But you didn't even know Trista and me then."

"That's where you're wrong, Todd. The newspapers were always writing about you. They wrote about your art shows and your company and your successes. And they wrote about what a lovely and loving couple you two were. Every time there was a mention of you, Trista's name was right there. And I just thought it was so wonderful how in love you two were. And when she died, my heart ached for you."

"So you found a way to hire on as my help and use my life for your story."

"It's not as sordid as it sounds." Again with the eyebrow. "Honestly, Todd. When I found out where I'd be working, who I'd be working for, the idea just kind of gelled. I'd been writing the story beforehand. You know how I like my happy endings." She actually got a smile with that. "But the story wasn't working. I didn't find it strange because my whole life was like that, but when I found out I'd be working for you, I thought, maybe I could get to know you, see what there was in you that made Trista love you and you love her back, and give that to my hero. That's all. I wasn't trying to exploit you at all. I… admire you."

He was mulling it over. And he was back to playing with the ends of her hair, so maybe he was losing some of his anger and hurt.

"I never meant to hurt you, Todd."

"I believe you."

He believed her.

"But it still doesn't explain the book," he added.

"I know. And I can't. I honestly have no idea how that happened. Maybe we should buy up the rest in Mr. Griff's store before anyone else sees it."

Todd shook his head. "He only had the one. I went in and checked after I saw what it was. After I'd read it."

He'd read it? "This just keeps getting weirder and weirder."

"I know. Kind of like my show tonight."

"Really? What's weird about it?"

"Mr. Griff was the one who mentioned the church benefit to me."

"What's odd about that?"

"When I called the lady at the church office, Angie someone, she seemed, I don't know, confused maybe, and had her boss call me back. I wondered at the time why she wouldn't know about it, if it was such a big deal, but then her boss was all over it, so that put an end to my questions. Plus, I was suddenly too busy to really concentrate on anything else."

"But why *those* pictures, Todd?"

He took a deep breath. "When I was passing your room that afternoon, I thought I'd heard someone talking. But it was just your cat having a daydream. I petted him to settle him down, but the damned thing ran from me and knocked your story off the shelf and onto the floor. When I picked it up, the words jumped out at me. Socked me right in the gut.

"After you left, I tried to paint someone else. Anyone. Jasmine sat for me, Earl, I paid the family next door, but I couldn't do it, Jolie. I couldn't get that something I had captured with you." He tucked a wayward strand of hair behind her ear and she tried to ignore the warm, melty feeling it stirred. "Then, Mr. Griff showed up and suggested I finish the pictures for the auction. I know I should have discussed it with you, but, honestly Jolie, I was still stung by your story. Then I read the whole thing—" he nodded to the mysterious novel—"and—"

"And you figured since I had gone ahead and done this, you could too." She sighed. "I can understand that. If I wanted my moment of fame, why not make it a big one and get back at me? I get it."

He lifted her chin. "No, you *don't* get it. That's not it at all. That makes me sound selfish and shallow, and I'd like to think I'm above all that." He put a finger over her lips when she started to speak. "No, I read that book and I thought about the title, *The Best Man*, and I saw the emotions in there, thought about you writing it, and then I thought about you, your life. I thought I'd known you, Jolie. Who you were, the person inside." He paused while his eyes searched hers. "The person who wouldn't intentionally hurt me.

"It took me more time than it should have to realize that. And with this benefit—a benefit for underprivileged and abused kids and homeless families, things you lived through, things that shaped you— I knew you'd want to help if you could. I had all these paintings of you taking up wall space—"

"You mean floor space."

"No, I mean wall space. I hung every one of them, Jolie, once I finished that book. All around my studio. Where I could see you all the time."

She had absolutely no comeback whatsoever to that.

"So, anyway, I had a bunch of completed pictures, a looming deadline and a cause near and dear to your heart. I honestly hoped to discuss it with you and get your agreement. I never doubted you'd approve."

"You're right about that."

He nodded. "I know. I know that about you. That's why I did the show, Jolie. Not to hurt you, but to help with a cause you care about. And I didn't show your face. Just like you'd asked."

Oh, the love she felt for him was flooding every cell of her body. He truly *got* her.

"Thank you," she whispered. "I really don't want that kind of fame."

"I know that, too. For the masses, you're just a nameless body on canvas. I want to keep what's between us, between us."

"What's between us?" She was holding her breath.

"You're parroting me again."

She bit her lip to stop the tears. He was teasing her. That had to be good.

"I have something for you," he whispered.

"You do?" What more could she possibly want than his belief in her?

He retrieved the paper-covered something, tore the wrapping, then stopped. "Jolie, this was never intended for the show. I started it that day… after the dinner at Bella's. Before the manuscript. I never hung it. No one's seen it but me."

She turned to fully face him, holding her breath. She'd never seen him this, well, nervous.

He tore the rest of the paper away and turned it around.

It was her. All of her.

She was on her side on that sofa, propped against pillows, with the drop cloth draped over her thighs. Her hair was mussed, falling over her breasts. Her lips were just a bit swollen as if she'd bitten them—or someone had been kissing them moments before. Her bottom leg was bent slightly, the upper one raised as if in invitation to discover what was beneath the cloth. And there was no doubt the artist already knew.

Everything she'd ever felt while they'd made love was there, in her eyes, looking out from the canvas. That *something* he'd wanted to capture.

This was a painting by a man who knew his subject in all her moods. And felt quite a bit for her.

Did she dare hope?

"Do you like it?" His soft voice wrapped around her like the silence of a moonlit courtyard.

She shook her head. "No. I don't."

The hope in his eyes faded and she couldn't let the teasing go on any longer.

"I love it, Todd." She touched his arm. "Almost as much as I love you."

"Thank you, God." He blew out a breath and set the painting aside, pulling her back into his arms.

She met him halfway, and then they were kissing each other as if they could make up for all the hurt and separation.

"I was so worried, Jolie," he said after, oh, ten minutes or so. "When you saw that picture, I thought I'd blown it. I hadn't had the chance to prepare you, and I knew you'd take it the wrong way. I would have."

It was her turn to raise her eyebrows.

"All right, I guess I did with your manuscript. I get it now, though the book thing does perplex me. Perhaps Mr. Griff will be able to shed some light on it." He linked his fingers with hers. "But it doesn't matter. We're together and that's what's important."

"Together."

"Forever."

"Forever?" Did he say the "F" word?

He pulled back. "You don't want forever? I thought you liked happily-ever-afters?"

"Is this one?" She was trying so hard not to get her hopes up in case she was reading too much into this.

He smiled. "Oh, yes, Jolie Gardener, this is one big happily-ever-after." He traced her cheekbones, then her lips, his eyes going all soft. "I love you. I want you in my life. Always." He slipped off the bench to one knee. "Will you, Jolie Gardener, marry me?"

Ohmygoshohmygoshohmygoshohmygosh—

"Yes!"

She threw her arms around his neck, her body into his, and she mauled the guy's lips as she almost crashed them to the terra cotta floor. He wanted to marry her! He loved her! They could have a family—

Oh boy. Now she was the one who pulled back.

"What?"

"Family," she squeaked.

"Mike and Barb already love you."

She shook her head as they resettled back on the bench. Good thing because Knees weren't able to stand yet. "No. Family. You and me."

"Ah," he smiled. "Yes, I want a family. Dozens of kids."

"Dozens?"

"Enough to have my own football team."

"I'm not sure that's physically possible for me, Todd."

"Well, then, we'll just have to adopt some, won't we?"

Honest to God, she loved this man. She honestly and truly loved him and she needed to crawl inside his skin and show him how much.

But not here. Obviously.

They needed to be in his house. Their house.

Their *home*.

He was right there with her as he stood, tugging on her fingers. "Come on, Jolie. Let's go home."

"But what about the benefit?" Not that she was complaining, but still… niceties and all.

"The pictures were sold the minute I unpacked them. My work here is done."

"Spoken like a true superhero." Their shared joke earned her another smile, then his eyes went all mossy green velvet.

She knew that look. And this was not the appropriate place. "Yes. Let's go home."

His smile reminded her of the one between Mike and Barbara. Between Bella and her husband. That "This is our world and we're the only two here" smile.

He picked up the painting as he intertwined their fingers.

"Where are you going to put that?" she asked.

"I thought since no one else will be sitting for me, I'd like to keep it in my studio." He kissed her fingers. "To be inspired. Okay with you?"

"You know," she said as they headed out the iron gate, dipping beneath shuttered honeysuckle flutes and traipsing through scattered rose petals, "I kind of like that idea."

"And I kind of like the idea of having a naked woman in my studio."

Yep, she tripped.

~~The End~~

The Beginning

M E M O R A N D U M

TO: Raphael, Archangel

RE: HEA, Case #TBJGB142156423360982019939.A8

As follow-up to reports A1-A7 concerning Charges, Todd Best and Jolie Gardener Best, I have the following updates:

1. Jolie Gardener Best has opened her own pastry shop, *Très Jolie Pâtisserie*, and continues to write romance novels. She has had fair reception from publishers and will continue onward to publication.

2. Todd and Jolie have three beautiful children—one for each bedroom in their home—and are in the process of adopting three more.

3. Jasmine and Earl Gray have moved in with them after Todd added an east wing to the house. The weekend the Grays went away was a bonanza for everyone: their son, Charles, and his wife are enjoying the set of triplets they added to the four children they already had. Not a spare inch of room for the grandparents, however. So Todd and Jolie forgave their well-intentioned interference and invited them to stay with them. Jolie has the family she's always wanted.

4. I have put off their questions regarding the book, *The Best Man*, that I submitted on Jolie's behalf, by saying the publisher, Beatus, Inc., went out of business.

5. Detective Phillips determined the fire that destroyed Jolie's apartment was indeed an accident. Maurice in 2B, a deaf man, had been making his wife an anniversary dinner and didn't hear the fire alarm when a stray white cat jumped in the window and knocked a ewer of oil that was sitting on the window ledge into a saucepan, and it kind of... exploded. A dishtowel went up, which then caught the curtains and the rest, well... It actually worked out rather well, despite the missing photographs and personal items. The insurance money came through, with a large fine for the landlord for having too many apartments in a building that wasn't up to code. A developer took over and built brand-new, affordable, good-sized condos for the residents. There is talk, by the residents, of thanking the mysterious

white cat.

6. Speaking of cats, Jolie was upset to find Boots missing, so St. Francis created a replica for them. I think Jolie may be suspicious, but since she thought she was imagining things when I was Boots, the replacement hasn't raised any untoward questions. No one ever came forward from the Found posters.

7. And, last, but by no means least, my wing buds have begun to itch.

Respectfully submitted,
Jonathan Griff, Guardian

Thank you!

Thank you for reading *Beauty and The Best*. If you enjoyed this story, please help others find it by posting a review on Goodreads, Amazon, Apple Books, Barnes & Noble… wherever you bought it. Feel free to share a link, tweet about it, Facebook it… All efforts are greatly appreciated.

I love to hear from my readers so check me out online and feel free to friend me!

www.JudiFennell.com
https://www.facebook.com/JudiFennell.Author/
https://www.goodreads.com/series/list/2778890.Judi_Fennell.html
https://www.bookbub.com/authors/judi-fennell

Sign up for my newsletter at:
http://JudiFennell.com/newsletter-signup/

Keep on reading for Bella and Reese's story in *If The Shoe Fits…*

If the Shoe Fits
Heaven
JUDI FENNELL

Once upon a time...

a long time ago
in a land far, far away,
there lived a girl by the name of Cinderella.

This is not her story.

This is the story of Lucinda Isabella Casteleoni,
who, like her namesake,
has a wicked stepmother, two tacky stepsisters,
and countless hours of hard work to (not) look forward to.
But unlike that fairy tale princess,
Bella's Prince Charming is nowhere to be found.

Until a little old man with sparkling green eyes
opens a shoe store down the street.

Then the magic begins...

And it begins…

Where was a fairy godmother when she needed one?

Bella Casteleoni gripped the railing on the steps outside the law office. Her stepmother was *not* going to send her little sister to boarding school if Bella had anything to say about it. Unfortunately however, the language she needed to speak was Cash since a custody battle required lots of it. And while Bella had been saving for one, she hadn't counted on it happening just yet. But Madeleine's latest threats had upped the stakes.

That witch had been using Sophia—as well as the family business—as a pawn for years. And now the woman wasn't just threatening to sell off the family restaurant, but also to send the fourth-grader away merely because, in the six months since Dad's death, she'd found single parenthood counterproductive to the life she'd become accustomed to since marrying their father.

Bella would show her counterproductive…

She picked up her pace, her pumps clicking on the stone steps. First thing tomorrow, she'd tell Giacomo and Guiseppe that the catering business she'd started on the side out of her family's restaurant was going to be more than just a *side* thanks to the discussion she'd just had with Uncle Vinny's lawyer. Without the resources she wouldn't be able to stop Madeleine from selling the business, but she could make sure she still had a business when it all shook out so she could still fight for custody.

She was going to have to ramp up the word-of-mouth campaign and set up sample tables at local events. Put out flyers. Build a website. Give referral discounts. Yes, she had a lot of ideas and she was going to do whatever it took to earn enough money to knock Madeleine's feet out from under her.

Like the dove that flew in her face did to her…

Bella missed the next step, stumbled down the last one, and found her skirt ripped up the middle when she landed butt-first on the pavement with one of her pumps flying off to God-knew-where.

Two seconds later, something—make that some*one*—ended up sprawled across her lap.

"*Ooomph!*"

A very large, very male someone.

Bella groaned as the big hunk of maleness hefted himself off her and got to his feet while she yanked the torn edges of her skirt together. Great. Add *mending* to her To-Do list. As if she needed more on it.

A hand appeared in front of her. "Here, I'm sorry. Let me help you up." The deep, husky voice resonated down her spine.

She looked up. Standing above her with broadly sculpted shoulders outlined against the afternoon sky, was one of the most gorgeous men she'd ever seen. Coffee-colored eyes, perfectly molded lips, sleek mahogany hair that showed just a hint of wave as it blew in the afternoon breeze, and those cheekbones. Good Lord. This guy could've been the model for Michelangelo's David, but with a much stronger jawline.

And clothing.

"Miss? Are you okay?"

"Um, yeah. Yes. I think I am." She looked around and spied her shoe on the next section of sidewalk. "Great," she muttered, taking the proffered hand.

"I said I was sorry."

At five-six, Bella wasn't exactly short, but he dwarfed her by a good eight inches. Tall, dark, and handsome. Like something from a fairy tale. Too bad she'd stopped believing in those ten years ago when a drunk driver had killed her mother and put Dad in a wheelchair and downward spiral of depression that had led to her and Sophia's current situation.

No. She couldn't go there. Fighting Madeleine was going to take every bit of strength she had. And some she didn't.

This guy looked to have some strength to spare.

She shook her head. Why drag someone else into her mess?

Speaking of mess… She brushed away a strand of blonde hair that had escaped the ponytail she'd scraped it into earlier. "I wasn't talking about you. My shoe." She nodded toward it. "Are you okay?"

"Yeah, thanks. Hang on, I'll get it for you." Tall, Dark, and Handsome crossed the three feet of concrete with the grace and speed of an athlete. Filled out those slacks pretty nicely, too.

Bella bit back a smile. Good to know Madeleine and her machinations hadn't sucked all the beauty from her world.

Then he rocked it with one hell of a sexy smile when he returned with her shoe.

Tall, Dark, and *Potent*.

Bella teetered on her one pump as she tried to put the other back on, the teetering having more to do with balancing on one thin heel than his potency. At least, that's what she told herself.

The hand he put on her waist to steady her, however, made her a liar.

"Here, let me," he said, slipping the shoe from her suddenly boneless fingers, then sinking to one knee and slipping it on her foot.

Charming, too. *Prince* Charming, maybe?

As his light blue dress shirt stretched across those strong shoulders and the unbuttoned collar gapped open to reveal a strong, corded neck, she took a deep breath. If only he really *were* Prince Charming...

She glanced heavenward with a silent plea, only to have to duck as the dove circled back around and nearly poked her in the eye with its wings as it headed toward one of the ornamental cherry trees lining the sidewalk.

Prince Charming stood and put his hands on his hips. "There. Shoe's in place. How 'bout everything else?"

"Everything else?"

His eyes skimmed her. "Yeah. Anything else broken? Missing?"

"Well, if you don't count the skirt, I guess I'm in good shape."

He quirked his eyebrows and she blushed at the double entendre she hadn't intended. Oh, God. He thought she was flirting with him.

She so wasn't. She didn't have time to flirt now, much less date, Prince Charming or not. Sophia's fifth grade year started in five months and Bella had to ensure that her sister stayed in that school. With all she needed to accomplish in such a short period of time, she'd be lucky to have time to sleep *alone*, never mind *with* anyone.

"I mean, yes, I'm fine. Thank you. Have a nice day." She spun on that heel, willing the stupid tingle his interest had sparked to go away, and headed toward her car.

"Hey, wait a minute." Prince Charming caught up to her and grabbed an arm. Awareness sizzled through her.

She took a deep breath and glanced over her shoulder. "Yes?"

"I'm Reese." His hand hadn't left her arm and his fingers were doing all sorts of wonderful twirly moves on her skin.

She tugged. She did *not* have time for this. Not now, not in the next five minutes, nor the next five years.

"And I'm late. Thank you for your assistance. Have a nice day." She gave him a slim smile and walked away. Another life, maybe.

"Hey, Cindabella!" called a nasal-y voice from behind her.

Drew. Bella missed a step, groaning while she tried to regain her balance. That stupid nickname. Her stepsisters found it funny. Bella did not.

But Drew would keep calling her until she turned around, so, resigning herself to three minutes of torture, Bella took another deep breath and turned around—

To find Prince Charming, er, Reese, with his arms folded, one shoe crossed over the other, and that mocking eyebrow almost touching his hair. "Cinda*bella*?"

"Don't ask."

He uncrossed everything. "On one condition."

"Huh?"

"I won't ask on one condition."

Drew was at the top of the courthouse steps and, even from there, the speculative gleam in her eyes was visible. Bella didn't have much time. "Fine. What's the condition?"

"Your name. Unless it really is Cindabella?"

She laughed in spite of herself. "No. It's Bella. Bella Casteleoni."

When he smiled she'd swear his eyes actually twinkled. "Now that wasn't so bad, was it?"

Darn, she didn't want to like him, but he was making it awfully hard not to. "I guess not."

"So, Bella—wait. Casteleoni? As in Casteleoni's Restaurant?"

"And Catering. Well, Bella's Catering." Might as well start the advertising now. She was going to need a lot of side jobs to fight Madeleine.

"Bella! Wait up!" Drew was a third of the way down the steps. "I need you to do something for me."

Of course she did. Both of her stepsisters took that stupid nickname to heart.

Bella looked between Drew and Reese. Even though she wasn't planning to get to know him, she didn't want him witnessing whatever ridiculous minutiae Drew was about to spew. And it was *always* ridiculous minutiae.

Reese glanced back at Drew, then nodded to the platinum Ferrari by the curb. "I could give you a ride somewhere."

Cool car, complete with convertible top and rearing stallion logo. Not one of those souped-up muscle-bound cars, but elegant, classy, and sexy as all get out. Just like him.

Which was reason enough to stay away. She needed to keep all her focus on the battle with Madeleine. "Thank you, but I can handle it, er, her."

"You're sure?"

They both looked at Drew who was now extremely interested in Reese. Which meant Bella could show no interest whatsoever. "I am. Thank you again."

Reese took one last glance at Drew who had changed the angle of her descent to head right toward him. "Okay. Right." In half a dozen steps, Reese reached the car and jumped into the driver's seat. "Good luck. It looks like you'll need it. See you around." The engine gunned to life and he peeled into traffic with a wave just as Drew sauntered to her side.

"Who's the hunk?"

"Oh, just someone I bumped into."

"Hmmmm." Drew flipped her hair back in that annoying affectation she thought made her look sophisticated. It didn't. "Listen, I need you to cater a party this Saturday."

Of course she did. Five days' advance notice was nothing to Drew. Matter of fact, Bella should probably be grateful for that much.

"What kind of party?" She'd love to tell Drew to take a hike, but the fact of the matter was, she needed the money. Even Drew's. And there was a certain irony in her stepsister contributing to the fight against Madeleine.

"Jimmy's mom is having a dinner party and her caterer cut out on her. I told her you'd do it." Drew had learned social climbing at Madeleine's knee; Jimmy DeLeo's mom was not only one of the wealthiest women in town, but also on every social committee there was—*including* the Arts board Madeleine was desperately trying to finagle her way onto.

Hmmm, this might just help her beat Madeleine at her own game.

###

Books by Judi Fennell

ROYALLY SUNK SERIES
Mermen and mermaids are just mythology, right?
Try telling that to the unsuspecting humans who fall head-over-heels for
those who don't always have heels...

In Over Her Head

Reel's a merman without a tail, and Erica's terrified of the ocean. Only one thing could get her into the water: a gun. And only one thing could keep her there: the sexy merman who saves her life, only to risk his own.

Wild Blue Under

Valerie's a mer princess landlocked in the middle of the country. Rod is the prince who sets out to rescue her. But can they dodge a usurper's plot and make it back to the ocean before his tail—and his claim to the throne—disappear forever?

Catch of a Lifetime

Logan ran *away* from the circus; all he wants is for his life to be normal. The naked woman who shows up on his boat is anything *but* normal. Especially when Angel turns out to be a mermaid—with an angry sea monstress after her.

Love on the Rocks

Princess Mariana isn't a poser; she really *is* an artist which she's about to prove with the statue she's carving on a deserted island. Problem is, Jace is hiding out there so the one thing that will set Mariana free from her royal prison is the one thing that will get Jace killed. Romance is rough enough, but when there's a tsunami in the weather forecast, love is on the rocks.

Making Waves ~ Outtakes

Read about The Incident that made Erica terrified of the ocean, the reason Valerie, the lost princess, was found, and how Logan's young son Michael found a mermaid The stories *before* the stories.

~~~

BOTTLED MAGIC SERIES

Careful what you wish for... it just might come true!
As these humans come to find out when a magical genie ends up their laps—literally—before they're whisked off to the most magical adventure of all... falling in love.

I Dream of Genies

Matt's luck has finally changed when genie Eden escapes her bottle and lands in his lap. Literally. And she vows never to go back in. Unfortunately for both of them, the guy who put her in there wants her back and he'll stop at nothing to get her.

Genie Knows Best

Samantha inherits her father's estate, complete with a genie who has one last master to serve before his indentured servitude is up. Sam's more than willing to set Kal free—until her greedy ex has decided that if he can't have Sam, no one can.

My Fair Genie

Zane's inherited the family mansion which he can't rid of quick enough to put the rumors of his family's crazy history to rest. Too bad the genie who's been the cause of those rumors has been set free to run amok once more. Only this time, it's his heart she's messing with.

Your Wish Is His Command ~ Outtakes

Find out how Kal came to be imprisoned in his lantern and why he needs to serve 1001 masters. It's the story before the story.

~~~

ONCE-UPON-A-TIME ROMANCE SERIES

*Once Upon A Time sounds good in a fairy tale, but real life isn't like that.
Or... is it?*
*With the help of a guardian-angel-in-training, these lucky couples will
find that falling in love is the greatest tale of all!*

Beauty and The Best

Jolie is a personal chef by day and a romance writer by night. So when she gets a gig for the hot reclusive artist, Todd, she has the perfect hero for her book. Until Todd finds out and kicks her out of his kitchen, his home, *and* his heart.

If The Shoe Fits

Once upon a time, a long time ago, in a land far, far away, there lived a girl by the name of Cinderella. This is not her story. *This* is the story of Lucinda Isabella Casteleoni, who, like her namesake, has a wicked stepmother, two tacky stepsisters, and countless hours of hard work to (not) look forward to. But unlike that fairy tale princess, Bella's Prince Charming is nowhere to be found. Until a little old man with sparkling green eyes opens a shoe store down the street. Then the magic begins...

Through The Leaded Glass (prequel)

An accidental trip to medieval England has ad exec Kate scrambling for a way home... But can she bring the hot knight in shining armor she's fallen in love with back with her?

~~~

</div>

<div align="center">

BEEFCAKE, INC. SERIES

</div>

Girls' Night Out never tasted so good!
Magic Mike has nothing on these guys.
*Sit back and enjoy the show as the guys of BeefCake, Inc. show you how
it's done...*

Beefcake & Cupcakes

Lara wants her cupcakes to be a success. Exotic dancer Gage wouldn't mind sampling them, but his work schedule to pay off his nephew's hospital bills doesn't leave him time to do so. Until a party where beefcake meets cupcakes and, *oh*, is it delicious!

<div align="center">

299

</div>
~~~

Beefcake & Mistakes

When Bryan mistakes Jenna for a hooker and she realizes he's her adopted son's father, the mistakes and misunderstandings start to grow. But something else is growing between them, too. Sometimes, one wrong turn can be oh so right...

Beefcake & Retakes

Tanner wants his ex-wife to be out of his life forever, but when her grandmother has a stroke and he has to pretend to still be in love with Juliet, can he risk a retake on the one woman who never stopped loving him?

Beefcake & Snowflakes

Gina's had a crush on Darien since forever—until the day he humiliated her in school. Fifteen years later, he leaves her cold. Exotic dancer Darien has come back to town to set a few things to rights. One is the mess he made for Gina years ago... and *maybe* rekindle the flames they'd once had. But the only way to melt the snow around Gina's heart is to turn up the heat, both on the job... and off.

~~~

MANLEY MAIDS SERIES

What happens when three irresistibly sexy brothers lose a poker bet to their enterprising sister? They get hired out for her housecleaning venture. Now, the Manley Maids are at your service. Satisfaction guaranteed.

What A Woman Wants

Resort owner Sean plans to buy an historic estate, making a name for himself and making millions, so he moves in under the guise of cleaning the place to thwart the one condition of the inheritance. But heir Olivia and her menagerie get under his skin, and he finds that the poker bet that got him into this mess isn't the only game-changer.

What A Woman Needs

Movie star Bryan wants fame and fortune, not a repeat of his penny-pinching "normal" childhood. After the publicity surrounding of her husband's death, Beth needs is a normal life for herself and her
~~~

children, and the movie star who lost a bet to clean her house—with paparazzi in tow—isn't it. But as flirtation turns into seduction, Bryan needs to convince Beth he's more man than a maid. Or actor. Because he's playing the lead in a reverse Cinderella story, and it might just be the role of a lifetime.

What A Woman Gets

Liam has no patience for women who spend a man's money without giving a thought to any actual work. But to make good on his bet, Liam must not only tolerate socialite, Cassidy, he'll have to clean up after her when her father cuts her off. With no money and no home for Liam to clean, Cassidy has no choice but to accept a job offer— as Liam's new maid. But when sparks fly between them, will it be true love or just another messy affair?

What A Woman

MaryAlice Catherine is all set to clean her grandmother's friend's house, only to find the woman's cocky grandson whom she'd had a crush on growing up—and he'd known all along—is living there and she's mortified. Jared remembers it differently; Mac was always a bossy little thing, but he's not going to let her call the shots now. But with the two of them living in one house, there's no telling who's going to come out swinging.

What A Guy Wants

Beckett is ready to pay up for his lost poker bet. He just didn't realize he'd have to do it with his heart. Jennifer is the one who got away and now she's right here in front of him. In her house. That he's here to clean. Jennifer can't believe the bad boy from high school she'd had a major crush on is in her home, but if there's one thing her ex-husband taught her, it's that she can't count on the bad boy. Until Beckett lays all his cards on the table and he turns out to be someone Jennifer can bet on after all.

www.JudiFennell.com

Here's Judi!

Award-winning, best-selling author Judi Fennell loves to laugh and loves love, so it's no surprise there's a little bit of each in every book she writes. Check out her fairy tales with a twist for a taste of her light-hearted, tongue-in-cheek paranormal and romantic comedies. From mermen off the coast of the Jersey Shore, to genies with magic carpets, to male strippers à la Magic Mike, and manly maids whose motto is *Satisfaction Guaranteed*, there's always a laugh and love to be had.

And, in her copious (?) amounts of spare time, she helps authors with all aspects of writing and indie-publishing with her formatting, cover and promotional design, editorial, consultation, and audiobook company, www.formatting4U.com.

Judi lives in suburban Philadelphia with a menagerie of four-legged friends, and the minute those creatures start A) singing, B) sewing clothing, or C) cleaning the house will be the day she retires from writing…!

www.ingramcontent.com/pod-product-compliance
Lightning Source LLC
Chambersburg PA
CBHW071727190726
48292CB00003B/647